DEADLY LITTLE SECRET

A British Murder Mystery

THE WILD FENS MURDER MYSTERIES
BOOK 16

JACK CARTWRIGHT

CP

CHESTNUT PRESS

ALSO BY JACK CARTWRIGHT

The Deadly Wolds Murder Mysteries

When The Storm Dies

The Harder They Fall

Until Death Do Us Part

The Devil Inside Her

Secrets From The Grave

The Wild Fens Murder Mysteries

Secrets In Blood

One For Sorrow

In Cold Blood

Suffer In Silence

Dying To Tell

Never To Return

Lie Beside Me

Dance With Death

In Dead Water

One Deadly Night

Her Dying Mind

Into Death's Arms

No More Blood

Burden of Truth

Run From Evil

Deadly Little Secret

Waiting For Death

The DCI Cook Murder Mysteries

A Winter of Blood

A Secret to Die For

DEADLY LITTLE SECRET

JACK CARTWRIGHT

PROLOGUE

THE DAY HAD BEEN LONG, and one Henry Hyde might have remembered fondly had he and his friends not made several poor decisions.

It had been warm enough that he hadn't needed to wear the hooded sweater his mum had forced him to take before he left that morning. It had remained tied around his waist the entire day, serving as little more than a cushion for when Liam, Gopher, and he had sat in the long grass on the far side of Sid James' field, where Gopher had produced a packet of his dad's tobacco and some rolling papers.

"Keep an eye out for Sid," Liam said. "You know what he's like. He'll drag us all back home behind his tractor, and I don't know about you, but I could do without my mum asking why I was over here."

Of course, the farmer in question wasn't actually called Sid James. That was just a name that somebody long ago had given him on account of him spending a lifetime under the wide Lincolnshire sky, causing his face to wrinkle like an old prune.

"Yeah, he knows my dad," Gopher said. "Last thing I need is my old man on my case. He's been in a right mood recently."

"Why's that?"

"Dunno," Gopher said. "I reckon he's seeing someone."

"Your old man's got a new girlfriend?" Liam said.

"What's wrong with that?"

"Well, he's a bit old, isn't he?"

"Same age as your mum," Gopher said, rolling onto his back and passing the pathetic-looking roll-up they had crafted after many failed attempts to Henry. "And yours, Henry. Anyway, it would be nice if he does. The place stinks."

Henry took a drag and immediately coughed. It was only once to start with, but it didn't take long for it to escalate enough that he pushed himself onto his knees and bent over with his forehead on the grass and his backside sticking up in the air, coughing his lungs up.

"Keep it down, Henry, will you?" Liam told him, taking a chance by peering up over the grass to see if Sid James or one of his farm workers were close enough to hear.

The field in question was several acres in size and almost rectangular in shape, and after a day of messing around in the woods and sampling Gopher's dad's tobacco, it was time for them to head home.

"It's getting late. We'd better get going," Henry said, spitting into the grass. "My mum will want to know where I've been, otherwise."

"Just tell her you were at mine," Liam said. "My mum's working all day. Just tell her you were at mine playing on the computer."

"I don't know," Henry said. "She knows when I'm lying, and what if she calls your house? It's best not to be late; then, she won't ask."

Liam groaned as if the day was coming to an end, and it was Henry's fault. He shoved himself up onto his knees and had another look across the fields for the farmer.

"All right, let's do it," he said, throwing the tobacco pouch and papers at Gopher. "Better put them back before your old man finds them missing."

They walked slowly, and although each one of them would never admit it, they were dreading returning to their homes. Going home, meant having a shower and going to bed, and that meant one thing; first day back at school in the morning.

"Do you reckon he really would?" Henry asked as they walked the flattened grass at the edge of the field.

"Jesus, Henry. Would who do what?" Liam said, leading them two steps ahead.

"Sid," he replied. "So, you reckon he'd really drag us back home?"

"My old man reckons he's a lunatic," Gopher said.

"Yeah, and my mum," Liam agreed. "Bloody looks the part, don't he? I doubt he'd drag us anywhere, though. He might give us a clip round the ear. Anyway, it's alright for you two. He don't know where you live. My house backs onto his land. He's bound to know me."

"Behave," Gopher told him. "It's not like he keeps a record of all the local kids."

"I didn't say he keeps a record," Liam said. "But I reckon he knows. Bloke like that?" He turned and walked backwards for a few steps, tapping his temple with an index finger. "It's all up there. I heard he killed his wife and kid."

"Oh, shut up, Liam," Gopher said.

"I did."

"He's not a killer. He's just a bloody farmer—"

"Alright, then," Liam said, bringing the pack to a stop. "Where are they?"

"Eh?"

"Where are his wife and kid?"

"I don't know. Maybe he doesn't have a family?"

"Yeah, not anymore," Liam said. "Because he bloody killed

them. Probably buried them out here where nobody would find them."

"You talk absolute—" Gopher started, but Liam's eyes suddenly widened, and he dived to the ground.

"It's him," he hissed. "Get down!"

Henry turned to see where he was looking, expecting to find nothing but an empty field and for the whole thing to be one of Liam's wind-ups. If he had laid down, then Liam would have teased him for being such a wimp.

But it wasn't a wind-up. He dropped to the ground beside Gopher.

"Did he see you?"

"Don't know," Henry told him. "Saw his tractor at the far end of the field. He'll be coming this way in a minute. He's bound to see us."

"I say we run for it," Liam said.

"No," Henry replied. "He'll definitely see us, then."

"Well, what do you suggest? We can't lay here all bloody night."

They looked to Gopher, who eyed them both, then nodded.

"We've got to run. The sooner we do it, the better."

"Right," Liam said. "Henry, you ready?"

"I'm slower than you two."

"On three," Liam said, ignoring his complaint. "Three."

Liam jumped to his feet, followed closely by Gopher, and they both tore off along the edge of the field.

"Wait up," Henry said. He made it to the corner of the field, where Gopher and Liam were hunched down, peering through the stems of wheat or barley, he never could tell the difference. "This looks like a good place. I say we wait here."

"Not on your Nelly," Liam said. "We'd be cornered. He'll be here in a minute. Look, he's turning back now."

"Oh, Jesus," Henry said, and without waiting for them, he got a head start.

They caught up with him with relative ease, both of them laughing. Perhaps it was the danger of getting caught and the unknown consequence, or maybe it was just their way of dealing with fear. But laughter was the last thing on Henry's mind.

"We're not going to make it to the track before he gets here," Gopher called out.

"In there," Liam said, pointing at the old, abandoned farmhouse that stood at the edge of the property, derelict and unchanged for as long as Henry could remember.

"No, keep running."

"He'll see and catch us," Liam argued as they ran.

Henry wanted to agree with Liam, but it was all he could do just to keep up with them.

"Sod it, I'm hiding in there. You two can get caught if you want," Liam said, darting off towards the building.

"Ah, for God's sake," Gopher said, pausing momentarily to check on Henry. They both glanced back at the tractor.

"He's coming this way," Henry said. "He's seen us."

"Run," Gopher said, dragging him along with him.

Twice, Henry nearly stumbled but somehow managed to stay on his feet until they neared the house.

They called it a house, but to Henry, it was little more than four walls with empty spaces where windows and doors had been and a tree growing out of where the roof had once been. It was a pile of graffitied bricks that, in his opinion, should have been knocked down.

They ran in through a small room and into a larger room, where they found Liam cowering beneath one of the empty windows. He held onto the ledge, peeking over the bricks as they joined him.

"Is he coming?" Henry asked.

"Dunno," Liam replied. "Can't see him."

"Shh, I can hear the tractor," Gopher said, wincing for them to be quiet. "It's getting closer."

"What are we going to do? We're trapped in here," Henry said, and he pressed his back against the wall, squeezed his eyes closed, and cursed himself for listening to the other two.

"My mum's going to find out where I've been," he said, hearing his own voice rise in fear.

"I think your mum is the least of our worries," Liam said.

"What do you mean?" he asked, and he peered past Gopher at Liam, who was staring across the room, wide-eyed, and, for the first time that Henry knew of, clearly terrified.

He followed his gaze, as did Gopher, and together they shared a moment of silent panic.

Until Gopher broke the silence.

"Jesus bloody Christ," he breathed. "Run."

CHAPTER ONE

"WHAT DO YOU THINK OF THIS?" She held a baby blue dress against herself. "I'll need some new shoes, of course."

Ben, who was slumped in the armchair in Freya's dressing room, glanced up from his phone and eyed the dress, then saw the look in her eye that dared him to criticise her choice.

"S'alright," he told her. "Not exactly practical, though, is it?"

He returned to his phone, on which was a reel of overhead videos showing farmers producing satisfying ridges and furrows in what he could only describe as challenging fields. His father had one such field, which required cultivation, ploughing, and sowing to be conducted in a particular way to ensure efficiency.

"It's not meant to be practical," she replied, turning to admire the dress in the full-length mirror.

"Well, I'll tell you one thing," he said. "If you wear that and we knock on a suspect's door, we won't have to worry about him answering. He'd rip the door off its hinges. Anyway, it's meant to rain tomorrow. I'd stick with long trousers."

"It's not for work, Ben," she said, taking a few moments to admire the dress from a different angle. "It's for the wedding."

He stopped the video.

She had turned away from him, but there was little doubt she was waiting for his response and had an argument prepared.

"What wedding?"

"Our wedding," she said. "Don't tell me you've forgotten."

"Our wedding? As in, you and me standing at the altar, exchanging rings?"

"That's usually what happens, yes."

"You're going to wear that?"

"I was thinking about it, yes," she said. "Well, it's either this one or the dark blue one. I'm leaning towards this, though. I like the neckline."

"Freya?"

"Yes?"

He shook his head, unsure which of the points he had to make should be made first.

"I'm not supposed to see it, am I?"

"See what?"

"The dress. It's bad luck."

"Oh, come on," she said, dismissing him exactly as he knew she would. "You don't believe in all that superstitious nonsense, do you?"

"Not really," he said. "But I'm not really keen to chance it. I don't walk under ladders, not because it's bad luck, but because... well, just in case."

"Oh, I wouldn't worry. Besides, who else am I going to get an opinion from?"

"What about Jackie? Or there's Denise or Anna—"

"Denise dresses like a grandma, Jackie only shops at Primark, and Anna dresses like a man in that leather jacket and jeans. She hasn't a feminine bone in her body."

"I'm not exactly a good substitute, am I?" he said. "I mean, look at me." He presented his check shirt and old jeans."

She followed his prompt and cast a scrutinising eye over him.

"No, you're right," she said.

"And if I could address the elephant in the room," he continued, waiting for her to stop admiring the dress and look at him again.

"Yes?"

"It's not white," he told her. "It's a cocktail dress."

"It's not a cocktail dress," she laughed.

"Well, whatever it is, it's not a wedding dress, is it?"

She inhaled, draped the dress over the back of a chair, and then picked up the dark blue option.

"I hope you're not expecting me to look like a princess, Ben."

"No, not a princess," he said. "But if you could look like a bride—"

"I've done all that," she said, toying with the shoulder straps as she held the dress against her. "I don't want to go through it again; all the hassle with the wedding breakfast, the cake, and God knows what else. I'm aiming for something far smaller. A few friends, exchange vows, and then we can sign on the dotted line and go to the pub for a few drinks."

"I see," he said. "I wonder if, at some point, I get to have a say in all this?"

"Of course you do," she told him. "When the landlord produces the bill for the drinks, you can pay it."

It was one of those throwaway statements that was light of heart yet carried a certain amount of truth.

"Freya?"

"Ben?" she said, distracted by her reflection. She continued to hold the dress against herself with one hand, and with the other, she toyed with her hair, pulling it across the side of her face that bore the scars. "I think it's long enough now."

"The dress?"

"No, my hair," she said. "I would have liked to have had it cut before the wedding, but I'll have to make do." She pulled her new hair into some semblance of a style. "I think I can make it work."

"You could just wear the wig," he said. "You've been wearing it for months, anyway."

"No," she said, and there was a strength to her voice. A determination. "No, not at my wedding." She turned to the mirror and traced the scar with a manicured fingernail, lowering her voice to a murmur. "I don't want any reminders. Not one."

Slowly, Ben shoved himself from the armchair, rising to stand behind her. He scooped her hair into a bundle, pulled it from her face, and then leaned in to kiss her neck.

"You know I think you're beautiful, right?" he said softly, to which she smiled a little.

"So you say," she replied, reaching for his hands to hold him there.

He looked up and held her gaze in the reflection.

"The light blue one," he said.

"Oh, really?" she replied. "And why is that? The neckline?"

"No," he said, letting her go and making his way to the door where he stopped and clung to the frame. "It'll go with the jeans I'll be wearing."

"Oh, you," she said, snatching up a hairbrush and launching it at him. He escaped the brush, which hit the door and then rolled to a stop.

"Want a drink?" he called up the stairs.

"Wine," she called back.

"As if I needed to ask," he muttered to himself in the kitchen. He flicked the kettle on, grabbed a fresh wine glass, and then poured her a drink, setting it to one side for when she came down. It was as he was preparing his tea that he really considered the conversation they had just had. He leaned against the work-top, mulling it over, and by the time she came downstairs, wearing her satin dressing gown and silky pyjamas, he had a dozen questions to ask.

But one in particular stood out.

Freya held her glass by the stem, eyed him curiously as she took a sip, then settled in opposite him, mirroring his stance.

"Go on, then," she said.

"Go on, what?"

"I know that face," she replied quietly. "Is it the dress?"

"What? No, of course not."

"What then? Look, I've been through this before. I don't want a big wedding—"

"It's not the wedding," he said. "Well, not that anyway."

"Well, what is it?" she asked. "Come on, we both know we're not going to bed until you've said what's on your mind, so you might as well say it."

He poured the water into his mug, strained the tea bag a little, and then dumped it into the bin. She passed him the milk, perhaps to hurry him along.

"Who do you have coming?" he asked.

"Sorry?"

"The wedding. Who do you have coming? I mean, I have family. I've got my dad and my brothers, and I think they've invited a few more, and then there's the team." He looked up at her. "Who is going to sit on your side?"

"The team," she replied. "Except Gillespie, he'll be up there standing beside you."

"No family then?"

"I have no family, Ben," she said.

"Yeah, I know that's what you say. But you must have an aunt or something."

She shook her head.

"No," she said. "No, there's nobody."

"Well, friends then. You must have a friend from back home."

"London?" She laughed. "No. I did have a friend, but she preferred the company of my ex-husband."

"Ah," he replied.

"Ah, indeed."

He shuffled his feet, aware that she could read his body language like a well-thumbed novel.

"You have another question," she said, to which he laughed once more.

"I have a dozen," he said, then let his expression stiffen. "Who's going to give you away?"

The winning smile she had worn faded, and her instincts took over. She drew her hair across her scar, then cleared her throat.

"Nobody," she said.

"Freya—"

"I don't need anybody to give me away. I don't have a father. I don't have a figure to look up to, somebody who can smile proudly at me. Somebody who, dare I say it, might even shed a tear or two." She shook her head again. "I have you, Ben. That's quite enough, thank you."

"What about—"

"Hold on," she said, raising a hand to stop him. She fished her phone from her pocket, answered a call, and all traces of their conversation were replaced by a familiar look in her eye. "DCI Bloom," she said. It was a hunger. A determination. A glaze that masked her inner feelings. "I see," she told the person at the end of the line. Ben sipped at his tea. It was too hot to drink, and something told him they would have left the house by the time it had cooled. "We'll be there," she said finally, then ended the call.

She dropped her phone into her pocket, sighed at the wine she couldn't finish, and then looked up at him apologetically.

"So much for an early night," she said. "Come on, you might as well get used to it."

"Get used to what?" he replied, tipping his tea into the sink.

"Disappointment," she replied. "Consider it marriage practice."

CHAPTER TWO

THE DISPATCH OFFICER provided them with an address in Billinghay, a small village to the east of Freya's village, Dunston. The journey was around fifteen minutes, enough time for Ben to settle into the Range Rover's luxurious seats and for his mind to ponder their previous conversation.

If there was one thing, however, that he had learned about Freya, it was that timing was everything when it came to pressing her for information.

A narrow lane off the main road led them past a single house surrounded by farmland, and after another kilometre, an abandoned farmhouse silhouetted against the amber sky came into view.

"Christ, look at this place," Ben muttered as they drew near to the lone police Astra that was parked nearby. A single uniformed officer raised a hand to them, guiding them to park in a space between two drainage ditches.

"It's not the place that bothers me," she replied, nodding at the familiar officer.

"Let's just let bygones be bygones," Ben told her.

Freya pulled the car to a stop nowhere near where the officer had suggested and killed the engine. Ben leaned forward to peer up at the old farmhouse. "Is that a.... It is. It's a tree growing through the roof."

"She's got a bloody nerve," Freya said, her tone sharp and bitter.

"We knew that already," he replied.

"I don't know how she managed to keep her job. If I'd had my way—"

"If you'd had your way, Freya," Ben interjected. "She would be out of a job, planning a full-scale investigation into us all." He let those words settle. "Detective Superintendent Granger saw fit for her to keep her job and for the whole thing to be forgotten. Let's keep it that way, shall we?" She shoved her door open, and Ben reached for her arm. "Let me deal with her." He held on until she looked him in the eye.

"PC Jewson," Ben said as he slid from the car. "On your own, are you?"

The young officer ignored him and started toward the front of Freya's car.

"DCI Bloom," she said.

"Sorry, Jewson, I'd prefer to get in and see the body if you don't mind—"

"Yes, but—"

"Thank you," Freya said, dismissing her as she strode towards the old, ruined farmhouse, which stood at the intersection of three drainage ditches with fields in every direction.

"Yes, but—"

"I've seen enough crime scenes to come to my own conclusions, thank you," Freya barked, drawing a line under the interaction.

"What's her bloody problem?" Jewson said to Ben while Freya was still within earshot.

"I'd suggest rephrasing that," Ben told her. "You'd do well to show a little respect for rank."

"Oh, I've got respect for rank," she replied. "But *her*? She's just bloody rude."

"I wasn't talking about DCI Bloom's rank," he said, which he followed up with a knowing look.

"Right," she replied.

"You had a chance to join our team," he reminded her. "You then systematically went about destroying that team and, very nearly, the career of a well-respected officer." Ben leaned on the front of Freya's car. "You're lucky to still be in uniform. You know that, right?"

"She's lucky the IOPC isn't involved."

"And what would that prove?"

"It would prove how bloody corrupt the police force is."

"It would prove nothing of the sort, and you know it," Ben replied. "Listen, I've been in the force long enough to know what corruption looks like, and this team is nothing like it. Not even remotely. The fact is, Jewson, you lack patience."

"I lack what?"

"Patience," he said again. "You want to be further along in your career than you are. I get that. I really do, but it takes time, and you don't get there by treading on others."

"You don't know me—"

"No, and if I'm honest, I'm pleased I don't know you. I've known enough officers like you, though."

"Like me? What's that supposed to mean?"

"Hungry for career progression," he said. "But lacking in both patience and..."

"And?"

"Teamwork."

"Teamwork?"

He smiled at her refusal to pay heed to his advice.

"Listen, there are two types of police officers: those who climb too high too fast and those who take one step at a time. You're aiming high. What do you want? Sergeant? Inspector?"

"Higher," she told him, with pride written all over her face.

"Do you know what that means?"

"Do I know what what means?"

"Do you know what it means to make Sergeant?" he asked. "Do you know what responsibilities it carries?"

"Well, yeah. I'd lead a team."

"And you know the law well enough, do you?" he asked. "You know the procedures better than any of your peers?"

"What I don't know, I'll pick up."

"No," he said with a laugh. "No, it doesn't work like that. You need to be doing the job you want for months, years even, before you're made up. If and when the day comes when you're made a sergeant, you will need to know the processes and procedures that fall under your remit, inside out, *before* you wear the stripes." He shook his head slowly. "If you don't, you'll crash and burn. You'll create anarchy in your team; you'll miss something or cause an investigation to fail."

"Is that right?"

"Yes," he said with another laugh. "Yes, it is. You know, before DCI Bloom arrived, I was in line for promotion. It would have been me leading the team. I was angry at first. I was angry at being held back. But the longer I was angry, the more insight I had into the role I would have performed." He shook his head again. "I wasn't ready. I would have failed, and there would have been no turning back. I couldn't have gone back to being a sergeant. Not in the same team, anyway. I could have transferred, I suppose, but it wouldn't have taken long for word of my failure to get about. The fact is that DCI Bloom saved me from that. I couldn't see it at the time, but I see it now. I could have played the sort of games you play and undermined her, but what would that have achieved? Nothing," he said. "Except failure."

"She's a bitch," Jewson said, then saw the look in his eye. "Sorry, but she is."

"She has a way about her," he told her. "The fact is, though, that when the time comes for me to take another step up the ladder, I'll be ready for it, and more importantly, I'll have the support of the entire team behind me. The moment you start stepping on people, going solo, as it were, you're on your own, and trust me, it's lonely at the top." He nodded at the derelict house. "She had to fight her way through misogyny. She had to fight to be recognised, and even then, she was still held back. You're lucky. You don't have that fight. Detective Superintendent Granger is probably the fairest officer in the force. You rise through merit and hard work."

She said nothing at first but showed no signs of having listened to a single word he had said.

"So, bide my time," she said. "That's what you're saying, is it? That's how I progress?"

"Not yet," he told her. "First, you need allies. You need people on your side. Your peers. That little game you tried with our team. Treading on Gillespie, calling out what you saw as weaknesses in us all? All that's done is have every officer in the station turn their back on you. You'll know when the time is right for you to move up because your peers will all be rooting for you. You'll have their support. Without it—"

"I come tumbling down?"

He smiled. Finally, she had listened.

"Be nice to people. Gain experience. Gain friends, allies, and support," he shook his head. "You've a long career ahead of you, but I'm afraid to say you've put yourself back a few years."

"A few years?"

"People will be talking about what you did for years, Jewson," he told her. "When they look at you, all they see is distrust. You need to change that before you do anything."

"Any other words of wisdom, Detective Inspector Savage?"

She spoke his rank with distaste, but he ignored her tone.

"Yes, as it happens," he said. "Turn your enemies into allies."

"What?"

"Turn your enemies into allies," he said again. "Those who speak loudest against you will often be the ones to speak loudest for you when the time comes." Those words hit home. He was sure of it. She pondered them silently, and in his peripheral vision, he saw Freya emerge from the abandoned farmhouse. "If I were you, I'd start with her."

"DCI Bloom?" she said, wide-eyed.

"You need allies on your left, your right, beneath you, and above you," he said, nodding at Freya, who was marching towards them, scowling. "Get her on your side, and that journey of yours will be far easier."

"Can I ask you something?" Jewson said, rushing to speak before Freya reached them. "Why are you helping me? After what I did, I mean. After what I said about you."

He took a breath. Freya was fifty yards away, leaving him little time to convey his thoughts.

"Because, Jewson, if you don't change, you will crash and burn. You'll be out on your ear," he said. "And when that happens, I'll have peace of mind, knowing that I gave you more help than you deserved. What you choose to do with the advice I've given you is entirely up to you."

"Jewson?" Freya called out, her voice shrill as she marched.

"Here we go," Jewson muttered.

"Jewson, what the bloody hell is this?" Freya waved a hand at the old house as she closed in.

"What's up?" Ben called out, but Freya didn't even look his way.

"Well?" Freya said, coming to a stop less than two feet from Jewson. "Are you going to say anything?"

"I tried guv," Jewson said, and she looked over Freya's shoulder to Ben, who could do nothing but raise his eyebrows, warning her to heed his advice. "I'm sorry. I should have tried harder."

"Am I allowed to know what's happened?" Ben asked calmly hoping to dissolve the tension.

"You can start by calling the medical examiner and CSI," she said. "Tell them not to bother coming."

"Sorry? What am I supposed to tell them—"

"Tell them not to come," Freya said, facing him briefly before returning to glare at Jewson. "Tell them it's a hoax."

"A hoax?"

"Yes, Ben," she snarled. "A hoax." She turned to Jewson once more. "There's no body."

CHAPTER THREE

THE ROOF TILES had long since been stolen or repurposed, and the roof beams had no doubt succumbed to the harsh elements, much like the first-floor joists and floorboards. The ground floor of the lonely old farmhouse consisted of two rooms, a kitchen, and a living space, both equally small in comparison to their modern-day equivalents. The brick fireplace was intact, though the iron features had been removed, as had the windows and their frames, leaving a single eye in each wall. The front window stared out across the fields in late dusk, while the window in the rear wall looked out into the thicket of trees and brambles that had claimed that side of the house.

That was as far as the house resembled any other. There were two remaining features that stood out in the living room if indeed that was what it had been. The first was the Alder tree that had sprouted from the ground to flourish where the roof had once been. Ben gauged the growth against those on his father's farm, surmising that it had been there more than twenty years, maybe even forty. For the seed to have taken root and enough daylight to have reached the ground, the roof and first floor had to have gone, and the floorboards had to have rotted away to reveal the bare earth. Though, to his untrained eye, the remains of the joists appeared charred, as if they had been claimed by a fire.

The second feature, and perhaps the most striking of all, was the tent that had been erected in the corner of the living space. The flaps had been unzipped and hung loosely, and when Ben, using a pen, pulled one back to peer inside, he saw only an old sleeping bag, a camping stove, and a few unopened tins of baked beans.

"If I didn't know better, I'd wonder if all this is yours," Freya said from behind him, to which he turned to question her remark. She grinned. "Baked beans. Your staple diet."

"Dinner of kings," he replied, standing to join her. "I don't get it. What is all this?"

"Well, the sleeping bag looks like it needs a good wash, and the stove isn't new. As for the tent—"

"Yeah, it's seen better days, hasn't it?"

"Looks to me like somebody in need of a home uses this place to escape the elements." She peered around at the old house in the dying light. "Have you cancelled Doctor Saint and CSI?"

"Doctor Saint, yes. I couldn't get hold of Southwell."

"Well, keep trying," she said. "We ask too much of her already. The last thing I want is to waste her time. You never know; she might reconsider favours when we ask."

"Oh, I think as long as we have Gillespie, she'll help out where she can."

"Just..." she started. "Just keep trying her."

"There's no need," a voice said from behind them, purposefully quiet.

Not only was Katy Southwell, the lead crime scene investigator, a force to be reckoned with, she was one of the few individuals to rival Freya's intelligence and was also in a relationship with Detective Sergeant Jim Gillespie, making her both a friend and a colleague whose allegiance was frail and easily scuppered.

"Katy," Freya said. "I'm so sorry; we seem to have wasted your time."

Southwell glanced around the gloomy space.

"There's no body," Ben explained. "Probably a hoax caller."

"So I see," Southwell said. "Well, there goes our quiet Sunday evening."

"Is Jim with you?"

"He came separately. He's outside with the rest of your team."

"Oh Christ," Freya muttered. "That'll mean overtime I'll need to explain. Ben, get out there and send them all away, will you?"

"As you wish," he replied. "Katy, I'll walk you out."

"No, it's okay," she replied, seemingly enthralled by the derelict building. She shone a torchlight over the old brickwork and the tree. "I'll stay for a bit if you don't mind."

"Suit yourself," he told her, then ducked into the kitchen to make his way out.

"Actually, Ben," Freya added. "I'll join you. There's something I want to ask." She waited until they were outside and a good ten metres from the doorway before speaking again. A few more cars had parked beside hers, and the sound of familiar voices could be heard. "What did she want?"

"Katy?" he said. "I don't know. Probably wants to look at the old building. You don't see many trees in somebody's front room, do you?"

"Not her. Jewson."

"Eh?"

"You were speaking to her when I came out the first time."

"What was I supposed to do? Ignore her?"

"It would have been preferable—"

"If you must know, she needed some advice."

"From you?" she said, to which she laughed.

"Is that hard to believe?" he replied. "And anyway, she didn't ask for advice. I just gave it to her."

"And what advice did you give her?"

"Just a few friendly words, that's all. Nothing to worry about."

Freya chewed on that comment for a few moments as they walked.

"Does she have plans?"

"If you're asking if she's going to pursue some kind of revenge or recompense, then no," he said. "I don't think so, anyway." He sighed. "Look. She's misguided. She needed steering in the right direction."

"And you steered her, did you?"

"I did my best," he told her.

"Why?" she asked. "Why bother?"

"Because Freya," he started, then sought the right words to use. "Because she needs help."

"That much is obvious—"

"As did I," he continued. "As do we all, sometimes."

"What are you saying?"

"Nothing," he said. "I just think that we all deserve a second chance. She did wrong, she was punished, and she's no longer our problem. If she continues down the path she's on, then I'll give her six months at the most."

"But?"

"But, if she listened to anything I said, then she might just stand a chance."

They came to a stop twenty metres from the cars, where Gillespie, Cruz, and Nillson were waiting. Jewson had retreated to the safety of the Astra, where she waited in the darkness, her face dimly lit by the interior light.

"Why do you care? So what if she messes up again and loses her job."

"Because, Freya," he said, "she reminds me of somebody. Somebody I happen to care about."

Freya's confused expression morphed into incredulity in the space of a heartbeat.

"No," she said. "You cannot align her to me. She's..." Freya fumbled for the right response, a little taken aback by what she perceived to be an insult. "She's—"

"A bitch?" Ben suggested.

"Yes, that, and a whole lot more."

"Remind you of anybody?" Ben said with a smile.

Lost for words, Freya brushed him to one side and strode over to the team.

"Gillespie, get hold of emergency services. Find out who took the call and see if there's any way of identifying the caller. The rest of you can go home."

"Guv?" Nillson said, perhaps sensing the mood that Ben had bestowed on Freya.

"It's a hoax. There's no body." She turned to Gillespie. "I want whoever called it in made an example of. That should keep you busy." She turned ninety degrees and strode towards the Astra. Jewson saw her coming and sat straight in the driver's seat. "And as for you, missy—"

"Freya?" Katy Southwell called out from beside the house. She waved her torch around to catch their attention.

"What is it?" Ben called back, seeing Freya come to a stop just feet from the Astra's door.

"Have you got a minute?" Southwell said. "I think you might want to see this."

CHAPTER FOUR

"You," Freya said, unable to hide the grimace that was forming on her face. "You, don't move a muscle."

"I tried to tell you—"

"Not a muscle," Freya said, cutting Jewson off. She stormed back to the house, ducked inside, then edged past Ben, who loitered in what used to be the small kitchen. Southwell was shining a black light across the exposed brickwork, and for once, the lack of daylight worked in their favour. "Blood?" Freya said, eyeing the spatter of luminescent droplets.

"I'm almost certain," Southwell replied. "I'd have to run tests, but—"

"How old?"

"Well, like I said," Southwell replied, crouching beside the area in question and spraying the brickwork with some kind of liquid. "I'd have to run tests if you want a definitive answer."

"What's that?" Ben asked, and he nodded at the bottle in Southwell's hand.

"Luminol," she replied, almost absentmindedly, and she offered no further explanation as if the name of the chemical in question would be enough to satisfy his intrigue.

"And what does that do?" he asked, and Freya got the feeling that Southwell was playing the '*you need me more than I need you game*', as was so often the case with intelligent specialists. It was only when individuals reached a certain maturity, like Doctor Saint, that they saw little need to demonstrate their abilities.

"Well," Southwell said, shoving herself to her feet. "Unlike semen or saliva, blood doesn't show up under a UV Light. Well, it shows up, but it doesn't glow. Before I sprayed the wall, it was just a series of black spots."

"Black spots?" Ben said.

"Blood doesn't reflect light naturally. Some might say it absorbs the light, kind of like when people tell you that wearing a black tee-shirt on a hot summer's day is a bad idea, as black absorbs the heat. It doesn't. It just doesn't reflect it, which is partly why black's a good colour for hiding a swollen tummy."

"Right..." Ben replied, his tone conveying his lack of understanding.

"So, when I came in here, I saw the spatter on the wall. Black dots, much darker than the surrounding brickwork. But that could have been anything. Cooking fat, paint, candle wax, anything," she said. "So, we spray it with luminol, which then reacts with the iron found in haemoglobin, and...well, to dumb it down a little, that's why it appears to glow."

"But you can't tell the age of the blood?" Ben asked.

"Not with any accuracy," she replied.

Freya pointed up at the gaping hole where the roof used to be.

"This place has been exposed to the elements for decades—"

"The effects of luminol dissipate over time. Haemoglobin doesn't last forever," Southwell said, sensing where she was heading.

"Right," Freya replied, nodding. "So, it's recent?"

"I'd say so," Southwell said. "The reaction was good. Of course, I'll need—"

"To take samples and run tests. Yes, you said," Freya replied. "Presumably, you could glean some kind of DNA from a sample?"

"I would hope so," Southwell said.

"What's the point?" Ben asked, and the two women stared at him. "There's no crime. It's a tent. You said it yourself. It's a hoax."

"Take the samples, would you, Katy?" Freya said, offering a pleasant smile that left little room for argument before she turned to Ben. "Have a look at that spatter pattern."

Ben did as instructed, then shrugged.

"So?"

"It's a lot of blood, isn't it?"

"So, where's the person the blood belonged to?" he said, and after a few seconds of hard stares and closing minds, they both lowered their gazes to the floor.

"Katy?" Freya said.

"Mm-hmm," she replied, busy searching for something in her case with a pen torch gripped between her teeth.

"I wonder if you could spray some of that…that chemical over here."

"Luminol?" Southwell said. "Well, technically, it's a mixture of luminol and hydrogen peroxide—"

"Just," Freya said, moving Ben out of the doorway. "Just spray the ground, will you?"

Southwell took a step over to them, dropped to a crouch, then sprayed the threshold. The reaction took mere seconds, and although it was fainter than on the wall, patches of dirt glowed what Freya could only describe as electric blue.

"Right, everyone out," Katy said almost immediately. She pulled her phone from her pocket and called a number as she ushered people out of the derelict house. "Pat?" she said into the phone. "Don't pack the van up. We're going to need markers, platforms, and the rest of the team." She waited for Pat to reply, then pocketed her phone. "Out. Come on. Shoo," she said to Freya and

Ben. "Unless you want to destroy what little evidence there is left. And we're going to need your shoe prints, along with whoever else has been in here."

She continued to spray the ground around them to identify areas where they could and could not walk.

"They were dragged," Ben said, pointing at the glowing trail.

"Never mind all that," Southwell said. "Out. Go. Go on."

Oddly, there was far more light outside than inside, on account of the pale moon that sat behind low cloud cover, as if somebody had placed a sheet of plain paper over a torch.

"Okay, what do we know?" Freya said.

"What do we know?"

"What did dispatch say when they called you?"

Ben shook his head.

"Only that whoever called it in had seen a man's body in there."

"It was a man, was it?"

"That's what the caller said," he replied. "I'm guessing the early night is still off the cards, then?"

"Put it this way," she said. "I'd be surprised if that bottle of wine is any good by the time we get home." The look on his face said all that was to be said. "Don't worry," she told him. "This is what married life is all about."

"Celibacy?"

She laughed.

"Evenings out together."

"You know, most couples spend their evenings out seeing a film or having dinner, not standing around waiting for crime scene investigators to finish picking fragments of dried blood from walls."

"I know, but we're not most couples, are we?"

"No," he replied as they walked, calling out to the team as they approached. "Gillespie, is Cruz about?"

"Aye, he's having a wee sit down in the car. Said his legs are knackered from the gym."

"Does his right foot work?"

"Somebody call?" A tinny voice sounded, and Cruz emerged from the darkness.

"Does your right foot work?"

"My right foot?" he said, his naivety as clear as the stars in the sky. "Erm, yeah."

"Good," Freya said. "We need coffee. Find somewhere, will you? And put that right foot of yours down."

"Oh, you're kidding," Cruz replied, clearly exasperated at pulling the short straw.

"Coffee?" Gillespie interjected. "I thought we were heading home. I just ordered Katy and me a Chinese."

"Well, you'd better cancel it then, hadn't you?" Freya said with a smile. "Either that or have it delivered here. I'm sure the rest of the team wouldn't mind. And get hold of the individual who took the call like I asked. I want that recording. Nillson, have our uniformed friends lock this place down, will you. When that's done, I'd like a search organised and can somebody get hold of the farmer who owns this land. I want to speak to them. With any luck, they'll give us permission without going via a warrant. The last thing I want to do is to upset the farming community." She looked up at Ben. "You know how sensitive they can be about doing things properly."

"There's no body," Gillespie replied. "Which means there's no crime, except for some wee scrote playing 999 pranks."

"Oh, there's a body, all right," Freya told him. "We just don't know where it is."

CHAPTER FIVE

"EMERGENCY SERVICES, POLICE, FIRE, OR AMBULANCE?" The operator said, calm and frustratingly controlled.

"Hello?" The voice was light. Prepubescent, male, and from the accent, local.

"What's your emergency, please?'

"Erm. I don't know."

The call handler followed a script, Freya knew that much. But there was often only so far that a script could take a conversation. Sometimes, the situation called for a little encouragement or even a distraction.

"Can I take your name, please?" The operator said, female, mid-thirties, and seasoned.

"We found something."

The operator hesitated, but her typing could be heard on the recording.

"What was it you found, please?"

"There's a bloke. A fella. He..."

"I'm afraid I'm going to need a bit more information, lovey."

"He was dead," the boy said abruptly.

"You found a dead man? Is that right?"

A silence followed, and the sound of a passing vehicle washed over the call before fading.

"It's in the old farmhouse down Labour in Vain Drove.

"Labour In Vain Drove? That's the name of the road, is it?"

"It's a lane," the boy said. "Near my...it's in Billinghay."

"And you're sure he's dead, are you?" No reply came, and the sounds of the operator multi-tasking came loud and clear over the noise of the road on the caller's end of the line. "Are you there?" The operator said. "Do you recognise him?" Silence. "Hello? I need to take your name—"

The line clicked, and the road noise died with it.

"That's all we've got, is it?" Freya asked. "Did we get the number?"

"It's a mobile," Gold said.

"Don't tell me, it's unregistered?"

"I'm afraid it is, yes."

"Okay," Freya replied. "Send it to Chapman. She can look into it in the morning. She has contacts with most of the providers. Excellent work, Gold."

"Ma'am."

"Ben, thoughts?"

Freya looked up at the man she was due to marry, keen to see if his mind was on the game or if he was still reeling over their lack of an early night.

"A few, actually," he said, leaning on Freya's car bonnet. "The caller is a young boy—"

"I can see why you made Detective Inspector, eh, Ben?" Gillespie cut in between swigs of his coffee. "Not much gets past you, eh?"

"He also said, 'we found the body'. *We*. Not me. Not I. *We*."

"I noticed that," Freya replied.

"And he nearly said something but thought better of it."

"And what was it he stopped himself from saying?"

"It was the bit about the location. He began saying that Labour in Vain Drove is near but then stopped himself."

"Do you think he was going to say near his house?"

"It's possible," Ben replied. "I mean, it's not near much, is it?"

Freya nodded her agreement. He had, as expected, picked up on the same things she had but had failed to notice one more key piece of information.

"He also made the call outside on the main road," she said. "I heard a large vehicle pass by."

"Probably a lorry," Cruz said, stating the obvious, to which the team offered a collective pitiful smile.

"There's only one main road here. If, as you say, Ben, this lane is near his house, then he must've made the call from the roadside somewhere here in Billinghay and...what's the name of the next town or village?"

"Tattershall," Ben said.

"What does that tell you?"

"He was walking along the main road on his way home?" Cruz suggested.

"Not necessarily," Freya said. "He was alone. Maybe he didn't feel like he could make the call from home. What time did he make the call?"

"Ten to nine this evening," Gold added.

"Ten to nine," Freya repeated. "What is he? Twelve, do you think? Thirteen?"

"Something like that," Ben said.

"And he's out on his own at nine o'clock in the evening?"

"We didn't all grow up in a manor house in the home counties," Ben told her. "That's not unusual."

"No, there was a nervousness to his voice, like he was betraying somebody. Betraying whoever he was with, or... I don't know. I need to speak to him."

"Oh God," Cruz said, and his shoulders slumped.

"Cruz, make a plan, will you?"

Cruz let his head fall forward in despair.

"I'm going door to door, am I?"

"In the morning, yes," she said. "We're looking for a boy who fits that description. But don't worry, you'll have Gillespie to keep you company."

"Ah, no way."

"Make a plan, and action it," Freya said. "I want you knocking on the first door at eight a.m. tomorrow morning. There can't be too many kids in the nearby houses."

As much as certain members of the team contested their tasks, they were, overall, responsive. But, before Freya could continue with the briefing, a few of them seemed to peer past her to the old house. Freya turned and found Southwell approaching slowly, respectful of interrupting.

"Anything?" Freya asked hopefully.

"Is it a good time?" Southwell asked.

"If you have news, Katy, then there's never a bad time."

"Good, well," Southwell started. "You were right about the floor, and as a result, I have a hypothesis if you want to hear it?"

"Does the blood trail lead to a body?" Ben asked.

"Blood trail?" Cruz said, demonstrating his lack of ability to think before he spoke. "What blood trail?"

"Sadly not," Southwell said, ignoring the interruption. "But it does give us an insight into what exactly happened."

Freya checked her watch. It was past midnight. She turned to address her team.

"Okay, let's get this place shut down, then you lot should get some sleep. If there are any developments overnight, then I'll need you on form."

"And if there are no developments?" Gillespie asked. "I mean, we don't have a body."

"If there are any developments overnight, Gillespie," Freya started, "they won't make a lot of difference to you or Cruz. You'll both be going door to door, so you won't learn of them until you're back at the station."

Gillespie could give as good as he got, but even he knew when and when not to put his point across.

"Aye, right," he said, perhaps a little embarrassed at being shot down in front of his girlfriend. The pair were usually particularly good at keeping their relationship and their professions separate, but he spoke to her directly. "Have you much to do, love? Worth me waiting, is it?"

Southwell sucked in a deep breath and glanced back at the old house.

"Given what we have here, I would suggest making me a coffee in the morning," she said. "I should just be getting home."

"Aye," he said, a little dejected. "Like passing ships, eh?"

"Shall we?" Southwell said to Freya, and she led the way back to the house. In the time it had taken to obtain the recording from the emergency services call centre, a few more of Southwell's team had arrived. Three of them were almost motionless, either scraping blood samples from the brickwork or the floor or applying various concoctions to the tent and its contents, while another fetched and carried to avoid too much movement. The platforms that Southwell had mentioned earlier had been set down outside the house, through the kitchen and all around the living room, providing a safe place from which the investigators could work without disturbing the evidence. "We've established a clear trail of blood from the brickwork over by the tent, in through the kitchen and out through the front door, or at least where the front door used to be. Right now, we're taking samples to check if the blood on the floor matches that on the wall. Assuming there is a match, then it looks to me as if somebody received a blow to the head over by the tent, which knocked them to the floor. They were then dragged out through the kitchen and beyond."

"Where does the trail stop?" Ben asked.

"Ten feet from the building," she replied.

"Ten feet? What did he do, get up and walk away?"

"With the amount of blood loss here, I doubt he or she would have been getting up and walking anywhere, Ben," Southwell replied.

"This hypothesis of yours," Freya interjected. "Does it include some kind of vehicle pulling up close to the house into which the body was loaded?"

"It seems a likely option," Southwell said. "We haven't had rain for a while, and the ground is dry as a bone."

"No tyre marks, then?"

"Nothing," she replied.

"And the blood on the wall," Ben said. "In your opinion, is this a knife wound? A slash, maybe?" He mimicked a slashing motion as if to support his question.

"It's possible," Southwell said. "But that would have involved a downward slash, given the direction of the spatter and its proximity to the floor." She shook her head. "I can't rule it out, of course, but I'm more inclined to go with some kind of blunt instrument. A bat or something. The victim would have been on their hands and knees, perhaps climbing from the tent."

"Surely the same could be said for a knife wound," Freya said, to which Southwell grimaced.

"Unlikely," she said. "If you have a knife and you're attacking somebody on the ground, then you're more likely to stab, and even if you did slash, I very much doubt the blood spatter would look like that." She pointed at the wall and shook her head. "I can't be certain, of course, but if you ask me, the victim was climbing from the tent, and the attacker hit them before they could rise to their feet. They then dragged the victim outside and loaded him into a vehicle. Whether the vehicle was already parked outside or not, I couldn't say."

"It makes sense that the vehicle had to be fetched," Ben said. "The killer could have..." he waved his hand around at the scene before them. "He could have done whatever he did here and then gone to get the vehicle to get rid of the body."

"Meanwhile, the boy and his friends come along?" Freya added, to which Ben nodded.

"They leave, the killer returns to remove the body, and then we turn up to find no body and therefore no crime."

"Will you be pursuing this?" Southwell asked.

"If you mean, will we be investing a significant number of resources, then no," Freya said. "But we'll get what information we can and keep an eye on missing persons. We'll also be conducting a search of the immediate area just in case." She edged past Ben on the platforms and then halted in the kitchen doorway before turning back to Katy. "If whoever that blood belongs to turns up, we'll need all the help we can get. We may be limited to whatever we find today."

"It's fine," Southwell said. "We'll leave no stone unturned."

"Thank you, Katy," she replied. "And when you see Gillespie in the morning..."

"Yes?" Southwell said, her head cocked to one side as if intrigued to hear what Freya had to say about their private life.

"Tell him I'll make it up to him," Freya said.

"Make what up to him?"

"Well, without wanting to put too fine a point on it, I think he was hoping for a quiet night in with the woman he so clearly adores," Freya said.

"He knows me better than that," Southwell replied. "Besides, it'll do him good to fend for himself for a change, although I'm dreading the mess when I get home."

"I've got something," the young female investigator said, who was half in and half out of the tent. She held up a brass photo frame, and once Ben had scrambled to pull on a disposable glove, he took it off her.

"What is it?" Freya asked, to which he simply held the frame up for her to see. "A family photograph?"

"The question is," Ben replied, handing the frame to South-well, who slipped it into a clear evidence bag and set to work marking the label. "Does the blood on that wall match any of these people? And if it does, then where the hell are they now?"

"There's something else," the investigator by the tent announced, and she held up what looked like an old scrapbook.

Ben accepted it and carefully let the book fall open in his hands.

"Ben?" Freya said, more than a little intrigued.

"It's some newspaper cuttings," he said quietly, perusing the old prints. He held the open book up for her to see.

"Good lord," she muttered to herself. "Well, at least we know why this place is empty."

CHAPTER SIX

"Ah, why on God's earth did I sign up for this?" Gillespie muttered with a yawn and a stretch that put a little too much strain on his old Volvo's driver's seat. Well, at least that's what Cruz thought he said. It was hard to understand him at the best of times, let alone when he was sleep-deprived. The lanky Glaswegian finished his stretch, swept the unruly mop of hair from his face, and rubbed his eyes like a child.

"You're one of them, are you?" Cruz said.

"One of what?"

"You know. You..." he mimicked the stretch and yawn. "You pandiculate."

"I what?"

"Pandiculate."

"I do no such thing," Gillespie replied, and the stubble on his neck rolls stood prominent as he pulled an offended expression. "What's pand...? What's that, then?"

"It's when you stretch and yawn. It's called pandiculating."

"For Christ's sake, Gabby," Gillespie said. "I've known you to come out with some crap in my time, but this? This takes the biscuit. So what if I stretch and yawn? We all stretch and yawn, don't we?"

"Well, yeah," Cruz replied. "But I just learned the word. It's nice to put it into practice, that's all."

"You want to learn words, do you? Well, I can give you words. Two of them, in fact. The first begins with F—"

"Alright, alright—"

"And I can give you another, too. It's the name of the place where you can shove your pan...whatever it was."

"Pandiculate?"

"Aye, that," Gillespie replied, and he grumbled some obscenities as he shoved the door open and climbed out. They were parked at the top of Labour in Vain Drove, where the main road ran right towards Tattershall and Coningsby and left towards North Kyme.

Slowly, Cruz climbed from the passenger seat and appraised the sky.

"Should be okay without jackets. What do you reckon?"

"I reckon if it rains, you can pull that dictionary from your backside and stick it on your head," Gillespie said, clearly still agitated at being outsmarted.

He pulled a sheet of paper from his pocket and unfolded it on the car bonnet, smoothing the dog ears as best he could. Cruz joined him and peered down at the sheet.

"That's your plan, is it?"

"Aye," Gillespie mumbled, and with his index finger on their position, he peered along the road and then pointed beyond the main road. "That dyke runs along the road. The way I see it, if the lad came up this lane, which, let's face it, he has to have done, he either lives in one of the few houses on the main road or he crossed the bridge further up the road and lives in one of the houses on the other side of the water."

"So that's our aim, is it? To find the boy who made the call?"

"My aim, Cruz, is to get through the day without having to endure living through an episode of Count-bloody-down."

"Surely it would be easier just to have Chapman run a report or look at the electoral register or something? She could tell us exactly who lives where, who has kids and who doesn't."

"Assuming the lad's parents actually vote," Gillespie told him. "Besides, there's a half a dozen houses on the main road and a few hundred on the other side of the dyke. Even if she did spend the next week ploughing through the data, the results would be questionable."

"Well, school records then."

"Can't do that," Gillespie said. "It's a GDPR thing, or safe-guarding, or something."

"What? We're the police. Surely, we can request the addresses of pupils that live in the area."

"Oh, right, and how would you go about that?" Gillespie asked, folding the map and stuffing it into his pocket. "You'd need a disclosure form to start with, and to obtain that, you'd need a crime number, and to obtain a crime number, you'd need a crime." Gillespie nudged his car door closed with his foot, then locked it. "And in case you hadn't noticed, Miss Vorderman, we haven't a crime. We've evidence of a crime, aye. But no actual crime."

"So, what the hell are we doing out here?"

"We're following orders, Gabby. For God's sake, man, you know how it works. The boss tells us to do something, we do it, and if it happens to be the wrong thing to do, the boss gets it in the neck." He started towards the first house and called back over his shoulder. "Then she diligently passes that wrath down to us in other ways. You can't say she isn't fair."

Cruz jogged a few steps to catch him up. The first house was just a few hundred yards along the main road.

"Do you think it's weird? You know, Ben and her getting married?"

"Weird? No," Gillespie replied. "I mean, I doubt there's many stations that would allow it. Actually, I think there's some kind of rule about it."

"So, how are they getting away with it?"

"Christ, Gabby, it's like having a five-year-old with me. *Why? Why? Why?*"

"I just want to know, that's all."

"Look, the Assistant Chief Constable has the final say, and I suppose Detective Superintendent Granger has had a word with him."

"Why would he do that?" Gillespie side-eyed him and sucked air in through his teeth. "I just want to know."

"Well, what choice has he got?" Gillespie said, coming to a stop and turning to face Cruz. "He can't stop them getting married, but he could force one of them to transfer, or he could force the boss into her office to prevent her from going out in the field, which, as a result, would limit the risk of their feelings for each other hindering an investigation."

"Oh, she wouldn't like that."

"Exactly. So, his options are to help them or lose one of them. And if he put his foot down and forced one of them to transfer, the chances are the other wouldn't be too happy."

"Right, so he's just going to let it go."

"Pick your battles, Gabby," Gillespie said, resuming his walk with a renewed sense of authority. "Pick your battles."

They stopped at the top of the first drive, and Gillespie waved a finger in Cruz's direction while he studied the house.

"What?' Cruz asked.

"Your thing," he replied. "You'll need to take notes."

"My notepad?"

"Aye, your notepad," Gillespie said. "And your erm..."

"Pen?" Cruz said slowly.

"Aye."

"Jesus, Jim. I mean, I don't expect you to know what pandiculate means, but notepad and pen? They're common items, especially for us—"

"Oh, shut up," Gillespie snapped. "It's been a rough night."

"I know, I was there, remember?"

"Aye, I know. I just didn't sleep too well."

"Oh, right. Waiting for the missus to get home, were you?"

"Kate? God no. It was gone six when she walked through the door," Gillespie said. "No, I've a few things on my mind, that's all."

"Like what??

"Like, mind your own business," Gillespie told him. "You ready for this, or what?"

"Just tell me what's on your mind."

Gillespie was clearly becoming frustrated at being pressed, and there were few things in life that pleased Cruz more than to see the big Scot squirm.

"Never you mind."

"Is it about your health?" Cruz pressed.

"What?"

"You know? You're getting to the age now, aren't you?" Cruz said, and he mimed a doctor slipping on a latex glove. "My old man had to go through it, but if it's any consolation, he said it wasn't as bad as you might think."

"It is not...that," Gillespie said. "If you must know, it's about the wedding."

"Ah," Cruz replied knowingly. "You're worried about the suit fitting." He reached out and grabbed a handful of Gillespie's midriff. "I wouldn't worry too much. You'll be surprised at what they can do now. I mean, they might need to add in a little more fabric to take to the strain—"

"I'm warning you, Gabby—"

"And you can always ask the photographer not to catch you side on—"

"It's the speech, you halfwit."

Cruz, delighting in Gillespie's reddening face, smiled up at him.

"The speech?"

"Aye, the speech," he said. He glanced up at the house to make sure nobody was listening. "I've got to make a speech. I'm the best man, right?"

"So? What is there to worry about? Get up, tell them how pretty the boss looks, mention how Ben is a good mate, and wish them luck in the future."

Gillespie stared back at him.

"You've not been best man at a wedding, I take it?"

"Well, no. Nobody's asked me."

"And you've not been to many weddings, I assume."

"Well, one or two."

"Right," Gillespie said as the front door of the house opened. "Well, until you have, I suggest you keep your suggestions to yourself. The speech is the highlight of the day."

"What? Of course, it's not—"

Gillespie suddenly lost interest as a young boy in school uniform emerged from the house. He left the front door wide open, suggesting that a parent was due to follow. The lad in question wore a school uniform as many youngsters did, with scant regard for pride. His shirt was untucked on one side, and his tie was pulled to the other. He ambled up the driveway apparently unaware of their presence, flicking through images on his phone.

"Alright, laddie? Is your ma or pa home?" Gillespie asked, and the young boy stared up at them wide-eyed and dumbstruck.

"Liam?" A woman called, presumably his mother. She pulled on a light jacket as she closed the front door. "Liam, leave them alone. Come on. Get in the car."

"It's alright, ma'am," Gillespie told her, and he held up his warrant card. "We're with Lincolnshire Police. Wondered if we might have a wee word."

"With me?"

"Actually, no," Gillespie said. "With the boy, here."

"With Liam? What do you want with *him*? He's done nothing wrong."

"Oh, he's not in any trouble, Mrs..." He beckoned for her to finish the sentence, and she hesitated for a moment.

"Jackson," she said eventually.

"We're investigating an incident, Mrs Jackson," Gillespie continued. "We wondered if Liam here might be able to help us." He stared down at the boy, and to Cruz's surprise, the big Scot's eyes softened. He even smiled a little. "You see, we had a call last night, Liam. From a young lad about your age, saying they saw something."

"What?" his mother asked. "What did they see?" Gillespie held his hand up to put her at ease.

"Was that you, Liam?" he asked. "Did you make a call last night? To the emergency services, that is. Did you call them?"

"Of course, he didn't," his mother cut in.

"And you can vouch for that, can you?" Gillespie asked. "You were with him, were you? You were with him at around nine-fifty pm last night?"

"I was working until eight, if you must know. But he was home, wasn't you, Liam?" She stared at Gillespie indignantly. "He has to be home by six."

"That right, lad?" Gillespie asked, to which the boy, once he had peeled his eyes from his mother's, peered up at him and nodded.

"S'right," he said, his voice light in tone. "I was here."

"But you had been out. Last day of the holidays, wasn't it? First day back at school today. I can't imagine you'd have been cooped up at home all day."

An awkward silence followed, during which the boy stared at his feet.

"Liam?" His mother said. "Tell the man where you were."

"I was here," he said.

"All day?" Gillespie asked incredulously. "While the sun was shining?"

"I was playing on my computer."

"On your computer? Alone?"

"No, Gopher came round for a bit."

"Gopher?"

"My mate," Liam explained. "And Henry, too. We just played here. I didn't make a call."

Gillespie searched for an untruth in the lad's eye, but from where Cruz was standing, there was none.

"I see," Gillespie said. "Well, thank you, and erm...have a good day back at school, eh?"

"Is that it?" the mother asked as she opened her car door.

"Aye, that's it," Gillespie replied as the boy made his way towards their Mondeo. Then Gillespie held his hand up one more time. "Actually, there is one more thing."

"Oh?" The woman said, her patience quite plainly being tested.

Gillespie pulled the folded map from his pocket once more, but instead of unfolding it, he flipped it over until he found a number scrawled in biro on the rear.

"Do you know Liam's phone number?"

"Sorry?" She looked appalled that he should even ask.

"He was on his phone a few moments ago," Gillespie said. "I just wondered if you know the number."

"My son has a phone for emergencies only, Sergeant," she said. "He doesn't have data, it's a phone call only SIM card, and I'm quite sure I'm not obliged to hand the number to any Tom, Dick or Harry that turns up on my doorstep."

"No, quite right," he told her, glancing down at the folded map. "Does the number end in two-three-three, by any chance?"

She waited a moment as if deliberating her response. Then, to put an end to the whole affair, she pulled her phone from her rear jeans pocket and navigated to the number.

"No," she said. "It's four-nine-one." She stuffed the phone back into her pocket. "Will that be all?"

"Aye," he replied as Cruz caught the lad staring at them through the windscreen. Gillespie followed Cruz's gaze, then cleared his throat. "I'm sorry to have disturbed you. You have a good day now."

They watched as Mrs Jackson pulled out of their drive and then turned right towards Coningsby.

"Believe him?" Cruz asked as she joined the traffic.

"Do I hell," Gillespie replied. "That's the problem with dealing with kids. They're all guilty of something."

"That's a broad statement."

"I didn't say he made the call," Gillespie said. "But he's guilty of something. He just didn't want to say in front of his mum. Could have been watching something on the internet or drinking her booze."

"What makes you so sure of that? He looked like a normal kid to me."

"Because," Gillespie said with a laugh. "I was a kid once, and was as guilty as any of them."

"So? I was a normal kid, and *I* didn't do anything I shouldn't."

"You're not a normal adult, Gabby," Gillespie explained. "I doubt very much you were a normal kid." He strode towards the next house, leaving Cruz speechless. He looked back over his shoulder as he walked. "Come on. You can do the next one. You never know; you might learn something."

CHAPTER SEVEN

"Oh, Christ," Freya said as she dropped into her chair and let her head fall back. Ben watched but said nothing.

"What's up?" Nillson asked, a question supported by both Chapman and Gold, who each looked on in concern.

"I've sent Gillespie and Cruz to knock on doors," she replied, and from the back of the room, Ben saw through her ploy and smiled to himself.

"That's okay," Nillson laughed. "We might not have a crime, but at least the office will be quiet for the morning."

"No, no," Freya said. "It's not that."

"Well, what then?" Gold asked.

"I would suggest she isn't too worried about Gillespie not being around," Ben said. "I suspect this is more of a Cruz issue."

"Cruz?" Gold said. "What's wrong with him being gone?"

"Ah," Nillson added, placing one foot decidedly out of Freya's trap. "Coffee."

"Coffee?" Gold said.

"Oh, that would be lovely," Freya told her, tugging a twenty-pound note from her bag. "Thank you, Gold. I'll have a flat white and whatever the rest of the team wants."

Gold wasn't just the nicest person on the team, nor was she simply the nicest person in the station. She was probably the nicest person Ben had ever met. A soft and kind-hearted soul. She laughed once and momentarily berated herself for falling for the trap.

"Okay, okay," she said, taking on the task far better than Cruz ever had. "Who wants what?"

"Black coffee for me," Chapman said.

"Cappuccino, please," Nillson added as Gold noted the requests down.

"Ben?" she said.

"Vanilla latte, please, Jackie."

"Sorry?" Freya said as if she hadn't heard correctly.

"Vanilla latte," he repeated.

"A *vanilla latte*? Since when do you have flavoured lattes?"

He felt the rest of the team watching, judging, and waiting for his response.

"Since I fancied one," he said. "Cruz always has it. Thought I'd try it."

"A week before your wedding?" Nillson said, pulling a face that suggested it wasn't a good idea.

"It's a coffee. I just want a coffee."

"Well have a coffee then," Freya said. "Just don't have syrup."

"I want a vanilla latte," he said. "Bloody hell. I'm a grown man—"

"Exactly," Freya cut in. "And if you grow much more, your suit won't fit." She turned to Gold while Ben scrambled for the words that conveyed his despair. "He'll have a skinny latte," she said. "No syrups."

"Right," Gold replied, and she avoided Ben's gaze as she strutted from the room.

"I don't believe you," he said as the doors swung closed behind Gold.

"Right, listen up," Freya said, ignoring him and addressing the room. "Whatever paperwork you have to finish up, do so by lunchtime, please. I'd like your full attention on last night's episode."

"I've got to follow up with the CPS on that hit and run last week," Nillson said.

"I should be clear by then, too," Chapman added.

Freya turned to Ben.

"Ben?"

"Freya?" he replied, unable to hide the icy edge to his tone.

"Will you be on top of your workload by this afternoon?"

"I don't know, Freya," he said. "I mean, I'm quite tired. I suppose it all depends on how good my coffee is."

She grinned, then laughed.

"Touche'," she said. "Make sure you are." She dragged the whiteboard into play, then spent a few seconds rubbing it down with the rag.

"I'd love to know what you're going to write on that," Ben said, which she duly ignored, then prised the lid off a marker. She narrated as she wrote, providing a summary of what they knew in list format.

"9:50 p.m.," she began. "Call comes in. Young male. Local. We." She circled the *we*, then turned to make sure they were all following. "Was he alone?"

"When he made the call or when he saw the body?" Nillson asked, to which Freya jabbed the marker in her direction.

"Good. Good." She continued writing. "Road noise. Main road?"

"Christ, Freya. Are we going through everything?" Ben said.

"Yes, Ben, we are," she said. "I've got a team of uniformed officers searching the immediate area, I've got CSI looking into the blood samples, and two officers going door to door. So, while all that goes on, it's down to us to go over everything we know."

"Alright, alright," he said, holding his hands up in defence. He sat back in his seat and accepted the decision was hers.

"What about the tyre marks?" Nillson asked, and again, Freya jabbed the marker in her direction.

"Tyre marks behind the house," she narrated as she wrote.

"Southwell took a look last night," Ben called out. "She's not hopeful. The ground is too dry to pull a print."

"Who said we need a tyre print?" Freya replied. "There was a car parked there, which means there's a good chance that whoever was staying there had access to a car."

"Right," Ben said.

"So, where's the car?" Freya added, and he had to concede that she had a point. She continued her narration as she wrote. "Tent, stove, food, scrapbook."

"Southwell is running them all for prints along with the DNA from the blood."

"Thank you, Ben. I was there when we agreed on a plan of action, if you remember."

He grinned to himself at being shut down. It was just her way of reasserting her position following the coffee incident. She would be right as rain when the two of them were alone.

"Speaking of blood," she continued. "Spatter on the wall. Trail of blood leading out to the threshold." She straightened, and at the top of the board, she drew a horizontal line from left to right. She marked six little lines starting on the left of the line. "Victim is killed," she said, noting the statement on the first of the lines. "Killer leaves to fetch vehicle," she said on the second line. "Boy/boys discover body," she said on the third line. She glanced back at them to make sure they were following, then settled on the fourth line. "Killer returns and moves body." Finally, on the fifth line, which was somewhere near the centre of the timeline, she wrote, "Boy calls 999."

She clicked the lid back onto the pen, tossed it into the tray beneath the board, then stepped back.

"Have I missed anything?" Gold said as she backed into the room carrying a cardboard tray of coffees.

"Nothing you didn't know already," Ben told her, much to Freya's chagrin.

She handed the coffees out, leaving Ben's until last, then returned to her seat.

"The point is that when the search has been conducted, when CSI have finished their tests, and when Tweedle Dum and Tweedle Dumber come back, we'll be able to slot whatever information they have into the timeline," Freya said. "In the meantime, Chapman, how did you get on with missing persons?"

"Nothing reported yet, ma'am," she replied. "I've got a reminder to check every hour."

"Good, thank you. Nillson, the search. How's that going?"

Nillson checked her laptop.

"I've got a message from the Sergeant leading the search," she said. "Nothing as yet. But they have had some pushback from the farmer who owns the land." She closed the laptop. "He says he's doing what he can but will need a warrant to access the fields."

"Ooh, tricky without a crime number," Ben added.

"Yes, thank you, Ben," Freya said, then addressed Nillson. "Tell him to do what he can, will you?"

Ben took a sip of his coffee to conceal his smirk and was pleasantly surprised to breathe in a delightful vanilla aroma. Gold remained facing forward, but there was little doubt she was smiling inwardly. He took a larger mouthful, let out a loud satisfied '*ahhh*,' then sat back in his seat, content.

Freya eyed him, and he was sure she was about to say something, but the doors opened once more.

"Good morning," Detective Superintendent Granger said, making a point of smiling at everyone in the room. "How are we all?"

"Very good, guv," Freya replied on their behalf. "We're just going through the events from last night."

"Last night?"

"Yes, guv. The Billinghay job. We're expecting some news this morning—"

"Well, I wouldn't put too much into that," he told her.

"No, guv. We're just getting prepared. I have little doubt that a crime has been committed, and so we're just getting one step ahead of—"

"I wouldn't put too much into that," he said, cutting her off. "In fact, let's drop it."

"Guv?"

"We've no body, Chief Inspector Bloom. With no body, we've no crime. I've a hundred other investigations I can put you on."

"Guv, I've got resources out there. Let's give it a day. If nothing comes in, we'll drop it."

He made a show of listening, and without raising his voice, he reiterated his position.

"Let's drop it, shall we?" He took a step forward and placed a new blue cardboard folder on her desk. "This one needs your attention."

"What's that?" Freya asked, and Ben noticed the entire team were craning their necks to see the file.

"It's a crime that needs investigating," Granger replied. "One with a body."

"I see," Freya said.

"While I'm here, I wonder if I could have a word?" he continued, and his eyes suggested a matter of some gravity. "In my office."

CHAPTER EIGHT

THE DOORS SWUNG CLOSED as Freya reentered the room, and the team, having seen the look on her face, busied themselves with work, refusing to make eye contact.

Ben offered an inquisitive look, to which she simply shook her head as she approached, and he prepared to be on the receiving end of her frustration.

But that frustration didn't come. Not in the way he had anticipated, anyway. She took one look at his stoic expression, stepped over to his desk and raised his coffee cup to her nose, inhaling long and deep.

She placed the cup back down with a defeated smile.

"At least we know where DC Gold's allegiance lies," she said, placing her car keys down on his desk. "You can drive."

She snatched up her coat and bag and left the room in an agitated flurry.

In turn, Gold, Nillson, and Chapman all turned to stare at him.

"What was all that about?" Gold asked.

"I have no idea," he replied. "But I'm sure I'll find out."

"Good luck," Nillson said with a grin.

"Ah, she'll be alright. Pre-wedding nerves," he said with a laugh that convinced nobody. He shoved his seat back, grabbed his bag, and swallowed the remainder of his coffee. He caught Gold's empathetic smile. "Cheers for the coffee."

"Was it worth it?" she replied.

He tossed the empty cup into the bin near the door.

"Every calorie," he called out as he made his way to the door.

He made his way down the fire escape stairs, then shoved through into the car park to find Freya leaning against the passenger door of her car, browsing what looked to be an open file in her hands. It was only when he had climbed in, adjusted the seat, and was preparing to move off that he saw what it was she was reading.

"For God's sake, Freya. You did hear what Granger just said, didn't you?"

Freya settled into the passenger seat.

"I did."

"Yet, you're still reading the copies of the scrapbook?" he said as he pulled out of the station car park and put his foot down to get her attention.

She jolted back a little, glanced up from the file, and then glared at him.

But instead of asking him to treat her car nicely, she cleared her throat and returned her attention to the pages before her.

"Did you know that building has been empty for nearly three decades?" she said. It was her usual tactic of diverting from the topic in question onto a more sedate and agreeable topic. There was little doubt, however, that the treatment of her car would be raised in a subsequent conversation - probably when he least expected it.

"Three decades? Wow," Ben said with mock enthusiasm.

"It says here that...oh God," she said, shaking her head. "A whole bloody family died in the blaze."

"Oh really?" he replied with far more sincerity. "Not kids, surely?"

"Two," she said. "Two girls and their parents."

"For God's sake."

"It says here that the blaze started in the kitchen and took hold in a matter of moments, leaving the family inside trapped."

"It doesn't bear thinking about," Ben told her, momentarily reflecting on how a tragedy could cut through a quarrel, putting life into real perspective.

"Interestingly, it does mention another child, whose name has been omitted for the purposes of child safety."

"Safeguarding?"

"The nineties equivalent, yes," she said. "He was twelve, and it says here that due to no known family to take him in, he will likely go into care."

"Swallowed by the system, then?" Ben said. "Don't tell Gillespie. You know what he's like about all that."

"According to this article, a local farmer named Frank Bowen was the first on the scene. He sent one of his labourers to call the emergency services, and despite his efforts to rescue the family, he was unable to. According to Bowen, when he saw the smoke from his field, he ran across and was able to hear the family inside… screaming." She paused, and from the corner of his eye, Ben saw her reaching up to the scars on her face, perhaps involuntarily. "The screaming soon faded, and then, as if to draw a line through any hope he might have had, the roof collapsed. How awful."

"I suppose that'll have to go into the archives," Ben said.

"Sorry?"

"The scrapbook," he said. "It'll have to be filed."

"I don't agree," she replied. "It should go to the next of kin. She scanned the rest of the old newspaper page. "It says here the summer is going to be the hottest on record."

"Don't they say that every year?"

"Feels like it, doesn't it? It's always the hottest summer and the coldest winter. Honestly, they think we're silly."

"It's not the heat or the cold people worry about around here," Ben added. "It's the rainfall. One bad season can put a farm into a slow decline. Did you see all those dykes by the farmhouse?"

"Of course."

"That tells you something," Ben said. "I've seen water sitting on fields for months. Half a farm, in some cases, underwater. That's like having one hand tied behind your back and being asked to cook a Sunday roast. You've got the tools to do it well, but you just can't use it."

"Well, in this case, a good douse would have served them well," Freya said, resuming her browsing of the scanned page. "It's funny, isn't it? We're still plagued by the same issues they faced nearly three decades ago." Ben glanced over, hoping to entice more from her musings. "I'm just reading the smaller headlines. One-year anniversary of a missing local girl, presumed dead. A spate of burglaries in Woodhall Spa reaches record high. Police call off the search for a missing man." She raised her head and stared through the passenger window. "You'd think we might have come on a little since then, wouldn't you? Honestly, this could be a newspaper from last month."

"Men will always be men," Ben said. "Some of us know the difference between right and wrong; some of us don't."

"Oh, I disagree," Freya replied. "I think you all know the difference between right and wrong. It's just that some men lack empathy and compassion."

"Well, most of us lack that," Ben replied.

"No. No, I disagree. Tell me, Ben, when you see a pretty girl, what is it that stops you from...attacking her? From taking what you want?"

"What? Freya, can we not—"

"Just answer the question. What stops you from assaulting her?"

"I would never do that. Most of us would never do that."

"Right, but why?" she asked. "*Why* wouldn't you?"

"Because it's wrong, Freya. Sorry, how have we somehow managed to be discussing my potential ability to—"

"Because it's wrong," Freya said. "That's why you wouldn't do it?"

"Yes," he said. "Because...because the girl in question would not only suffer the ordeal of the moment but for years to come. How many times have we seen that?"

"And if I told you that there are some men out there that would never dream of hurting a young girl and taking what they want by force, not because they can empathise, as you do, but because they fear the consequences?"

"I suppose there must be men like that—"

"There is," Freya said. "The only thing that stops those men from committing a terrible crime, is the fear of prison. Not empathy, not compassion. Just fear of prison."

"Well...I'm not one of them."

"No, you're not, and thankfully, nor are most men. But there are also those who not only lack empathy and compassion but also do *not* fear prison. The threat of the consequence is overshadowed by their selfish demands. They know the difference between right and wrong, yet they still continue to..." She cleared her throat and checked her reflection in the sun-visor mirror, then slapped it closed. "Those are the men we hear about. That's who this man here was." She jabbed a manicured fingernail at the newspaper cutting. "The same can be said about burglaries. There isn't a barrister in the land that could argue a burglar was unaware that his actions were wrong."

"Although, you could argue that crimes like burglaries and theft are driven by need," Ben said as they pulled into a little lane on the border of Tattershall and Billinghay. "When times are hard, people get desperate. It's a choice of starving or risking prison."

"Fifty years ago, I might have agreed," she said. "But these days, people can get help. There are food banks, benefits—"

"So, you're saying that nobody is starving in this country, are you?"

"No, if you listen, Ben, I'm saying there's no reason for people to starve, and there's certainly no reason for people to commit crimes in order to survive." She pointed ahead to where two police cars were parked on the track between two fields. "There. Looks like we're late to the party."

Ben pulled the car up behind one of the police Astras and killed the engine.

"Christ," Freya said, and he followed her gaze. "Granger wasn't wrong about there being a body, was he?"

The sight before them was one of tragedy, devastation, and suffering. Four uniformed officers were present; two were standing with their backs to the crime scene, one was speaking into his radio by one of the Astras, and the fourth was white as a sheet, doubled over with a string of vomit and saliva hanging from his mouth.

"Get Gillespie on the phone, will you?" Freya said quietly.

Ben checked his watch. "He's probably only a dozen houses in—"

"Just..." she snapped, then calmed herself. "Just get him on the phone."

A few moments later, with three of the uniformed officers staring at them, waiting for an instruction, Gillespie's voice came through loud and clear over the call.

"Aye, Benny boy. How's it going?" he said. "What a glorious day, eh? The sun's shining, and I've already got my ten-thousand steps in. Should have done this one yourself, you know, what with the wedding and all that."

"Gillespie, it's me," Freya said, her voice taut as a drum.

"Eh? Oh, sorry, boss," he said. "Listen, we're running a wee bit behind schedule but should be back by mid-afternoon. I'll get my report typed up as soon as we're back, but to be honest, we've got bugger all right now—"

"I need you here," she said.

"Eh?"

"I said leave it. Abort. I need you here. Ben will send you our location. It's just down the road from where you are."

"Well, alright, boss. If you say so."

"I do say so. We're going to need everyone on this," she replied. "And for you in particular, I have a particular job in mind."

She reached out and ended the call before Ben could add anything to soften the blow.

"Are you going to tell me what Granger said?" he asked, to which she simply stared out of the window at the fields beside her.

"No," she replied curtly, shoving the car door open. "There's nothing to say."

CHAPTER NINE

THE SMELL that hung in the mid-morning air was putrid and nauseating. It was unique. Unmistakable to those who had smelled it before. It was leathery yet subtly metallic, the way the iron taste of blood lingers on one's palette.

Birds sang just as they would have on any other day. As if the sight that had captured Freya's imagination was insignificant.

Just another day.

But to those living, things both blessed and cursed with empathy and compassion, the sight was a travesty. A grotesque demonstration of just how broad the humanity spectrum could span.

"They're here," Ben muttered as a car rumbled along the track somewhere behind her. The engine noise died, and on any other day, the morning would have returned to that of bird song. And indeed, the birds still sang, perhaps calling to each other in warning of an approaching lanky, mop-haired Sergeant Gillespie.

But it wasn't the bird song that took centre stage. Sure, they might have provided a light morning chorus to cheer the sombre mood, but it was the bass notes that were building to a distant crescendo.

Flies.

Great swathes of them.

Huge blow flies that thrived in the fertilised fields now feasted on the carcass of one poor man, and when one lost its place on the prize, it buzzed around, searching the masses for another way in or ventured further afield to where Freya and Ben stood. Twice, one of them had landed on Freya's lip, perhaps attracted by the scent of her balm, and twice she had swatted it away. With the second swipe, she had actually made contact with the slow and cumbersome creature and had been surprised at its weight as it connected with her palm.

"Can't we do something?" Ben asked, apparently immune to the swarm. "Everyone's here now. Gillespie and Cruz are just parking up, Nillson is two minutes out, and I think I can see Doctor Saint's Jag coming down the track."

"What about Southwell?"

"I imagine her and her team are fast asleep after last night."

"Have you called her?"

"I've left a message," he said.

"Good. Well, let's not rewrite the playbook. Have Nillson close the roads off. Gillespie can organise a search of the immediate area, and when he's done that, he can come and see me."

"I think the Duty Sergeant might have something to say about that," Ben replied. "You've got half his officers up the road in Billinghay."

"Yes, I know. I was hoping we might have a last-minute discovery to give Granger an 'I told you so,' but it seems I am beaten," she said and waved off another dozy fly. "Have them moved over here. I'd like to start as soon as possible."

"I'll call the Duty Sergeant, then."

"No," she said. "No, move them first. I don't want him taking the opportunity to strip me of resources. If they're here and working, it'll be far harder for him to argue."

"You really are a piece of work, aren't you?"

"It's just experience, Ben," she replied, and finally, she turned away to escape the inquisitive blowflies. Doctor Saint, the region's Forensic Medical Examiner, was retrieving his case from the boot of his car. "Good morning, Peter."

She strode over to him, savouring the relatively cleaner air.

His smile never wavered, not even when, while shaking her hand, he glanced over her shoulder at the devastation beyond.

"Thanks for coming," she muttered, and he took a deep breath.

"Well, I could hardly refuse, could I?" He looked across at Ben and offered a friendly nod. Already, the sight behind Freya had cast a sombre tone.

"You might wish you had," Ben said.

"Where are we?" Saint asked.

"It's as we found it," Freya said. "He was found by a woman walking her dog. According to one of the uniformed officers, she didn't have her phone with her. She went home to report it immediately. We've got her address, and we'll be sending somebody round. So far, that's about as much as we know. We haven't touched him for obvious reasons."

"Well, that's one thing. I presume we've been in touch with Katy Southwell?"

"We've left a message. She was on call last night, but I'm hopeful she'll respond soon."

"Jesus, would you look at that," Gillespie said as he walked by, shaking his head.

The interruption caught Saint's attention, and he saw the urgency in Freya's eyes.

"Okay, let's get started," Saint said.

"You weren't kidding about this one, were you?" Gillespie said to Freya as the threesome returned to the scene. Ben peeled off and took Gillespie to one side.

"Jim, listen I need you to pull the resources from Billinghay and get them here without causing too much of a fuss."

His voice faded as Freya and Saint approached the body and the flies.

"How long's he been there?" she asked, to which he sucked in a deep thoughtful breath.

"Hard to say. Under ordinary circumstances, the flies wouldn't come in until putrification. You might get the odd one or two, but nothing like this."

"But?"

"But he's been severely burned. They're attracted to the raw flesh and blood."

"So?"

"So, I can't say," he said. "Not without examining him. What are your thoughts?"

"My thoughts are that some kind of accelerant has been used, petrol perhaps. His jeans appear to be scorched. A shoe is missing, and you can see the difference between the singed flesh on the top of his foot and the...ordinary flesh below."

"Yes," Saint said. "Yes, I'd have to agree. His face seems to have gone untouched for the most part. Does that mean anything to you?"

Freya took a few steps to one side to view the body from a new angle. The air was thicker, and in the shade, the flies seemed even more persistent, so she held a handkerchief to her mouth and nose.

"I noticed that," she told him. "You might be forgiven for thinking it was due to his clothing. Only those parts of him covered by clothing have been burned. But clothing doesn't burn like that. In fact, it takes a fair amount of heat to burn denim. Anything polyester would have simply melted to his skin and frazzled away like molten plastic, which I suppose it is." She took a few careful steps forward for a better view, then retreated to Saint's side.

"But?" he said. "I sense a but coming."

"I've seen this before," she explained, and he cocked his head to one side. "And I'm not referring to my own injuries. I saw this in London once when I was in the Met. It was a gang thing. The perpetrators wanted to inflict as much pain as possible."

"And this?" he asked.

"Well, I doubt it's gang-related," she said. "Not round here." She stared up at the gentle giant. "But given that his face has, for the most part, been saved," she said. "I would suggest that whoever did this wanted him to suffer. They wanted him to see his body burning. They wanted him to feel every inch of him ablaze."

"A notion you're familiar with," Saint said softly.

"No, I was unconscious when my...when my accident happened," she said. "This man was alive and conscious. He would have seen every lick of every flame, and he would have felt everything."

"Do we have photos?" Saint asked.

"Ben has taken some. CSI will take more."

"Well, given the circumstances, if you're happy, I think we should begin."

Freya stared at the body one more time, then nodded and turned to the uniformed officers nearby.

"You two," she said, and they glanced at each other before tentatively edging closer. "Come on, he won't bite."

Saint waved a fly away, and the officers came to stand beside them both.

"Ma'am?" The first officer said.

"Summon the help you'll need," she said, studying the anguish that had been seared into the man's eyes moments before he died. She turned to face them once more. "Then cut him down."

CHAPTER TEN

THE REMOVAL WAS CONDUCTED with as much taste as possible, providing the victim with all the dignity the men could salvage. Three officers bore his weight, while a fourth mounted a ladder sourced from a nearby farm, and cut through the rope.

The activity did little to dissuade the flies from their feast, forcing the officers to don heavy jackets, gloves, and face masks, which made the difficult task even more of a challenge.

They eased him to the ground, away from the tree, to preserve as much of the evidence as possible. A plastic sheet had been laid out for him, which served as little more than a target for the flies which seemed to come in droves.

"We'll need to be quick," Saint said. "We can wrap him until the CSI team gets here."

"They're on their way," Gillespie cut in, then turned to Ben. "Kate messaged me a while ago. They were just unloading the boxes from last night. Should be here any minute."

"Right. Can I have some space, please?" Saint asked. "Freya, Ben, you can stay, but if we can ask the others to move away, I'd be grateful."

"Right then, lads," Gillespie said to the officers. "Good work.

You've earned yourselves a nice cup of tea. How does that sound, eh?"

Even Gillespie's upbeat, motivational tone did little to cut through the officers' moods. What they had been asked to do had been horrific, traumatic even. The fact was that somebody had to do it. There was an argument that suggested the task should have been done by CSI in conjunction with paramedics. But in Freya's opinion, the man needed to be cut down sooner rather than later. The longer he was up there, the greater the chance of a member of the public seeing him, and that could have had serious consequences.

Doing what he could to motivate the officers, Gillespie took their jackets, masks, and gloves and, with Cruz's help, led them off towards the cars.

Saint busied himself with the medical side of his examination, taking internal and external temperatures and assessing crucial details that may or may not translate into causes of death.

Freya and Ben, meanwhile, remained silent, each of them making their own mental notes and assessments.

He caught Freya looking his way and raised his eyebrows expectantly.

"Tattoo," she said and nodded at the little cross on the right side of the man's neck. It wasn't a complex tattoo or a detailed cross. Simply two lines, as if a friend had done it, or even a fellow inmate during a prison sentence.

"I saw that," he replied.

Typically, in moments such as these, they would notice fresh wounds or abrasions, perhaps from a scuffle. A grazed knuckle or a defensive wound, maybe even bruising on the neck or throat. But given that more than ninety per cent of the man's body was either charred or inflamed and angry red, such details were almost impossible to identify in situ.

"Pockets are empty," Saint called. "No jewellery, phone, watch, or any other accessories."

"Robbed?" Ben suggested, to which Freya gave a rather non-committed shrug.

"Tattoo on the side of his neck. Looks old," Saint continued. "I'd say he was in his late thirties, early forties, well-groomed, clean fingernails."

"Not our camper, then?" Freya muttered.

"Sorry?"

"Nothing. Sorry, Peter."

He nodded and eyed Ben before continuing. "Given the manner in which he was discovered and the haemorrhages in his eyes, I think it's safe to say that he died from strangulation, although I would caveat that with the possibility that his heart gave out before strangulation took effect."

"Can we be sure?" Ben asked.

"Not here," he said. "Pip should be able to tell when he's on her bench, but without opening him up, I'm afraid all I can give you is a best guess. But I will say this. I pray his heart gave out long before the rope around his neck did its job."

"Why do you say that?" Freya asked, to which he shrugged and gathered his various implements into his case.

"Have you ever heard of the long drop?" he asked.

"Of course," she said.

"Well, the long drop was implemented because of the terrible suffering caused by the short drop," he said, waving a hand over the body. "This was a short drop." He shook his head with pity. "It can take anything up to fifteen minutes for a man to die like this. In the meantime, he becomes brain damaged, clinging onto life by a thread, and all the while he is more than aware of his circumstance, and even more aware of the pain."

"You paint a vivid picture, Peter," she said, but he had yet to finish.

"You, more than any of us, are aware of the pain caused by fire," he said, and she stiffened at the reference. "As awful as your injuries were, Freya, they pale in significance to what this man endured. He was hanged by his neck, doused in fuel of some sort, and set ablaze. I can't say if he was already swinging when the flames took hold or if the killer waited until he was ablaze before hauling him up there. But I know this." Again, he waved a hand over the victim. "The pain this man endured was beyond that which any of us could possibly imagine. *Any* of us."

"You said he could have been hauled up," Ben said. "Do you mean he was lying on the ground, and the killer pulled him up?"

"That's exactly what I mean."

"That would take considerable strength."

"It would," Saint said. "Of course, it would also mean that he would have to tie the rope off once the victim was swinging freely."

"And, of course, doing that while the flames were going would have added more of a challenge," Freya added, to which Saint nodded his agreement.

"This is all hypothesis, of course. We can never know for certain."

"In case you're not aware, Peter, pretty much all of what we do is hypothesis. Very rarely do the pieces of the puzzle fit together nicely first time around."

"I will say this, though," Saint added. "In terms of the practicalities surrounding the..." he waved a hand again, his hand as limp as sombre as his tone. "It's not uncommon for a horse or a vehicle to be used in these circumstances. In the US, slave owners would employ the additional power to string up individuals who failed to toe the line."

"Of course," Freya said. "That would mitigate the need for outside help."

"There are heavy abrasions on the man's neck, which, although could be due to the swinging motion, could also be attributed to being dragged into the air."

"So, one rope was tied around his neck, slung over the tree branch, and then tied to the tow bar of a car or something?" Ben said. "Then he's hauled up there, the noose is slipped over his neck."

"That's about the size of it," Saint agreed. "The rope is nothing out of the ordinary. You'd find this in nearly every garage or shed. But the knot is interesting. It's an actual noose."

"What does that mean?" Freya asked.

"Well, you'll have to excuse me here, but I've seen more hangings in recent years than I care to remember. Most of them were suicides due to the pandemic and the economic crisis. The world is a cruel place right now."

"It is," Freya agreed.

"I can count on one finger the number of times the victim has tied a real noose like this," he said. "They usually just tie a slip knot. It holds. Does the job, if you know what I mean?" He held the knot, which was still tied around the man's neck, for them to see. "This appears to be a real noose."

"What's the significance of that?" Ben asked.

"Well, if I gave you a length of rope right now, could you tie me a noose?"

Ben shrugged.

"I suppose I'd need a bit of time to remember how to do it, but—"

"Precisely," Saint said with a smile. "If my opinion carries any weight—"

"Which it does," Freya said.

"Then this noose was prepared in advance. He knew what he was doing. This whole thing was planned."

"He wanted him to suffer," Freya muttered.

"He did," Saint agreed. "And I'm sorry to say, he got his wish."

A few moments of silence passed as each of them imagined the horror the victim had endured, and Ben was more than a little grateful to feel the vibration of his phone in his pocket.

He stepped away from the threesome, leaving Freya and Saint to consider the man's final moments.

"Chapman?" he said quietly, hoping to convey the sobriety of the scene.

"Ben, we've had a call come in," she said over the line. "It's a missing person not far from where you are."

He glanced back at Freya and Saint, who were now in contemplative silence.

"Send me the details, will you?" he said, more than a little distracted.

"It's a Mrs Dean. Says her husband didn't come home on Saturday. He's been acting strange all week."

"Thanks Chapman—"

"She also said he went out to the shed before he left. She thinks he might have done something stupid."

Her words painted a picture that Ben imagined with ease.

Her silence added the weight needed to press the matter home.

"I'll go and see her," he said, ending the call as he strode back to Freya and Saint.

"Peter, can I ask a question?" he said, seeming to rouse them both from their imaginations.

"Of course," Saint said, checking his watch before giving his undivided attention.

"In your opinion," he began. "Has our victim suffered any head wounds? Or any other wounds, come to think of it." He eyed Freya, who was clearly thinking along the same lines. "Has he experienced severe blood loss?"

Saint's eyebrows raised like two caterpillars dancing to some unheard tune.

"From what I've seen," he said at last and then shook his head. "No. No, he did not."

CHAPTER ELEVEN

"WHAT'S HIS NAME?" Freya asked as they pulled up outside the address Chapman had provided. Ben checked the messages on his phone.

"Tommy Dean," he replied. "Been missing since Saturday."

"And it's her husband, you say?"

"That's what the report said," he told her. "With any luck, he's done a runner."

"Gone for a pint of milk, you mean?" she said, offering a wry smile while she adjusted her hair in the mirror. A few months ago, she would have pulled it across her face to mask the scar. But with the help of some makeup tutorials and the healing powers of time, she was slowly leaving more of her damaged skin exposed. It was a positive sign, but Ben knew better than anyone not to bring it up, as she would no doubt resort to keeping that side of her face in shadow. She snapped the sun visor closed. "Shall we?"

"Quite possibly the worst part of the job," he said as they walked up the garden path. He distracted himself with the garden. The beds were well kept, the driveway free of weeds, and the soil had been turned over. Such details would never stand up in court as evidence, but they did give the experienced eye an idea of who they were dealing with.

"We don't know it's him yet," she reminded him, coming to a stop at the front door, where she waited for Ben to ring the bell.

They heard footsteps in an instant, as if whoever it was had been waiting close by.

"Yes?" she said when the door opened. "Are you the police?"

She was a pretty woman in her mid-forties, wearing a long floral dress. Her hair had been pulled back, and her moist brown eyes were blazing red.

Freya held up her warrant card, and Ben followed suit.

"I'm Detective Chief Inspector Bloom, and this is my colleague Detective Inspector Savage," she began. "May we come in?"

"Of course, of course," the woman said. "I'm so sorry to have bothered you all. I just..." She held the door and averted her eyes as she fought to keep her emotions in check. "I'm just a bit worried, that's all."

"It's understandable," Ben told her as he followed Freya into the house. The hallway was what he had expected from the exterior: large and clean, with the stairs ahead of them, doglegging up the right, and various doorways leading to various parts of the house.

"It's just not like him, that's all. He never does this." She led them through to a modest lounge, where a single sofa and an armchair waited for them. She took the armchair, leaving Ben and Freya to settle on the sofa.

Ben flipped to a clean page of his notepad while Freya waited for the right moment to begin. During the time he had known her, he had come to learn her strategy for such occasions, which was to let them speak, to get things off their chest before dialling into specifics.

She waited patiently while the woman spilled everything she knew.

"He went out on Saturday. He's been a bit down recently, so I figured he needed a bit of time. We've no kids, so it's not like he left me in the lurch."

"I see," Freya said, encouraging her to continue.

"He wasn't home when I went to bed at ten, so I figured he was in the pub. You know, blowing off steam." She paused for a moment and stared at her hands. "But then he wasn't here when I woke up. I tried to call him, but it just rang and rang."

"And his phone isn't here, anywhere?" Ben asked for clarity, to which she shook her head emphatically.

"He always takes his phone. He never leaves without it. Never." She added. "I sat here all day yesterday, waiting. I called the pub. They hadn't seen him. I called everyone I knew. Nobody has seen hide nor hair of him."

"What about his work? His colleagues?" Ben said, coaxing her on.

But she shook her head sadly.

"He's out of work," she replied.

"Hence, him being a little down?" Freya asked, and again she nodded.

"Right, well, let's start with the basics," Freya said. "We've got him down as a Tommy Dean, but we weren't given your name."

"My name? Oh, sorry. It's Julie. Julie Dean."

Ben made notes while Freya picked up the questioning.

"And he's been missing since Saturday, has he? What time, exactly? Do you know?"

"No. I popped to the Co-op at around midday and had to run a few errands. He was gone when I got back."

"And you said he was feeling a bit down?

"Yes," she said. "I asked him if he was okay. But you know what men are like." She looked up at Ben. "Sorry, I don't mean to generalise, but—"

"It's fine," Freya said. "We're all grown up enough to appreciate certain characteristics. Don't worry; we won't accuse you of being sexist."

Mrs Dean smiled a little, but it faded fast.

"He always bottles things up, you see? He's like an emotional rock. Never speaks about anything. It's so bloody....frustrating," she said, then squeezed her eyes closed. "I just wish he'd call, or... or something. I just wish I'd pressed him harder."

"Mrs Dean, you mentioned he was out of work. How long for?"

"Oh, a few months," she replied. "I mean, I should have been upset by it, but if I'm honest, I was quite pleased. It was killing him."

"How so?"

"Well, when I met Tommy, he was training to be an accountant. He had a job in town and did quite well. But when the pandemic struck, the firm he was working for started to make cutbacks. They opted to use an outsourced accountancy firm to save money. Not just him. It was HR and a few others, too. Scraping money off their bottom line." She sucked in a breath and released it slowly. "Tommy wasn't too fussed. Not as much as me, anyway. He took the opportunity to start fresh. Said he wanted to work outdoors." She gave a little laugh to conceal her truest thoughts. "He was putting on a bit of weight, you see. Felt unhealthy, if you know what I mean?"

"I can understand that," Ben agreed.

"Got himself a job on a nearby farm. They were struggling because all the foreign workers had to leave, so it worked well. I think he enjoyed it. His dad was a farm worker. Worked on the same farm back in the day."

"It's gratifying work," Ben added, which raised a polite smile.

"Tommy drove a lot of the machinery but also had to get stuck into the heavier stuff. Some days, he'd come home and could barely walk, but he'd always play it cool. He'd tell me he was okay, but I could see it in the way he moved and the way he sat down or stood up. It was doing him in."

"So, what? Was he not fit for the job? Is that why he lost it?" Freya asked.

"Oh, God no," she said. "No, it was the boss. The farmer, I suppose. Never paid his wages on time. Sometimes, not at all. It caused all sorts of arguments with us. In the end, I told him that if he didn't have a word, I'd go and have it for him."

"I bet that went down well," Ben added.

"I would have, you know?" she said adamantly. "But Tommy had this thing, see. He didn't want me upsetting the boss. In the end, they had words and came to an agreement."

"Which was?"

"Tommy got the money he was owed and then gave it up. The farmer said something about cash flow being a problem, what with the cost of fertiliser and whatnot. Don't get me wrong, Tommy would have been paid. But it wouldn't have been a regular thing. First, he blamed the pandemic; then there was the war. His latest excuse was the pressures the government has put on farmers. I mean, how hard can it be? If you hire people, then you need cash in the bank."

"It has been a challenging time for farmers," Ben agreed. "But you're right. Any employer has a duty of care to their staff."

"Well, I wasn't having any of it. We're not in a position to wait until harvest to get paid; the bloody mortgage can't wait, can it? And what about his other men? Surely, they can't all be waiting for pay." She shook her head. "No, I didn't believe a word of it. I told Tommy he was being taken advantage of. Anyway, they parted company. He's just been struggling to find anything else. I mean, he could have gone back into accounting, but he was adamant."

Freya waited a few seconds for Ben to finish taking notes and for Mrs Dean to stop her rocking back and forth.

"So, you've spoken to everyone he knew, including family?" she asked.

"Everyone," she said. "I'm at a loss." Now that the story was out, she had little to distract her from her imagination, and her eyes welled once more. "I just hope he hasn't done anything..." She wiped at her eyes with her cuff. "I was just worried. I'm really bloody worried about him."

Freya nodded and glanced around the room, settling on a framed photo.

"Is that him?" she asked. "With the dark, curly hair?"

"Yeah, that's him. It's shorter now, though."

"Mrs Dean, does Tommy have any identifiable features?" she asked. "I don't know, a scar or a—"

"A tattoo," she said. "He has a tattoo. Why? Why do you ask?"

"Can you describe this tattoo?" Freya asked gently.

"Yes, it's a cross. It's on his neck. I always hated it. But him and his mates did them when they were kids."

Freya nodded, and Ben noted the description, picturing the tattoo on the hanged man's neck they had seen less than an hour before.

"Mrs Dean, there's no easy way to say this," Freya began, and Julie Dean's expression played through a series of expressions, ending on defeat. "This morning, we attended a call to a field not far from here."

"No," Mrs Dean said. "No, don't say it—"

"I'm sorry," Freya said. "But there's a chance it could be Tommy."

"No," Mrs Dean blurted out. "No, no, no."

In a rare moment of compassion, Freya reached out and took Julie Dean's hand.

"Mrs Dean, I need you to be strong now," Freya said. "We don't know for sure."

"I do," she replied between sobs, and she raised her head to stare at Freya. "I think I've always known."

CHAPTER TWELVE

PROCEDURE DICTATED that Mrs Dean be subjected to a hideous rigmarole designed by somebody with little to no experience of grief. Hence, Freya felt duty bound, as she so often did, to manipulate the processes to allow for as much empathy as the procedures allowed.

"See that she's okay," Freya whispered to DC Gold, who, in the capacity of Family Liaison Officer, had attended the house at Ben's request. She glanced up the stairs to see the bathroom door was still closed. "See if there's a family member or somebody to come and be with her. But I want you to stay, okay?"

"Will do, ma'am," Gold said, her soft Edinburgh accent marking her out as the most suitable for the job.

"Any luck with the dog walker?" Freya asked, to which Gold shook her head.

"No, she didn't get close. She saw him hanging and ran home to call it in."

Freya nodded. It was an understandable reaction. She pointed upstairs, where Julie Dean was in the throes of grief.

"We've taken a brief account, but you know how it is. She might say more, so feel free to make notes," Freya continued.

"Doctor Bell is going to need the rest of the day with the body, but we can't begin the investigation in an official capacity until she's identified the body."

"Is she up to it?" Gold asked, to which Freya shook her head.

"Would you be?" she replied. "But I'm afraid she's going to have to, and if I'm right, then she'll want to."

"Why's that?"

Freya glanced up the stairs once more, then beckoned Gold into the living room. Ben remained by the door to keep watch.

"She was frightened he might do something stupid. According to her, he was quite down," Freya explained. "So, I made the decision to tell her that the man we discovered had not committed suicide, that we believe there was a third party involved."

"Jesus," Gold hissed to herself. "How did she take it?"

"She's been upstairs ever since," Freya said. "But I think you can push her to formally ID the body tomorrow morning. Do you think you can manage that? She's torn between it not being Tommy and, if it is, then resentment at whoever did this. I explained that we can't start the process until we know for sure."

"I'll see what I can do," Gold said.

"Good," Freya replied. "I'm sorry to leave you like this—"

"It's fine," Gold said. "I'm used to it. In fact, it's better if we're alone. I can get to know her. See if she'll open up."

"Well done," Freya said, giving Gold's shoulder a squeeze. "In the meantime, we'll pay a visit to his former boss to see if Tommy has been in touch and to see if the story she told us matches. Unfortunately, until we know for sure it's him, our hands are tied. We can ask questions, but we cannot pursue a line of enquiry. So, I'm afraid it's on you."

"I get it," Gold said, and she opened the front door for them. "I'll call if there's any updates."

They stepped out of the house, and Freya breathed in the fresh air.

"Oh, and Gold," she said before the front door closed behind them. The young Detective Constable checked the stairs as Freya had, then leaned out of the door in waiting.

Freya considered her words, hoping to convey the delicate nature of the topic.

"I haven't explained to Mrs Dean yet exactly how we discovered the victim. I told her the man had a tattoo on his neck, but I've said nothing of the burns or...or the manner in which he died."

"I see," Gold said, but Freya thought otherwise.

"If we're pushing for a formal ID, then it would be best to forewarn her, as it were. She should know what to expect before she goes in. Can you do that for me, or would you like me to talk to her again?"

"No," Gold said. "No, I'll take care of it. I'll find a suitable moment. You're right; she should know beforehand."

Freya gave her a sympathetic nod, then turned and led Ben away.

"Poor woman," Ben said.

"Mrs Dean?"

"No, Jackie," he said. "If there's one job I just couldn't handle, it's FLO. I think you need to be a certain type of person."

"And how do you think she would fair doing your job?" Freya asked as they approached the car. They each climbed into their respective seats and slammed the doors closed so nobody could overhear them.'

"Honestly? I don't think she'll ever make Sergeant."

"Well, there you go then," Freya replied. "We all bring something to the table. Remember that. For me, Chapman has the role I couldn't bear to do."

"Chapman?"

"Yes. She's tied to a desk all day, researching evidence, checking alibis, making calls, and listening to us lot squabble." Ben started the car while she spoke. "You know, I often think she sighs with relief when we all leave."

He laughed at the comment.

"I know what you mean. She makes out she's happy to see us, but I think, really, she just enjoys having the radio on and keeping busy," he said. "Speaking of which." He pulled his phone from his pocket and dialled Chapman's desk phone. It was answered within two rings. "Chapman, it's me."

"Oh, hello," she replied. "How did she take the news? Or shouldn't I ask?"

"You could probably use your imagination," he replied. "Listen, she mentioned a previous employer."

"Frank Bowen?" Chapman replied, and both Ben and Freya frowned. "Sorry, I took the liberty of doing a few checks while you were talking to her."

"And what else did you find?"

"Not a lot. He owns a farm nearby," she continued, and they heard her flicking through her notepad. "Brinkleview Farm. Oddly, it's the same farm you attended last night."

"Brinkleview?" Freya said, and she eyed Ben curiously.

"That's right. Are you on your way? Did you want me to line up some support?"

"No," Freya told her. "No, I want to get back to the scene before the body is removed. With any luck, Southwell is there. Do me a favour, though, will you?" She checked her watch. "It's midday now. Get everyone back to the incident room for four pm. I want a full debrief from them all before the close of play. We've asked Gold to push Mrs Dean for a formal ID tomorrow, but I want to get in there beforehand. Call Pip, will you? Set the postmortem up for eight-thirty and the ID up for ten. Which means that by this time tomorrow, we should A know if it's Tommy Dean or not, and B have some kind of lead to follow."

"Will do," Chapman replied, no doubt noting down the instructions.

"We'll go and see Southwell and then this Bowen character," Freya said. "We'll see you at four."

Ben ended the call, put the car into drive, and started back towards the crime scene.

"So, what have we got," he asked as he drove, which, in Freya's experience, was his way of controlling the situation. It was a two-minute drive to the crime scene, therefore going over the few facts they had would fill that space, whereas Freya, who had been going over them since the moment they saw the body hanging from the tree, would have a moment of silence to put her musings into some semblance of order. "Man hanged from a tree and set on fire. I agree with Doctor Saint. It screams revenge to me. If it does turn out to be Tommy Dean, then we must assume that somebody held a grudge against him. That doesn't exactly align with the whole farmer thing. If anything, he was the one who was disgruntled."

"Is that what you think?" she said, more to keep him talking so she could focus on her own thoughts than anything else.

"We're talking about a man being hoisted into a tree by a car or something and then having a noose slipped over his head," Ben continued. "And don't forget, that noose was pre-tied. This whole thing is premeditated. It's not an emotional reaction like most murders are. They didn't have a fight that went too far. Somebody planned to kill him. They tied the noose. They lured him to the tree where nobody would see him, they strung him up, and then, using petrol they must have taken with them, they set light to his writhing body. It's sick, Freya. It's bloody sick."

"Well, for once, I agree with you," she replied as Ben turned into the lane. The crime scene was a good five hundred yards ahead of them, but from that distance, it was just a collection of vehicles and people.

"What are you thinking?" he asked. "You're unusually quiet."

She smiled to herself.

"I'm unusually quiet," she said, "because I've been over everything you just said a hundred times, and I've drawn my own conclusion."

"Which is?" Ben said, pulling the Range Rover up behind one of Southwell's white vans.

"Well, it's not a conclusion; it's more of a pragmatist's concern," she said, and she smiled across at him. "What if..."

She hesitated, then shook her head.

"What? What if, what, Freya?"

She looked across at him, and he knew her well enough to recognise the glint in her eye.

"No," he said flatly. He shoved open the car door and started towards Southwell and her team.

"We don't know the two incidents aren't linked," she told him, and rather than run after him, she waited at the front of the car, knowing full well what he would do.

And he did.

He stopped, looked up at the sky, and then turned on his heels to close the gap between them.

"You heard what Granger said. We leave it. We drop it. There's no body, Freya."

"It's one mile away, Ben."

"Saint said there was no sign of a wound. No sign of blood loss, Freya."

"It's one mile away," she said again. "A boy finds a body, and then it's gone. The next thing you know we're called out to another crime scene." She watched him process the information. He could see the logic in what she was saying. He must do. He's an intelligent man. It was one of the reasons she loved him.

He gave it some thought, glancing back at the group to make sure they were still alone.

"We follow the leads," he told her. "That's what we do. If those leads lead us to Billinghay, then so be it. But we cannot venture down the route of making evidence fit our narrative. We can't Freya. For all we know, the blood we saw at the old house was...I don't know, a dog's, or...or I don't know. But we don't know anything. It could be nothing."

"It could be everything," she replied.

"Freya, please," he said, and she knew by his tone his frustration was growing. "I just want to talk to Southwell, see the farmer, and get back to the incident room. We can't do anything until we've confirmed it was Tommy Dean hanging up there. Let's see where it leads us, eh?"

"And if Southwell's report confirms the blood was human?"

"Then we wait until we have a body to match the crime," he said. "Look, we've got less than one week until we get married. One week, Freya. Do you really want to cut our honeymoon short or postpone it because we still have a live investigation? The way I see it, this is a God send. We have a body with a recognisable tattoo, and a woman who has reported her husband missing, who, by the way, has the same tattoo. We can close this off by Thursday, sort the CPS paperwork out on Friday, and then enjoy our wedding day, and then after that, we can enjoy our honeymoon."

"Our holiday, you mean?"

"Freya!"

"Okay, okay," she said, holding her hands up. "But if I am right."

"If you are right, Freya," he said. "I will gladly investigate. I'll even call it a holiday. How does that sound."

"Like a deal," she told him, brushing past him. "A deal you just lost."

CHAPTER THIRTEEN

"HELLO AGAIN, KATY," Freya called out as she approached the group of investigators and her team. She looked around at them all, pausing on Gillespie. "Are you still here, Gillespie? Cruz?"

"Aye," Gillespie replied. "We were just holding the fort until you got back."

"No, you weren't. You were talking to your girlfriend, no doubt trying to impress her with your knowledge of crime scenes and procedures."

"Eh?"

"Go on," Freya said. "You'd better get started."

"Get started?"

"Door knocking," she told him. "Make a plan and start knocking."

"But—"

"But, what?"

"But you said you had a special job for us. We were knocking on doors in Billinghay this morning. You told us to get here because you had a special job for us."

"That's right," she said. "Door knocking."

"You're kidding!"

Cruz let his head fall back but was intelligent enough to recognise when arguing was futile.

"Come on. Toot sweet," Freya said, turning to Nillson. "How's the search going?"

"The team have arrived from Billinghay. We've got them going over the immediate area before we go wide," she replied. "I was thinking we start on the area surrounding the track from the main road."

"Good idea," Freya said. "Anything yet?"

"A length of rope," she replied. "Looks like the same type used to...used for the noose. Other than that, nothing really. An old coke can, some old rusty wire, and a bunch of rotting roses."

"Well, that's something," Freya told her. "I'll leave that in your capable hands." She made a show of smiling at Southwell and her team, then hesitated before looking back at Gillespie and Cruz. "Still here?"

"Come on, Gabby. Let's get our steps in, eh?" Gillespie said, with a brief goodbye nod to Southwell. "At this rate, I won't need a belt for my wedding suit. I'll need a bloody elastic band."

Their voices trailed off, and Southwell's team shared an uneasy look.

Southwell, who knew Freya better than any of them, grinned.

"What's the plan?" Freya asked as Ben joined them.

"Same as always," Southwell replied. "Doctor Saint has gone, so before the body is removed, we'll get in and flag any footprints. There won't be many. The ground's too dry, but you never know." She took a deep breath and let it out slowly. "We've got the ropes, which will undergo a full analysis, and we'll swab the exposed areas of skin prior to him being taken away. That should give us a head start. Saint suggested the perpetrator hauled him up with the longer length of rope attached to his vehicle, then stood on his vehicle to put the noose around his neck. There are signs a vehicle has been through here, but again—"

"The ground is too dry?"

Southwell grimaced apologetically.

"We may be able to determine the wheel centres, which in turn should give us a shortlist of vehicles, but we have no way of—"

"Connecting them to the actual murder," Freya finished for her. "Yes, I see that. Any number of farm vehicles could have come through here," she sighed and imagined how the murder might have played out. "What about the petrol used to burn him?"

"We have a sample of his clothing. We'll run some tests. My guess is that it's nothing out of the ordinary - unleaded petrol that anyone who has a petrol lawnmower would have in their shed."

"This shed seems to be a significant factor," Ben added. "The rope, the petrol. It might help us later down the line."

"Unfortunately, we need help now," Freya told him, returning her attention to Southwell. "Ideally, we'd like to confirm the series of events. We'll need you to work closely with Pippa Bell. If he was hauled up with the longer rope, then there should be signs of that on his body, under his arms, maybe."

"That's if she's able to get at his skin," Southwell said. "His skin and his clothing have...fused, for want of a better word. I doubt she'll be able to identify a few grazes caused by the rope."

"Never say never," Freya told her. "Anything else?"

"There is one more thing," Southwell said, and she led her away from her team and Ben. "When I spoke with Doctor Saint, we went over the *most likely series of events*, as you called it."

"Okay?"

Southwell eyed Freya's scar, then averted her eyes.

"This isn't what we're used to dealing with. This isn't some heat-of-the-moment attack," she said. "If we're right, then it was planned. I needn't explain to you the pain this man must have been put through."

"I'm not sure how this is relevant to your role as crime scene investigator, Katy."

"I know," she said. "I know, it's just...well...Jim and I—"

"Sergeant Gillespie, you mean?"

"Yes, we were just worried it might be a bit close to home for you."

"I'm sorry."

"It's not impertinence," Southwell explained. "We don't want to overstep the mark. Well, Jim didn't, anyway. He's just a bit concerned about you, that's all. He doesn't want this to bring up memories of your accident."

"Sergeant Gillespie? Worried about me?"

Southwell smiled at how ludicrous it sounded.

"He's got a big heart; and believe it or not, he's a big fan of you. Ben, too, come to think of it," she said. "And what with the wedding coming up. He...no, *we* wanted you to know that if all this does bring up unwanted memories, shall we say, well, you should come to us. Or me, at least." Freya cocked her head and studied Southwell's eyes for sincerity, finding it with ease. "You've got friends. I suppose that's what I'm trying to say."

"How...how lovely," Freya replied, keenly aware of how she had spoken to Gillespie. She gave a little laugh. "I must admit, part of me wants to tell you to mind your own business." She watched and marvelled at Southwell's lack of reaction - a sure indication of maturity. "However, I have to say, I'm quite touched. I'm fine, though. I can deal with it, but you're right. It's nice to know I have someone to talk to."

"Are you ready for it?" Southwell asked. "The wedding, I mean."

"I'm ready for the wedding," she replied. "It's what comes after that concerns me most."

"How so?"

Freya smiled it off with a shake of her head.

"Nothing," she lied. "It's funny. Ben and I were discussing the ceremony. I think it means more to him than me if I'm honest. I've been through it all before. But we were talking about who will sit on which side, and I was reminded of the fact that everyone here was Ben's friend long before I knew them."

"Everyone but me," Southwell said. "I'll be right behind you. Not that you'll need support."

"No, but I will need a stiff drink."

"Consider it done," Southwell replied with a friendly smile.

Freya paused for a moment, then gave in. It wasn't often that somebody spoke with such earnestness. Not to her, anyway.

"Thank you, Katy," she said. "I...I suppose I should make it up to Gillespie at some point."

Southwell touched her shoulder and gave it a squeeze.

"You don't need to thank me," she said as she turned to walk away but then stopped and half-turned. "And I wouldn't worry about Jim," she beamed at Freya. "He thrives on banter and abuse, you know?" Again, she started off, and again she stopped herself. "Oh, and one more thing. About last night."

"Yes, I'm sorry about that," Freya told her. "We have been given very clear instructions to drop the matter for the time being. This one takes priority. I'm afraid you had a late night for nothing."

"Ah, it's all part of the job," Southwell said, brushing it off. "But, for the record, the blood on the wall and the ground..."

"Yes?"

"Human," Southwell said. "No DNA match. Whoever it belongs to is either out there somewhere, or they managed to reach a hospital."

"They're not in hospital. We've checked," Freya said. "Ben is keen to get this one dealt with so he can enjoy the wedding."

"And you?" Southwell asked.

"I just...I suppose I want to make him happy," she said. "But don't tell him that. I don't want him running away with the idea that I have a heart."

Southwell gave a laugh. She had a beautiful smile, and it wasn't hard to see why Gillespie had fallen head over heels for her.

"We have to keep them on their toes, don't we?"

They almost parted once more, but this time, it was Freya who held Southwell back.

"Southwell," she said. "That is, Katy." Freya smiled an apology. "I wonder. Could I ask a small favour of you? Well, actually, it's not a small favour. In fact, it's rather large."

CHAPTER FOURTEEN

IF BRINKLEVIEW FARM was a sprawling patchwork quilt, then the seams of each patch were deep dykes, channelling the runoff into the River Witham that meandered through the county towards Boston, where it joined the River Haven, eventually spilling into the North Sea.

Freya elected to drive, and as she made the turn off the main road, following the old wooden signs, the farmhouse came into view, a white dot on an otherwise green and featureless landscape. The lane was almost central to the crime scene and the old derelict house they had attended the previous night. Somewhere, beyond the fields to Freya's right, was the old house with the tree growing out of its roof, with its blood trail and spatter, the camping equipment, and a plethora of apparently meaningless evidence. While somewhere to her left, more than two dozen officers and investigators were working on a seemingly simple crime.

The track was narrow enough that, when they came upon a tractor coming the other way, Freya had to pull onto the sparse verge, risking her near-side wheels nearing the dyke in order to let it pass.

"Am I okay?" she asked Ben, who was peering down through his window.

"Plenty of room," he said. "You've got another eight inches or so."

"Eight inches?" she said and slammed the brakes on before seeing the humour in his eyes. "I bloody hate these dykes."

"I know," he grinned.

The tractor driver was more elderly than mature and was wise enough to slow as he approached. She lowered her window and waved to get his attention. Using the full width of the verge on his side, he came to a stop, shoved open the window and glared down at them, saying nothing.

"I wonder if you can help me," she called out to be heard over the noisy old diesel engine. He made no sign of hearing her. He just stared back at her, his gaze vacant.

"Oh Christ, here we go," she muttered to Ben, then called out again. "I said, I wonder if you can help me." The old man peered down at her still, then a slight raise of one caterpillar-like eyebrow hinted at her words having made their way through. "We're looking for Frank Bowen."

"You what, love?" he called, his accent immediately marking him out as London-born.

"Frank Bowen," she said. "We are looking for Frank Bowen. Are we in the right place?"

"Frank?" His voice was as gruff as his complexion suggested as if his throat were lined with the very gravel beneath the car.

"Yes, Frank Bowen."

The old man craned his neck to view Ben, then sneered, and as if the interaction justified a break, he began rolling a cigarette, perhaps taking pleasure in making them wait. Eventually, he clicked open an old Zippo lighter, lit his cigarette, and inhaled a lungful of smoke.

"He's at the barns, ain't he?" he said. "He's loading up. That's where he'll be. That's where you'll find him."

He started to close the window, and Freya caught him just in time.

"Thank you," she started. "I wonder if you could tell me where the barns are?"

"The barns?"

Freya sighed. It was as if the man had been sent purely to frustrate her.

"Yes," she said, doing her best to refrain from conveying her truest thoughts. "Where can I find these barns?"

He gave her a quizzical look, then looked over his shoulder.

"Follow the track," he said, then closed the window as he brought the conversation to an end. "Can't bleedin' miss 'em."

"Charming," Freya said as the old man put his foot down, coughing out a great plume of red diesel smoke. Ben grinned to himself. "What?"

"Oh, nothing," he told her.

"No, go on. What? Don't tell me you're going to stick up for the rude old sod. I could barely understand what he was saying."

"And he probably felt the same way about you," Ben said. "Smart car, a well-spoken woman in fine clothes. He probably thought you're with HMRC."

"Well, I was going to show him my warrant card," she said. "But, he'd have been on the phone to this Frank Bowen before he'd finished his fag. I'd prefer to have the element of surprise on my side."

She eased the car off the verge and only put her foot down when all four wheels were firmly on the gravel track, fully aware of the cloud of dust the big car was kicking up in their wake. Just as the old man said they would, they eventually came across a collection of four barn-like structures, each opening onto a large, central concrete pad. A large grain trailer was parked to one side, and a few digger-type machines were to-ing and fro-ing, loading it with some type of crop from the barn.

"Turnips?" Freya said, and Ben laughed again. "I wish you'd

stop making fun of me. We weren't all raised on a farm, you know?"

"They're sweet beets," he told her. "Turnips are in the summer. Although, he's a bit late. My dad had his up last month." He watched with an experienced eye, none of what he was seeing seemed to intrigue him at all. "He probably stores them. A farm this big would have the storage space." He sat back and began looking about the car, presumably searching for whoever looked to be in charge. "Most farmers get shot of them as soon as they're up. Get the revenue in before year end."

"What does that mean?"

"Well, why sit on a crop when it can be bringing money in unless you have enough of it to spread out the sale? The price would have been low last month, with every farmer wanting shot of them. Looks to me like he's waited a while. New tax year, less supply. He could have got a few more pounds per ton." Freya watched him and waited for what he had just said to align with the investigation. "Hold on," he said.

"There we go," Freya grinned, pleased to have the upper hand once more.

"If he's held onto them for a month, he can't be that short of cash. This time of year, most farms are screaming for income."

"Let's find our man, shall we?" she suggested, and she pulled the car over to one of the barns where the machinery was not likely to hit it.

It was as they climbed from the car, that one of the huge tele-handlers came to a stop, its driver watching them through the side window.

"That's our man," Ben said, nodding to indicate the big yellow machine.

"What makes you so sure?"

"He stopped," Ben explained as he made his way over there. "You work on a farm; you don't stop unless the boss says so."

The telehandler's door opened, and a man climbed out slowly.

Just by his movements, Freya ascertained his approximate age, placing him in his mid-fifties. When she approached, her judgement was proved right. He was slight yet strong and wiry. His whiskers were grey, and the skin around his jowls hung loose with age more than obesity. And like Ben's father, who had farmed his entire life, the man's expression was serious, and his intelligent eyes roving - never missing a trick.

"Now then," he called out, his voice almost robotic.

Ben let his warrant card fall open and introduced himself as Freya closed in.

"I'm Detective Inspector Savage, and this is Detective Chief Inspector Bloom. Nice set-up you have here."

Ben gestured at the buildings around them and the team of men loading up.

"Well, I—"

"We're looking for a Frank Bowen," Freya said before the two got into a heavy discussion about farming. It was bad enough listening to it on those odd occasions they visited his dad, let alone with a complete stranger.

"S'me," he replied, his frown deepening.

"Is there somewhere we could talk, Mr Bowen?" she asked.

"Here do?"

"Somewhere a little quieter," she said, and as if to make her point, one of the other telehandler drivers revved their engine as they raised a large crate of sweet beets up to the trailer.

The old man nodded but made no effort to conceal his displeasure.

"This way," he said gruffly and led them to the barn close to where Freya had parked her car. There was a pair of large sliding doors, no doubt made for the large machinery, and a smaller pedestrian door, which he shoved open. The walls were little more than a thin steel cladding, yet it blocked most of the noise out, enough for them to have a discussion. "Right then. Ain't got long. This about last night, is it? Told your girl she'd need a warrant. I'll not have two dozen nosey coppers treading my fields."

"I'll get straight to the point, Mr Bowen," Freya said. "We're looking for a Thomas Dean. Or Tommy Dean, as I believe he's known."

"Tommy?" he said. "Yeah, I know Tommy."

"He worked here, is that right?" Freya asked. "Until recently."

"S'right," he said. "Left a few months ago, now."

"And, have you seen him since? Has he been back at all?"

Bowen shook his head and pulled a face that seemed to drag his weighty jowls into creases like an unmade bed.

"'Fraid not."

"I see. Would any of your employees have seen him? Was he friends with any of—"

"No," Bowen said sharply. "No, Tommy wasn't really chummy with anyone. Kept himself to himself, if you know what I mean."

Freya took a moment to appraise his expression and to consider his choice of words, wondering if those rolls of prickly old skin concealed his truest thoughts.

"He hadn't worked here long, had he?" Freya said.

"I'm sorry. What's all this about, then? Has he done something? He in trouble, is he?"

"No," Freya said. "No, he's not in any trouble. He's been reported missing."

She watched for a flick of an eyelid or a twitch of his lip. But nothing came.

"Missing?"

"Since Saturday."

He nodded, then turned to eye Ben, letting his eye wander over him from his shoes to his eyes.

"Chief Inspector..."

"Bloom," Freya added, and again, he nodded before turning back to Ben.

"And you were..."

"Detective Inspector Savage," Ben said.

"Savage?" he replied. "Local, are you?"

"I am," he said. "If you recognise the name, then you might know my dad."

"Ah, yeah. Now, I see," he said, nodding again. "I don't know him, but I've heard the name well enough."

"Mr Bowen," Freya started, "perhaps we can—"

"It seems odd to me that you two should turn up for a missing man," he said, cutting Freya off.

"Excuse me?"

"That what you do, is it? Send a chief inspector out, and a..." he gestured at Ben, "an inspector. Seems unlikely if you ask me. I mean, I'm not an expert, but for a missing man, I would have thought—"

"No, you're quite right," Freya said, tugging the reins from him. "How very astute, you are. In fact, we're investigating a murder. Near to here, as it happens. On the edge of your farm."

"A murder, you say? On my farm?"

"On the edge," she replied. "Tommy hasn't been seen for a few days. We're just trying to connect the dots."

"So, you came to see me, did you? Who put you onto me?"

"His wife, if you must know," Freya told him. "She said he left after some kind of financial conflict."

"With one of the lads, you mean?"

"With you, Mr Bowen. She stated that they couldn't survive without a regular salary. Something you couldn't provide him with."

"Well, well, well," Bowen replied, and he cleared his throat, which made no difference to his gruff tone. "Tommy came to me a few years back. It was during the lockdown. You remember, do you?"

"Vividly," Freya told him.

"Said he wanted a fresh start. Said he was getting fat and wanted to work outdoors," Bowen explained. "I'd lost all my seasonal workers. They'd all gone back to Europe. So, I took him on. Had one of my boys show him the ropes. Hold his hand, as it were. He did me a turn." He looked up at Ben. "You'll know from your old man's farm how hard it was, back then."

"It was a tough time all round," Ben said rather diplomatically.

"He did me a turn, and I did him a turn," Bowen said. "But I can assure you. I paid him fair and square every single month."

"That's odd," Freya said. "His wife was certain you hadn't."

"Listen, lady," he said. "My family's been on this farm for nigh on a century," he said. "We ain't done that by not paying a fair day's wage for a fair day's work."

"So, you paid him, did you?" Freya asked. "Each month?"

"If you're looking for a reason for somebody to do the lad in," he replied, opening the door for them, reintroducing the noise of the machinery outside, "I suggest you look elsewhere."

CHAPTER FIFTEEN

"RIGHT, LISTEN UP," Freya said before Ben had even followed her through the incident room doors. Then she peered around the room at the empty seats, finishing on Chapman. "I thought we arranged a debrief for four p.m.?"

"We did, ma'am," Chapman replied. "Jackie is still at Mrs Dean's house, Gillespie and Cruz are still walking the streets, and Nillson is on her way back. Should be here in the next few minutes."

"Right," Freya said, and that part of her mind where reason was housed released a little of its quarry. "I apologise. It's my fault for not being clearer."

"Jesus," Ben said. "Did you just confess to making a mistake?"

"It wasn't a mistake, Ben," Freya told him. "It was an oversight." She turned back to Chapman. "Get them on the phone, will you? Group call."

"Ma'am," Chapman replied, then set to work.

Leaving the details from the previous night's mystery on the whiteboard, she flipped it to the other side, then set to work wiping it clean. It was a habit of hers to wipe any details from the board after each investigation, but what with the wedding and the distractions of life, she hadn't done so. So, she busied herself with the task, fussing over the tiniest mark, telling herself, as she always did, that it was best to begin with a clean slate. A fresh mind. An unblemished opinion.

But of course, her judgement was blemished with what lay on the other side of the board.

Chapman put the phone on loudspeaker and began dialling the team in as Freya set to work on the clean board.

She had only written two words, *hanged* and *burned*, when the first phone joined the call.

"Ah, Chapman, Chapman, Chapman," Gillespie's voice sang out. "Am I glad to hear from you."

"Gillespie, I—"

"This morning, I have been plagued by a half-wit who goes by the name of Gabby Carol Vorderman Cruz, I've walked more miles than a sodding postman, and I've been belittled in front of Katy by the boss. I'm not having a good day, I can tell you," he continued. "Anyway, what can I do for you? Don't tell me, the dragon has breathed fire all over the incident room, and you're wondering where the fire extinguisher is."

"Actually, Gillespie, I was rather hoping for a debrief," Freya called out. She grinned and winked at Chapman to avoid any embarrassment, then savoured Gillespie's desperate attempts to excuse his faux pas.

"Boss? That you?"

"The very one," she said, then waited.

"Ah, I was just kidding, you know?"

"Really?"

"Aye, you know how it is. A wee bit of banter never hurt anybody, did it?"

"No," she agreed. "No, I agree. A little office banter never hurt anyone."

"Ah, good. Anyway, I suppose you want an update?"

"Hold that thought, Gillespie," she told him. "Chapman needs to dial the rest of the team in."

She gave Chapman the nod, who then set about dialling in Gold and Nillson, leaving Freya to focus on the board. She drew lines from the word *hanged* and at the end of each of those lines, she wrote three words: *rope, method, significance*. She then did the same to the word *burned*, adding the words, *petrol* and *ignition*.

"Hello?" said a voice, light in tone, and although Scottish like Gillespie, her accent was far softer and more approachable.

"Jackie, it's me," Chapman said, and then, perhaps to avoid further embarrassment, added, "you're on loudspeaker with DCI Bloom and Ben."

"Oh, am I? Is everything okay?"

"Everything is fine, Gold," Freya called out. "Is it a good time?"

"Actually, yeah. Julie's having a quick bath. What's it all about?"

"I just wanted a debrief. If you hang on a minute for Anna to join."

She nodded at Chapman again, and then returned to the board, drawing a circle around both of the root words, *hanged and burned*. She then drew three more lines, and added the words *suffering, planned*, and *why*.

"Chapman?" Nillson said when the call connected.

"You're on loudspeaker," Gillespie called out, and from his seat at the back of the room, Ben laughed aloud.

"Eh?"

"Hello, Anna," Freya began. "It's a group call. I just wanted an update from you all."

"Oh, right. Well, I'm nearly back at the station."

"That's fine. We're here now, so Gillespie and Cruz, perhaps you can begin?"

Gillespie cleared his throat.

"Aye, well. It's not looking too good," he began. "We've

knocked on..." there was a short pause, and Freya imagined him waiting for Cruz to help him out.

"Oh, erm, forty-five," they heard Cruz say in the background.

"Forty-five doors," Gillespie continued. "Not a single person saw or heard a thing. A few of them saw the blue lights and asked questions, but nobody saw or heard anything unusual. Not even Tommy Dean's neighbours."

"Did anybody see him leave the house?"

"No," he replied. "The lady opposite, a..."

"Mrs Greaves," Cruz added.

"Right, a Mrs Greaves. She saw him on Friday morning. He left and came back twenty minutes later with a Co-op bag."

"We think he popped out for some shopping," Cruz chimed in.

"Really?" Freya said, with more than a hint of sarcasm. "Where are you now?"

"We're on the other side of town," Gillespie said. "We've got three houses left before we venture into the realms of scratching at hope. Anybody further out than this is unlikely to even recognise him, let alone remember seeing him."

"Okay," Freya said. "Well, just remember to write up your notes. You never know; something might be significant later on, and the last thing you want is an old dragon like me chasing after you."

"Aye," he said quietly.

"Gold, what do we have?"

"Well," Gold started. "I can't really get much out of her. The marriage is fairly good. They had a rough spell when he lost his job during lockdown, and they had to make some lifestyle changes when he got the job on the farm, which caused a bit of friction, but otherwise, they seem to be okay."

"Well, clearly they aren't okay," Freya said. "He's missing."

"I know, but if there's something deeper than that, she's not saying so."

"What about the ID? Is she willing?"

Gold took a deep breath, and when she exhaled, her breath rasped across the phone's microphone.

"She is," she said. "I managed to convince her to do it. I told her I'd be with her; I hope that's okay?"

"Of course," Freya said. "Whatever it takes." She looked to Chapman for confirmation, who peered down at her notes.

"Postmortem is scheduled for early doors tomorrow morning," Chapman said. "Formal ID at ten am."

"Can you be there for nine forty-five?" Freya asked.

"I can," Gold said. "I'll pick her up. We can't expect her to be in a fit state to drive after that."

"Speaking of which," Freya said. "Do we know if Tommy Dean had a car of his own, or did they share the one on their drive?"

"He had his own," Gold said. "A Toyota pickup. She said he bought it when he started at the farm."

Again, Freya looked to Chapman.

"Have a look into that, will you? DVLA records, ANPR. You never know; it might have been picked up somewhere."

"Will do," Chapman said.

"Good work, Gold," Freya said. "Stay with her. See if she's got a friend who can come and sit with her this evening, and of course, make sure she has your number in case she remembers something."

"Already done," Gold said. "A neighbour is popping over later on."

"Nillson?" Freya said. "What do *you* have?"

They heard Nillson apply her handbrake, and Freya glanced out of the window and found her car in the car park down below.

"We've done a fingertip search of the immediate area, and aside from the rope, there's nothing."

"No matches or a lighter?" Freya asked. "What about the missing boot?"

"Nope, nothing," Nillson replied. "The ground was too hard

for any prints to be made, but we do have the wheel centres from the flattened grass. I need to go through the database, but to be honest, it's not going to give us anything concrete to go on."

"I agree," Freya said. "But do it anyway, will you? We're going to need anything we can get on this."

"Will do," she continued. "We also scanned the area on either side of the track and in the dykes."

"I'm assuming if you had found something, you would have highlighted that at the start of this conversation?" Freya added.

"Yep, nothing. Whoever did this knew what they were doing," Nillson said.

"Either that, or they had given it considerable thought," Freya argued.

"How so?"

"Well," she said, and she turned to her board. "And this is for all of you to pay attention to," she said. "We have a man found burned and hanged from a tree. As far as leads go, we're hopeful that Katy's team can give us something on the rope and the accelerant found on the clothing. With regards to the MO, our current school of thought is that either two individuals were responsible or one man with the assistance of his vehicle. He used one rope to haul the victim into the air and the other to hang him with. What does that tell you?"

"It wasn't a reaction," Gillespie said.

"You've been talking to your better half, haven't you?" Freya replied.

"Aye, well. We tossed a few ideas around, you know?"

"Well, you're right. This wasn't, as most of the murders we deal with are, a heat of the moment thing. There are two types of murder most often dealt with by teams like ours. There are the emotional and reactive murders, which includes accidental murders, and then there are those that are premeditated. If it was emotional, then the data tells us that the killer will either give himself up due to the weight of the guilt or try to cover his tracks.

He may even leave the country, although that's not as common as the TV would have you believe." She took a breath and stared at the board once more. "If it was premeditated, however, our man will be one step ahead of us. He will have an idea of our approach. He will know we'll be searching the fields and the dykes. He will know we'll be talking to neighbours, and he will know we will be asking questions. If he's smart, then he's put barriers in place to ensure our efforts lead nowhere."

"What about the rope?" Nillson asked. "He just tossed it into the dyke. If he knew we'd checked there, then surely—"

"The rope matches the rope used to form the noose," Freya said, cutting her off. "It would be directly linked to the murder. If we found that in his vehicle or his property, that would be evidence against him." she shook her head, visualising the decision the killer took. "No, he would have worn gloves. The rope will be clean. The best we can do with the rope from the dyke is match it to the noose and maybe find out where it was bought."

"It was old rope," Nillson said. "It wasn't new, so I doubt we'll get him on camera buying it."

"In which case, the only thing we can hope to find is some kind of DNA, a hair, or blood. I don't know."

"So, what's the plan?" Gillespie asked.

"Then there's the motive," Freya continued, ignoring Gillespie. "We've all seen the body, aside from Chapman, and I think we can agree that whoever did this wanted the victim to suffer. To me, that screams revenge or hate. They're bitter, but over what, I don't know. But if you put all of that together, we have an individual, or individuals, who hated the victim and wanted to see him in pain. They're one step ahead of us, so they've covered their tracks."

"Wow, I can't wait to meet him. Sounds like a right barrel of laughs," Gillespie joked, but nobody laughed.

"Until we have a formal ID, our hands are tied," Freya continued. "Gold, I need an update from you as soon as you're out of the hospital."

"Will do," Gold replied.

"And while you're at it," Freya said, "question her and find out the reason Tommy lost his job."

"Erm, okay. Why's that?"

"Well, we paid a visit to his employer, Frank Bowen. He seems to think he paid salaries on time."

"That's not what she said."

"Do some digging, will you? If it is Tommy Dean, then we can access his bank records and see for ourselves. Either way, somebody isn't being honest."

"What about us, boss?" Gillespie asked.

"Finish up there tonight," Freya said. "Then do your reports in the morning. Aside from Gold, I want everyone here with a clear desk when Ben and I get back from the postmortem. Understood?"

A series of yeses and ayes followed, and Freya looked to Ben for anything to add. He shook his head.

"I'll see you all in the morning," she said. "Oh, and Gillespie, one more thing."

"Aye, boss?"

"Bring your walking shoes to work in the morning, will you?" she said, smiling at Ben, who, again, shook his head in dismay. "I have another of those special tasks for you."

CHAPTER SIXTEEN

"GO ON, THEN," Ben said when they entered Freya's house. He dumped his bag down and flopped into one of the armchairs. "Are you going to tell me what Granger said? You've been in a mood all day."

"I was invited to attend a private meeting with my superior officer, Ben. You can't expect me to share every detail of my work life with you."

"Fair enough," he replied. "What do you have in store for Gillespie, then?"

"Oh, nothing really," she replied, making a beeline for the wine rack. She smiled back at him. "I just want him to dread coming into work. A few uncomfortable hours of trepidation should be enough to make him think before he speaks."

"That's just cruel."

"The funny thing is," she said, holding up a spare glass, silently asking if he wanted wine, "dragons are clearly impervious to fire." He held up his hand to decline the offer and watched as she poured a glass for herself. She finished and sat politely in the armchair opposite him. Deftly, she raised her hair, which hung over one side of her face. "Which I clearly am not."

He remembered the scar in its early days, when it had been angry and red, and the entire side of her face had been swollen. With very little effort, he could recall seeing her skin smouldering and her hair succumbing to the flames in an instant. But now, her injuries seemed part of her. A smooth and shiny patch of skin on her cheek that seemed not to yield when her expression changed. She sipped at her wine and caught him staring.

"I'm not a dragon, am I?" she asked.

"I hope not," he replied.

"I'm being serious," she said. "I know, in the past, I've been difficult. And I know I can rub people up the wrong way, but..."

"But what?"

She smiled a little, then set it free.

"I'm trying," she said. "I think I've changed, don't you?"

"Christ, that's a loaded question."

"Don't mock me," she said, and perhaps for the first time, there was a neediness to her expression.

"What's up?"

"Nothing. I...I just...I don't know. I'm just trying, that's all, and I suppose I want to know that my efforts are being noticed. I don't want to be remembered for being difficult."

"Well, I don't think there's a member of the team that would argue with you being trying."

"I mean it," she said, and the sip of wine she took verged on being more of a gulp. "This whole thing. The accident. It's changed me. You know, I can count on one hand the number of officers who were genuinely nice to me when I was in the Met."

"Oh, come on, it can't have been that bad."

"It was," she said. "Sure, most of them were civil and up for a laugh, but genuinely nice? Nice enough to go out of their way to help you or to see if you were okay?" She shook her head. "Honestly, a handful. No more. Yet here we are in the middle of Lincolnshire, and I can count on one hand the number of officers who haven't been nice."

"Jewson, you mean?"

"For one, yes," she said. "And then there was Standing."

"Yeah, well, the least said about him, the better."

"I've had a lot of time to reflect."

"So have I," Ben told her, and he shoved himself out of the chair. "And do you know what I've come to realise?"

"Go on?"

"That I'm hungry. What are we eating?" he asked as he made his way towards the kitchen.

"No, I can't eat," she said. "Not yet, anyway."

Ben pored through the cupboards, but nothing jumped out at him. It all seemed either a faff to cook or would take too long.

He leaned against the kitchen doorframe.

"You alright?" he asked, with a little more sincerity than before.

"I suppose," she replied, with far less sincerity than before. Then she caught him staring. "I spoke to Katy earlier."

"Right?"

"She said something, and now I feel guilty."

"Blimey, Freya. An apology and guilt all in one day."

"Oh, sod you," she said, delving into her wine.

"Sorry. Go on. What did she say?"

Freya set her glass on the coffee table, then tucked her feet beneath her, the way that only the female anatomy allowed.

"She said that Gillespie was worried about me."

"What? Jim, worried?"

"That's what I thought, but somehow, I don't think she was lying. I don't know; I don't think she would. As much as she loves Gillespie, I don't think she would lie for him. She seems quite adept at keeping her professional and personal lives separate. Anyway, she said he was worried about me, I don't know, being reminded of the accident."

"By the burned man, you mean?" he said, to which she simply looked at him, no reply needed.

"It was moments after I had *shown him up* for want of a better phrase."

"Which time was this? It's a daily occurrence, isn't it?"

"Don't," she said, rubbing her forehead. "I feel bad enough."

"My God, should I call the doctor?" He joked, and she glared at him. "An apology, guilt, and now you feel bad for something you said. That's a full set of human traits, Freya. You should go and have a lie-down."

"I knew I shouldn't have spoken to you about it—"

"Alright, alright," he said, calming her down.

"I just find it difficult, you know? I mean, Anna Nillson, Jackie Gold, Denise Chapman, and even Cruz. They all work bloody hard and rarely put a foot out of place."

"But Jim does, does he?"

"Both feet," she said. "And often."

"But *does* he?" Ben asked. "Does he really? I mean, yeah, he shouldn't have called you a dragon earlier, but would you have him any other way?"

"No," she admitted. "No, I wouldn't."

Ben stepped back into the kitchen, looked briefly at the fruit bowl, and then resorted to yanking the bread bin open. He dragged two slices onto a plate, then snatched up the butter dish and a knife.

"Listen," he said as he retook his seat and set the butter and knife down. "Jim is like a...I don't know, a farm dog."

"A farm dog?"

"Yeah, you can belt him and berate him, and you can shout and scream, and he'll still come back to you. He'll still sit by your feet, tongue hanging out and tail wagging."

"He *is* thick-skinned."

"You forget," he told her. "He was raised in more than a dozen care homes. He had a new brother or sister every month, and most of them bullied him or worse. He thrives on it. He loves it. That's why he's so harsh on Cruz, because that's all he knows. But you know, if Cruz was in trouble, Jim would be the first one to help him out."

"You think?"

"I think you should go easy on yourself. He's alright, is Jim."

"Are you saying that because he's your best man?"

"No, I'm saying that because he's my best mate. And it's true, believe it or not. You can give him all the stick you like. It won't make a blind bit of difference to him. But if it makes you feel better, maybe you could give him a nice job every now and then."

"More carrot, less stick, you mean?"

"Exactly," Ben replied, holding the plate out in front of her. She peered down at it, then looked up at him questioningly.

"What?" she said. "Is that for me?"

"No, not at all," he replied. "I was wondering if you could breathe on it for me. Save me firing the toaster up."

CHAPTER SEVENTEEN

"RIGHT, ONE MORE HOUSE," Cruz said, and for the umpteenth time, Gillespie checked his watch. "I don't know why you're worried about getting home. It's not like your missus is going be home anytime soon."

"So what? I do enjoy a bit of me time, you know?"

"Ah, right," Cruz said. "I can only imagine what that entails."

"Yeah, yeah," Gillespie said. "At least I have somebody to go home to."

"Ooh, that was below the belt."

"What is Hermione doing these days, anyway? I wonder if she looks back fondly at the time she was with you—"

"Anyway," Cruz said, cutting him off. "Shall we?" He presented the garden path of the last house on the street with a wave of his arm. It was a modest semi-detached house, and although it pained Cruz to judge, it was hard not to when they had visited nearly fifty houses in one day. The windows were in need of care and attention; the white UPVC had lost its whiteness. The render that covered the brickwork had crumbled away in a few areas, most likely causing a spot of damp, and the block-paved driveway was home to a spread of weeds. He might not have had the same amount of experience as Gillespie or any of the others, but there was a correlation between those neglected houses and the attitude of the occupants. Not to say that every house in need of some love was home to less than polite individuals, but more often than not, when somebody gave them stick or simply slammed the door in their face, the house was not in its prime. There were, of course, houses Cruz would have loved to own with immaculate facades and beautiful gardens, with owners who slammed the door in their faces, but they were rarer. "You can do this one."

"I thought I gave the orders?" Gillespie said as he reached up and pressed the doorbell.

"It wasn't an order," Cruz said. "And anyway, I thought we were taking it in turns."

"We are taking it in turns," Gillespie replied. "And it's your turn."

"No, I did the last one."

"You started the last one, then made a comment about the carpet, so I had to take over."

"Yeah, well. It was a nice carpet, that's all. My mum has the same one in her hallway. I didn't ask you to speak over me."

"If I'd have let you continue, Gabby, we'd have another death on our hands. Honestly, the next time you start telling a total stranger about your mum's decor, I'll have to call for an ambulance to follow us about."

The door opened before Cruz could respond, and Gillespie smiled up at the man. He wore a baggy tee-shirt with dark patches around his armpits and loose-fitting shorts. His feet were bare, and his toenails were nothing short of barbaric.

"Yes?" he said, staring at them both, eyes wide in expectation.

Gillespie, making a show of keeping his mouth firmly closed, turned to Cruz, who sighed and cleared his throat before letting his warrant card fall open.

"Sorry to bother you, sir, but we're investigating—"

The man took one look at his ID and shook his head before starting to close the door.

"Wait, wait," Cruz said, and he stopped the door from closing with his boot, which gave the man more than enough cause to give him a questioning look. "Sorry, it's important. We're just wondering if you can help us with our enquiries, that's all."

"Doubt it," he replied.

"It's a serious incident, Mr…" Cruz said, and he fumbled for his notepad and pen. The man hesitated and then gave in.

"Godolphin," he said.

"Godolphin? As in—"

"Go dolphin," he replied. "Do you want me to spell it?"

"Mr Godolphin, we're looking into a serious incident that took place over the weekend in the fields between Tattershall and Billinghay," Gillespie cut in.

"Oh, right."

"That doesn't seem like a surprise. Did you see anything?"

"I saw the flashing blues over in the fields, that's all. What was it? Anybody hurt?"

"It was a serious incident," Cruz explained, hoping that would convey that they were not at liberty to divulge much more information.

"I see," Godolphin replied. "Well, if you can't tell me what happened, how am I supposed to tell you if I saw anything?"

"We were just wondering if you saw anything unusual over the weekend. Possibly an abduction."

"An abduction?" he replied. "What do you mean? Somebody stuffing somebody else into a van or something?"

"These are initial enquiries, sir. I'm sure you can imagine there's a lot to consider. We're just asking questions now in case somebody saw something unusual."

"And if I saw somebody forcing somebody into a car or something, am I likely to have not called you lot?"

"Mr Godolphin," Gillespie interjected again, but he was cut

short when a young boy peered around the man. "Oh, hello, young man."

"Benjamin, get back inside, will you?" the man said. "Sorry about that. It's my son. He's nosey. Like his mother." He turned back to his boy. "Go on. Haven't you got homework or something?"

"First day back, Dad," he replied. "Won't have homework 'til tomorrow, probably."

"A likely story," he said. "Go on. Get out of here."

"Actually, Mr Godolphin," Cruz said. "Maybe he saw something?"

"What?" the boy said.

"We're looking into an incident that happened this weekend," Cruz started.

"He saw nothing," Mr Godolphin said, pulling his son into his side. "Ain't that right, lad?"

"I just thought it was worth asking—"

"He saw nowt," the father replied. "Besides, he ain't allowed over Brinkleview. Not allowed past the river, are you?"

"No, dad," the boy said.

"As it happens, the victim was from Tattershall. Maybe he saw a scuffle or somebody having strong words?"

"He saw nowt," Godolphin said again, a little louder this time. He glanced down at his boy. "Did you, eh? See owt, did you?"

"Are you police?" Benjamin asked.

"We are," Cruz said, and for the first time, his short stature played in his favour. "I'm DC Cruz, and this is DS Gillespie. Nobody's in any trouble, so don't worry. But there was a serious incident, and we're just asking the neighbours if anybody saw or heard anything." He grinned at the boy, who seemed to pale in their presence.

"Told you," Godolphin said. "He saw nowt. So, if you don't mind."

"Before we leave," Cruz said, and from his inside pocket, he fished a contact card and held it out to him. "In case you remember something or maybe hear anything."

Godolphin accepted the card, scanned it, and then leaned inside to toss it onto what Cruz could only imagine was a bureau or table of some sort.

"Right then," Cruz said. "Well, thanks for your time. If you do happen to remember anything."

"I'll call," Godolphin said, though Cruz doubted that he had any intention of helping the constabulary. He was just one of those men. Helping the police would be considered as betraying his kind.

Cruz looked up at Gillespie in case he had anything to add, but he was just staring at the man.

"Shall we?" he asked, but Gillespie was transfixed. "Jim?"

Godolphin also caught Gillespie staring, and his eyes narrowed.

"What do you want, a photo?" Godolphin asked, which seemed to rouse Gillespie from his daydream.

"Eh? Oh, sorry. I was just...thinking."

"Right."

"Finished thinking?" Godolphin asked.

"We'll be seeing you, Mr Godolphin," he said and started back up the footpath.

The owner of the house watched them leave, and it wasn't until Cruz was back on the footpath and had caught Gillespie up two doors away that Godolphin finally closed the door.

"What the hell was all that about?" he hissed. "And you accused me of acting weird."

"Did you see it?" Gillespie asked, checking back to make sure Godolphin wasn't listening.

"See what?"

"On his neck," Gillespie said, and he leaned in close to Cruz and spoke with gritted teeth. "The bloody tattoo."

CHAPTER EIGHTEEN

THE TUESDAY MORNING FELT FRESH. The sky was a glorious blue, and the air as Freya and Ben walked across the hospital car park was as fresh as could be. Summer was a month or two off, yet after such a long and gruelling winter, spring had clearly had a positive effect on peoples' dispositions.

It hadn't been that long ago when Freya and Ben had walked across that same hospital car park en route to see Pippa Bell, and people had been wrapped in heavy coats, bracing against the cold wind and rain.

"You ready for this?" Ben asked her.

"For Pip?" she let a small laugh escape her lips. "I'm not sure if ready is the right word to use. But, if it means anything, I'm more looking forward to seeing Pip than I am the body. As far as bodies go, this is probably one of the worst we've seen for a while."

"I think they're all the same," Ben replied as they walked through to the main reception. He spoke quietly so as not to draw attention to themselves from the visitors and patients who seemed to loiter in the area. "Once she's opened them up, let's face it, what does the outside matter?"

"It's funny, isn't it?" she said, musing on his comment. "I've seen countless bodies, and I can't remember the last time one had any real effect on me. Yet, when the flesh is damaged like that..."

"You going to be okay with this?" Ben asked.

"Yes, yes, of course. It's just...I don't know. It just seems unnatural, doesn't it?"

"Unlike when she's pulled their chest open, you mean?" he said. "Maybe we're just not used to seeing that kind of damage. I wonder if, like you said during yesterday's debrief, this one is different. The attack wasn't emotional. It was savage. This isn't simply somebody throttling somebody else and lashing out in a state of frustration or a moment of madness. This is planned. Whoever did this knew what they were going to do. They knew where the victim would be; they knew what they would do once the job was done. He probably had a place lined up to go."

The sun shone through the glazed walkways, warming Freya's face. But still, the thought of what had been done to the victim sent a chill through her veins.

"Which leads me to think the worst," Freya replied as they entered the corridor that led down to the mortuary.

"He's going to do it again?" Ben asked.

"No. Well, maybe. But that wasn't my initial thought," she said. "No, my initial thought, when you take all of that into consideration, is that whoever did this might not even be local. It's probably the worst possible scenario for us. We've got the body of a man who's been brutally murdered by somebody who knew what they were doing and were following a plan, which means that we're missing our one advantage."

She hesitated, waiting for Ben to suggest what that advantage might be.

"Surprise?" he said.

"Emotions," she corrected.

"Emotions?"

"Think about it," she continued as Ben reached up and pushed the buzzer to let Pip know they were there. "If you had a moment of madness and lashed out at me, and I died as a result, you'd be terrified. Not that that would ever happen, of course."

"No, I dread to think," Ben replied with a smile, which she ignored.

"So, when it comes to questioning you, you'd either break and confess, or your emotions would work against you. You'd be scrambling around to cover your tracks; you'd be lying, sweating, digging yourself further into a hole or trying to behave normally."

"So, the killer in this instance, according to your theory—"

"It's not a theory, Ben; I'm just verbalising my thoughts. We have to be prepared for these things. I don't think it's going to be as easy as developing a shortlist and then working through them. Not this time."

Ben laughed and averted his eyes.

"What?" she asked.

"Nothing."

"No, go on. What is it?"

"It's just that...I can't help but wonder if you're hoping for something a little more challenging," he said. "Something that might drag on and delay our honeymoon."

"Our holiday, you mean?"

"Not yet, it's not," he said.

"And that's what you think, is it?"

"Like you said," he replied, "I'm just verbalising my thoughts." He grinned at her as the door began to open. "We have to be ready for these things."

Usually, when the door to the mortuary reception opened, they were greeted in a number of ways. Either Doctor Pippa Bell would be in a good mood, a sour mood, or a cantankerous mood. But today, Pippa didn't greet them at all. Before them was a fresh-faced young man wearing a bright blue smock over a clean white tee-shirt.

He looked up at them expectantly.

"We're looking for Pip," Ben told him.

"Doctor Bell?" His voice was delicate, as were his hands, and he held onto the door as if a strong gust of wind might blow him into the middle of next week."

"Ah, it's you two," Pip called out from behind him. Doctor Pippa Bell was a stout middle-aged woman who spoke in a strong Welsh accent that provided both warmth and colour to any conversation while doing little to dull her tongue's keen blade. "Sorry about that. I was just getting the room ready." She came to stand at the door. "I see you've met my little prodigy, Andrew. He's going to be helping me out for a while."

"Helping you out?" Ben said. "What do you mean, like a work experience thing?" He peered down at the lad.

"She means as a locum," Freya told him, and she extended a hand. "Welcome, Andrew. I'm Detective Chief Inspector Bloom, and this is Detective Inspector Savage."

"You'll have to watch out for these two," Pip told him. "They'll cause you no end of headaches." She made her way towards the large, insulated doors that led into the morgue, leaving them with Andrew. "Don't be too long. I don't want him warming up now."

She was, of course, referring to the victim, and took great pleasure in allowing her comment to plant vivid images in Freya's mind.

The heavy doors closed with a swish behind her.

Ben had already begun delving into the cupboards to get PPE for them both, and he tossed a set onto the couch for Freya.

Andrew watched them curiously.

"What's your story, Andrew?" Ben asked as he set about getting himself into the gown.

"My story?"

"I mean, where are you from? What's your full name? What are you doing here? Are you enjoying it?"

"It's Fox," he replied. "Andrew Fox."

"What he really means," Freya cut in, "is, how are you finding working with Pip?"

"Oh," he replied, slightly hesitant to disclose his truest thoughts. "She's okay. A little eccentric."

"Eccentric, how?" Freya asked, toying with the young man's naivety.

"Well, I've never come across a pathologist who listens to Iron Maiden while they work."

Freya laughed. She didn't mean to; it just sort of came out.

"Sorry. You'll get used to her," she said. "And where are you from?"

"Essex," he replied. "I'm waiting for a permanent position somewhere. Just filling in where I can really, to get my experience up."

He was warming up. His comments were far less jittery than they had been. Perhaps he was realising that Pip was not the display model of everyone in the area.

"So, when do you qualify?" she asked.

"Me? I'm done," he said.

"Done? But you're what? Twenty-two? Twenty-three?"

"I'm thirty," he replied, a confused look emerging on his young and hairless face.

"Thirty?"

"I know, I've got a baby face. Can't help it. Runs in the family."

"And what made you choose this line of work?" Ben asked, to which he shrugged.

"I'm not sure, really. Dad was a doctor. Mum's a nurse. I suppose it just sort of rubbed off on me."

"Specifically, a pathologist," Ben pressed, and Andrew shrank a little.

"I'm...not really a people person," he explained. "And I don't like loud noises." He smiled apologetically. "Or busy places."

"Right," Ben said. "Well, that answered my question."

The door opened again, and Pip leaned into the reception.

"Will you be much longer?" she asked. "Only, the patient's getting bored."

Freya grinned at her.

"We'll be right in," she told her, and Pip looked across at Andrew suspiciously.

"Been bothering you, have they?"

"No," he said. "No, they've been quite nice."

Pip looked at Ben and Freya in turn. Her eyes narrowed, and she nodded slowly as if she knew they weren't telling her something.

"Shall we get going?" she asked. "Before I'm knocked off the top spot on your favourites list."

"Oh, there's not much chance of that," Freya told her as she edged past Pip's stout frame into the morgue and braced against the freezing air. She winked at Andrew and stopped beside Pip. "You have to be on the list in the first place to be knocked off the top spot."

CHAPTER NINETEEN

PIP HAD ALREADY PREPARED the victim. He was laid out on the gurney with a sheet up to his midriff, presumably to preserve his dignity. She had created the standard Y-shaped incision, with a cut from below each ear to the centre of his chest, and then a single cut down to his naval. A pair of clamps held the cavity open, exposing his internal organs.

"You've been busy," Ben said.

"No, I've been waiting," she replied tautly. "That's what I've been doing while you lot have been in there gassing."

"Well, then, shall we get started?" Freya said, as Andrew joined then, tugging on a mask, and as if the final part of his PPE had induced a transformation, he had gone from a quiet and shy young pathologist, who had replied in succinct sentences, to a man who clearly was no stranger to death and procedure. He snapped on his latex gloves, dragged a stainless-steel trolley over to them, and prepared the tools they would need.

"Did you manage to read Doctor Saint's report?" Freya asked, and Pip nodded.

"Poor fella," she replied.

"The victim?"

"No, Saint. Didn't stand a chance with this one. You know, his trousers were damn near melted to his skin. His socks, too." She shook her head. "It's a wonder his face was intact."

"Well, I'm sure all the grisly details can be discussed a little later, can't they?" Freya said, nudging her on.

"Saint posed me a question," Pip continued. "He wondered if he died from the hanging, or if his heart gave up."

"And?" Freya asked, and Pip hesitated, letting the tension build.

"He died of strangulation," Pip replied quietly, knowing full well what that statement meant.

"Jesus," Ben said, clearly horrified.

"Presumably, you came to that conclusion from the haemorrhage in the eyes and the lungs?"

"And there was me thinking *I* was the pathologist," Pip said, to which Freya rolled her eyes. "Or does the cause of death fall under your remit, now? Have I taught you so much, that you can pretty much do this by yourself?"

Perhaps it was the idea of being belittled in front of her new assistant, or maybe it was just Pip's unrelenting hunger for conflict. Either way, Freya knew where and when not to upset her. She would bide her time and, if Gillespie's description was accurate, would fight fire with fire when the moment arose.

"We're just keen to progress this, Pip," Ben said, clearly trying to ease the new tension. Freya inwardly cursed herself for falling foul of Pip's entrapment but let her continue.

"As for the rest of the theory," Pip continued her tone low and sombre. "I'd say it's pretty much spot on." She indicated some bruising around the man's armpits, then gestured for Andrew to step in and help. Carefully, he rolled the victim onto his side, allowing Pip, with the use of the multicoloured pen from her breast pocket, to indicate the bruising continuing down his back. "Ropes," she said. "He was hauled up using rope of the same, or similar diameter as that which was used to hang him."

"We found another piece," Ben said. "A longer length."

"There you go," Pip added, and she produced a clear bag with the remains of the blue noose. "Had to cut this off him. Tighter than a camel's backside in a sandstorm, it was. He struggled some. I'll give him that. Didn't die easily."

Above his mask, Andrew's eyes widened, and he cleared his throat loudly, as if to distract himself from Pip's choice of analogy.

She gripped the knot through the bag to demonstrate its girth.

"This is off to the lab later today, along with the swabs we've taken from his skin," she said. "But I agree with Saint. This wasn't hurriedly cobbled together on the fly. This is a work of art. See how neat it is?"

She held the bag up for them to see, and aside from a neat coil of rope, Freya failed to be impressed.

"Do you have anything to add regarding the noose, Pip?" Freya asked.

"Not the noose itself," she replied. "But the placement."

"The placement?" Ben cut in, to which she nodded.

"See, Ben, in the good old days, when a murderer could expect to swing, the executioner would position the knot just here." She demonstrated an area on the side of Andrew's neck. "That ensured that when the ill-fated prisoner reached the bottom of his drop...snap!" She made a loud click with the side of her mouth, holding his gaze. "His neck broke. Death would be instant."

Ben, who, despite falling into most, if not all, of Pip's conversational traps, was not one to be affected by gruesome details.

"Too quick for some, in my opinion," he told her.

"You're a fan of capital punishment, are you? Now, Ben. You do surprise me."

"I'm a fan of proportionate punishment," he replied flatly. "Sadly, all *we* can do is find them, gather the evidence, and hand them to the CPS. We have no say after that."

"And would you like a say?" Pip replied, seeming to enjoy this deep dive into Ben's opinions on all things judicial. "Could you manage the weight of another man's life in your hands?"

"I wouldn't want it," he replied. "Not for all of them, anyway." He gestured down at the body before them. "But there are some cases where I would dearly love to be holding the gavel."

She smiled a cold and knowing smile.

"You and me both," she said.

"Anyway," Freya cut in, nudging them on again. "So, our man suffered. His neck did not snap, and he hung from the rope whilst ablaze, did he?"

"She likes to paint pretty pictures," Pip explained to Andrew, whose eyes revealed no judgement. She frowned at the lack of reaction, then turned back to Freya. "Yes, Freya. That is what happened. There's a significant amount of tissue damage to the lower areas, signifying that he was alive while the fire blazed."

"Is that conclusive?" Freya asked.

"Had he been dead," Andrew said. "His flesh wouldn't have reacted that way. It wouldn't have reacted at all. It would simply have just burned."

"Freya's more familiar with the effects of fire than any of us, Andrew," Pip told him, and Freya steeled herself and turned her face to reveal her scars. With only his eyes to go by, he seemed not to react at all. Instead, once he had had a good look, he turned back to Pip. "Once the killer had him hauled into the air, which, by the way, in addition to the bruising, fractured two of his ribs, we can assume he then climbed onto something to attach the second rope." She raised the bag again as if to support her statement.

"Then he set light to them?" Ben said.

"He did. I'm certain he or she used a petrol-based accelerant, but you'll have to speak to Katy Southwell about which one it was. All I can tell you is that his upper half was not doused."

"Sorry?" Freya said.

"His upper half, Freya," she repeated. "There's no petrol or whatever it was on it. His clothes were scorched but not burned to a cinder. Not like his lower half. What does that tell you?"

"The killer wanted him to suffer," Ben said. "We've been over this a few times."

"Not necessarily," Andrew cut in, then his eyes widened as they each stared at him. "Well, think about it. The poor man's hanging from a tree. How high was he?"

"Nine or ten feet," Ben replied.

"That's about three metres in new money," Pip explained, and Andrew nodded.

"Well, presumably, the killer used a car or something to haul him up there and then stood on it to put the noose over his head."

"Right?" Ben said, and Freya fell in with what he was going to say.

"He had to move the car or van, or whatever it was," she said. "Which meant that when it came to dousing him in petrol, he couldn't reach the top half. There was nothing to stand on."

"Right," Andrew said, as if the answer was obvious.

Ben looked at them all as if they'd lost their minds.

"He tied a rope to a man, tossed the rope over a tree branch, then hauled him into the air," Ben said. "He then put a noose around his neck and prepared to set light to him. I don't care if he couldn't splash the upper torso with petrol or not. He wanted him to suffer. If he wanted him to die quickly, he wouldn't have gone to such lengths, would he?"

"I agree," Freya said. "But I don't think this is the place to ascertain his motive, do you?" She turned to Pip. "Time of death?"

She referred to her notes and flipped to another page.

"I know Doctor Saint suggested otherwise, but let's face it, this isn't your run-of-the-mill—"

"Pip?" Freya said before she went off on a tangent.

"Saturday night through to the early hours of Sunday morning," she replied. "Internal temperatures, rate of cooling, rate of digestion all gives us a six-hour window. I can't be any more specific than that. All we've got to go on is the progress of livor mortis, the current stage of rigor mortis. He's still within the rigor mortis window, but livor mortis was well and truly set in when he was cut down." She indicated the man's feet, which were a deep red where blood had pooled.

"But he could have been there longer," Ben said. "It's possible, is it?"

"Well, that's why we take internal temperatures," she replied. "We can get an approximate calculation from the rate the body cools."

"Anything else to support that?" Freya asked.

"I can show you what he had for dinner," Pip said, and she referred to the chest cavity.

"An explanation would suffice," Freya said, refusing to be led into Pip's world.

"Steak and chips," she replied. "I think there's some onion rings in there, too."

"I get it," Freya told her.

"Unless he had steak for breakfast," Pip continued. "He might have been on the Atkins diet."

"I think we've got enough, don't you?" Ben asked.

"No," Freya said. "No, I need to know if he suffered any other wounds."

"Like?" Pip replied.

"Blunt force trauma, maybe?" Freya said, to which Pip shook her head.

"No. Not as far as we've seen, and we've been over every inch of him."

"No cuts or anything?"

"Isn't this enough?" Pip said, slightly incredulous. "The man suffered a hideous death—"

"I know," Freya said. "I was just—"

"She's just checking the facts," Ben cut in, and he gestured at the door with a nod of his head. "We'd better get back."

Pip checked her watch.

"Oh, would you look at that. Time flies with you two, I must say," she said. "We'd better start getting him ready. Can't put him out like this, can we?"

"There is one more thing," Freya said, raising a hand to stop Pip from pushing them out.

"Go on," Pip said, checking her watch again.

"You're familiar with tattoos, aren't you?"

Despite her position as a respected forensic pathologist, she made no effort to confirm to societal norms. Not only was she the most tattooed pathologist Freya had ever met, but she was also the most tattooed person she had ever met, full stop. The largest of which, to Freya's knowledge at least, was the great Welsh dragon that protruded from her black tee-shirt across her chest and onto her throat.

"Referring to the cross, are you?" she said, and Freya stepped closer to peer down at the small, blueish-green mark.

"It's not professional, is it?"

"It doesn't look it," Pip agreed. "If you look closer, you can see it was done with a series of marks. A needle, probably, with some bottled ink."

"Have you seen this before?" Freya asked.

"Not this particular cross," she replied. "But a modern tattoo machine has lots of needles, depending on the one in use. There are so many, that you can't really isolate them. But this?" She shook her head, reached up, and dragged a huge magnifier down that hung from a mechanical boom. She positioned it for Freya to get a better look. "See what I mean? The lines aren't straight. None of it is uniform. Used to do this back in the day, they did. Would have taken hours. Hardly seems worth it, does it? Small cross like that."

"But does it mean anything to you?"

"I'm a pathologist, Freya, not a semiotician."

Freya looked closely. She could almost make out the individual marks the tattooist made. The cross was no bigger than an inch yet comprised of hundreds of tiny marks.

"You were quite happy to discuss the motive and the method," Freya said. "Does that fall under your remit, too?"

Pip said nothing. She dragged the magnifier up and out of the way, before gesturing for Andrew to begin preparing the victim.

"Anything else?" Pip asked abruptly. "His wife will be here, soon."

"Actually, there is one more thing," Freya said.

"And what's that?" Pip asked.

"The fact that his face and torso are untouched," she began. "You're right, it might be due to the height at which he hung. But personally, I think that's circumstantial."

Pip, never one to be beaten, busied herself by covering the victim with the sheet.

"Go on, Freya," she said. "Enlighten us."

"It was intentional," Freya said. "He wanted the victim to suffer, and he achieved that."

"We established that—"

"But he also wanted him to be recognisable," Freya continued. "But I wouldn't have expected a pathologist to understand that."

CHAPTER TWENTY

"Bloody cow," Freya muttered under her breath as Ben closed the insulated doors behind them. "Did you hear her?"

"Freya—" Ben said.

"Honestly, just because she's got a new toy boy in tow, she thinks she can make a fool out of me?"

"Freya," Ben said, and he cleared his throat. He flicked his eyes across the room and furrowed his brow.

It took a microsecond for Freya to understand the meaning, but a few seconds more for her to regain her composure and formulate a plan. She untied her gown, pulled the string over her head, then turned, making a show of leaving it neatly on the couch.

"Oh, hello, Jackie," she said, injecting as much surprise as she could. She glanced across at the woman Gold was standing with. "Julie. How are you doing?"

Julie Dean said nothing at first, then sought assurance from Gold, who gave her shoulder a squeeze.

"Yeah," she said. "Yeah, I'm alright. Jackie's been... Well, she's been great. I don't know what I'd have done without her, to be honest."

"You're not the first one to say that," Freya replied, and the steel resolve Julie Dean had tried to convey cracked like glass.

"Oh God," she said as she frantically fumbled in her handbag for a tissue. Gold, as always, was ready. She slid an arm around her and slipped a tissue into her hand, whispering something in her ear that seemed to calm her down, something that neither Freya, Ben, nor the rest of the team, for that matter, could have achieved with such ease. She wiped her eyes, stared up at Freya with blood-shot eyes, then shook her head slowly from side to side. "I don't know what I'm doing here. I mean, we were okay. Everything was okay. It wasn't great, but we got by. Why didn't he just come home? Why didn't he just tell me?"

"I can't tell you," Freya told her flatly, and even as she spoke the words, she heard how cold they sounded. "I wish I could. Honestly, I wish I could make all this go away. But I can't, Julie." She stepped closer, and Gold gave them some room, like some informal dance routine. "I won't put them on the spot, but I'll bet DC Gold and DI Savage feel the same," Freya continued, and she took a deep breath, preparing herself for the statement that had the potential to shatter that facade, sending her crumbling to the floor. "I asked Jackie to explain the situation. Did she do that, Julie?"

"The situation?" she said through sobs and sniffed loudly.

"The man we found had been attacked. Quite brutally," Freya said, and Julie nodded, forcing her head upright so that she peered down the length of her nose at Freya. "I need you to be ready, Julie. I need you to go in there and..." She softened. "I need you to remember him how he was. Remember him as you met him, when you laughed together, and those moments you shared that nobody can ever take away. Can you do that for me, Julie? Can you remember those moments? Can you remember his smile?"

Julie nodded slowly, and the frown embedded into her fore-head smoothed for a moment.

"I can," she whispered.

"Good," Freya said. "Because we need you to be strong. He needs you to be strong. When you're done, we'll be right here."

"Alone? I can't do this alone—"

"We can't go inside with you," Freya explained. "But the pathologist will be with you. Doctor Bell."

"The cow?" Julie said, forcing a laugh.

"No," Freya said softly. "No, I'm afraid the only cow in here is me. Well, if I'm honest, I'm more of a dragon, and if you don't believe me, you ask DI Savage. He'll back me up on that."

"She breathes fire," Ben said, and Julie's lips straightened, not quite arcing into a smile.

"But that's okay," Freya continued. "It's good to have a dragon on your side. Because I'll fight, and I won't stop until every resource available to me has been exhausted, every door has been knocked on, and every possible lead has been torn to shreds."

"The rear door opened, and Pip, wearing a clean smock over a smart blouse, waited in the doorway.

"He's ready," she said.

"We need you to do this," Freya said, and Julie nodded. She didn't speak. Everything she needed to say was written in her glazed and reddened eyes.

Jackie led her to Pip, who invited them both into the back room, where the Chapel of Rest was located.

Then the door closed, and the tension that had built inside Freya was released in a single breath.

She heard the click of saliva as Ben opened his mouth to speak.

"Don't say a word," she said before he could, then let her head fall back onto the wall. "Please. Don't say a word."

She took a few paces towards the door, listening for a sign, but her impatience got the better of her, and her legs just seemed to carry her around the room. She didn't walk fast. It was more of a thoughtful stroll, but if she stopped, then so too would her mind, and if that stopped, the ideas, the scenarios, the theories.... they would all come tumbling down like a house of cards, leaving her with little more than doubt. Doubt in her own abilities, of the conclusions she had already drawn, and of her own mind.

She had completed less than one full circuit under Ben's curious and watchful gaze when the door opened again. It was quick. Too quick.

Jackie Gold entered first, and Freya sought some indication from her expression, but Julie Dean followed closely behind and then Pip.

"Is everything okay?" Freya asked.

Julie was taking deep breaths. She faced the wall, gripping one hand with the other, perhaps to stop herself from shaking. Eventually, she turned to face Freya, wiping her eyes one last time.

"Julie—"

"He's still out there," she said, with a new worry weighing heavy in her voice. "It's not him. It's not my Tommy."

CHAPTER TWENTY-ONE

FREYA HAD HOPED to unveil some meaning to the spider-like spatter of words she had written on the whiteboard the previous day. Yet, she found her scribblings cast deeper into shadow. The room was silent behind her. Even Gillespie refrained from whispering an insult to Cruz or a playful dig at Nillson.

Despite how hard she stared, the words remained unchanged, meaningless, and unrelatable, like stars in the night sky. They were there, right in front of her. But they were so very far from providing any real purpose.

"Are we all ready?" she asked quietly, still facing the board.

"We are," Ben replied as spokesperson, and she imagined him checking each face in the room for an argument.

"Good," she sighed. "Well, the good news is that Julie Dean's husband is very likely still alive. Before we move on, I think it's worth mentioning that DC Gold did a sterling job as FLO. I think you've really found your stride."

"Thank you, ma'am," Gold murmured, unused to such praise.

"The truth is, Gold, had it not been for you, we'd still be looking into Tommy Dean."

"Aye, but he's still missing," Gillespie said.

"Yes, and the last time I looked, missing persons were not part of our job description." She turned to Chapman. "Anything from the hospitals or news from the front desk?"

Chapman shook her head.

"Nothing," she replied. "I need disclosure forms for Tommy Dean's financial details, but—"

"Put that to one side for the time being," Freya told her. "We'll be requesting warrants soon enough. I don't want those we do need sitting beneath a pile of warrants we no longer need."

"Got it," Chapman replied.

"Well, actually, they might be useful," Gillespie said.

"Oh?"

"Well, you see, I was...that is, Cruz and I were on our wee walk yesterday. It was the last house, as it happens. Fella named Geoff Godolphin. Had a wee lad about eleven or twelve years old. Anyways, neither him nor the lad saw or heard anything."

"Is this a talk of disappointment, Gillespie? We do have rather a lot to get through, namely finding the identity of the victim."

"Aye, well. See, Cruz gave him a card in case he remembers something. He leaned in to toss the card onto a table, and that's when I saw it."

"Saw what?"

"The tattoo," he said. "On his neck. Clear as day."

Freya wanted to ask, but remembering what Ben had said, she hesitated, prompting Gillespie to embellish the statement.

"It was a cross," Cruz cut in. "Just like the one on the victim's neck. Same place and everything."

"Nice one," Gillespie said. "Remind me the next time you want to deliver a bombshell, and I'll be sure to ruin your punchline."

"Sorry," Freya said, doing her best to cut through the noise. "He had a tattoo?"

"Aye," Gillespie told her. "Just like the one on...you know. The fella."

"A cross?"

"Homemade, too, by the looks of it."

"What did you say his name was?" Freya asked, with a glance at Chapman to suggest she should take notes.

"Godolphin," Gillespie replied.

"That's Go dolphin," Cruz said. "As in the mammal."

"Mammal? You halfwit. It's a fish," Gillespie said, but Freya was too preoccupied to correct him. She stared at Ben. Who, by the look on his face, had come to the same conclusion.

"Julie Dean?" she asked him, and he nodded thoughtfully.

"Eh?" Gillespie said.

"Chapman, look into this Godolphin, will you? See how far you can go back."

"Anything worth sharing, boss?" Gillespie pushed.

"Gold, access the crime scene photos. See if you can blow up the tattoo," Freya said. "Print it, will you? Let's have it up on the board."

"Something caught your attention, boss, has it?" Gillespie continued. "Anything we can help with?"

"Nillson, while Chapman's looking into Godolphin, get onto the DVLA and check ANPR for any sign of Tommy Dean's Toyota pickup truck."

"You know, sometimes I feel like I'm saying stuff, but nobody can hear me," Gillespie said.

"Gillespie," Freya said, finally putting him out of his misery.

"Boss?"

"I've got a job for you."

"Oh, aye?" he said, the statement causing more trepidation than excitement.

"I want you to go and see this Godolphin again," she said. "Invite him in for questioning."

"Voluntarily?"

"Voluntarily," she said.

"When's a good time for you?" he asked. "This afternoon? It

was around five-ish when we spoke to him, so I might be able to get him here for five-thirty."

"Whatever suits you," she said.

"Well, not really. If I'm going to convince him to come in voluntarily, then I'll need to make sure you're here. His type's not a huge fan of the law, if you know what I mean. He's not going to hang around waiting, but I think if we play it right, we can get him on side. I think he might be useful."

It was perhaps one of Gillespie's more mature statements and pleasantly surprised Freya.

"Get him here whenever it suits you, Gillespie," she said, and she caught Ben's curious gaze in the corner of her eye. "It's you who will be interviewing him."

"Me?"

"And Cruz, yes," she said. "I want you to focus on the tattoos. First of all, let's confirm the connection between the two men. There's a slim chance that the victim, Tommy Dean, and this Godolphin character having the same tattoo is a coincidence, although I can't see why anybody in their right mind would do that. If there is a connection, find out when they were done? Who did them? Why did they do them? I want to know if he's seen Tommy Dean recently or if he knows of any reason why Tommy Dean might be missing."

"Right," Gillespie replied, tapping his pockets for his notepad. "Do we want his DNA?"

"Why would we want his DNA?"

"Well, I mean. There are three fellas with the same tattoo. One of them is dead. The other one's missing. Stands to reason the CPS will want him either ruled out or ruled in."

Freya nodded, and Ben shrugged, nodding to say it seemed to make sense.

"Don't force the matter," she said after deliberating. "Request a swab as a matter of procedure, but if he is, as you suggest, the type that has little respect for what we do, then he'll know his rights. We don't want to get his back up. Not yet, anyway."

"No, I'll save that for you, boss," Gillespie replied, and Freya stilled at the comment. "I mean, if we end up nicking him. You can get his back up when you charge him."

"I see," she replied, and a wash of red crept up Gillespie's face.

"I've got a question," Cruz said, and he screwed his face up in confusion.

"Yes Cruz?" Freya said.

"If three blokes all have the same tattoo, it makes sense that they went to the same place to get it done and most likely did it together."

"It's an assumption, but yes, one that I'd agree with, tentatively."

"Well, you'd think they were good friends, wouldn't you?"

"Yes, go on. I assume you do have a point to make."

"Well, if they're good friends, then why didn't Julie Dean recognise him?" Freya thought about it, then turned to Gold, initiating a wave of turning heads and expectant gazes.

"She didn't say anything," Gold said.

"Did you ask?" Nillson said.

"Well, no, I mean. She was upset and relieved more than anything—"

"It's okay, Jackie," Ben told her. "We were there, and we didn't ask either. It never even occurred to me."

"Nor me," Freya said. "You'd think she would have said something."

"Unless..." Gillespie added.

"Unless what?"

"Unless she did recognise him," he said.

"Are you going to embellish that statement, Gillespie, or are you taking lessons in stating the obvious?"

"Well," he said, laughing her comment off. "Where is she now?"

Again, everyone looked to Gold for an answer, who shrugged.

"I took her home. She said she needed to get on. Her work has been good so far, but she needs to carry on as normal and just hope that either he turns up or we find him."

"The former rather than the latter, I assume," Freya mused. She had an idea of what point Gillespie was trying to make, but preferred it to come from him. "Gillespie, are you suggesting she's not being entirely truthful?"

He took a deep breath, smoothed his shirt, and picked at a non-existent piece of fluff.

"She said Tommy Dean was down in the dumps, right?"

"Yes," Freya said.

"He's been out of work since, what late last year?"

"Have to admit, I was pleasantly surprised at your insights into Godolphin, Gillespie, but I'm finding this rather tedious—"

"What if Tommy had some kind of grudge against our victim?"

The words mirrored the thoughts that circled in Freya's mind like buzzards over a dying lamb. It was a large leap to make and one she was sure would have come to light when they had more to go on. But now that he had aired the thought, the sentiment seemed even more plausible.

"You're suggesting that she's either in the know or suspects that he's responsible."

"Tommy Dean isn't a victim here," Gillespie said, shaking his head, and he stabbed at his desk with a large index finger. "He's our bloody killer."

CHAPTER TWENTY-TWO

JACKIE GOLD WAS STICKING an enlarged image of the tattoo on the whiteboard. The image meant nothing to Freya or anyone else in the room, she assumed, but it would serve as a constant reminder of the one element they had that linked the victim to another individual, or in this case, individuals.

Gold caught Freya staring and shied.

"Looks bloomin' awful this close, don't it?" she said, and Freya stepped closer, recalling what Pip had shown her with the aid of the magnifier.

"Pip said it could have been done with a needle."

"Stick and poke," Nillson called out.

"Stick and what?"

"Poke, boss," she replied. "That's what they used to call it."

"When did who call what stick and poke, Nillson? Come on, just because Gillespie has left for the day doesn't mean we need to fill the gap with more vagueness."

"It's a method," Nillson said, as she typed into her computer before turning the laptop around for Freya to see. "You get a needle, stick the dull end into a cork or something you can grip, then wrap the cotton thread around the sharp end to act as a kind of wick."

"I see," Freya said. "And you did this, did you? You don't strike me as the type of woman who would do something like that to your body, Nillson, I must say."

"I didn't do it, personally," Nillson replied. "I prefer piercings, myself." She smiled, and Freya resisted from delving deeper into whatever body enhancements lay beneath her clothes. "But a few of the lads at school did. Not on their necks, mind. But they did it. They dipped the sharp end into some ink, then just make a shape or a pattern with loads of tiny little pricks."

"Well, that seems like a suitable word to use," Freya muttered.

"The cotton soaks up the ink and kind of drips it onto the end of the needle," Nillson continued, and she stood to join them at the board. "Look, you can see it here." She identified the individual marks that Pip had spotted. "Looks like what the boys I knew did if you ask me. It hurts, and if it's not done well, there's always a chance of infection."

"That probably explains why it's so small," Gold added. "What is that, two centimetres?"

"What about the shape? A cross. Does it mean anything to anyone?" Freya asked, putting the question out to the room and receiving a series of head shakes in return. "Is it gang-related, do you think? Did they have gangs around here back then? It's certainly the kind of silly thing kids would do down in London, but up here? Ben?"

"Not really," he replied. "Any gangs have usually been the problem of the city lot. Sure, they'd come out here and cause trouble, but as far as I know we've never really had any gangs based around here."

"A cross," Freya said again. "A cross. Why a cross?"

"Because it's easy," Nillson said.

"Sorry?"

"It's easy," she replied. "To tattoo, I mean. Everyone can draw a cross, can't they?"

"You don't get a tattoo on your neck purely because it's easy to draw, surely?" Gold said.

"You don't get a tattoo on your neck, full stop," Freya said. "Unless you're a half-wit."

"That's a bit strong," Ben said.

"Is it?" she said. "Do you think they gave a thought to future job interviews?"

"It's low enough a collar would have covered it—"

"Even so," Freya said. "It's there for life. It doesn't even look good. It doesn't even look finished, for God's sake." She paced, then came to the conclusion that they had exhausted the discussion on the tattoo until they knew more. "Well, all hopes of answering our questions on the tattoo lie in the hands of Gillespie and Cruz."

"Jesus," Nillson muttered.

"Have you had any luck with Tommy Dean's car?" Freya asked her.

"No," she replied. "ANPR alerts are set up, and according to the DVLA, there's nothing out of the ordinary. He pays his tax and insurance, and it's MOT'd."

"That's what I thought," Freya said, then turned to Chapman. "Any luck on Godolphin?"

"Nope," she replied. "He's an engineer. Works for a firm that repairs farm equipment. No previous record, owns his own house, he's on the electoral register, and married with one child. A boy named Benjamin."

"Shame," Freya said almost to herself but loud enough for the others to hear. "I was hoping we could keep him here when Gillespie brings him in."

"I might have something," Ben called out. He was over by the rear wall, looking up at the map of the area. Curious, Freya strode over to him, followed by Nillson and Gold.

"Go on," Freya said, and Ben pressed his index finger into a spot on the map.

"The crime scene," he said, and he searched around him for a pin, which Gold dutifully found and handed across to him. He pressed the pin in, then stood back and searched the stationary tray on the desk behind him. He snatched up a pencil, then duly set to draw a line on the map.

"What's that?" Freya asked.

"This line," he said, as he finished drawing, "denotes the boundary of Brinkleview Farm."

"Brinkleview?"

"Frank Bowen," he said, giving her a look that suggested it should mean something to her. And it did.

"The abandoned house?" she said, and his shoulders sagged. He held his hand out to Gold, who placed another pin into it. He then pressed the pin into the map.

"This is the abandoned house," he said. "But that wasn't what I was getting at."

"Well, what *were* you getting at?"

"Well," he said and pointed at the area of the map where the line he had drawn skimmed past the crime scene. "Bowen's land ends on one side of the track. Everything from that point on belongs to Hawes Farm up the road."

"So?"

"So, Julie Dean told us that Tommy hadn't been paid or wasn't being paid regularly," he explained. "That was why he left the farm."

"But Bowen said he didn't know why he left and that there was never any issue with payment," Freya finished.

"Right," he said. "Bowen would know this land. That spot..." he banged a finger at the crime scene again. "This is the perfect place. You can't see it from the road; you can't see it from the farm, or anywhere. Nobody can hear you."

"They might see a bloody great fire, though," Nillson said.

"No. How would they see it?" Ben said. "There's no angle from which you could possibly see the place from outside the farm."

"And no way of hearing the screams," Freya added. "I take it from your subdued excitement, Ben, that you're implying that Tommy Dean came across this place whilst working on the farm."

"Yes and no," he said. "I think that anybody who works or worked on the farm would have cause to know about this place."

"But?"

"But I don't think it's limited to Tommy Dean," he said. "In fact, the more I think about it, the more I think we should be looking at Frank Bowen or his employees." Freya opened her mouth to speak, then stopped herself. Rather than add complexity into the mix by mentioning the abandoned house, she allied herself to his enthusiasm.

"But you're of the opinion that the site was selected, are you?" she said instead. "That any of Bowen's workers would know of the place."

"Tommy Dean definitely would have," Gold said, and Freya turned to question her.

"Go on."

"Well, it was something Julie said," Gold continued. "When lockdown hit, he was working in the office job, but from home, like most people. He used to take himself for walks." She collected one of the pins from the container and pressed one into the Dean house on the outskirts of Tattershall. "She said he used to watch the tractors. His dad used to work there, so he used to go over and watch them, and that's what gave him the idea of a new start."

Ben traced the route he might have taken from Tattershall to the crime scene.

"If he followed that footpath, it would have taken him right to the spot," he said.

"Do you still want to look into Bowen and his band of merry

men, Ben?" Freya asked, to which he hesitated while considering his response.

"I think we shouldn't limit our options," he replied, and he looked back at the whiteboard on the far side of the room. "I think we have names, now, and that's much better than what we had an hour ago."

"I've got something," Chapman called out, the only one of them not to be standing beside the map. She waited for the team to give her their attention, then turned her screen for them to see. "It's Frank Bowen."

"What about him?" Freya asked. "Is he worth looking into?"

"According to this," she replied. "We'd be stupid not to."

CHAPTER TWENTY-THREE

GILLESPIE AND CRUZ waited in the custody suite. Sergeant Priest, the custody sergeant, was at his place behind the custody desk, where he could usually be found with a biro poking from between his lips, and typing with just his index fingers. It was painful just to watch him, Cruz thought. Every now and again, Priest would tut and grumble to himself before hitting the keyboard several times in quick succession, which Cruz put down to him, deleting entire words or sentences.

"Which room we in, Mister P?" Gillespie asked as they waited for him to finish typing the word or sentence before he looked up at them.

"Two, Jim," he replied. "One's out of action."

"Oh, aye?"

"Clarkson's in there now with the full hazmat suit and a bucket of bleach."

"Sounds like a good night in," Gillespie joked.

"One of the CID lot left a suspect in there earlier, who then decided to...redecorate, shall we say, in protest."

"Charming," Cruz said.

Priest was a Yorkshireman through and through. He was tall.

Taller than Ben and Jim most likely, Cruz mused, remembering that back when he would have joined the force, there were height restrictions which had become more relaxed over the years.

Instead of relaxing the height restrictions, however, Cruz wondered if they would have been better introducing girth limits. Priest, who Cruz thought to be in his late fifties, had expanded somewhat even in the few years he'd known him.

He had perpetual rosy, red cheeks as if he'd just walked in out of the cold, despite the warm weather, and what was left up top had been spread so thin it reminded Cruz of the meagre wipe of butter his mother used to apply to his sandwiches.

"You call it charming," Priest said. "I call it downright bloody filthy. Who brings these people up like that, eh? Who does that?"

"Ah, come on," Gillespie said. "You've seen worse, eh? The clientele you get in this place, you should count yourself lucky it wasn't worse."

"I've got human faeces on the walls, Jim," Priest grumbled, then leaned on the desk. "I'm not sure how it gets any worse than that. I don't know. Maybe I'm just getting tired of it all. Seen enough pee and...well, you know what else, to last a lifetime."

"Ah, come on, Mister P. You can't retire. You're what, thirty-six, thirty-seven?"

Priest laughed, and as always, it was a sight to behold. He had a beaming smile and full cheeks that squashed his eyes closed when the two worked in tandem.

"Ah, Jimmy, you always know what to say, don't you?" he replied as the doors to the car park opened.

Godolphin entered first, followed closely by two uniformed officers, one of whom looked up at Gillespie and stared at him with nothing short of hatred.

"PC Jewson," Gillespie said to the young female officer who, just a matter of weeks ago, had been inches from destroying Gillespie's career.

Cruz, who, due to years of being on the receiving end of Gillespie's fractious moods and maddening musings, had become tuned into the big Glaswegian well enough to know when to take control.

"Thanks for coming in, Mr Godolphin," he said, hoping to God that neither Gillespie nor Jewson started bickering. The slightest little remark from the young PC would be enough to put Gillespie on the offensive. "If you could follow me."

"Not booking him in?" Priest asked from behind the custody desk.

"Nah, it's just a chat," Cruz replied. "Mr Godolphin is here voluntarily. He's just helping us with our enquiries. Room two, you say, yeah?"

He held the door to the corridor open for Godolphin, hoping that Gillespie would follow suit.

"Not going to process him, then?" Jewson asked, and Godolphin stopped in his tracks.

"No, PC Jewson," Cruz told her. "No, like I said, he's here voluntarily as a potential witness. He's not a suspect. We don't process witnesses."

"What does she mean, process?" Godolphin asked.

"She's asking why we're not taking your fingerprints or your DNA," Gillespie cut in. "Apologies, Mr Godolphin, our young colleague is still learning the ropes."

"Wouldn't hurt, though, would it?" Jewson said.

"Jewson!" Priest said, his voice a barrelling bass, had enough of an eye to warn her not to get involved. "Haven't you got something to do?"

"Coming up to the end of my shift, sarge," she replied.

"You're not fingerprinting me, are you? I don't have to give you my DNA, do I?" Godolphin said.

"You don't have to do anything unless you want to," Cruz said.

"Well, I don't. It's bad enough I'm here. I'm not being processed, or whatever you call it. I've done nowt wrong."

"It's fine," Cruz said. "It doesn't apply to you."

He shared a look with Gillespie, who was seething at Jewson's interference.

"Actually," Gillespie said. "I thought I heard Clarkson was looking for you. I think he's in interview room one. Said he could do with a hand."

"Oh yeah?"

"Yeah," Gillespie said. "That's right, eh, Cruz?"

"Oh, yeah," he said. "He's got a right tough nut in there."

"Aye," Gillespie added. "Tell you what, you'd learn a lot from being in there on that one. The type that gets up your nose, if you know what I mean?"

"Sign the car back in, Jewson, and then get down there, will you?" Priest said, nodding for Cruz and Gillespie to make their escape.

Gillespie turned to Cruz, winked at Priest, and then politely led Godolphin into the corridor.

Neither of them said another word about it, but inwardly, Cruz was grinning madly.

He extended an arm to invite Godolphin into the room and caught Gillespie leaning into the next room.

"You alright, Clarkson?" he said.

"Been better, Jim," came the reply.

"We've just arranged a little help for you. Got some spare gloves there, have you?"

"Got the gloves, the tools, and the bleach," Clarkson said. "All I'm missing is the will to live."

"Ah, well. Maybe when the help arrives, you can go and take a break, eh? Let them finish it off."

"Cheers, sarge," Clarkson replied.

"What was all that about?" Godolphin asked. He entered interview room two and took the seat Cruz proffered.

"Ah, it's nothing," Cruz told him. "Can I get you a water or a tea or something?"

"No, let's make this quick, eh?" he replied. 'Got to be at the workshop this afternoon."

"Sorry about that," Gillespie said, closing the door behind him. "Have you offered him a drink, Gabby?"

"I'm fine," Godolphin said. "Look, what's this all about? You knock on my door, scare the bejesus out of my boy, and now you drag me down here."

"Before we begin, I just want to make it clear that this interview is voluntary. You're not under arrest, and are here purely to help with our enquiries. You are free to go whenever you choose."

"What's the point? Look, if you've got something to say, then now's the time. I'd rather not have you knocking on my door again, and I definitely don't want you turning up at my work again."

"Well, it's just a few enquiries," Gillespie started.

"You said it was related to a serious incident when you were on my doorstep."

"Aye, it's related to a serious incident. But all we're looking for from you is a little guidance."

"Guidance? You want me to tell you how to do your job?"

Gillespie cocked his head to one side and peered at the man's neck.

"That's an odd tattoo you have there," he said. "What is that? A wee cross, is it?"

Instinctively, Godolphin raised his hand and covered the little blue-ish mark.

"It's nothing," he said, and Cruz made a note in his pad.

"What are you writing?"

Cruz looked up innocently.

"That the tattoo is nothing," he said.

"What does it matter about my tattoo? It's just a tattoo. It's nothing."

"You do that yourself?" Gillespie asked, making no attempt to hide the fact that he was vying for a better look.

"It's just a tattoo. Look, have you got me down here to talk about...whatever this is, or my tattoo?"

"Well, as it happens, both," Gillespie said.

"What?"

"It is, isn't it?" Gillespie continued. "That's a homemade tattoo. What do they call it? Poke and jab or something?"

"My mate did it," Godolphin said. "We were eighteen. It was a mistake. I'm sure you made mistakes when you were eighteen?"

"Aye, but no tattoos," Gillespie said, then turned to Cruz. "You, Gabby? Any tattoos?"

Cruz shook his head. "No, never fancied it, really. Never really saw the point of them."

Cruz noted the points as they came, filtering the frustration from fact.

"Why a cross?" Gillespie asked. "Is that significant? Are you religious?"

"No, I'm not religious."

"Well, why a cross, then?"

"Why not a cross?"

"I don't know. It just seems...well, symbolic or something. I always thought that if I had a tattoo, I'd have the lyrics to Wish You Were Here across my chest. Do you know the song? The bit about the lost souls swimming in a fishbowl?"

Godolphin shook his head slowly in disbelief and then nodded.

"Yes, I know the song."

"Either that or a sunrise," Gillespie said. "You know, like a new beginning. Symbolic, aye?"

"We did crosses. I don't know why. I can't remember."

"We?" Gillespie said. "Who's we?"

"Me and my mates," he said.

If Cruz were to categorise the man's disposition, he would have said it was more bewildered than frustrated, with a heavy dose of angst.

"Mates, plural?" Gillespie continued.

"What?"

"Mates, plural," he said. "As in, two mates. Meaning, there were what, three of you? Four?"

"Three," he replied. "Look, I don't know if this is how you do things or if you're just trying to be friendly, but this is a bit weird. Can we just get to the point?"

"Aye, sorry," Gillespie said, then let the silence fill the void. "What were their names?"

Whether purposefully or not, Gillespie had driven Godolphin to the limits of his patience. He thrust his hands into the air, shoved himself out of the seat and started towards the door.

"I'm done," he said. "You asked me to come without telling me why, and I came. I can't be fairer than that. I gave you every chance to ask me questions, and all you want to talk about is a poxy tattoo I had done when I was young and dumb." He stopped at the door. "I'm free to go, right? You said I was free to go when-ever I choose."

"That's correct," Gillespie told him, making no attempt to stop him.

"Well, if that's all. Have a good day," Godolphin said, and he snatched at the door handle.

"There is one more thing," Gillespie called out, stopping Godolphin in the doorway. He turned to face him. "Tommy Dean."

It was one of those moments that, as a police officer, you only get one chance at. The reaction. The moment a suspect hears a name or a fact, they react subconsciously. Never again would they get that chance, and although reading the reaction can only ever be described as subjective, it was often enough to convince the officer in question of being on the right track or not.

Godolphin's face paled, and his eyes widened just a little, but enough.

The reaction lasted no more than a second-microseconds

probably-but it was long enough. Cruz saw it, and Gillespie would have seen it, too.

"Sorry?"

"Tommy Dean," Gillespie said. "He was one of your mates, was he not? Has a wee tattoo on his neck just like that one."

Godolphin looked between them both, then glanced along the corridor as if deciding on the best course of action.

"I don't know what you're talking about," he said eventually. "I've never heard of him."

CHAPTER TWENTY-FOUR

"TOMMY DEAN, James Godolphin, and Frank Bowen," Freya announced once she had written the names on the whiteboard. She replaced the cap on the marker, then turned as the incident room doors opened slowly, and a somewhat despondent Gillespie entered with Cruz following close behind. "Ah, just in time. How did it go?"

Gillespie slumped into the chair, and Cruz made every effort to avoid her gaze.

She waited, sidestepping over to her desk, where she perched and folded her arms. Dragging an ugly truth from its cave was rarely beneficial. It was far better, in her experience, to lure it out with silence.

Gillespie shook his head.

"Sorry, boss," he grumbled. "I really thought we could get him to open up, but..."

"Well, what happened? He must have said something."

"Oh, aye. He said something alright. He said there were three of them that had the tattoos. He didn't say why they did them or why they had crosses."

"They were eighteen," Cruz said. "He did give us that much."

"And how old is he now?"

"Forty-one," Chapman said, and she waved a thin file in the air, which presumably comprised of the research she had gathered on him so far.

"And Tommy Dean? Is there a link?"

"Yes," Gillespie said. "There's a link. I mean, he said he didn't know the name, but I saw it, boss. I saw it in his eyes when I mentioned it. He bloody knows him, alright."

Freya nodded. As much as Gillespie often played the fool, there was no questioning his experience and capability when he put his mind to it.

"Alright," she said. "What about DNA and fingerprints? Was he happy to give them up?"

"Don't know," he replied, slapping his hands palm down on the desk. "Didn't get the chance to talk him into it. I mean, if I'd done it my way, I'd have made him feel comfortable, got to know him, you know? I'd have given him a bloody pipe and slippers if I thought it would help."

"But?" Freya said, and she inhaled long and deep.

"But Jewson managed to stick her bloody size fives into it, didn't she?"

"Sorry, Jewson? What the hell has she got to do with this?"

"Well, we called him to see if he'd be happy to answer some questions on a voluntary basis. Said we'd meet him at his work if there was somewhere private."

"I doubt he'd be up for having us lot in his workplace," Freya said. "Not if he is as you described, anyway."

"He's not a bad bloke," Gillespie said. "I just think it's a...I don't know, a society thing, or a community thing. Nobody wants their neighbours to think they're a grass, do they? Nobody would trust you."

"True," she replied. "So, you sent somebody to pick him up, did you?"

He grimaced.

"I didn't think it would be Jewson. Never even crossed my bloody mind."

"Gillespie, what did she do?"

"Oh, nothing you could reprimand her for," he said. "She's too sly for that. She just questioned if we'd be processing Godolphin. It was a valid question had she been involved, but if I'd done it my way, I'd have got him on side first."

"Little cow," Freya hissed. "I'll have a word with Granger. The little minx needs bringing down a peg or two."

"Ah, I wouldn't worry too much," Gillespie said, and that old smile she'd come to enjoy made an appearance. "In fact, it's probably best if we steer clear of the topic for a wee while."

"What did you do?"

"Well, nothing really. CID had a bit of a nutter in one of the interview rooms. Left him alone too long, and he decided to... redecorate."

"What does this have to do with anything?"

He grimaced again, that sheepish boy-like grin in full bloom.

"Clarkson was cleaning it up," he said. "I didn't think it fair."

"You what?" Nillson cut in. "You made her clean it up?"

"I did no such thing," he said, taking mock offence. "I just told her that Clarkson had quite a challenge on his hands and that she could learn a lot by volunteering to help him in interview room one."

"Oh my God," Gold said. "Is she down there now?"

"I've got to see this," Nillson said, shoving her chair back.

"Nobody is going anywhere," Freya called out before the entire team left the room to witness the spectacle. "I'm sure we'll get a full account from Sergeant Priest."

Gillespie grinned at his accomplishment, and the team settled down again.

"As suitable as the punishment might be, we're still left in the same position," Freya said.

"I see you've got the farmer down as a suspect," Cruz said. "Is he back in the picture?"

"He was never out of the picture," Freya replied. "We just didn't know quite how to paint him."

"And now?" Gillespie asked.

"In broad strokes," she replied. "Ben seems to think the site of the murder was chosen specifically due to its privacy."

"Makes sense," Gillespie said.

"Which means that few people would have known about it," Freya continued. "You can't see it from the road, so the only people that would know about it are dog walkers and hikers or those who work or have worked on the farm."

"Such as Tommy Dean," Cruz said. "

"Such as about a dozen men," Freya corrected him. "Ben and I are going to pay him another visit when we're done here. In the meantime, who's our mystery man? If Godolphin is saying there were three of them, then who is the third man, and why is he being so coy about knowing Tommy Dean?"

"I can put some pressure on if you want," Gillespie said. "We've played nicely so far, but if we have a good reason for suspecting him—"

"No," Freya said. "No, you did the right thing, letting him go for the time being. All we have on him is the fact that he has a similar tattoo to the victim. We need to prove a connection."

"How do we do that?" Cruz asked.

"Social media?" Gold suggested.

"You can try," Freya said. "He's a middle-aged man with a wife and a child. I doubt very much he's the type to photograph his dinner and put it up for the world to see."

"His boy might," Cruz said, and Freya pondered that thought for a moment.

"You're suggesting we investigate a young boy's social media?"

"Just an idea," he said.

"I'm sure the ethics police would have something to say about that," she told him.

"Benjamin Godolphin, Tattershall?" Nillson said. She was sitting back in her chair with her phone in her hands.

"Nillson, what are you doing?"

"Browsing social media," she replied, as if daring Freya to make an argument she knew would work against them. "Here we go."

"Nillson!"

"Not much on here," Nillson said. "Him and a couple of mates playing on a computer, some screenshots of a shoot 'em up game, presumably he was proud of his score." She flicked through, shaking her head. "Just a normal kid. Here's one of him washing his dad's car with his mates. I suppose they were trying to earn a few quid." She leaned back on the chair and held the phone out for Gillespie to see. "That's him, right?"

Gillespie leaned across to meet her and peered down the length of his nose for a better view.

"Aye, that's him," he said. "But that's not his dad's car. His dad had an SUV of some kind, not a Mondeo."

"A Mondeo?" Cruz said. "That lad's mum had a Mondeo."

"What lad?"

"The one in Billinghay."

"What lad in Billinghay?"

"For God's sake, Jim. It was yesterday. The lad we spoke to."

"The computer kid?"

"Yeah. Show me that photo."

Nillson held the phone up, and for a moment, Freya thought she would stand and walk over to him. But, with three older brothers, she had clearly learned when and how to exercise power.

"I'll come to you then, shall I?" Cruz said, shoving himself out of his seat to get a closer look. "Yeah, that's him. The kid in the middle."

"Jesus, you're right," Gillespie said. "But why...?"

"I wonder if at any point either of you will be updating the rest of us so we can all share this particular revelation," Freya said.

"Alright," Gillespie said, his eyes squeezed closed as he put the details into some sort of order. "When Gabby and I went door knocking in Billinghay—"

"For the hoax caller?" Ben asked.

"For the blood-stained abandoned building," Freya corrected him. "Go on, Gillespie.

"Well, one of the houses we knocked at, which was what, a few hundred yards from the lane the old farmhouse is on, had a wee lad living there. We spoke to him. I even asked him if he'd been anywhere near the farmhouse, but he said him and his mates were indoors playing on the computer."

"Right," Freya said. "What did you expect him to say? Yes, it was me who called the police. The boy was probably terrified."

"No, no, it's not that," Gillespie said. "It was his mates. He told us their names."

Cruz pored through his notebook, looking for the right page.

"Liam," he said. "His name was Liam."

"And his friends?" Freya asked.

"Henry," he replied, still scanning the page. Then he looked up at them, perplexed. "And Gopher."

"Gopher?" Gold said.

"That's what it says."

"Maybe you wrote it down wrong?"

"Or maybe you can't write very well?" Nillson added.

"No, it was Gopher," Gillespie said, cutting them all off. "But I doubt very much that's his real name."

"No, it's a nickname," Ben said from the back of the room. "It's short for something."

"Godolphin?" Cruz said. "Bloody hell."

"Want us to get down there, boss?" Gillespie said, already packing his things away.

"No, Ben and I will go while we're out that way," she replied, fishing her car keys from her handbag and tossing them at Ben. "Ben, I'll meet you by the car in five minutes."

He caught the keys and waited for some kind of explanation, which Freya wasn't ready to give. Instead, she waited for him to leave and then addressed the room.

"Three names," she said. "Tommy Dean, James Godolphin, and Frank Bowen. Find everything you can. By the time Ben and I get back, that list is going to be significantly longer, so make use of the time."

"Gabs and me can take Godolphin," Gillespie said.

"No, come with me," Freya said. She snatched up her bag from her desk and strode over to the door, where she peered back at him and smiled at the fright evident in his eyes. "I've got a special job for you."

CHAPTER TWENTY-FIVE

"WE'RE TREADING on thin ice here," Ben said as Freya pulled onto the farm track. They passed the spot where they had spoken to the old man in the tractor and made their way to the conclave of buildings in the distance. "If he is involved, then by the time we actually have something on him, he's extremely unlikely to cooperate."

"Then we must apply leverage," Freya replied, and Ben dreaded to think what that might entail.

"You're going to bring up the past, aren't you?" he replied. "You did hear what Chapman said, didn't you? Nothing was proven. He wasn't charged."

"I shall use every tool at hand to crack the nut," she replied, bringing the car to a stop in the same place they had before. "However old and tenacious that nut proves to be."

Unlike their previous visit, there were no telehandlers moving back and forth, loading farm trucks and trailers. There wasn't a soul to be seen.

"I imagine they're out in the fields," he said. "Busy time for them."

"Well, I'm sure he'll have time to speak to us," she replied. "Where do you think he'll be?"

Ben shrugged.

"In the fields, somewhere, I suppose."

"So, which way?" she said.

"I don't know. If the map is correct, then Brinkleview Farm is massive, Freya. Bigger than my dad's. He could be bloody anywhere."

The clatter of a steel-clad door closing rattled around the concrete pad, and Ben craned his neck to find the source of the noise, settling eventually on the building to their right.

"I'll go," he said, shoving the car door open.

"Let's just wait. Somebody is bound to come along."

Ben glanced over to the barn.

"I'll just have a look."

He marched across the concrete to the pedestrian door that stood alongside the huge closed shutters. "Hello?" he called out once inside the barn. "Anybody here?"

He waited for a response, but nothing came.

"Anyone in here?"

Most of the barn served as a grain store, and Ben remarked on how clean it was. He recalled the machinery loading the trailer the previous day and noticed that the floor had been swept since. It was good habits like that, he thought, that ensured the farm passed any inspections and received the little red tractor symbol on its produce, which Ben knew meant it would receive the best price.

He backed out of the building and was about to call over to Freya when he saw her talking to somebody by her car. He strode over, recognising the old man who had been driving the tractor.

"Everything alright?" he asked as he approached.

"He's in the west field," Freya said, then nodded her thanks to the old man. He wasn't a tall man, just an inch or two taller than Freya. He wore a pair of old dungarees over what, at one time, had been a white tee-shirt, and the leathery skin on his face and arms gave him the look of somebody who had been hewn from the ground by the elements.

"Anyways," he grumbled, his lips barely moving. "I best be off, be waiting for me, won't they?"

"Thank you," Freya said, then stared at Ben with an expression that was nothing short of unbridled smugness. "Had a good look around, did you? While I was working."

"It's clean," he replied as he climbed back into the car. "Can't fault the management of the place."

"It's not his management that I'm keen to understand," she said once in the driver's seat. She started the car and headed over to the space between the west-most barn, where a wide track gave access to the fields. "According to the old boy, they're out here somewhere. Can't miss them, apparently."

There were no tractors in sight, not even a trailer in the distance. But a faint cloud of dust hung in the air a thousand metres away or more, the source of which was obscured by thick hedges that lined the fields, serving as windbreaks from the incessant gales that tore across the open landscape.

"There," he said, pointing at the dust. "Follow the track. It should lead us there."

But Freya didn't set off. Instead, she stared in the wrong direction through the passenger window at an old caravan that had been dumped onto a small patch of land behind the barns. It shared the space with old cultivators and blades that had been left to rust in the unkempt grass.

"The graveyard," Ben said when he saw what had caught her eye. "My dad has one too. I expect most farmers do. Most farmers of my old man's generation, anyway."

"Oh?" Freya replied as she started towards the dust clouds, and Ben thought how to explain the situation to somebody of Freya's ilk.

"Will you drive this car until it falls to pieces?" he asked.

"What? No, probably not. It'll last me a couple more years, I expect."

"Yeah, see, that's where you and my old man differ," he explained as she slowed for a series of deep potholes in the track, and their heads rocked from side to side as the Range Rover navigated them. "See, he'd drive it until it broke, then get it repaired. He'd be looking to eke out the investment over as many harvests as possible. If something costs, say, ten grand, and it lasts ten harvests, then that's a grand per harvest. But if he can stretch that to fifteen or twenty..."

"That doesn't make sense," she said. "Surely it's better to sell it on while it still has some resell value?"

"I told you. It's a generation thing. He still uses the same pen he did when I was a kid. Did you know that?"

"A pen?" she said. "But wouldn't it..."

He grinned.

"So, he's tight. Is that what you're saying?"

"No, I'm just saying that he's from a different generation," Ben explained. "We live in a throwaway world these days. You and I would think nothing of replacing an old sofa. My dad, and most likely Frank Bowen, too, wouldn't dream of chucking anything out until it fell to pieces."

The track they were on was blocked by the source of the dust, several tractors, trailers, telehandlers, and half a dozen men working on the track itself.

"My God, what on earth are they doing?" Freya asked as they dropped in and out of a particularly deep rut, rocking them both from side to side.

"Have a guess," he said.

"Ben, I know you enjoy this sort of thing, but I don't. I'm just grateful I've got an off-roader."

"They're repairing the track," Ben said. "And this is not an off-roader."

"Why are they repairing the track?"

"Because come harvest time, they'll be a dozen tractors out here ferrying what the combines collect back to the grain stores. If the tracks aren't in good nick, it'll slow them down, and once they start, there's no stopping. If a dodgy track causes a puncture on a trailer, it could put them back a day while it gets fixed," he said, peering out at the workforce ahead of them. Bowen had seen them but made no attempt to stop working. "No, they're doing the right thing. He's a good farmer, is Bowen."

"He might be a good farmer," she replied, both of them staring at the quarry through the windscreen. "But he's an awful liar, and I intend to prove it."

"Did you bring your nutcracker?" Ben asked, which raised a wry smile. She hesitated before opening the car door.

"You miss it, don't you?"

"Miss what?"

"Farming," she said, gesturing at the land around them. "You miss it."

"I was never a farmer," he replied. "I worked on my dad's farm, sure. I know what I'm doing, but I was never a farmer. Not at heart."

"Would you ever consider going back to it?" she asked.

"What? Give up playing second fiddle to my wife, you mean?"

"I'm not your wife, yet—"

"Well, alright. Give up being your whipping boy in return for spending my days in the fresh air, doing manual work with honest men? I'd be mad to."

"They're not all honest," she told him, and she eyed Bowen as he watched a dumper spill its load of gravel onto the track. A telehandler moved in to spread the load, and a roller waited nearby to flatten it. "As no doubt we're about to find out."

"I know what you're doing," he said. "You're trying to link this back to the old farmhouse, aren't you? You're trying to win the bet."

"Trying?" she said as she slid from the car. She smiled up at him. "I don't need to try."

"You can't bear being wrong, can you?" he said, joining her. "You really can't bear it."

"I don't know," she replied, beaming at him. "I have no experience of the sensation."

CHAPTER TWENTY-SIX

"I THINK we're in the right place," Gillespie said as an RAF Typhoon rose up from behind RAF Coningsby's main building on take-off and soared up into the clouds, shaking every window in sight.

"Jesus Christ, imagine sitting in that?"

"I expect it's quieter for the pilot," Cruz said, leaning forward in his seat for a better view.

"What? Quieter? How do you work that out?"

"Well, isn't it something to do with the air?"

"It's bugger all to do with the air," Gillespie told him, "And more to do with the two sodding great engines on either side of him. What a racket."

The road into the base split into two, and a large sign told them that non-passholders should stay to the left. The brakes gave a light squeal as the car came to a stop at the barrier, where Gillespie lowered his window and met a grim-faced officer.

"Now then," Gillespie said, adopting the standard Lincolnshire greeting. But his efforts were met with an inquisitive gaze that seemed to penetrate his very soul. "Looking for Group Captain Shaw. Is he in?"

"Is *he* in?" the man said as if Gillespie had just walked dog's muck across his carpet.

"Aye," he said, revealing his warrant card. He held it up for the officer to see. "He about for a quick word, is he?"

"As it happens, Group Captain Shaw is in *her* office," the officer replied. "I heard she's been refusing meetings all day in the hopes that some scruffy sod from the local police force comes knocking."

"Oh, aye?" Gillespie said, turning to Cruz. "You're in luck, Gabby."

"No," the man said. "That was sarcasm. You'll need to make an appointment."

As they spoke, another officer inspected the car's underside with a mirror on a long stick.

"I couldn't get in there, then?" Gillespie asked. "For a wee chat?"

"If Group Captain Shaw had time for a wee chat, as you put it, I very much doubt she'd be doing her job. What's it concerning, anyway?"

"A murder," Gillespie said flatly.

"A murder?"

"One of your lot," he said. "Could look bad for the base."

Gillespie smiled up at him, daring him to make another challenge.

"What's his name? This individual."

"Well, if I told you that, I doubt I'd be doing my job very well," Gillespie replied, which somehow induced a little laugh from the man in the hut.

"Stay there," he instructed, then slid the window closed, through which Gillespie watched him pick up a phone and make a call.

"Do you have to annoy them straight away?" Cruz said. "Christ, we're not even through the gates, and you've managed to make an enemy."

"Ah, he's not an enemy,' Gillespie told him. "They're alright this lot. RAF Police. They do what we do."

"What drive around with idiots annoying people?" Cruz replied.

"They ask questions, Gabby," he said. "They make enquiries. Follow up on leads. That sort of thing."

"And anyway, what did you mean by telling him it was one of his lot? We don't know that."

"No, but he's on the blower, eh? He's making a call. What would you have done? Make an appointment? You'd be lucky to speak to this Shaw lass before next week."

Cruz shook his head in dismay, and Gillespie laughed at how easy it was to wind him up.

The window slid open, and Mr Grim stared down at Gillespie. He leaned out of the window to hand him two visitor's passes.

"You're in luck," he grumbled, and the officer inspecting the car gave him a nod. "Follow the road around to the main entrance. Park in the visitor's parking and ask for Group Captain Shaw at the reception."

"Ah, you're a legend," Gillespie told him. "So, she was waiting around for a scruffy police officer after all, was she?"

The officer straightened, offering little more than malice in his glare.

"Don't run off with those, neither," he said, gesturing at the two passes, which Gillespie passed to Cruz blindly.

"Much obliged," Gillespie called out as he eased the car into drive before waving him goodbye through the rising window.

They passed the fighter jet parked at the entrance, which served as a reminder of the seriousness of the facility. From outside the reception, none of the workings of the base could be seen. There were only offices and old RAF houses for the serving men and women. That sober feeling was even more present in the small reception, where a young man behind a desk invited them to wait. They had barely sat down on the proffered chairs when a smart-looking lady entered the room, and the man behind the desk nodded at Gillespie and Cruz. Her uniform was immaculate, and Gillespie wished he had rubbed his shoes on the backs of his trouser legs to smarten himself up. Her hat or cap, or whatever they called it, had a string of what looked like bird's muck across its peak but no doubt identified her as a senior officer.

She approached confidently but with slight trepidation.

"I'm told you want to see me," she said, extending her hand for them to shake. "Group Captain Shaw."

Gillespie rose to his feet and showed his warrant card.

"DS Gillespie," he said. "This is DC Cruz." She nodded and waited for him to continue. Gillespie produced the scanned copies of the scrapbook found at the abandoned house from his folder. He flicked to the page showing a photo of a group of RAF officers standing before the very fighter jet they had passed. "I was wondering if you recognised any of these people."

She took the scrapbook from him, rather than edge closer for a better view, and then handed it straight back to him.

"Yes, I do."

"Which ones," he asked.

"All of them," she replied. "I recognise every one of them."

"All of them?"

"It's my job as Station Commander," she replied. "I'd appreciate it if you could just get to the point. I do have a busy schedule—"

"We think one of them might be the victim of a serious crime," Gillespie said.

"Murder?" she said. "That's what the guard said. Is that right?"

"It's possible," he replied. "We've not a lot to go on, hence our impromptu visit—"

"Follow me," she said, and as if she was used to her orders being followed without question, she turned and headed back along the corridor from which she had come without looking back. They followed dutifully, and she led them into an office, which, on reflection, Gillespie thought to be not much nicer than Detective Superintendent Granger's. The budget was certainly similar, but a different shade of blue had been used as an accent.

"Please," she said, gesturing at the visitor's seats while she took the seat behind the desk. "You've got five minutes."

"Right," Gillespie replied. "Well, we received a 999 call on Sunday night, directing us to an old burned-out house on a farm in Billinghay. When we got there, there was no body, but our CSI team discovered a trail of blood on the wall, leading out of the house and inside the tent—"

"What tent?

"The tent inside the house," Gillespie explained.

"There was no roof," Cruz added.

"Right," Shaw said, clearly still none the wiser.

"This was found in the tent along with a few possessions. We believe that the crime took place there, and due to another nearby incident—"

"Another murder?"

"Aye," he said, not seeing any point in withholding anything now. "It was a mile or so away in Tattershall. Our boss thinks they might be linked."

"And you think that whoever owned that tent is in this photo, and therefore, that I might be able to provide a name?"

"We've not got too much to go on," he replied. "The victim we discovered in Tattershall had a tattoo on his neck."

"On his neck?"

"Aye, a small cross. Handmade. Not professional."

"Anything else?"

Gillespie shrugged and took a deep breath.

"Mid-forties, male, six feet."

"So, aside from the tattoo, he fits the description of forty per cent of the serving RAF personnel."

"We think the tattoo might be pertinent," Gillespie said.

"And he's the victim, is he? Not the perpetrator?"

"If we're going to be one hundred per cent transparent, Mrs Shaw—"

"It's Group Captain," she said.

"Aye, sorry."

"But if you have this photo and presumably you have a body, then why can't you simply match the body to the photo?"

Gillespie winced a little at the memory of that poor soul they had cut down from the tree in Tattershall.

"There was significant damage to the man's body," he explained. "And besides, if he's in the photo, then he's wearing a hat."

"A cap?"

"Aye, a cap," he said. "We've tried to match him, as you say, but not with any confidence."

"And you thought I'd be able to point him out, did you?"

"Aye, well, we're clutching at straws here. If you couldn't, then perhaps his boss, officer, whatever you call it."

She sat back in her chair, appraising them both with a lick of her thin lips.

"You know who he is, don't you?" Gillespie said, recognising the look in her eye as that which so many men and women had worn in interview rooms over the years. She was deciding whether or not to reveal any information and the possible consequences to her station.

"Has either of these incidents been revealed to the press?" she asked, confirming Gillespie's suspicions.

"No," he said. "No, we prefer not to go public unless either we've exhausted our leads or somebody leaks it."

She nodded.

"Will this link back to the force in any way?"

"That depends," he replied. "Is he still serving?"

She hesitated, then shook her head.

"No. No, if it's the man I'm thinking of," she said, leaning forward and placing the tip of her index finger on the photo. "It's this man."

Both Gillespie and Cruz leaned forward, glanced at each other, then across to Shaw.

"You know him?"

"He retired a year or two ago," she said, a little sadness in her tone, as if the marking of his death had touched her somehow. "He was in logistics. A good man."

"You're sure, are you?" Gillespie asked. "I mean, how sure?"

"I take pride in knowing my staff," she replied. "We don't have many anymore. Not as many as we used to. But I like to meet them all."

"But you must have met so many. How can you be sure?"

"Because I've seen this man half-naked," she said, to which Gillespie couldn't help but sit back in his seat, speechless. "He was our boxing champion." She removed her finger but remained staring past the photo. "His name was John Tyler."

CHAPTER TWENTY-SEVEN

"Now then," Bowen grumbled, a practised look of disdain spreading across his weathered chops as Ben and Freya approached. A few of the machines came to a stop, and the drivers looked on with interest until Bowen issued a stern, "back to work, the lot of you."

"Hello again, Mr Bowen," Freya said, and Ben recognised the undertone the statement carried, even if Bowen didn't. "I wondered if we might have a word."

"Another word? What about?" he said, as he noticed the driver of the telehandler was still idle, which in turn had caused the roller to come to a stop. "Go on, with you. Need this done by tonight. We've half a mile to do yet."

The telehandler jumped into life, and the driver set to dragging the stones from the pile the dumper had made, roughly across the track, ready for the roller to flatten.

"This about Tommy again, is it?" he asked. "Well, I told you. I've nothing much to say on the matter. It's sad. Course it is. But it's not my doing."

"It's about several matters," Freya told him, having to entice his attention from the workers back to her by stepping between him and his crew. "One of which is Tommy Dean, yes."

"Well, go on," he said, then issued a shrill whistle to the dumper driver. "S'enough. Back it up. Come on, let's keep it moving."

"Is there somewhere quieter we can discuss this?" Freya asked, to which he placed his hands on his hips, looked up and down, and rubbed at his bristled chin. "Look, lady——"

"We all have jobs to do, Mr Bowen," Freya said. "And I'm quite certain that you are familiar with the procedures that we have to follow."

His head cocked to one side.

"You what?"

"Given that you were the primary suspect in a murder enquiry." The machinery was loud enough that there was little fear of the statement being overheard, but still, he peered back at his men to make sure no heads had turned. "One of our researchers did a little digging, Mr Bowen, so you can imagine our surprise that you hadn't mentioned it when we last spoke."

"Dragging all that up again, are you?"

"I'll drag up whatever I have to if it means you answer my questions candidly," she said, then glanced back over her shoulder at the workers. "In a suitable environment."

"We can't talk here?" he asked, and she shook her head as if she was sorry for the disappointment.

"My place or yours?" she asked.

"I'll not go to the police station if that's what you're asking."

"Your place it is, then," she replied and presented the way back to her car with a sweep of her arm.

Ben felt for the man. When Freya had the bit between her teeth, there was very little room for manoeuvre.

"Farm office," he said, nodding back at the bumpy track they had travelled down, on which an old pickup was making its way towards them. The driver was the old man they had spoken to,

and he pulled onto the edge of the field to park beside Freya's
Range Rover.

"Take over for me, will you, Les," Bowen called out as he
approached the pickup. The old man left the engine running and
the door open and, with a curious look at Ben and Freya, resumed
where Bowen had left off. Bowen climbed into the driver's seat,
crunched the pickup into reverse and leaned out of the window.
"Follow me."

He didn't wait for Freya to turn around. He sped off along the
track and was out of sight even before Freya and Ben had got
back into the car. Progress on the track came to a temporary halt
as the drivers of the telehandler, dumper, and roller each waited
to witness Freya's attempt to turn around on the narrow track. If
he were honest with himself, even Ben was wondering how she
would fair. But never one to place herself into a situation that
might compromise her credibility, she didn't even attempt a
three-point turn. Instead, she put the car into drive, pulled the
wheel onto full lock, and put her foot down, tearing a wide arc
through the edge of the field. Ben winced at the damage to the
crops and imagined the disappointed looks on the workers' faces.
But he had to hand it to her. She hadn't given them a reason to
laugh or mock her. Once back on the track, she settled into a
moderate pace in Bowen's wake, checked her reflection in the
mirror, and overall, seemed rather pleased with herself.

The pickup was parked outside the northernmost barn, and
the pedestrian door had been left open for them. Inside, to Ben's
surprise, a small room had been created with stud walls clad with
ply to house a desk, a few filing cabinets, and an eclectic spread of
chairs that looked like they had been plucked from various skips
over the years; an old office swivel chair, a wooden carver much
like his father had in his kitchen, a plastic folding chair that could
have been from Ikea, and a cushioned occasional chair that
appeared to been ravaged by a dog or two.

Bowen took his seat, which, although more comfortable than

the rest of the offering, was in no better state. He slid his phone onto the desk, then interlinked his fingers across his gut.

"Come on then, let's hear it," he said.

Freya, who was never one to be led, considered her response long enough for the pendulum of power to return to middle ground, where she grasped it firmly.

"I thought we could start with Tommy Dean," she said.

"We've been over him," he replied as if he'd been expecting the starting point.

"Not in detail," she replied. "Not nearly enough detail for me, I'm afraid."

"What's to say? He came to me during lockdown. Asked for a job."

"And you just gave him a start, did you? As easy as that?"

"No," he replied. "No, I turned him down, first off."

"So, he just came here and asked for a job? Or did he knock on your house door?"

"Neither," Bowen replied. "Saw me out in the fields. Stopped me and asked then."

"That seems rather random, doesn't it?"

"They were strange times," he replied. "Half my workforce had gone back to Europe, social distancing, and whatnot. Strange times, indeed." He settled into his seat, perhaps succumbing to the fact that he would be there for some time. "Caught me out on the edge of the farm. Waved me down, he did. He had some gumption; I'll give him that. I don't take kindly to people on my land." He glanced across at Ben. "Expect you'll know all about that. The damage people do with their dogs. Kids on bikes, and God knows what else. Scant respect, that's what they have. Don't realise they're treading on the food they'll have to eat."

Ben nodded.

"But you spoke to him, nonetheless?"

"Aye, I did," Bowen said. "He knew me by name, so I had to hear what he had to say."

"Is that unusual, Mr Bowen?" Freya asked. "People knowing you by name, I mean."

"Not really," he said. "Most know me round here. There was a time when I knew them, too." He shook his head sadly. "Not now, though. Those days are gone. Anyways, he asked for a start. I told him no. He asked again, and…I don't know. There was something in his eye."

"Hunger?" Freya suggested, which Bowen dismissed with a wave of his hand.

"Desperation," he replied eventually. "Started him on minimum wage, had one of the lads spend some time on him, and that was that. He was alright, was Tommy. For someone who hadn't ever done owt like this, he was alright. Picked it up fast."

"And then, just like that, he packed it in?" Ben said.

"Just like that," Bowen replied. "No thanks, no goodbyes, no token of appreciation for getting him out of a hole. Just upped and buggered off."

"And you stand by your claim of paying him in a timely fashion?" Freya asked, to which Bowen didn't answer directly. Instead, he turned sideways, opened the little filing cabinet beside him, and after a moment or two of fingering files, dragged a folder out and plopped it onto the desk."

"Every payment to every employee," he said.

"In the past year?" Ben asked.

"In the past twenty-odd years, I would imagine," he replied.

"May we take this?"

"Will it put an end to this nonsense?"

"That depends on what we find, doesn't it?" Freya replied, sliding the folder closer to Ben. Bowen made no effort to conceal his feelings.

"That's got a back to it, you know?"

"You'll get it back," she said. "Once we've made copies. Every employee, you say?"

"Every employee," he said. "Nobody's ever accused me of not paying them, not now, nor will they. Are we done?"

"Well, I'm sure once we've had a look, we'll draw the same conclusion," Freya said, again summoning that smile that suggested they were far from finished. "Now, I'd like to talk about the incident that took place in the nineties."

"What's the point?" he asked. "You asked about Tommy. I gave you what you wanted."

"Because, Mr Bowen, the body of a man was recently discovered on the edge of your land," she said. "And this is not the first murder investigation you've been embroiled in, is it?"

CHAPTER TWENTY-EIGHT

THE HOUSE WAS A LARGE, detached building set between two terraces, which led Cruz to believe that it was either built to fill the space by a budding developer, or it was the original house that had perhaps sold land off, which had then been developed into the terraces.

Judging by the age of the place, he deemed it to be the original. The windows were arched with wooden sashes, and three chimneys protruded from various parts of the immense and intricate roof.

"Jesus, it's like something from a movie," Gillespie mused aloud.

"What type of movie?" Cruz asked.

"The type where young children are lured into the basement, Gabby," he replied, and he widened his eyes, presumably trying to look ghoulish, "and never seen again."

"It's funny," Cruz said as they each climbed from the car. "You see a horror movie, and I see something entirely different."

"Oh, aye? What do you see? Don't tell me; it's some kind of period drama, where the wee bairns are put to bed by the nanny, and the men always wear a three-piece suit?"

"No," Cruz said. "I was just thinking about the heating bill. Look at those windows. Must be bloody freezing in winter."

Gillespie laughed and dismissed the idea with a shake of his head.

"That's your problem," he said. "You've no imagination. You're all about…I don't know, words and feelings, and the world you live in is black and white."

"I've got an imagination," Cruz replied, then berated himself internally for falling into one of Gillespie's traps.

"Oh, aye? What do you see, then? If you were to see this place on TV, what would it be? A horror? Maybe a crime drama?"

"Gardeners World," Cruz said, peering at what little they could see of the gardens from the roadside. "I'll bet it has a little gate with a secret garden and everything."

"There you go," Gillespie said. "A bloody period drama."

The drive that led them down one side of the property was more of a wide path covered in stones than a finished drive, and somehow, the look suited the place. A perfectly proportioned driveway with paving blocks just wouldn't suit it.

There were five steps that led up to the large front door, in which was a window that comprised of coloured glass to resemble a rose and surrounding green foliage. The doorbell beside it could have been installed when electricity had first been implemented into houses. It had been painted over several times, and it took some serious effort for Gillespie to press it home. On the third attempt, they heard a distant ring.

"You know the trouble with you, Jim?" Cruz said quietly as they waited for somebody to come. "Everything in your world goes wrong."

"Eh?"

"Everything goes wrong," Cruz repeated. "You manifest it. You see the worst of everything, and then you get the worst of everything."

"Aye, it's called real life, Gabby."

"It doesn't have to be like that. There is some good in the world. You just have to look for it, and you have to...recognise it when it happens."

"Jesus," Gillespie mumbled. "Do you think they've a stable in the back with a unicorn in it? Maybe the walls are made of gingerbread, and they've pillows made of candy floss. You should ask them."

Cruz would have replied, but a form appeared beyond the coloured glass, and the door opened to reveal a mature woman who Cruz placed in her seventies, retired but mobile.

"Hello, I'm sorry to bother you," Gillespie started, allowing his warrant card to fall open for her to see. "I'm Detective Sergeant Gillespie, and this is Detective Constable Cruz. We're looking for a Mrs Hall."

"That's me," she said, clutching the collar of her knitted cardigan together at the neck. "Is everything okay?"

"Well, that's what we're hoping to find out," he told her. "Would you mind if we came in?"

She seemed hesitant at first, then relented, stepping aside but clutching the door as if it were a lifeline.

The hallway was as broad as it was long, and Cruz noted how the staircase was set as far back as possible to provide light and space, unlike modern houses where you fall onto the stairs as soon as you enter the house.

"It's a lovely place," Cruz remarked, earning himself a glare from Gillespie, who then adopted a cheerful expression for Mrs Hall's benefit.

"I'll get my husband," she said, then stopped mid-step. "That's okay, is it?"

"I'd prefer it," Gillespie replied, then watched her leave.

"It's a lovely place," Gillespie muttered, mocking Cruz for his comment. "Honestly, you're not Kevin bloody McCloud."

"Well, it is," Cruz hissed at him, keeping his voice as quiet as he could. "It doesn't hurt to be nice to everyone. You don't have to get everyone's back up, you know? I'm surprised that bloke on the RAF base didn't turn us away and report us."

"Ah, he's alright. Imagine the boredom he has to deal with on a day-to-day basis. I probably made his day."

"Is everything okay?" somebody said from the end of the hallway. If Cruz could have drawn Mrs Hall's husband from the imagination Gillespie accused him of not having, the picture would have resembled the man who stepped into the hallway, clearly on the defensive. He also wore a cardigan, although his was not knitted. His shirt was buttoned to the collar, and to Cruz's delight, he was wearing a tie. Had it been nineteen-seventy, he would have had a smoking pipe in his hand with which he would have gestured with to make a point. "My wife said you're with the police. Is that right?"

"Ah, Mr Hall," Gillespie said in a polite tone that Cruz knew he reserved for when they had to deliver bad news. "DS Gillespie. This is my colleague, DC Cruz."

Mrs Hall returned to stand by his side, still clutching her collar.

"Is there somewhere we can sit?" Gillespie asked, and suddenly Mrs Hall jumped into life, fussing them into a room to one side of the hallway through a pair of glazed doors. The furniture could have been plucked from a nineteen-seventies sitcom, and they were invited to take the two-seater sofa, placing Cruz far closer to Gillespie than he would have liked.

They waited for the couple to take their respective armchairs, Mr Hall beside the window with the best view of the television, and Mrs Hall closest to the door, within reach of the telephone.

Cruz imagined they lived as they had decades ago in a far more misogynous world than today. Mr Hall would go out to work while Mrs Hall managed the household.

"We've been given your details by a Group Captain Shaw," Gillespie started, then pointed over his shoulder. "She runs the RAF base up in Coningsby."

"Okay," Mr Hall said, intrigued, then looked across at his wife. "Shall we have some tea, dear?"

"Actually, it's better if you're both here," Gillespie said. "Do you recognise the name?"

"Shaw?" the old man said, shaking his head. "Should we?"

"She was John Tyler's senior officer," Gillespie said, then silenced to witness the name resonating between the couple.

"Our John?" Mrs Hall said. "Is he in trouble? He's not, is he?"

"I'm afraid we, potentially at least, have some bad news, Mr and Mrs Hall," Gillespie continued. "A man matching his description was found dead on Monday morning."

"Oh," Mrs Hall said, letting go of her collar to cover her mouth. "Oh no. Not our John."

"I realise it's not something you were ready to hear, but—"

"How?" Mr Hall said, stoic but clearly moved.

Gillespie waited for a moment as if deciding how much to divulge. For all Gillespie's flaws, Cruz knew that at such times, there were few people more qualified to deliver bad news, and in this particular instance, he was better suited than anyone.

"He was...he was found hanging."

"Oh, good lord," Mr Hall said, and to Cruz's surprise, he stood to comfort his wife.

"Group Captain Shaw managed to find his records. You both were listed as his next of kin. Is that right? You were his family?"

Mrs Hall dragged a box of tissues closer, and Mr Hall, with his arm around his wife's shoulder, nodded but was quite unable to voice a reply. He gave himself a few seconds, checked on his wife, and then spoke.

"He was twelve when he came to us," he replied. "We knew he was the one for us within a matter of months."

"You adopted him?"

Hall nodded.

"He was thirteen or fourteen when it finally went through."

Gillespie smiled empathically.

"Seems like he landed on his feet with you," he said, then sought to explain. "I was in the system, too. I was one of the unlucky ones. Ferried from home to home until...well, until I was old enough to ferry myself."

Mrs Hall peered over her tissue, perhaps studying Gillespie in a new light.

"Are you sure it's him," she said between sobs.

"Group Captain Shaw has agreed to formally identify the body," he replied.

"We can do that—"

"In this instance, maybe it's best to leave it to her. She's a lovely woman. She clearly has a heart and was quite fond of him."

"But can we see him? Is that allowed, or..." her voice trailed off as she realised there may be a reason why a third party was identifying him. "Oh," was all she said when she had drawn a conclusion. "But even so. I'd still like to. *We'd* like to. Wouldn't we, dear?" She looked up at her husband, pleading with him, and Mr Hall jutted his lower lip out in defiance.

"Yes," he croaked. "Yes, we would."

"Had he been to any homes before he came here?" Gillespie asked. "As a young man, I mean. Was he like me and lost in the system?"

"No," Mr Hall said. "No, he came to us soon after the fire."

"The fire?" Gillespie said.

"Yes, didn't you know?" Mr Hall said, squeezing his wife's hand. "His entire family died in a fire not far from here. His parents and his two sisters. It was...nothing short of a tragedy."

"This fire," Gillespie said. "I'm sorry, I realise you're processing this, but where exactly was this?"

"Up the road," Mr Hall said as if it was common knowledge. "Brinkleview Farm."

CHAPTER TWENTY-NINE

"ALICE NEAL," Freya said, and Bowen's eyes glazed at the mention of the name. "Do you want to tell me about her?"

"Look, I—"

"Have lots to do. Yes, I know. So do we, Mr Bowen. So, let's just get this done, shall we?"

He sighed, and the rigidity in his arms seemed to wane.

"I'll tell you what I told them back then," he said. "I know nothing about her. I knew nothing then, and I know nothing now."

"She was reported missing, wasn't she? Where was she last seen?"

"It was more than two decades ago—"

"But I'll bet it feels like yesterday for her poor parents," Freya cut in. "I'll bet they relive the events of those days on a daily basis. I'll bet they jump every time the doorbell rings. I'll bet that, even after all this time, a glimmer of hope raises its ugly head at the sound of footsteps on the garden path."

"It's not working, you know?"

"I'll bet her mother lies awake at night, imagining what she might look like now. More than two decades on. How she might

have grown. How her hair might be. How tall she had grown, or...
if she still remembered her mum and dad. Perhaps she can even
recall the hugs. They would have had special memories, too. The
way she enjoyed having her hair stroked, or perhaps one of those
rituals that families develop. At dinner time, perhaps. A certain
seat that she sat in. Maybe even a favourite meal."

"You don't know what you're saying—"

"I wonder if anybody has sat in that seat since," Freya continued. "I wonder if they even have that meal anymore or if perhaps
the memory invokes an unsavoury flavour. An aftertaste, so bitter
that it would take days to wash away." She smiled sadly. "Perhaps
not even then."

"It's sad," Bowen said. "It was a sad time on all accounts." He
grimaced, but his eyes were keen and hard, belying the shine that
now coated them. "They lost a daughter. More than that, most
likely. I imagine their world came tumbling down."

"I imagine so, too—"

"But so did I," he said, and he appeared slightly ashamed of
saying so. "Of course, it's insensitive of me to say so. I was the
man everyone was looking at. I was the man the papers tore into,
wasn't I? Even three months later, when they finally released me, I
was still guilty. In the eyes of the world. I was still a..." His mouth
downturned as the sour memories took hold. "A monster. Who
could I go to, eh? Who could I go to when I was freed? When I
came home and found my wife gone, my boy gone, and my entire
world flattened like...like a bloody roller had driven over it." He
gave a laugh and shrugged, a helpless display of conflicted
emotions. "Nobody, that's who. Nobody cared." He nodded, a
bitter snarl curled his upper lip, and those keen eyes narrowed.
"So, you talk to me about loss, missy. You talk to me about how
her poor mum stroked her hair, where she sat and what her
favourite meal was. Because you know what?" he said, stabbing at
his chest with a fat index finger. "I still remember where my boy
sat. I still remember what his favourite meal was, his favourite toy,

the way he used to curl into a ball when he slept, the way he hated wearing socks and would pull them off the first chance he had, and the way he used to hug me. You talk to me about that, and just imagine that I haven't lived it, that I haven't imagined what her mum and dad have been through."

"Your boy wasn't presumed dead, Mr Bowen—"

"No, but he might as well be. I'm dead to him. To his mum. I've not seen him, and I very much doubt I ever will. So, what's the difference? You talk of loss like it's a commodity. A bloody grain you have to work at and earn through grief, and water with tears, then harvest when the time is right. They didn't deserve the grief they went through, but neither did I, lady. So, if you've anything more to say, just say it, just get it over with, because when you say her name and speak of that time, all you do is pull my little boy's face from in here," he said, slapping his chest. "And you stick it right here." He finished by stabbing his finger into his temple.

"You're very eloquent," Freya remarked. "Tell me, Mr Bowen, why was it you were the primary suspect?"

"You've read the files, no doubt. You tell me."

"It might surprise you to learn that I have yet to read the files in detail," she replied. "In fact, it might surprise you to learn that I'd rather hear the story from you. Reports can often be biased, one way or another. I'd prefer to come to a balanced conclusion."

She was pleased to have broken through his hardened shell to expose the soft nut inside, but there was very little to gain from crushing the nut. Instead, she mused, it was far better to nurture that soft inside, to identify its true flavour.

He shrugged.

"Circumstance," he said, a single word that somehow summarised the root of two families' heartache and the altered paths they now trod. "Somebody saw her near my field. Not sure who. Don't suppose it matters, now."

"And you?" Freya asked. "Did you see her?"

He hesitated, and when he spoke, his voice was dry and cracked.

"Aye, I saw her," he replied. "At least, I think it was her. I was out in the north fields. She was on the path from Tattershall."

"Did you get a good look at her?"

"No. No, she was too far away, I was too busy, and she was one of a dozen people I might have seen every day. Dog walkers, hikers, local kids. They all used to cut through my land. Bird watchers, too."

"They don't cut through anymore, then?" Ben asked, and Bowen looked his way. "You said they *used* to cut through your land, by which I assume they no longer do. Is that part of the fallout from the investigation and the accusation?"

"No," he said. "No, it's old news now." He straightened in his seat. "They don't cut through anymore because I don't let them. It's not a public right of way, and well, look what happened the last time I turned a blind eye. Do you think I want that again? You think I want you lot turning up on my doorstep?" He laughed, but it wasn't rooted in humour. "The funny thing is, I've nothing left to lose, anyway. So, go ahead. Make all the accusations you like. I did nothing back then, and I've done nothing now."

Ben nodded, made a note, and then beckoned for Freya to continue.

"The problem I have, Mr Bowen," Freya started, "and I hope you can understand, even if you aren't in agreement, is that a man's body was found a stone's throw from your property. A man who was known to you and until recently, worked for you, has been reported missing. And as if that wasn't quite enough, regardless of the outcome, you were previously investigated for murder."

"I was released. Innocent. That's what they said—"

"You were not proven innocent, Mr Bowen, you were found not guilty. The prosecution failed to convince the jury of your guilt. There's a marked difference."

"Thought you said you hadn't read the reports."

"I don't need to read the reports," she said. "If your innocence had been proven, you would have stated the reasons behind it the moment I mentioned Alice's name. But you didn't."

"You're twisting it," he said, and a new emotion was fed into his tone. Panic. "You're doing what they did back then. You're twisting everything to make it look like I'm guilty—"

"I'm just doing my job, Mr Bowen," she said. "But it strikes me that there's an awful lot of death on this farm, and somehow, you seem to be embroiled in it all."

"I didn't kill them," he said. "I didn't kill Tommy, and I didn't kill the girl. So, if you don't mind, I've better things to be doing with my time."

He slammed the filing cabinet closed and shunted his seat back to stand.

"Out of interest, Mr Bowen, where were you this weekend? Specifically on Sunday evening."

The question stopped him in his tracks. He stared down at her with nothing short of malice in his eyes for daring to ask the question he surely must have known was coming.

"At home," he said.

"Where's home?"

"Up the track," he replied. "As far from where you found Tommy Dean as possible."

"And can anybody vouch for you?" she asked. "Or were you alone?" He said nothing. There was very little he could have said. The look on his face told Freya everything she needed to know. "I thought so." She scooped up the folder, nodded at Ben, and then stood. "Don't go anywhere, Mr Bowen. I have no doubt you'll be hearing from us again."

"Well, you'll know where to find me then, won't you?" he told her as he marched towards the door.

"I just pray that we find Tommy Dean alive," she said, and his footsteps halted.

"You what?"

He had taken the bait, and she refrained from grinning as she turned to face him.

"I said, I just pray that we find Tommy alive."

"But you said—"

"That he had been reported missing, yes. It's a terrible shame. His wife is most upset, as I'm sure you can imagine."

He paled. Even from afar, Freya could see the blood draining from his face.

"Then who—"

"Who indeed, Mr Bowen," she said, watching for his reaction. "Who, indeed?"

CHAPTER THIRTY

"THE BOSS WON'T BE happy about this," Cruz said, and Gillespie recognised that little tinge of fear in his voice. A tremble. Like a violin's vibrato. "Shouldn't we call her?" Gillespie ducked through the doorway of the abandoned house into what used to be the kitchen. "Jim, did you hear me?"

"Just..." he said, irritated by Cruz's whining. "Just give me a minute, will you?"

"Well, I'm not having anything to do with it," Cruz carried on, and as Gillespie's imagination played out the events that Mr and Mrs Hall had described, the whining faded.

In the daylight, the building was much as it had been a few evenings before but bathed in fewer shadows.

"They said it started in the kitchen," he called out, marking the spot where the Aga would have stood. What remained of the plaster was black, like a tattoo that two decades of rain and the worst weather imaginable had failed to cleanse as if the walls themselves held onto those last moments.

"I'm not listening," Cruz replied, his voice faint. "You're on your own."

Gillespie let the scene he had imagined return. The door he

had entered through was the only exit. The house had been built in a world where health and safety were designed to protect the rich, usually at the cost of the poor.

He looked up at the bright blue sky overhead, noting the charred remains of timbers that had once been the first floor and the roof joints above them, which now jutted from the brickwork like rotten teeth.

"Jesus," he said to himself. "It must have been hell in here." With Cruz blocking the exit, he moved through to what would have been the living room. There would have been a set of wooden stairs leading up to the first floor, maybe some seats. Nothing fancy. Enough for a small family to sit around the fireplace or watch the box.

Now, there was just a tent, and aside from patches of blackened plaster on the walls and a spatter of blood, he could picture the scene.

And then there was the tree. A seed that must have blown in from the trees to the rear of the property and taken root in the soil that had once been covered with floorboards. Untested and protected from the elements, it now grew out of the roof space. It was alien to see in the house, yet somehow, it looked as if it was meant to be there. It was a paradox.

There were two window spaces, one to the front of the house and one to the rear. The front looked out onto the spot that Katie had suggested the victim had been dragged to. The other looked out into the small copse of trees behind the house. The wood and glass had most likely succumbed to the fire, but the holes were there, and they posed a question Gillespie couldn't quite fathom.

"Why didn't they get out of the windows?" he called out to Cruz. He didn't expect an answer, and as much as he tried to paint the picture in his mind in black and white, possible and impossible, the variations he created were nothing short of obscene.

"What was that?" Cruz said, stirring him from his mind, and

Gillespie turned to find him in the doorway to the kitchen, looking around as if he was viewing a house he might rent. "What's up with you?"

"Eh?"

"Are you crying?"

"No," Gillespie replied, turning away.

Cruz came to stand beside him, peering up to see his face despite Gillespie's efforts to look away. He hadn't quite realised the impact the scene had had on him, alone with his thoughts, and he half expected Cruz to mock him. Perhaps he would even do his best to make sure the rest of the team found out about it. So, he was as surprised as he was touched when Cruz touched his arm.

"You alright, mate?" he asked.

Gillespie turned to look him in the eye, braved a smile, then nodded once.

"Ah, don't mind me, Gabby," he said. "I was just..." His thoughts took over, and whatever he was going to say was lost to them, like ashes to a strong wind.

"Is it the girls?" Cruz asked gently. "The Halls said they were found upstairs, huddled together." They both peered up into space, but Gillespie said nothing, and Cruz continued to fill the void with Mr and Mrs Hall's account. "The parents were found in the kitchen, but they were up there." He moved across the room, stepping around the tent and the narrow tree trunk. "It must have been like a tinderbox," he said. "There's no way a mother would leave her children upstairs. She would have at least tried to save them, and if not save them, then be with them." He shook his head at the theory. "A place like this would have gone up in seconds."

"It's not them," Gillespie said. "I mean, aye, it's beyond belief what those wee girls must have...it doesn't bear thinking about. It's the lad I'm thinking of."

"John Tyler?"

"Aye. Imagine it," Gillespie said. "You come home from school, get to the top of the lane, see the smoke, and know it can only be coming from one place. There's nothing else here." He moved over to the rear window and leaned on the brickwork to peer outside. "Imagine what he must have been thinking as he ran down the lane? Imagine it, Gab? Your whole life gone in the blink of an eye."

"I know, it must have been—"

"He was twelve, Gabby. Twelve years old. Can you imagine that? Can you imagine having to watch as the fire brigade did whatever they could and came out carrying...carrying the bodies, Gab. Stiff and charred..."

"Don't—"

"And then, as if that isn't bad enough, some do-gooder takes you by the hand and dumps you into the arms of strangers."

"They seem lovely enough—"

"Strangers, Gab. Strangers. They could have been Mother Teresa and Gandhi, but they still would have been strangers."

"I see," Cruz said.

"Do you?" Gillespie asked, testing his statement. "Do you really see? I do. That kind of thing has a profound effect on a man—"

"Your circumstances were different, Jim—"

"Aye, my family didn't die; they just didn't want me. They might as well have been dead," he said. "And the homes I went to were awful, but they might as well have been the same. They were still strangers. It was still a bunch of people I didn't know."

"I can't imagine it," Cruz said honestly. "Honestly, I can't. You've told me about it before, and I've never been able to fathom it. But, Jim, you can't let it get to you—"

"Oh, aye?"

"No, you can't," Cruz said. "Look at how far you've come. Look at the people around you. You did that. You've done more than most people do, and you were on the back foot. Just as John Tyler was."

"Oh, right, and it all worked out for him, didn't it?" Gillespie said. "Landed in the laps of two strangers, joined the RAF, and what happened? He retired from the Air Force, and a few months later, he's found hanging from a tree."

"Jim—"

"No, Gabby. You said it earlier. You summed it up all so well. I think the worst. I manifest this stuff, probably like John Tyler did. Maybe I'm destined to be a bitter old man. That's if I make it that far."

"Oh, look, you can't—"

"What's the point of it all, Gabby?" he said, and he shoved himself away from the window, kicked the stove across the room, and took hold of the tent in both hands, tearing it from where it stood before hurling it at the wall. "That's the point. That's what men like John Tyler and me are destined for, Gabby. A poxy tent, some old baked beans, and scrapbook filled with what could have been."

"Jim?"

"You know, he'd have been better off in the house with the rest of them. It would have saved him a lifetime of misery and a bloody awful, lonely death—"

"Jim!" Cruz said a little more urgently.

Gillespie let his head fall back, and he closed his eyes to the sky.

"Aye, what?" he said, expecting some kind of motivational rubbish to spill from Cruz's lips.

"Look," he said, and Gillespie cast his eyes downward, finding him pointing at the ground where the tent had been.

"Jesus," he whispered, and he stared wide-eyed at Cruz. "I think you were right."

"About what?"

"About calling the boss," Gillespie said, all the bitterness swept from his mind. "We need the whole bloody circus back."

CHAPTER THIRTY-ONE

"I DO HOPE you haven't trampled on any evidence, Gillespie," Freya called out as she ducked into the old house. She barely even took in the kitchen in daylight before bursting into what was once the living room. She glanced about the place. The little camping stove was over near the wall to her right, and the tent was upside down against the back wall. "Well, that answers that, doesn't it?"

"I think the evidence has already been trampled, boss," Gillespie replied, and he glanced down at the ground where the tent had been. "In fact, I think it's been buried."

"Is that—?"

"Could be," he said.

Ben followed Freya into the room, edged past her, and took the scene in with a look of horror on his face. He said nothing but followed their gazes to the ground, where the earth was far darker and fresher than its surroundings.

"Is that—?"

"We think so," Freya replied, cutting him off. "Make the calls, please. We're going to need Southwell, diggers and GPR."

"Ground penetrating radar?" Ben replied. "Surely we know where to dig?"

"Oh, we know where to dig in here," she replied. "But if this is what we think it is, then who's to say there aren't more out there somewhere?" She gestured outside and waited for her words to broaden his imagination.

"Actually, boss," Gillespie said. "I've already made the calls."

"To Southwell?"

"Aye, sorry. I figured we'd need her."

"And the dig team?"

"They're sharpening their shovels as we speak."

"GPR?"

"Same team, boss."

"What about Doctor Saint?"

"Eh?"

"Well, if this is what we all think it is but hope it is not, then we'll need him, won't we?" She turned to Ben. "Call him. Have him on standby, will you? God knows how long it'll take to dig this lot out. I expect there will be a bundle of red tape to get through before even we get going."

"Right," Ben said, and she stared at him expectantly until he got the hint and left the building. "Okay, okay."

She waited for him to go, then watched through the hole where the window was as he paced across to the adjacent barn with his phone pressed to his ear.

"Well?" she said to Gillespie and Cruz. "What news?"

"It's a long story, but I can summarise."

"Do," she said. "You've got until Ben gets back."

"Well, in the late nineties, a wee twelve-year-old lad walked home from school. He got to the top of that lane," he said, pointing behind him. "And saw the smoke. He ran the length of the lane, but by the time he got here, this place was an inferno."

"He lived here?"

"With his mum and dad," Gillespie said. "And his two wee sisters."

"Christ, it's the story from the newspaper article."

"The bairns were found upstairs," he continued. "Mum and Dad were in the kitchen. None of them stood a chance." He took a breath as if preparing himself for the next chapter in the story. "They all died. He watched the firemen carry them from the house." He paused, unable to meet Freya's gaze.

"Gillespie?"

"They put him..." He cleared his throat. "They put him into care, boss."

"Ah," Freya said, for want of a better word. "I see."

"Bloody care. Not a family member or a...I don't know, a friend or something. Bloody care."

"I read that there was nobody," she said softly.

"Aye, maybe. He just became another lad in the system. Another burden on society."

"And did he fall into a life of crime?"

"No, boss," he said. "No, he joined the RAF at eighteen."

"So, there are at least two success stories," Freya said, and he looked up at her to suggest he understood the inference. "He retired a few months ago. Well, he left the RAF, anyway. We don't know what he was planning on doing."

"Quite a few of them learn a trade," Cruz said. "My mum had a plumber who was ex-forces. Bloody good, too, he was."

Cruz waited for somebody to respond, then took the silence as it was intended.

"We spoke to a Group Captain Shaw down at RAF Coningsby," Gillespie continued. "She knew who we were speaking about as soon as we mentioned the tattoo."

"It was below the collar line, wasn't it?"

"He boxed," Gillespie replied. "Good as well, apparently. Anyway, she's agreed to a formal ID."

"Have you lined it up?"

"I said I'd call her boss. I didn't know if you wanted to be involved."

"No, you take care of it. Line it up and keep me informed."

"There's more," Gillespie said. "She put us onto the couple that took care of him. They're not far from here, so we paid them a visit."

"And?" she asked. "Are they as bad as..."

He shook his head and inhaled long and hard.

"No, they're alright, as it happens. On the surface, anyway. Seemed like a nice couple. It wasn't a kid farm like the homes I was sent to. They actually adopted him."

"So, he was loved?" Gillespie said nothing. He stared at the ground, cheeks puffed out as he sought to control his emotions. "Cruz, would you mind giving us a minute?" Freya asked, and although the young DC left without a word, he did reach out and squeeze Gillespie's elbow. It was one of those tiny, almost imperceptible gestures that carried more weight than words ever could. "Is that what this is, Jim? Has it...invoked memories?"

"Ah, don't worry about me, boss—"

"Well, it's my job to worry about you, so I'm sorry, but I will," she told him, luring his eyes from the ground. "Are you upset because he was loved, and you...well, you had a very different experience?"

He shook his head.

"Sorry, boss—"

"Well, what is it?" she asked. "Look, I'm not letting a single person into this room until you tell me. I don't care if it delays the investigation. I'd have the entire Lincolnshire police force waiting outside if necessary. We're not leaving until I understand."

He laughed at the prospect, then sighed.

"It's not that he was loved, and I wasn't," he said eventually, and to his credit, he held his emotions back, although they were evident in his eyes. "It's that...boss, all my life, I've felt like I was on the back foot, you know? I felt hard done by, and compared to most, I was. You know, I used to sit on my bed, wherever the bed might be, whichever home I was in, and I would pray for a home like the wee lad. I'd pray for somebody to give me a hug. To show they cared, you know?"

She nodded, but she could never actually know.

"I thought," he continued. "I thought that my life could be so much better if it was just me and a couple of doting carers. No beatings from the other kids, none of the abuse. I'd be a different person."

"You're an amazing person—"

"But I'd be different. I'd have a different outlook. I don't know; more positive, maybe. Maybe I'd be less, I don't know, abrasive, sharper, smarter. I mean, this lad, he lost everything. I always knew I had parents; they just didn't want me or couldn't afford me, I don't know. But this lad lost it all. He watched them being carried out." He opened his mouth to speak, but the only sounds he emitted were the gasps of frustration as he sought the right words. "I would have done anything for that."

"Sorry?"

"To know that I was wanted, boss. That I was wanted, but they were just dead. I could have moved on. Maybe I wouldn't be so bitter. And he had that. This lad. He had that. He had a home. He was loved, and I'm not saying it was easy for him because, Jesus, it must have been bloody awful for a wee lad to go through it, but he had love. He had the things that I've spent my life wishing I had, and then what? He winds up hanging from a tree, torched. What's it all about?"

"Gillespie," she started, then corrected herself. "Jim. Do you want to take some time off?"

He shook his head.

"No, it's okay. I'm just being daft—"

"I can arrange it. Full pay. You can take a few days—"

"No," he said. "No, I'm just...I'm being selfish. People have died, boss, and here's me moaning about my lot."

"No, it's fine," she said. "I think that perhaps the news of him being in a home has stirred up some memories."

"Boss, he had everything I could have wished for and still..." He shook his head, and they heard the crunch of tyres outside and the rumble of a diesel engine. "What's the point, boss? What's the point in dreaming and hoping if, at the end of it all, we're just destined for misery?"

She smiled, and as Cruz had done, she touched his arm.

"You're not destined for misery," she told him. "And I know you won't believe me when I tell you this..."

He looked up at her, eyes glazed.

"Aye?"

"I wouldn't have you any other way," she said. "You are one of the strongest people I have ever known, and I know for a fact that every one of the team looks up to you."

"Aye," he said, with a laugh, dismissing the notion.

"I mean it," she told him. "So, if you're not going to take a few days, then I suggest you pull yourself together. Go and get some air, and when you're done, if you're up for it..."

She waited for him to look up at her. She wanted to see how hungry he was.

"Aye?"

"It looks like I'll be busy here for a while," she said. "So, I want you to run the investigation for me."

"Seriously?"

She nodded sincerely.

"I can't think of anybody more qualified for the role," she told him. "By the way, what was his name? This boy. What was he called?"

"His name was John," he replied. "John Tyler."

"John Tyler. Well, I'm sure, as somebody with an idea of what he's been through, that you'll do his memory justice," she said softly, then peered down at the ground, at that patch of dark and disturbed earth. "I just hope I can do something similar."

CHAPTER THIRTY-TWO

"You know what this means, don't you?" Freya said, and Ben braced himself for one of Freya's theories, which would be far-fetched but somehow contain an element of fact. She would then, at some point in the very near future, remind him of how right she had been, and he would no doubt be forced into accepting that he was wrong.

"Go on," he said, stepping to one side to allow Southwell's team inside. "Enlighten me."

"I was wrong," she said.

"Sorry? Can you say that again?" he fumbled for his phone and then navigated to the voice recorder. "Loudly and clearly, please. I'll save the recording."

"We were all wrong," she said, evidently mildly amused. "We theorised that whoever the blood spatter belongs to was hit, most probably in the head by a blunt instrument." She caught Katy Southwell's attention. "That was right, wasn't it, Katy?"

"That much still holds up," Southwell replied without looking up. She was crouched with her team, examining the area of soil in question.

"And then he was dragged outside where he was loaded into a vehicle of some kind."

"Right," Ben said. "I remember. It was only two days ago."

"Ah-ha," she said, raising a slender index finger in the air. "That's the part that was wrong. It's reversed. What if whoever that bloody spatter belongs to was injured somewhere else? He was driven here and unloaded from a vehicle of some description right outside?"

"And then he was dragged in here and...buried?" Ben said.

"Solves a puzzle, doesn't it?"

"What puzzle was that?"

"Whether or not the blood that Katy found is linked to the hanging," she replied. "It's okay. I know you hate it when I'm right."

"No, no," he lied. "But I think we should wait and see."

"It's okay," she said, taunting him, and even Southwell looked up at him with a wry smile. "We can discuss it while we're away." He knew then what was to follow. "On our holiday," she added.

"Katy?" Ben said, ignoring Freya's smugness. "What do *you* think?"

"What I think," she replied. "Is that it's a good job we had a late night on Sunday. There's nothing left for us. At least, not until the diggers have been in."

"Think it could be?"

"It's possible," she replied. "There's a variation in the PH of the soil compared to the ground we are standing on. The exposed ground."

"Could that be due to the area being covered by the tent?"

"Not really," she replied. "Not to the extent it is, anyway. The soil beneath our feet has been exposed to sunlight, rain, and God knows what for God knows how long—"

"Two decades," Freya said.

"Right," Southwell replied. "The soil beneath the tent has a different composition."

"Worms?" Ben said, seeing where she was leading them.

"And other organisms, yes," Southwell said. "There are thousands of microorganisms that live in the soil, all of which excrete, all of which extract nutrients, and all of which thrive at varying depths."

"Without inviting David Attenborough to interpret all of that, Katy, are you able to tell me in English?" Freya said.

"What I mean is," Southwell started. "If I were to dig down beneath your feet, I'd get to a level where the soil matches the soil over there where the tent used to be. Which means—"

"That the area has been dug recently?"

"In short, yes."

"Oh good," Freya replied. "Well, let's get them in, shall we?" She looked up at Ben, eyebrows raised, and he took the hint and started towards the doorway.

"We'll just pack up and get out of the way," Southwell said. "Myself and Pat will stay on site. I'll send the rest of the team back to the lab."

"Actually, I thought you might like to check on your boyfriend," Freya said, and Ben tuned in. "In fact, I think it might be wise."

Southwell's usually stoic expression turned to one of curiosity, but if there were any emotions stirring, then she did a good job of concealing them.

"We can finish up here," one of her team said, and she smiled a thanks before stepping outside.

"What was all that about?" Ben asked, to which Freya made a point of not replying.

"How's the dig team coming along?" she asked, then smiled politely before following Southwell outside.

"Right then," Ben said, as he ducked through the doorway and waited for the assembly to quieten. Southwell was heading towards Gillespie, who was on his own over by the junction of the three drainage ditches. Cruz, Gold, and Nillson were huddled together as if conspiring, and the dig team, who were no doubt used to waiting, were spread out by their vans. Slowly they came together to better hear what Ben had to say.

"We'll start with the Ground Penetrating Radar," Ben called, nodding at the relevant team. "If there is a body in there, I'm not expecting it to be deep, but it'll be good to know what we're dealing with before we put the spades into the ground. When you're done, I want you to cover every inch of the surrounding area, including the barns."

"Are you expecting more?" one of the men called out.

"Put it this way," Ben replied. "We aren't expecting more, but the way my week is going, I wouldn't be surprised."

The man nodded and looked around at his team to make sure they were all ready.

"Once the GPR team is out, let's get some spades in there. We need to go slowly. I want every spadeful of soil sieved and studied. Any finds go to Katy Southwell and her team. The moment you find evidence of a body, I want you to stop. From that point on, this place officially becomes a murder scene."

"What is it now then?"

"Now?" Ben said. "Now it's a bloody headache. It's a theory. A bloody expensive theory that, sadly, I think is about to be proven." The group nodded but said nothing, and Ben continued. "Doctor Saint, the FME, is local. He can be here in under half an hour. Alongside Katy Southwell, he'll observe the remainder of the dig and coordinate the removal of the body. At that stage, there's likely to be a significant wait while CSI and the FME do their things. Note. This is not your call to leave. If shifts need to be put in place, then team leaders, please do so. This has the potential to be linked to another investigation not far from here, so I'm hoping you understand what that means?"

"What?" somebody said but Ben couldn't see who, so he addressed all two dozen of them.

"It means two bodies," he said. "Double trouble, double the

pressure, double the work, and double the paperwork. We need to get this right. I need continuity and joined-up thinking. Feel free to insert any other buzzwords you can think of. The point is there are multiple teams here, and that means that a single point of failure could make this even more of a nightmare for us all. Got it?"

"I think we get the gist, Inspector," one man replied, maturer in years and somebody Ben recognised from a previous investigation.

"Sergeant Nillson. Gather any uniformed officers you need and lock this place down. Gold, can you help her, please? I need you to stay on top of the proceedings. We might need you to visit Mrs Dean again."

"What about me and Jim?" Cruz called out.

"Oh, don't worry," Freya interjected, and she beamed at his dismay. "I've got something special lined up for you both."

Cruz cringed, and a few of the wider team laughed amongst themselves.

"Right then," Ben called out, checking his watch. "It's three p.m. Let's see if we can all be home by midnight, shall we?"

CHAPTER THIRTY-THREE

THE ALERT SPREAD through the workforce like an unwanted disease.

The man with the spade stopped working, looked up at his colleague who was waiting to shovel the soil out and nodded. The man with the shovel turned to the two individuals sifting through the pile of dirt, one of whom stood and stepped outside.

"Boss?" she called to her team leader to get his attention, then passed the nod onto him. It was at this stage that the message seemed to spread through the air, penetrating every subconscious with delicate tendrils that did little more than tickle the intrigue inside. Almost every man and woman there picked up the vibe, and the hum of chatter, the whirr of the GPR, and the crackle of radios came to a stop.

Freya was with Ben, leaning against her car, when her curiosity was piqued.

"I'm just saying," he said. "GPR might have picked up on a signal, but that doesn't mean the murders are connected—"

She held up a hand to stop him, and shoved herself off the car, peering over to the individual who was standing half in and half out of the doorway to the house.

Her expression said it all.

"I think we're about to find out," she said. "Did you call Doctor Saint?"

"He's ten minutes out," Ben replied as they made their way over to the house. They walked slowly. It wasn't as if they were in a hurry to find out if there really was a body buried in the house. They knew there was. It wasn't as if they were in a hurry to bring the various teams together to increase their chances of bringing the murderer to justice. The fabled and critical twenty-four-hour window was long passed. Right now, there was more to be gained from composure than hasty decisions and conclusions.

Southwell split from the discussion she was having with her colleague to join them, and one by one, the threesome stepped inside. The workers stepped back or to one side to allow them access, waiting for an order but no doubt intrigued by the next steps.

"I felt it," the man with the spade said. "I didn't stab down hard, but I felt it." He pointed to the area he had been working on, and Ben dropped to one knee. The hole was maybe a foot deep, eighteen inches at the most. He snapped on a latex glove from his pocket, and keen to investigate, Southwell stooped beside him. She handed him a brush, which, unlike the range of expensive specialist equipment she carried in her little van, was little more than something that came with a dustpan for two pounds from any discount store.

He brushed lightly at the soil, until the strokes felt somewhat different. There was more resistance, and the way he moved his hand altered to compensate.

And then there was colour. A deep red, vivid against the surrounding earth.

"It's a shirt or a jumper," he breathed rather than spoke, then handed the brush to Katy and sat back on his haunches.

Freya offered a weak smile and watched Katy resume the excavation. Although she was careful, she moved far more soil than Ben had, perhaps having done something similar before.

"Nobody touches him until the FME arrives," Freya reminded them. "Just expose what we can without disturbing him."

To free the body from the dirt would take time. They all knew that somebody had a long and tedious job ahead of them. The important part, the part that mattered to Freya, the part that would enable them to move forward with an investigation, was the priority, and it took less than two minutes for Katy to partly answer the question on Freya's lips.

"There," she said, moving out of the way to reveal her work. A full arm had been exposed, from the clenched fist to the twisted shoulder, covered with what looked to be a red sweater. With one gloved hand, Katy eased the collar of the sweater back and carefully rubbed the soil from the cold, pale skin.

"A cross," she said quietly, then peered up at them. "It's the same, or as near as damn it."

Ben let his head fall back. He closed his eyes to the world, and Freya watched him. Now was not the time to remind him of how right she had been. Any humour they might have shared while discussing the theory was long past. It was the unspoken, undocumented reality that TV shows and films never seemed to depict a sober truth. The man, presumably Tommy Dean, had been murdered, and as if that wasn't bad enough, the killer had gone to great lengths to conceal the body.

"It takes a certain type of individual to do that," Freya said, shaking her head at the idea of dragging somebody, half-dead from their car, into the house and then beating them to death before digging the hole, dragging the body inside, and then covering it. The covering was the worst part. Anybody, under the right amount of pressure, could beat somebody to death. She had interviewed women who wouldn't say boo to a goose but had been taunted, abused, and prodded and poked so much that one day, that valve that retains the pressure had given in. People, regardless of their size and weight, were capable of almost anything.

"Hello?" a voice called out, cutting the tension like a blade through warm bread.

"In here, Doctor Saint," Freya replied, and they heard his waterproof jacket rustling long before he emerged, stooping to duck through the doorway. He took in the scene with indifference, then settled his gaze on the exposed arm. "Oh, I see."

"Sorry, we're not quite ready for you."

"No, no," he said, as polite as ever. "No, take your time. These things must be done right."

"Thanks for coming," Freya told him. "We've just exposed the arm. It'll be an hour or so before you can...well, before you can get to him as you need to."

"It's fine," he said, and his smile was as reassuring as the sunrise on a summer's day. "It won't be the first time I've worked in a hole."

CHAPTER THIRTY-FOUR

FOR BEN, the slow and painstaking reveal was akin to completing a jigsaw he neither wanted to see nor wanted to complete. He knew what subject the final result would reveal, yet knew not the form it would take. He might not have had decades of experience, but he had seen enough of these puzzles to know that Tommy Dean, if indeed it was Tommy Dean, would not be lying peacefully on his back with his arms folded across his stomach as if placed there by the tender hands of an undertaker. Whoever had dragged the body into the hole had done so in haste and without finesse or care; the weight of the soil, regardless of time, would have had a profound effect on the limbs, causing them to rest at unnatural angles. But perhaps the most dreaded piece of that grotesque jigsaw that Ben didn't need to see would be the face, with the owner's final moments etched into every line and muscle and the pain he must have endured painted in those dead eyes.

Yet, as Katy's delicate strokes brushed the earth from the form, exposing the image inch by inch, he found some macabre curiosity held his gaze firmly on the pale white flesh.

The entire arm was in view, pinky finger up, suggesting the victim was lying on their side or partially on their front. It had been Freya who had raised that particular theory, which had been confirmed by Doctor Saint when the elbow fully came into view. The upper arm and the shoulder were next, and it was only now that Ben made a mental comparison between the two men. The hanged man had been toned and muscular, not overly, but he had been healthy and strong. Where the man that lay at their feet was what Freya would call a soft body, his upper arm was loose and undefined, and his shoulder boyish.

An ear began to show itself, just the tip, but with every stroke of Katy's brush, it emerged like some kind of hairless rodent from the soil, and with it came hair. A mass of unkempt, short, dark curls, and he felt Freya look up at him. She said nothing, but he knew what words were coiled on her tongue, ready to pounce, as he recalled the framed photo from the Dean's house.

Perhaps it was because Katy knew what they really wanted to see, or perhaps she just wanted them out of there so she and her team could work without an audience. Whichever the reason, she concentrated her endeavours between the ear and the shoulder, revealing more of the man with every tactile stroke until they saw it, almost vivid against the pale flesh.

"It's him," Freya said, and for the first time, she crouched for a better view.

Ben saw no need to crouch. It was as if a balloon had burst inside him. A balloon that had inflated puff by puff with every stroke of Katy's brush.

It wasn't the losing of the bet that burst that balloon; it was by no means the first bet he'd lost to Freya, and it certainly wouldn't be the last. Even her smug comments were bearable; her tenacious desire to win every aspect of life was one of the things he adored about her. No, it was the very meaning of Tommy Dean's death that troubled him. Had there been no little cross on the neck, there would be no definable link between the murders, leaving them with little option but to work the investigations independently, the only connection being coincidence.

But to have the links between the deaths confirmed meant complexity, which meant time and resources, and far more work for him and his team, far more heartache for the victims' families, and a far more callous and cunning murderer.

"Thank you," Freya said as she rose to stand beside Ben.

"What are you thinking?" she asked.

"Me?" he said, taking a deep breath. "I'm thinking that whoever we're dealing with has gone to great lengths to cover his tracks."

"That's funny," she said. "That's precisely what I was thinking."

"Yet, he didn't go to such lengths with the other one," Ben replied. "It's almost like he wanted us to find the hanging."

"John Tyler," Freya said, and she caught the question in his expression. "I sent Gillespie and Cruz to speak to the Group Captain at the RAF base."

"Right," he said. "Presumably because of the photo in the scrapbook?"

"Precisely," she said.

"Which, at the time, wasn't linked to this place."

"Again, precisely."

"Hence why you chose to keep it from me."

"Three out of three, Ben," she said. "You really are getting quite good at this."

"Well," he said. "I'd like to see how the timeline looks in your report to Granger, who, might I remind you, specifically told us to leave this place alone."

"Yes, I can't wait to see his face when he learns that he was wrong, and I was right," she said, and Southwell glanced up at them with a smirk. "Perhaps you could have a word with him beforehand? Maybe you could give him some tips on how to handle it. You are, after all, quite experienced in that regard."

He laughed and shook his head. There was so much he wanted

to say, but all of it was pointless and would only serve to strengthen her position.

"Anyway," she continued. "Gillespie is arranging for John Tyler's formal ID in the morning. If we can get Tommy Dean out tonight, with any luck by the end of tomorrow, we can have Mrs Dean do the same."

"Which means that we should be in a position to start piecing all of this together."

"Here we go," Doctor Saint said, interrupting them.

The uppermost third of the body was now exposed, and Katy was just cleaning up the remainder of the head.

"I did as you suggested, by the way," Freya continued to Ben as a closing statement.

"You called Alcoholics Anonymous?"

"No," she replied, her tone rising in pitch like a mother warning a child. "I set Gillespie a task. I gave him some autonomy. He'll be running the John Tyler investigation while we focus on Tommy Dean."

"It's...one investigation, Freya," he said. "I know I'm feeding your ego here, but you were right. It's one investigation."

She stared up at him with a curious smile and licked at her lower lip as if deciding how to respond. Her conclusion, however, was to say nothing and leave him with a wink with which to draw his own conclusions. She dropped to a crouch, and Ben, still deciphering that curious wink and smile combination dropped down beside her.

Doctor Saint took an internal temperature from the victim's mouth, noting his findings in a notebook while Katy deftly brushed more soil from the lowermost eye. Much of the head was still beneath the earth, as was the remainder of the body. It was as if the victim had been swimming front crawl and mid-stroke in the earth rather than water.

"Severe petechial haemorrhaging," Saint said, verbalising his findings as he shone a little Maglite into the victim's exposed eye.

"Haemorrhaging?" Ben said. "He was strangled?"

"Possibly," he replied, then moved back to allow Southwell room to work. But no sooner had he made room than he stopped her. 'Wait.'

Taking care not to dirty his gloves and therefore risk contaminating other parts of the body, he fingered the man's hair, using feel more than sight.

"What is it?" Freya asked.

He pulled his hand away and glanced up at Katy.

"Would you expose more of the head, please?" he said. "I think we have a fracture of some kind."

Southwell focused on her efforts on the area in question.

"A fractured skull?" Freya said. "So, not a strangulation?"

"Just saying it how I find it," Saint replied.

"Could the haemorrhaging in the eyes be a result of blunt force trauma?"

"It's possible," Saint replied. "Petechial haemorrhaging occurs as a result of pressure. Hence it is a visible sign of strangulation or hanging, and while it's not implausible that it could occur from blunt force trauma, in this instance, which is quite severe, I would suggest he endured some kind of strangulation, whichever form that might take. We'll know more when his neck has been exposed and he's cleaned up."

"Another visit to the delectable Doctor Bell," Freya said, her cheerful tone flavoured with sarcasm.

"Peter?" Southwell said, having exposed more of the head, and he set to work, feeling his way around the skull, nodding to himself as he did.

"Yes," he said. "Yes, it's a fracture. Severe. Three to four inches. There's also significant swelling, which could only have occurred while the victim was alive." He thanked Southwell with a curt nod, then retracted his hand. "It's not easy to say for sure, but I would suggest, given his internal body temperature, the conditions in which we've found him, and the progress of rigor mortis, that he's been dead for at least two days. Death occurred either by strangulation or that blow to his head. Given the swelling, I'm leaning towards blunt-force trauma. Doctor Bell will advise on the size and shape of the weapon."

Ben moved over to the blood spatter on the wall.

"How about if he was beaten somewhere else, enough to cause a wound of some sort? He was driven here, dragged from the car—"

"Which left the blood trail," Freya added.

"Right," Ben said. "The killer delivered the final blow here while Tommy Dean was on his hands and knees. He dug the hole and buried him, leaving the tent over the top to cover the scene."

"It's a start," Freya agreed.

"The question is, who died first? Tommy Dean or John Tyler?"

"No," Freya said. "No, the question is, who killed Tommy Dean and who killed John Tyler?"

"Sorry?"

"You said it yourself," Freya told him. "Different MOs, different measures with which to control the scene. John Tyler was hanged and burned and left for us to find. Tommy Dean was beaten to death and buried." She found that smile Ben had yet to interpret. "We're dealing with two different killers, Ben."

CHAPTER THIRTY-FIVE

"COME ON THEN," Ben said as they entered Freya's house. He kicked his shoes off with a loud groan, then flopped into an armchair. "Let's hear it?"

"Hear it?" Freya replied, feigning ignorance. She made her way to the kitchen, sought a fresh bottle of wine from the cupboard, grabbed two glasses, and then made her way back into the lounge. She set them down in front of Ben and even fetched the bottle opener from the drawer on the coffee table. "You'll have to explain yourself a little better if you expect some kind of response, Ben."

"You were quiet all the way home," he told her. "You've been quiet since yesterday morning. Something's on your mind."

"Something's on my mind? Oh, really. I wonder what that could be?"

"Maybe it's got something to do with a certain holiday we're about to go on?"

"Close," she replied, standing over him.

"Or maybe it's got something to do with two dead bodies?"

"Ooh, colder," she said, stepping over his outstretched legs.

He cocked his head to one side, narrowed his eyes, then

reached out for her hips. She swiped his hands away, then slid her knees either side of him. "Keep guessing."

He raised his hands again, and this time, she held his wrists, pinning them to the armchair.

"Does it have something to do with Gillespie and Cruz?"

"Oh, God, no," she spat, then started on his shirt buttons. "Come on. Use your imagination."

"I can't believe you're thinking about this after today."

"What about today?" she breathed into his ear.

"Freya, less than an hour ago, we were standing beside a hole with a dead body in it."

"Doesn't it make you feel...alive?"

"Not really," he said as she forced his shirt from his shoulders.

"Can't you put it to one side for a while?" she asked. "Surely there are better things to think about."

She ran her hands across his chest, admiring the taut muscles beneath her fingers.

"I might need a little motivation," he said, to which she responded by digging her nails in. Not hard. But enough to force whatever image was in his mind into a dark corner.

She eased off and ran a nail across his skin, and he tensed, waiting for the onset of pain. She watched his eyes curiously, watched his chest rise and fall, and his nostrils flare.

And then she dug once more, savouring that little groan he gave as he controlled the focused pain.

"You're a piece of work, Freya Bloom."

She leaned in again until her lips teased at his ear lobe.

"Forget about work," she replied. "Forget about what we saw and forget about what those two men did. I want you to forget about every face you know, apart from mine." Her fingers rested on his belt buckle, and again, he reached for her, only for her to sit up, stare at his hands, and then give him a warning stare until his hands dropped to the armchair in submission. "What are you thinking?"

He shook his head but said nothing.

"Work?"

He didn't respond, so she moved back to his belt buckle.

"Now?"

"Dead bodies," he told her, and she slid the loose end from the buckle.

"Still?"

"Cold and pale," he replied with a smile.

She tugged until the belt's prong came free, then waited.

"And now?"

"Blood," he replied. "I told you, I'm going to need some help here."

She released the belt and tugged it free of his trousers, taking it in both hands before him and bringing the soft leather to a snap.

"Freya?"

"Don't speak," she said, and she playfully struck his bare chest with the curled belt.

"No, Freya," he said.

"Just close your eyes—"

"I can't," he said, and she stilled.

"Excuse me?"

"I can't," he said, turning his head away.

"Ben, if there's a problem—"

"There's no problem," he replied. "Except that...well, I've already explained what the problem is."

"Ben, it's work. It's just work."

"I know, but it's...well, it's not like we work in insurance, is it? I can't just finish work and turn it off?"

"It's never been a problem before," she said. "Is it me?"

"No, of course not. It's...I don't know. I know this is how you put things out of your mind, alright? I know. And believe me, I'm more than happy to help, but this time? This time, it's...difficult," he said, to which she nodded.

"Do you want to talk about it?" she asked, dropping the belt onto the floor and reaching behind her for the glasses. He took them, one in each hand, while she reached for the bottle and the opener, and he waited patiently while she worked the cork.

"What is there to say?" he asked. "I can't shake the image of Tommy Dean from my mind, and when I do—"

"You see John Tyler?" she suggested.

"I see John Tyler," he replied. "I don't know. For some reason, it's got to me this time."

"Got to you? How bad?"

"Not bad, bad," he said. "But enough that I can't...you know?"

"Would music help?"

He laughed and held one of the glasses up for her to fill.

"No, Freya. Not really."

She nodded and poured the second glass.

"I could close the curtains," she suggested. "Make it darker."

He laughed again.

"What, and deny the neighbours a view?" he shook his head. "Listen, I'm okay. I'm just not...I'm not in the mood."

"So, what then?" she asked, setting the bottle down and taking one of the glasses from him. "Do you want to talk about it?"

"No—"

"What about this?" she asked, and with one hand, she unfastened the top button of her blouse.

"Freya?"

She took his hand gently and pressed it against her chest, squeezing his hand closed around her as she sipped her wine. She held it there for a moment but felt nothing from him. He hadn't stirred.

"Sorry," he said, and she released her grip on his hand.

She watched him, trying hard to remember the last time she had seen him vulnerable enough that he couldn't look her in the eye.

"No," she told him. "No, it's me who should be sorry." She

sighed heavily and rested her glass on his chest. "It's not unusual, you know?"

"What isn't?"

"You know? Not being able to—"

"There's no problem," he said. "Everything works just fine. It's just that today, tonight, I can't." He took a mouthful of his wine, reminding her that she still had some work to do on him.

"There are three types of people who drink wine," she said.

"What?"

"The first type are cretins," she continued, and she held the glass at the base of the stem. "They hold the glass like so."

"What are you talking about?"

"The second type are animals," she said, moving her hand to the bowl of the glass. "Uncivilised and uncouth."

He stared down at his hand on the glass.

"So, I'm an animal, am I?"

"The third type," she continued, moving her hand to where the bowl meets the stem. "That's who you want to be."

He moved his hand to where the bowl meets the stem and held the glass to her as if toasting her.

"Am I an animal?"

"Consider yourself tamed," she told him, and she leaned forward to kiss him. "Whereas I..." She leaned back, smiling at him. The glaze in his eyes had gone, and the definition in his tense shoulders softened. "I still need taming."

"Some beasts aren't meant to be tamed," he told her.

"Aren't you up for the challenge, Mr Savage?" she asked. "And here was me thinking you're the man for the job."

"I couldn't tame you," he said, and he reached up for her wrist, stopping her from taking a drink. He held it there as if he were demonstrating some kind of power. "I wouldn't want to change you."

He released her wrist, and she grinned at him as she drank.

"Are we okay?" she asked, sensing the moment had abated.

"Let's just get through these next few days," he told her. "I'll be fine once this one's over."

"Once that ring is on my finger, you mean?" she said, and he bit down on his lower lip in thought.

"You know, in a few days' time, you'll be Freya Savage." He cocked his head again as if imagining the not-too-distant future.

"Excuse me?"

"You'll be Freya Savage," he said again. "How does that make you feel?"

"It doesn't make me feel anything," she replied. "I won't be changing my name."

"Eh?"

"I'm not changing my name," she said.

"But—"

"But nothing. I like my name."

"But I thought—"

"What? Did you think that I would give up my father's name just like that? I have no brothers or sisters, Ben. I'm the end of the line."

"But we're getting married, Freya. We'll be husband and wife—"

"So, change *your* name, then," she said. "If it's that simple. If all you want is for people to recognise our marriage, *you* change *your* name."

He said nothing but shrugged his shirt back onto his shoulders.

"Not so easy now, is it?" she said, shoving herself to her feet and sinking the remainder of her wine. She set the glass down on the table, waiting for him to say something. But he just stared out of the window. "I'm going for a bath." She waited again. "Care to scrub my back?"

"No," he said. "No, I'm going to stay here and think."

"What about Mr Bloom?" she asked but failed to raise a smile.

He hesitated but eventually turned to face her.

"Dead people," he said. "I'm going to think about dead people."

There was a serious tone to his voice. One she knew not to question.

"Suit yourself," she said, dragging her hand across his bare chest to, if nothing else, remind him that there were no hard feelings.

"Freya?" he said as she reached the stairs. His voice had lightened. It was almost boyish, and she turned.

"Ben?"

"You do realise," he began, "that if we don't sort this out. If we don't put this one to bed, we'll be in the middle of a double murder investigation while we get married?"

"The thought had crossed my mind."

She held onto the bannister, mindful that he was demonstrating some underlying sensitivity that she hadn't seen before.

"Is that who we are? Is that what we'll remember whenever we look back at our wedding day?" he asked. "Not the dress, not who took whose name, but two bloody awful murders."

She gave it some thought; then slowly, she moved back across the room to him. She touched his shoulder, ran her fingers along the length of his arm and took his hand in hers, tugging him gently until he stood. She held him, and he held her back, and it felt good. It felt right.

"There's a line we must draw between work and...and us," she said. "I know it's hard, and I know we're not in insurance, but we have to. Most coppers can't talk about it to their spouses. Most of them have to bottle it up." She pulled away from him just far enough to look him in the eye. "We have to close it off. We have to shut it out so, as you said, so we don't become...that. So, we remain us."

He nodded slowly.

"Easier said than done," he replied, and she squeezed his hands.

"Come and have a bath," she told him, leading him towards the stairs. "You can think about what we're going to do."

"When?" he asked. "What we're going to do, when?"

"In a few days time," she said, and she stopped at the stairs again, coaxing him to lead the way. It was only when he was three steps ahead of her that she delivered the blow that was sure to raise a smile. "On our holiday."

CHAPTER THIRTY-SIX

A TENOR HUM emanated from the incident room when Ben and Freya pushed through the doors from the fire escape stairwell into the first-floor corridor. The entire team was present, and the cars in the station car park told Ben that much. Yet, he prayed that the hum was, at least in part, related to the investigation. Freya's mood had been fractious all morning, mostly, Ben thought, due to the previous night's disappointment, although she hadn't said so, not in so many words, anyway.

But her mind was unmistakably distracted and had been since the moment Granger had taken her into his office. It was one of those things, he supposed, that spouses learn to pick up on. A sense, fuelled by her silence, her reluctance to look him in the eye, and the mute curse she breathed when she had caught a nail on her blouse.

It was at such times, that Ben had learned that it was best to carry on regardless, not to press for a response, not to ask what the matter was, and not to let her mood spoil his day. If she wanted to speak about it, then she would do so in her own time. If she chose not to discuss whatever the issue happened to be, then so be it.

Still, he prayed that the incident room was a haven of efficiency and progress, right up until the moment he pushed through the double doors and all his hopes smashed on the floor like a pile of Greek dinner plates.

"What do you mean, you half-wit?" Nillson called across the room, her venom focused solely on Gillespie. "We all stretch and yawn. It's not a bad habit or an affliction. It's just a...I don't know, a thing we all do. We wake up, and at some point, we stretch and yawn, and if, like me, you happened to be with a team of uniformed officers searching a bloody field all night, then you'll continue to stretch and yawn until you get a good night's sleep. And by the way, a common by-product of being tired is being short-tempered, so I'd think twice about getting on my nerves, Jim."

"What's going on here?" Freya asked nobody in particular as she marched across the room to her desk, where she set her bag and jacket down.

Ben dumped his bag on the floor, dropped into his seat, and closed his eyes, readying himself for everything he had hoped would not happen.

"Anna got out of the bed on the wrong side," Gillespie said.

"Jim learned a new word," Nillson replied. "He's moving onto adjectives tomorrow, and by the end of the year, he might be able to string a sentence together."

"I see," Freya said. "Well, for what it's worth, Gillespie, we all pandiculate, as do dogs, cats, and most mammals." She turned to Nillson. "I presume this yawning and stretching is a result of a long night?"

"It is boss."

"Anything worth mentioning?"

"I need some new batteries in my torch," she replied. "But I won't need to restock on evidence bags."

Freya nodded and turned her back on them as she studied the board, and Gillespie took the opportunity to berate Cruz.

"I blame you," he hissed.

"Eh?"

"You. You and your bloody—"

"John Tyler," Freya announced, as a schoolteacher might gain the attention of a classroom rabble. "Hanged and burned sometime on Saturday night. She wrote the name and drew a horizontal line across the board, positioning Tyler somewhere near the centre. She moved to the right side of the line and marked a spot with an X. "Nine-fifty on Sunday night," she continued. "Call to emergency services."

"The wee lad?" Gillespie said.

"The wee lad, indeed," she replied as she marked another X. "Eleven-thirty. We arrive at the crime scene to discover the old farmhouse empty."

She stepped back to take the board in.

"We think the body we discovered yesterday is Tommy Dean," she said. "Gillespie, what time is your ID?"

"Twelve, boss," he said. "Doctor Bell is expecting you at nine-thirty for the PM."

Ben glanced up at the wall clock, noting it was eight-thirty and a good half-hour drive into the city.

"Well, she'll be disappointed, then," Freya replied. "I want you and Cruz to attend the PM. It'll take an hour or so. After that, while Pip prepares him for the ID, call in and give me a debrief."

"Want us to wait around to meet Mrs Dean?" Gillespie asked.

"No," she said and turned to Gold. "Would you?"

"Of course," Gold replied.

"Good. I think a friendly face will help," Freya said. "But I want you to do some digging. Get close to her. She trusts you."

"Okay," Gold said slowly, as if she, like Ben, was expecting Freya to provide a reason.

"If it was Tommy Dean in that hole, and Doctor Bell provides a time of death after Saturday night when John Tyler was killed, then I'd like to examine the possibility that Tommy

Dean killed John Tyler, and as a result, he was subsequently murdered."

"Any reason for thinking that?" Nillson asked. "Just so we're on the same page."

"Well, firstly, the murders are vastly different," she replied. "One body was left for us to find; the other was buried so that we wouldn't find it. One was a considered act of extreme violence designed to inflict as much pain as possible; the other was, if Doctor Saint is right, little more than an act of emotional violence. A venting of frustration and anger, after which the killer panicked. Whoever killed John Tyler would have needed considerable strength, whereas whoever murdered Tommy Dean needed little more than a vehicle and something heavy to whack him with. My guess is that it was a shovel or spade, which was then used to dig the hole."

"Hence, why you want me to get close to Julie Dean?" Gold cut in, and Freya smiled. "Do you really think she could have killed her husband?"

"It's nice to see that some of us are awake," she replied. "Talk to her about the prospect of her house being searched. Watch for a reaction. I'm not looking into her yet, but I'm certainly not ruling her out."

"Freya, if it is him, then she'll be in a bit of a state. Do you think it's worth saving that for tomorrow?"

"I thought you were keen to get this over the line, Ben," she said, and then, when he didn't respond, she turned back to Gold. "Frame it like we're looking into his death. We'll need access to his personal effects, a diary if he has one, and the shed and the garage. I'm sure you'll find a way to get the message across far better than I."

"Right," Gold said, and when Freya turned back to the board, she frowned at Ben, suggesting the task was borderline lunacy.

He shrugged and offered Gold an empathetic smile.

"Freya, why on earth would she murder her own husband?" he asked.

"I didn't say that she did," Freya replied. "I merely suggested that it's plausible. She claimed not to recognise John Tyler, yet we know that John Tyler had been friends with her husband since they were kids. She claimed he left the farm job due to being paid late, yet Frank Bowen suggests otherwise. Speaking of which," she said, and she took the file from the farm and dropped it onto Chapman's desk. "Some light reading for you. Do a background check on everyone inside that folder for me, would you, Chapman?"

"Yep, sure. Are we looking for anything in particular?"

"Criminal records would be a good start," Freya said.

"Time served," Ben added, and Freya turned to him, eyebrows raised in question. "I think that we should consider the prospect of Tommy Dean dying before John Tyler."

Freya considered the idea and then held the board marker out for him.

"Show me how that would work," she said.

He stood, walked across the room, and took the pen from her. At the left of the line, he placed an *X*, as she had. Above it, he wrote TD death. Between that and *John Tyler death*, which Freya had already written in the centre of the board, he made another mark.

"TD is taken to house," he said, narrating as he wrote, just as Freya often did. He then moved on to Freya's writing. "John Tyler death." He then moved across the board, making more marks as he went. "Boy finds body. Body buried. Boy calls 999. We arrive. No body."

Freya nodded slowly.

"In which case, is it plausible that John Tyler killed Tommy Dean?" she asked.

"Entirely," he said.

"And as a result, somebody killed John Tyler?"

"Again, it's plausible."

"Except that John Tyler's death was considered. The theory doesn't stack up with the MOs. If somebody murdered John Tyler out of revenge because he killed Tommy Dean, then surely, they wouldn't have gone to the trouble of hanging him and burning him. It would have been emotional. Reactive."

"I'm just saying we can't rule it out," he said, then moved over to the list of names they had on the board and added Julie Dean's name. "Geoff Godolphin. He's the only one we know that had the same tattoo—"

"And he bloody lied to us about knowing Tommy Dean," Gillespie added.

"Right, so he knows something or at least suspects something."

"Or he's guilty of something," Gillespie cut in again.

"Let's keep an open mind, shall we, Jim?" Ben said, tapping the next two names on the board. "Frank Bowen, previously investigated for murder, found not guilty."

"We're not supposed to let previous investigations cloud our judgement," Freya said.

"But we do," he countered. "We just can't reference it as evidence when we hand the case over to the CPS." He looked up to the board. "Both him and Julie Dean have conflicting stories about why Tommy Dean left the job. She, as you rightly said, Freya, claims not to recognise John Tyler."

"To be fair, I doubt his own mother would have recognised him," Gillespie said. "With his tongue hanging out and his face all swollen."

"Anyone else?" Ben asked. "Any more suspects?"

"Not unless Chapman discovers Fred West in Frank Bowen's employee records," Freya replied.

"So, let's agree on a theory," Ben said. "If Tommy Dean died first, there's a good chance that John Tyler killed him and was then killed as a result. But if John Tyler died first, then there's a good chance that Tommy Dean killed him—"

"And died as a result," Freya finished, nodding. "Yes. I think if anybody is going to seek justice for Tommy Dean, then it's his wife."

"And if anybody is going to seek justice for John Tyler?" Ben asked. "Who loved John Tyler enough to kill for him?"

"The Halls?" Gillespie suggested. "They were his only family, albeit adopted. I mean, Mrs Hall is quite frail and soft, but the fella? He would have been capable."

"If we're venturing down that route," Nillson added. "Presumably, Godolphin knew them both."

"Right," Ben said. "So, what we're saying is that either John Tyler killed Tommy Dean or Tommy Dean killed John Tyler, and subsequently, either Julie Dean killed John Tyler for murdering her husband, or Mr Hall killed Tommy Dean for murdering John Tyler."

"Or Godolphin killed whichever one of them killed the other," Gillespie added, smiling at the confusion.

"I think it's time we nailed this timeline," Freya said, singling out Cruz and Gillespie. She checked her watch. "Call me as soon as you have a time of death."

They both stood, grabbed their things, and started towards the door, and as a final taunt, Nillson made a show of stretching and yawning as Gillespie passed her.

"Who do you think died first?" Ben muttered so that only Freya could hear him.

"John Tyler," she said. "You?"

"Tommy Dean," he said, and she glanced up at him curiously. "Double or nothing?"

CHAPTER THIRTY-SEVEN

"Ah, Christ, I hate this," Gillespie said. They came to a stop at the mortuary doors, both him and Cruz unwilling to reach up and push the buzzer. "I think the best thing to do is just stay professional. Say nothing unless it's about the body. We want the time of death, the cause of death if she can, and nothing more. Let's get in and out before she has a chance to accuse us of anything."

"Agreed," Cruz said. "Although I quite like her."

"Eh? Pippa Bell?" he said. "You like Pippa Bell?"

"Yeah, she's alright. I mean, she's a bit of a nutter."

"A bit?"

"Yeah, but you know. She's alright. She's harmless, really."

"Harmless, aye. Like barbed wire or a landmine?" Gillespie replied as he pushed the buzzer. He stepped back and looked down at Cruz. "In and out, remember?"

"In and out," Cruz confirmed.

The lock turned, and Gillespie braced himself. But to his surprise, it wasn't Pippa Bell who opened the door; it was a bloke. He wore a similar smock to those that Pippa Bell always wore, but in place of Crocs, he had what looked to be white plimsolls on.

There were no tattoos, no piercings, and his hair was parted to one side. If anything, he looked on the nerdy side, like somebody Gillespie would avoid at a party, but compared to being faced with Pippa Bell's scowl, he'd take that.

"Help you?" he asked, his voice matching his appearance in tone and colour.

"DS Gillespie," Gillespie replied. "This is DC Cruz. We're booked in for a PM. I called yesterday—"

"Ah," he said cheerfully. "Come on in."

"You new?" Gillespie asked as they pushed into the little reception. He tapped Cruz's shoulder, pointed at the cupboard where the PPE was kept, and then waited for the man to answer.

"I'm a locum. Just waiting for a permanent position. Somebody up high thought it would be a good idea if I help out here for a while to give Doctor Bell a break." He opened the insulated doors to the mortuary. "I'll see you inside."

"I tell you what," Gillespie called out, pulling his gown on. "You're a sight for sore eyes. Thought we'd have to deal with Pippa for a wee while, didn't we, Gabs, eh?"

"We did," Cruz said with very little enthusiasm.

"Thought we'd have the old Welsh dragon breathing down our necks, eh? Meet her yet, did you? Right piece of work, that one, I tell you. You know, this one time, the daft cow—"

A shadow formed on the floor by the man's feet, growing in length by the second. Gillespie eyed it, then watched as a plump hand gripped the door Andrew was holding and opened it fully.

Pippa Bell stepped into view wearing what Gillespie could only describe as hell on her face. It was as if she had just woken up from a century-long slumber and had yet to have a coffee.

"Sergeant Gillespie," she said, that Welsh accent of hers squeezing every torturous drop from every syllable.

"Doctor Bell," he said. "What a nice surprise. I was just saying to, erm..."

"Andrew," the man said.

"Aye. Andrew. I was just telling him about…" his voice trailed off, and he swiped the air with his hand. "Ah, what does it matter? Shall we get started?"

"No, go on," she said. "I'd like to hear it."

"Hear it?"

"What you were going to say," she said. "The part about the dragon. Go on. I'm sure Andrew would love to hear it, too. Isn't that right, Andrew?"

"Ah, well," he said, making a show of checking his watch. "We really should—"

"Tell me," she said, raising her voice. "Tell me what you were going to say. Come on. You've started now. You might as well finish. I want to hear all about this dragon you spoke of."

"The dragon?"

"The dragon," she replied, and Gillespie sought support from Cruz, who seemed to be enjoying every moment of his agony.

"Aye, well," he began, looking at Andrew. "I mean, have you met her yet? My boss. Our boss, that is. Freya Bloom, or DCI Bloom, I should say. About so high…" he held his hand up to shoulder height. "Blonde with a wee touch of red—"

"He's met Freya," Pip said.

"Aye, well. You'll know what I mean then, eh? Right piece of work, that one. I mean, I could go on. I could tell you some stories, eh? Believe me…" He let the statement fade and eyed Pip for some sign that she had fallen for what he had said. She gave nothing away. Instead, she just watched him, her left eye narrowing as she took every movement he made and every noise that spilt from his lying lips.

"He's inside," she said, leaving him with a final glare. Andrew followed, and Gillespie let a long breath escape.

"Jesus," he hissed at Cruz. "You could have backed me up."

"I know," Cruz replied as he edged past him. He stopped for a moment in the doorway and looked back at Gillespie. "But I was having so much fun."

It was as if Pip had known it would be Gillespie and Cruz attending the post-mortem and had decided on the path she would take, even before Gillespie's faux pas. The body was laid out on the gurney as it usually was, but instead of being covered with a sheet, which was her usual practice, she had removed it entirely and had even opened the chest cavity with the Y-shaped incisions. On the little trolley between her and Andrew were several stainless-steel dishes, each one containing what looked to be organs of some description.

"Christ," he muttered. "You don't hang about, Pip." He turned to Cruz, whose mask inflated and deflated with his deep breaths.

"His wife is coming in a few hours," she told him. "We've got to get this done, put him back together and clean him before then. Unless you want her to see him like this?"

"Nobody needs to see him like this," he replied. "Least of all her."

"Well then," she said. "Cause of death? Blunt force trauma. There's some swelling to his skull, which is fractured as a result." She used a pen from her pocket to highlight the area in question, but there was little need. A three-inch gash in the man's hairline and skin revealed everything Gillespie could have done without seeing before lunch.

"Weapon?" he asked. "Any ideas?"

"Buried, wasn't he?" she asked.

"He was," he replied, to which she nodded knowingly.

"Andrew?" she said, then invited him to take over with a sweep of her hand.

"Yes, I'm sure," he said casually. "Doctor Bell and I are both of the opinion that he was hit with a large, flat object with a keen edge."

"A what?"

"A spade," he said. "Or a shovel, of course. It's hard to be sure, but what we can see, if you look closely..." he reached up for the overhead light and pulled it into position, "is a slight grazing on one side of the wound."

"A grazing?" Cruz said, leaning in for a better look.

Andrew straightened, then waited for them both to do the same.

"Imagine if I hit him with a...I don't know, a baseball bat."

"Aye?" Gillespie said.

"A bat is curved. The point of impact would be fairly even. Whereas imagine if somebody were to swing a spade or a shovel. The sharp part of the weapon would graze the wound a fraction before the point of impact. Does that make sense?"

"Aye, it does. But, I mean, we could be talking about anything with a flat surface here. An iron, a golf club, he could even have whacked his head on a table." He felt the edge of the gurney as if to make his point.

"Was there a table or a gurney at the crime scene?"

"Well, no, but there was no spade either—"

"Was there a hole?"

"Alright, I hear you," Gillespie replied, knowing when he was beaten. "You're sure, are you? I mean, I don't want to have to go back to the boss with another theory. We've enough of those already. She needs facts."

"Of course she does," Pip said. "I mean, you wouldn't want to wake the dragon, would you?"

She stared at Gillespie, and her crow's feet deepened as she smiled under her mask.

"We also have some soil samples taken from the grazes," Andrew said. "In addition to that, we can also tell you which way the spade or shovel was travelling due to the damaged blood vessels to one side of the wound."

"Go on," Gillespie said, intrigued.

"Well, we believe he was much lower than the killer, perhaps on his hands and knees. The killer brought the weapon down in a diagonal motion, like so," he said, mimicking the action. Then he stopped and, as if to accentuate the brutality of the attack, added a single word. "Twice."

"Twice?"

"Two grazes," he said. "One fracture. The second blow finished him off."

"Bad day for him then, eh?"

"It was a bad day," Andrew continued. "Before he endured the final blows, he also suffered part strangulation, plus some fairly significant blows to his body. Three broken ribs, two broken fingers, a punctured lung, and if you look here." He highlighted the victim's midriff. "A small stab wound."

"A stab wound?"

"Nothing major. But he would have lost blood."

The wound was less than half an inch across but was clear as day in the bright light.

"Screwdriver?" Cruz suggested.

"Possibly," Andrew replied. "More than likely, in fact, given the shape of the entry point. A flat-headed driver, driven in a few inches."

"Christ," Gillespie said, nodding. "Alright, I suppose all this will be in your report, aye?"

"It will. I'll send it to your office," Pip said. "I'll make it out to the dragon, shall I?"

She watched him for a reaction, but he brushed the comment to one side and focused on Andrew.

"Time of death?" Gillespie asked. "Any ideas?"

"Hard to say for sure—"

"I imagine you want to know if he died before or after the other one, do you?" Pip cut in before Andrew could finish.

"Aye, it's kind of a key part of the investigation," Gillespie replied. "We've a couple of potential leads, but it depends on when he died as to which one we press on with."

"I see," she said again before Andrew could intervene. "The other one died on Saturday night. Is that right?"

"Aye, it is."

She looked up at Andrew as if conferring silently, but it was all a ploy to wind Gillespie up, and he supposed he deserved it.

"And knowing your team, some of you think this one died first, and some of you think the other one died first. Right, am I?"

"You are," he said, making no attempt to hide his boredom. "What do you want from me, Pip, eh?"

"And which side of the fence do you sit on, Sergeant Gillespie?" she asked. "Do you think he died first or second?"

"I think we should—" Andrew started but silenced as soon as Pip raised a plump digit.

"First or second, Sergeant?" she teased. "I'll tell you if you're right or wrong."

CHAPTER THIRTY-EIGHT

THE SCHOOL that Chapman had sent them to was on a side street in Tattershall, and as far as schools went, there was very little out of the ordinary about it. The road outside was marked with yellow lines to prevent parents from blocking the main thorough-fare during drop-off and collection times, and seeing as the car park gates were closed for security purposes, they had to find a street to park and finish the journey on foot.

"How do you think they're getting on?" Ben asked, not that the question needed answering. He was more interested in seeing if Freya's mood had abated or if the eggshells she was expecting him to walk would cut into his feet.

She checked her watch.

"Well, it's ten-thirty," she replied, offering no indication as to her mood. "I'd hope they'll be finishing up soon. Pip will need some time to get him ready, I imagine. Cruz will need a few minutes to stop laughing, and Gillespie will need a corner in which he can hide away and lick his wounds."

"She'll eat him alive," he said. "Is that what you're saying?"

"Ben, she eats you alive, and you're one of the mildest-mannered men I've ever come across."

"Oh? Is that a compliment?"

"No," she said as they crossed the main road. "It's an observation."

The statement was curt, leaving Ben in the dark, so he pressed on regardless. There was very little to gain from hounding her. She would either come around or she wouldn't.

The pedestrian gate was unlocked, and as they made their way towards the main entrance, Freya seemed preoccupied with her phone.

"News from Gillespie?" he asked.

"No," she replied distractedly. "Nothing yet."

"Well, no news is good news," he replied as he pressed the buzzer to gain entry. "Amazing, isn't it? This place is as secure as the station. The kids can't get out, and we can't get in. In my day, anybody could have walked in, and they did, too."

"The times are changing, Ben," she said, dialling a number on her phone.

"Reception," the tinny voice said from the speaker on the wall.

"Hello, I'm Detective Inspector Savage. I'm with Lincolnshire Police. Here to see the head."

"The police? Do you have an appointment?"

"We rather hoped we could cut in between meetings," Freya called out. "It's regarding a serious incident."

The lock buzzed, the electromagnet released, and Ben held the door for Freya, then followed. They came to a little window in the wall, beyond which a pretty receptionist peered up at them quizzically.

"I'll just need you to sign in," she told them, sliding a pen through to them along with two visitor passes on blue lanyards. Then she snatched up her desk phone, hit a speed dial button, and mouthed to them to show their IDs.

They both held their warrant cards up for her to see while she spoke.

"Sorry to bother you, Mariam," she began. "I've got the police here." She leaned forward to read their names. "A Detective Chief Inspector Bloom and a Detective Inspector Savage. They said they need a word with you." She silenced, presumably while the head asked questions. "I don't know," she said. "Something serious, I think."

"We just need ten minutes," Freya assured her.

"They said they just need—" She silenced again and nodded as she listened before replacing the handset.

"You can go through," she told Ben and Freya, gesturing at the doors to their right. "Up the corridor on your left, second door on the right."

She reached beneath her desk, and the doors to their right buzzed.

"Thank you," Ben said, seeing as Freya had clearly left her manners at home. He followed her through the doors, where they found a stout-looking woman heading directly towards them. "Here we go."

"Hello?" she said as she closed in. She held out a hand for Freya to shake and then moved on to Ben. "I'm Mrs Jacobson. Is there a problem?"

"Actually, we are wondering if we could have a word with one of your pupils and possibly his friends," Freya said.

"Who? Which ones?"

"A Liam Jackson," Freya said. "I was led to believe he attends this school."

"He does," Mrs Jacobson replied. "But I must say, I find it hard to believe that he's caused any trouble. He's a quiet boy."

"He's not in any trouble," Freya assured her. "None of them are. "Does he have any friends? A Benjamin Godolphin, maybe?"

"Benjamin," she said, nodding. "Benjamin Godolphin, but again, they're both well-mannered boys."

"Anybody else?" Freya asked. "Or are they a well-mannered duo? I was led to believe there's a boy named Henry."

"That's right," Mrs Jacobson replied. "That's the threesome."

She peered past Ben to the receptionist, who had evidently chosen to perform some tasks or other at the end of the reception office nearest to where they were standing. "Samantha, would you mind sending somebody to fetch them?"

"Fetch who, Mariam?" The receptionist replied, feigning no knowledge.

"You know very well who," Mrs Jacobson replied, smiling up at Freya. "And if you could arrange for some tea. We'll be in my office. Thank you, Samantha."

She spoke exactly as Ben expected a head teacher to speak. It was a derogatory tone that she used, and the way she drew out the final words of each sentence.

She led them to her office, invited them to sit, and took her own seat, making a show of closing all the open windows on her PC screen, presumably for the purposes of GDPR or safeguarding.

"I'm terribly sorry about this," Freya said. "Just to give you a bit of background, we're investigating a serious incident that took place not far from here, and we believe one or more of the boys might have seen something."

Mrs Jacobson was sharper than most. She listened intently, and behind those intelligent eyes, her mind whirred.

"Presumably, it's easier to speak to them here, as a collective, rather than at home, where their parents might make that more difficult?"

"My thoughts entirely," Freya replied. "We have spoken to one of the fathers, and by all accounts, he's...disinclined to help us for one reason or another."

"I understand," she said. "I'll need to be here. I hope that's okay. I can't leave you alone with them. To be honest, we should make a record of this."

"Oh, I'd prefer it if you stayed, and it's an informal chat, that's all," Freya told her, just as there was a knock on the door. The receptionist came first, placing a tray on the desk. She straightened, then turned to the open door.

"Come on," she said. "In you come."

"Thank you, Samantha," Mrs Jacobson said, and she smiled politely offering more than a hint that the receptionist's presence was superfluous to requirements.

The three boys were nothing short of ordinary prepubescent lads, no different to how Ben was when he was their age. Their ties had been tied but either hung at jaunty angles or had yet to be pulled to the collar. In Ben's day, he mused, they stuffed the tie between the top two buttons so that only the knot showed, preventing that annoying habit school friends had of peanutting, which involved somebody yanking the tie hard so that the knot grew so tight that at times, it had to be cut off.

"Hello," Freya said to the boys. "Before I begin, I want to assure you that there's absolutely nothing to worry about. None of you are in any trouble. In fact, we were hoping you could help us."

The three lads exchanged glances and sought some kind of feedback from Mrs Jacobson.

"Relax," the head said as she poured three cups of tea. "Detective Chief Inspector Bloom here just needs to ask you a few questions, and in case you're worried about what your parents might say, I can assure you I'll remain here. So, there's nothing to worry about, okay?"

"Miss," one of them said by way of confirmation.

"Now," Freya said, clapping once. "Which one of you is Liam?"

The two boys on the ends looked to the boy in the centre, who slowly raised his hand.

"Me, miss."

"Thank you. I understand you spoke to one of my team earlier this week. A tall Scottish man?"

"That's right."

"And you told him that the three of you were at your house playing on your computer on Sunday. Is that right?"

"Yes, miss."

Freya winced at the salutation but let it go, presumably for the purposes of momentum.

"And do we have a Gopher?" she said, and the boy on the left raised his hand.

"Me, miss," he said quietly.

"Can I call you Ben?" She asked, to which he nodded. "I understand you have also spoken to one of my team. The same man, in fact."

"That's right, miss. He came to our house. Spoke to me dad."

"And as I understand it, your father explained that you aren't allowed beyond the bridge at the end of Tattershall without his consent. Is that right?"

"S'right, miss."

"Thank you," Freya said. "Which leaves you, Henry, is it?" she said to the last boy, whose throat rose and fell with anticipation.

"Don't worry," Freya said, smiling at them all. "We're investigating a rather serious incident that took place not far from your homes at the weekend."

"It weren't us, miss," Gopher said. "We were at Liam's house."

"As you explained," she replied. "But isn't Liam's house on the other side of the bridge, all the way up in Billinghay?"

The boy paled.

"You won't tell my dad, will you?" he said. "We didn't do nothing—"

"I'm quite sure that part of the tale can be kept between us," Freya said, and Ben mused on how easy life would be if everyone they interviewed could hand over their trust so effortlessly. "We did, however, receive a call to the emergency services on Sunday night, at approximately nine-fifty p.m." She left those words hanging for a moment to gauge their expressions. If she identified any telling signs, then she was better than Ben, who saw absolutely no shift in their faces at all. "The call came from a boy around your age. He was on a main road, but sadly, he left no name."

"I was in bed," Henry said.

"Yeah, me too. We had school on Monday."

Freya raised a hand to stop the alibis from coming.

She eyed them all curiously.

"So, neither of you made the call. Is that right?"

They looked at each other, each one shaking their head with vehemence.

Freya plucked her phone from her pocket, but Ben couldn't quite see what she was doing.

And then it made sense.

A gentle buzzing came from one of the school bags, and the boy named Gopher closed his eyes.

"Is that yours, Benjamin?" she asked, gesturing at the offending bag on the floor by their feet.

He nodded, and his face turned plum red.

Freya held her phone up for them to see.

"Do you know what number I'm calling?" she asked, then before either of them could answer, she continued. "I'm calling the number that made the call to emergency services, stating that the caller had discovered the body of a man at an abandoned farmhouse in Billinghay."

A look of utter surprise came over his friends' faces as they put the pieces together, and before either of them could berate Gopher for his betrayal, Freya continued.

"Did you make that call, Benjamin?" she asked. Avoiding his friends, he stared at the floor and nodded. "I think you have some explaining to do, don't you?"

CHAPTER THIRTY-NINE

THE NOISE of a phone ringing sang through Gillespie's car speakers, much as it had for the past fifteen minutes.

"Still not answering, then?" Cruz said from the passenger seat.

"Aye, Gabby. He answered. Didn't you hear him? We had a wee chat about the weather, and I went into detail about how the lad died."

"Alright, there's no need for sarcasm," Cruz replied, turning his face away. "Why don't you try the boss? I mean, if Ben isn't answering, maybe she will."

"Not on your Nelly, Gabster. It's bad enough that I've been burned by one dragon this morning, let alone invite another to torch my backside," Gillespie said. "No, he'll call back. I expect he's just busy."

"The boss won't like it," Cruz said as they pulled into the familiar street and stopped outside the familiar house with the familiar walled garden and gravelled driveway. "She said to call as soon as we left."

"Aye, well," he said. "Maybe you should call her then."

"Eh? Me? You're the bloody Sergeant."

"Ah, see? Not so full of it now, are you?"

"If I was in charge, then I'd call her," Cruz said. "What's the worst she can do on the other end of the phone? Besides, it's not like we're calling with bad news, is it?"

"It doesn't matter what news we're delivering, Gabs. It's the tasks she sets us when we're done delivering said news."

"Eh?"

Gillespie sighed and settled into his seat.

"Look, the way I see it, we know the order of events, and we're able to pursue a line of enquiry as per her original instructions."

"Which was?"

"To investigate John Tyler's death, Gabby. Come on, wake up, will you? If we call her with the news, she'll then no doubt dream up some grand plan, of which I can guarantee you this: we, namely you and I, Gabby, will be on the receiving end of the short stick."

"I don't get it."

"She'll give us all the crap," he said. "Knocking on doors or something equally as mind-numbing."

"So why call Ben?"

"I was calling Ben so that I could fulfil my obligations to deliver the news and make a sharp getaway before the boss gets wind of it and puts us onto something else." He straightened in his seat and tugged his collar into shape. "He's got five missed calls from me. He'll call back. In the meantime, it's down to you and me to continue investigating John Tyler's murder."

He nodded at the big house, and Cruz shook his head in dismay.

"This is typical of you, Jim. You try to outthink everyone, and it nearly always backfires. Just call her. If she assigns us another duty, then so what? At least we won't land ourselves in bother."

"Ah, Gabby. You'll get nowhere with that attitude," Gillespie told him as he shoved the car door open.

"Because you've climbed to the top of the ladder, haven't you?" Cruz replied, joining him on the driveway. "Sergeant Gillespie."

"Aye, well. It's not about rank," he said. "It's about vision." He spread his hands before him. "If you can see where you want to be, if you can manifest it, you'll get there. It might take a lifetime, Gabs, but you'll get there. The point is to never stop trying."

"Right," Cruz said, sounding less than convinced. "And where is it exactly that you want to be?"

They climbed the steps, and Gillespie reached up for the ancient doorbell.

"I don't know, really," he said. "I've never thought about it."

The lock turned, and the door opened, and standing before them was Mr Hall, who clearly recognised them in an instant.

"Can I help?" he said.

"Aye, do you remember us, Mr Hall?" Gillespie asked, displaying his warrant card for good measure.

"How could I ever forget?" he replied, seemingly astonished that Gillespie should even feel the need to ask.

"I appreciate it's not a good time, Mr Hall," Gillespie continued. "We've a few questions we need to ask you. Relating to...well, you know."

Hall glanced over his shoulder, stepped out of the front door, and held it closed behind him.

"It's not really a good time," he said quietly. "It's my wife, you see? She's taken it quite badly."

"I'm sure," Gillespie said. "And I realise how difficult this must be, but, well, without putting too fine a point on it, this is a murder investigation. If we're to get to the bottom of why and how your son died, Mr Hall, we need to move fast. The first twenty-four hours were critical, but I'm afraid they've been and gone. The longer it takes, I mean statistically speaking, the poorer our chances." He watched the man digest the information. "It would be a great help."

"So, it's him, is it?" he said softly.

"It's not been formally confirmed yet, but for the purposes of expedience, we're pressing on. There's no time to lose, Mr Hall, as you can imagine."

"Alright," he said eventually, and he reached into the house, grabbed a cardigan that was hanging close to the door, and joined them outside, tugging the front door closed behind him. "We can walk in the gardens. She's having a lay down, so I can give you five or ten minutes."

"I'm grateful, Mr Hall," Gillespie said, and he let the homeowner lead the way.

"You've got a wonderful garden," Cruz said, to which Hall smiled a brief thanks, but hadn't the composure to show his full appreciation.

"It's a necessity more than a passion," he said, then embellished his statement. "My doctor recommends it. High blood pressure, you see?"

"Ah," Cruz said knowingly. "They say gardening is good for the soul, don't they?"

"What is it you need to know?" he asked, clearly unwilling to waste time discussing the merits of gardening. "Have you any idea who might have done this yet?"

"We've some leads we're following up on, but..." Gillespie stopped and waited for Hall to follow suit.

"But?"

"I'm sorry. Please don't take this the wrong way, but in order for us to progress, we need to build a picture of the night in question."

"The night in question? I'm not following."

"We need to understand the whereabouts of everyone who was close to John."

"Excuse me—"

"I know, it's never an easy topic to broach, but we need to broach it nonetheless, Mr Hall. You see, if we fail to supply the CPS...that is, the Crown Prosecution Service, with every detail, if and when we charge somebody, their defence team will highlight the fact that we failed to undertake a thorough investigation. They'd suggest to the jury that there's plausible doubt that the defendant is guilty." Gillespie shook his head but held the older man's gaze. "It's a terrible thing, Mr Hall. What happened, I mean. And what follows is...well, it does little to ease things or help you grieve. But we need to know, Mr Hall. If you were home, then that's fine. If you can vouch for your wife, and your wife can vouch for you, then great. That's all we need to know."

Hall bit his lower lip so hard that his entire lower jaw seemed to tremble with anger. His nostrils flared, and his chest filled.

Then, those early indicators of a forthcoming torrent of verbal abuse faded. His lower lip protruded as he seemed to suck on the inside in thought, and eventually, he nodded once.

"I see," he said. "Well, like you said, we were here."

"All night?" Gillespie asked. "Sunday evening? You were both here, were you?"

"We were," he said.

"And would your wife, if we asked her at some point in the future, agree?"

"Listen to me, son," Hall said, his voice lowering in warning. "If you come anywhere near my wife again, I'll make sure you're back in uniform and walking the streets. Do you understand? She's frail. She doesn't need to hear any of this. If I tell you we were both here, then we were. You can take my word for it. Write it down if you need to. But you don't talk to my wife. Not ever."

Cruz's questioning glare burned into Gillespie's temple, and he met it briefly to put his mind at ease.

"Thank you, Mr Hall," Gillespie said. "For making your position ever so clear."

"S'alright," he replied. "Now then. Is that it?"

"Actually, no," Gillespie said. "There was something else that was on my mind."

"Go on?" Hall replied as a message came through on Gillespie's phone. He glanced down to read it. "She'll be wondering where I am," Hall said, urging him to hurry up.

"Sorry," he said, pocketing his phone. "I was just wondering when you last saw John. When was he last here?"

Hall shrugged and peered around his garden, perhaps for distraction.

"We haven't seen John for some time."

"Weeks?" Gillespie asked. "Or months?"

"Years," Hall said, his eyes burning red.

"Years?" Gillespie said far too loud, and Hall looked up at the upstairs windows to make sure his wife hadn't heard. "Does that not strike you as odd?"

"It's not a topic I'm comfortable discussing, Sergeant..."

"Gillespie," Gillespie said. "I'm sorry, but I find it odd that a man who lost everyone he ever loved should shun, for want of a better word, the very people that took care of him." Gillespie posed the question and then adjusted his position to stand before the man, giving him little else to look at but his inquisitive face. "Now, why would that be, Mr Hall?"

CHAPTER FORTY

IT WAS as if Benjamin Godolphin had studied the behaviour of guilty children and had practised well. He stared at the floor, his foot working a hole into the drab and already worn carpet, while his two red-faced friends appeared to communicate through various alarmed expressions.

"I'll reiterate my previous point," Freya said. "None of you are in any trouble." The boys remained silent, most likely, Freya thought, while they concocted some kind of fabrication of the truth. "Now," she continued, "I'm going to give you a version of events. Once I'm done, I'll ask each of you to either confirm if I'm right or if I'm wrong in any part." She spoke quietly, well aware that tone was everything, and the audience in question was not a great ape, like Gillespie. It was three boys who had, most likely, seen something each of them would carry for the rest of their days. "I believe that for one reason or another, either you, Benjamin, or the three of you, were at Brinkleview Farm on Sunday. Judging by the guilty looks on your faces, Liam and Henry, I would hazard a guess that the three of you were there. For one reason or another, you entered the old farmhouse where you made a certain discovery."

It was the word 'discovery' that instigated the strongest reaction. Benjamin raised his head and looked up at the ceiling; Henry peered along the line at him while Liam simply bit his lower lip in anticipation.

Had a jury witnessed the reaction, there would be little need for the prosecution to say anything further.

"Now," Freya continued, "I was once young, like you, and I also kept secrets with my friends, so I do realise what is at stake here, but believe me when I tell you that this is serious beyond the wrath of your father, Benjamin. I think you know what I'm talking about, and we'll come to that in a moment. Before then, I'd like to understand the sequence of events."

"The what?" Henry asked.

"The sequence of events," Mrs Jacobson replied. "The order in which the events took place."

"Thank you," Freya told her, regaining control. "I believe you three argued somewhat. Am I right? Did you argue about whether or not you should tell anybody about what you saw?" The boys remained silent, none of them wishing to be the one who spoke first, but when they did, Freya was sure they would build momentum. It was a case of removing the little boy's finger from the dam. "In the end, you agreed that, for fear of your parents finding out where you had been, you should keep quiet and hope that the problem would go away by itself. However, at nine-fifty p.m. on Sunday night, you, Benjamin, were overcome with guilt. You made the call, and rightly so, I should add." She sat back in her seat and appraised them fully. "Now, how accurate is my theory?" she asked.

Benjamin shrugged and looked to Henry, who in turn looked across at Liam. Eventually, he turned to Freya.

"Yeah, it's pretty much right," he said, to which Freya smiled.

"You left your house, presumably to avoid your father overhearing," Freya said. "And you made the call from the main road? Is that right?"

Again, he shrugged.

"Dad weren't home," he said. "He popped out. I was in bed, and I heard him leave. The front door woke me up. It bangs, like."

"And does your father often leave you alone in the house?"

"No," he said. "I thought he might have a girlfriend or something. He popped out the night before, an' all."

"I see."

"But..." he hesitated and again gave his friends an apologetic look. "I've seen it on the telly. I thought that you lot could trace the call, and the last thing I wanted was for...well, you know?"

"For us lot to come knocking?" she replied. "I see you've inherited your father's distrust of the police, Benjamin."

"It's not that. It's just...I don't know. People talk, don't they? He don't want..."

"Us lot?"

"Right. He don't want you knocking on the door. He worries what the neighbours will think."

"Okay, that's fair," Freya told him. "But perhaps we can go back a few steps. Why were you at the farm? What time did you get there?"

"Most of the day," Benjamin said. "We went out in the morning, and I don't know, we just messed about."

"And this messing about led you to the old farmhouse, did it?"

"No," Benjamin said. "No, we were out in the fields. It's just that, well, old Sid James was out. We saw his tractor."

"Sid James?"

"The farmer," Benjamin said. "That's not his real name. My old man calls him it. I think he was an actor or something. Had a wrinkly face."

"That's right," Freya replied. "He was very popular in the sixties and seventies, I think. Do you know the farmer's name? His real name, I mean."

"Yeah, it's Frank something."

"Bowen," Liam cut in. "Frank Bowen."

"And you believe that he wouldn't have been happy about seeing you three in his field? Is that right?"

Benjamin nodded.

"Why is that, do you think?"

"Cause he's a miserable old—"

"Liam!" Mrs Jacobson cut in before he could finish his sentence.

"How would you know? Have you had previous encounters with him? Is this some kind of ongoing saga in which you tease him, and he chases you?"

"No," Benjamin said. "No, it's nothing like that. Everyone knows what he's like. He's just a bit...well, grumpy, that's all."

"Yeah, and he'd probably tell our parents," Henry added.

"So, none of you are allowed over there? It's not just Benjamin's dad. It's all of your parents, is it?"

Liam nodded.

"My mum reckons he did something years ago. She never said what, but always tells me to steer clear of the place, but how can we do that? His farm is massive. It's the only place to go except the woods, and the only way to get there is to walk through the farm."

"It's okay," Freya said, holding her hand up to calm him. "Nobody is in any bother here, but I am keen to understand if all of your parents have the same distrust of Frank Bowen, and if so, is it for the same reason?"

"Pretty much," Benjamin said, and he looked at Henry who nodded his agreement.

"Is it true then, miss?" Liam asked. "Did he do something?"

"Not to my knowledge," she replied as honestly as she could. "And I'm not about to say anything in contrast to your parents' wishes. If they tell you to steer clear, then I think you should do exactly that in the future. Although, I dare say you won't be venturing over to the farm anytime soon."

"Not likely," Liam muttered.

"So, if you can help me some more," Freya said. "What time was it that you entered the old house?"

Benjamin offered the shrug he had called upon so many times already.

"Dunno," he said. "Late afternoon, I suppose. I was home by six, and it's about a forty-five-minute walk from Liam's house, which is near to the top of Labour in Vain Drove, where the house is. So, what? Five-ish? Something like that."

"Thank you," Freya said. "And now for the sensitive part. Now, I know what you saw, and for what it's worth, I'm sorry you had to see it."

"What was it?" Mrs Jacobson asked. "What did they see?"

Freya turned to her and hoped her expression suggested patience. She would find out soon enough.

"It was a bloke," Liam said, and he stared at Freya. "He was dead."

"Oh my—" Mrs Jacobson started, but Freya intervened before her hysteria became contagious.

"May I ask how you know he was dead?" she asked the boys, Liam in particular, who adopted a surprised expression, nodding fearfully.

"Well," he started, "he had a bloody—"

"Liam, I've warned you once about your language," Mrs Jacobson said.

"Sorry, miss," he told her, then looked sheepishly at Freya. "He had a gash in his head and was as white as that piece of paper there." He pointed to Mrs Jacobson's desk, on which was a stack of A4 papers.

"And did you make any attempts to check?" Freya asked tentatively."

"Sod that," Liam said.

"Mr Jackson—"

"It's fine," Freya said, settling Mrs Jacobson. "Really, I think in the circumstances we should let the truth out, unfiltered.

These boys have witnessed something quite traumatic, and I'd hate for our presence here to have a negative effect on their wellbeing."

"Well, yes," she replied. "When you put it like that."

"Go on," Freya told Liam. "In your own words."

"Well, that was it, really," he said. "We ran into the house, ducked behind the wall and peered out of the living room window."

"Checking for Frank Bowen."

"Right," he said. "We heard his tractor, so he must have seen us. Then, when the tractor got close, we ducked down out of sight." He licked his lips, and his unblinking eyes found Freya's. "That was when we saw it."

"And what did you do?" she asked. "What did you do when you saw it."

"Legged it, miss," he said. "Sod Bowen. We just ran and didn't look back."

"Is that accurate?" she asked the other two, who nodded sincerely.

"We ran to the top of the lane. Gopher...I mean, Benjamin had to go right to his house, and me and Henry had to go left. Henry lives over the river, see?"

"Thank you," Freya said warmly.

"So, I suppose that's when we argued about what we saw. Gopher...sorry. Benjamin wanted to call 999, but...well, Henry and me, we thought it best to just keep quiet."

"Because of your parents?" Freya asked.

"Yeah," he said, glancing across at Henry, the shortest but heaviest of the three. "Ain't that right, Henry?"

"Yeah," he said but sounded more than a little unconvincing to Freya.

"Thank you, boys," she said. "You've been a great help, and if I can, no promises, but if I can, I'll try to keep you from further questioning. But no promises, okay?"

"Cheers, miss," Liam said, and they each looked to Mrs Jacobson for permission to leave.

"Go on," she said. "Straight back to class with you."

"There is one more thing I'd like to understand," Ben cut in. He'd been quiet during the entire interview, presumably not to overwhelm the boys. But he spoke now, and the boys stopped, turned and waited in a state of pensive anticipation. "I want you to think clearly and be honest with me. This is important."

With their rush for freedom paused, the boys stood wide-eyed, while Ben considered his next statement.

"What is it, sir?" Liam asked.

"I want to know if, when you saw the man," Ben started, "any of you recognised him?"

Liam, whose voice had been loudest during the interview was brazen in his response, and shook his head, turning his nose as if a bad smell had crept in.

Benjamin, who had been slightly more apprehensive, also shook his head.

"No, sir," he said.

But it was the quietest of the three who grabbed Freya's attention. Henry. He neither shrugged, shook his head, nor said anything to indicate a response one way or another. It was the pale colour of his skin and terrified expression that said everything Freya needed to know.

"Is there something you want to tell us, Henry?" Ben asked, his eyes narrowing as he appraised the young boy. "Did you recognise him? Henry? Do you know who he was?"

CHAPTER FORTY-ONE

"OH, WHAT DO WE HAVE HERE?" Freya said as she navigated her car through the various parked liveried police cars, Nillson's car, and one more, which was an old Volvo estate with a coffee cup wedged between the windscreen and the dashboard. "I wondered when we'd hear from him." She checked her watch. "I asked him to call me as soon as he came out of the PM."

"To be fair, Freya," Ben replied. "I've got five missed calls from him, so he has tried."

"Bloody coward," she said. "I hope he's got something good for us. We seem to be collecting evidence and theories, and none of them are connected."

"We're doing alright," he told her. "It's not an easy one, this."

"No, when are they ever?"

Nillson saw them and nodded to acknowledge them, too cool for school to wave. She was on the edge of the field, and it was only when Ben and Freya made their way towards the old farmhouse that she started towards them, issuing a command to the team of uniformed officers performing their search.

"How's it going, Anna?" Ben asked.

"Want the good news or the bad news?"

"Give me some good news, Nillson," Freya said.

"Well, we've just about covered every inch of the lane and the track."

"And the bad news is that you haven't anything to show for it except a nice colour on your arms?"

Nillson checked her arms and laughed a little. Rarely did she ever laugh out loud.

"No, the bad news is that we can't go onto the fields."

"Excuse me?"

"The old man turned up. Told us to come back with a warrant if we want to trample his fields."

"Bowen," Freya said, and Ben heard the hiss of air she sucked through her teeth. "I should have expected that."

"I'll call Chapman," Ben said. "I'm sure we can get something sorted out."

"Put her on loudspeaker," Freya said, then turned to Nillson. "Where's Gillespie? I saw his car."

Nillson nodded at the house and Ben followed her gaze just as Gillespie and Cruz came to the living room window.

"Ah, it's a full house," Gillespie called out. "Apart from Gold, that is."

"And Chapman," Nillson corrected him.

"Oh, aye, but she doesn't leave the office, does she? I don't even know if she can walk. It's like she was born with a swivel chair stuck to her backside."

"Have I interrupted you, Gillespie? I was expecting a call."

"Ah," he said. "I couldn't get through to you, so I tried Ben a few times. Figured you'd be coming here. How did you get on, anyway?"

"Here we go," Ben cut in, holding the phone out. "Chapman, are you there?"

"I'm here, Ben," Chapman replied.

"Let's get inside," Freya suggested, then called out to Chapman. "Can you dial Gold in? She should be out by now."

"Will do," Chapman said as the three of them moved into the house.

"Come in, come in, wipe your feet," Gillespie said, feigning the host. "Gab, stick the kettle on, son."

"Eh?"

"Right," Freya called out, cutting the chit-chat and setting the tone of the meeting with a single syllable. "Are we all here?"

"We're here," Chapman announced over the phone.

"Okay, Gold. Let's start with you, please."

"She's in there now," Gold replied over the phone. "Pip came out a few minutes ago. It's him. It's definitely Tommy Dean."

The news had not only been expected but also welcome. It wasn't that Freya was glad Mrs Dean had lost her husband, but a small part of her anticipated a negative ID, which would not only traumatise the poor lady further but also throw a large spanner into the works.

"Thank you, Gold. Take her home when she's done. Spend the rest of the day there if need be."

"Cozy up to her, you mean?"

"You'll need to tread a fine line," Freya said. "You'll need to understand her movements over the weekend and have them confirmed. If she can't prove where she was, then we'll need to find some way of eliminating her. I'm not in the habit of kicking somebody when they're down, but we need momentum on our side."

"What about the search?" Gold asked.

"We'll need to do that regardless," Freya said. "I'm afraid you're going to have to find a way of breaking the news to her. Focus on elimination. She's already aware that there were two bodies—"

"I know, she's seen them both."

"Explain to her that it's procedure. We need to eliminate Tommy from our enquiries, and to do that, we'll need to have a look around. Given the circumstances, we won't be sending an army of uniformed officers round there to break the door down, but rather, we'll be sending Gillespie and Cruz—"

"Eh?" Gillespie said.

"Gillespie is leading the investigation into John Tyler's murder," Freya continued. "And I know he can be tactful when he puts his mind to it." She eyed him to drive the message home. "Can't you, Gillespie?"

"Aye," he said dryly, then cleared his throat. "Aye, boss. I can."

"Naturally. I'd expect you to remain with her, Gold. Gillespie has a habit of failing to pass on critical information, so you can be my eyes and ears on the ground."

"Will do," Gold replied, her smile evident in her voice. "Hey, listen. I think she's coming out."

"Stay in touch," Freya said, and they heard the line click as Gold left the call.

"And then there were six," Gillespie said, presumably to fill the void.

"Chapman, Nillson has met some resistance from Frank Bowen with regards to searching his land. Can I leave it to you to arrange the necessary warrants?"

"You can," Chapman said, and Freya imagined the diligent young lady making a neat note on a fresh page in her notebook.

"And how have you got on with Bowen's employees?"

"It's pretty straightforward," she replied. "I ran a background check on them all, and aside from a few minor offences—"

"Such as?"

"Possession of a class B drug, drunk and disorderly, affray, disturbing the peace, assaulting a police officer—"

"Christ," Gillespie said. "Sounds like a good night out."

"That's more than two dozen men," Chapman said. "And some of the offences go back to the two-thousands."

"Anything recent?" Freya asked.

"Nothing," Chapman replied. "There's nothing here that would support an inquiry into any of them."

"So, Bowen is the only individual with any serious charges against him."

"And even that was quashed," Ben added.

"Yes," Freya replied. "Well, if he played any part in either of these instances, he won't be getting away with it this time. You mark my words." She stepped over to the window and peered out, watching as Nillson's team of uniformed officers regrouped. "Anything else?"

"Yes, we've had the report come through from Southwell."

"Which report is that?"

"The first one, ma'am. Regarding the old house. I think it was put on hold when Granger handed us the hanging. I suppose there was no body, so we couldn't put a crime number to it."

"I didn't instruct her to open it up again," Freya said.

"Ah, no, that was me, boss," Gillespie said. "I had a wee word with her last night."

"You did what?"

"I'm running the John Tyler investigation, and there was potential evidence sitting in her lab, boss."

"I see," Freya said. "Well, I don't see how I can argue with that, but next time, do let me know." She peered out of the window again. To see an expanse of the area they were unable to search and an entire team of uniformed officers standing idle was frustrating, to say the least. "Nillson, how much more can you realistically do until a warrant comes through?"

"We're pretty much done," she replied.

"And there's nothing? Not a single thing?"

"At the moment, boss," Nillson said. "Every shred of evidence is in this house."

"Ben, you know farming. Surely there's a way to speed this up."

His laugh set the tone for his response.

"It's private property, Freya. You wouldn't want somebody trampling over your business, would you?"

"If a body was found on my property, I'd expect it to be trampled, pulled apart, and every aspect of my life exposed."

"Your property isn't accessible by the general public," he said. "If we trample his crops and later discover he had nothing to do with the crime, we'll be looking at his loss of earnings. If a judge grants a warrant, which I can't see them not doing, it becomes somebody else's problem, namely the CPS."

"Aye," Gillespie said. "And given Bowen's experience with the establishment, he'll be well-versed in his rights."

"It's his experience with the law that makes me wonder what he's hiding," Freya said, then reset the conversation. "Right, we are where we are. Nillson, you'll have to keep those lot out there busy. Have them check the dykes again. We don't want some jobsworth in the station getting wind of them standing around."

"Want me to go now?" Nillson asked.

"No, stay for a bit," she said. "We might as well all hear Gillespie's news. Given that he's been keeping it so close to his chest, I can only assume he's planning a marching band and fireworks." She looked to Gillespie, who leaned casually against the rear wall. "So, come on, Gillespie, let's hear it."

CHAPTER FORTY-TWO

"Actually, we do have some news," Gillespie said. Had he taken centre stage and paced the room, savouring the limelight like Ian McKellen playing Macbeth, then Freya's hopes might have been elevated. But given that he remained leaning against the wall on the other side of the room, as far from Freya as possible, those hopes of hers sank to the ground, then dug themselves a hole beside the makeshift grave.

"Go on," she said, catching Ben's cautious stare.

"First of all, Group Captain Shaw has been to see Pip," he said. "Pip messaged me a while ago. It's him. It's John Tyler."

"Well, there's a box ticked," Freya muttered. "Alright, well, I suppose we all hoped it was, didn't we? Is that it? Is that the sum of your findings?"

"No, actually. Moving on to body number two. Tommy Dean, or whoever it is, was hit with something like a spade or a shovel."

"So, I was right?" Freya said. There was little need to look at Ben's expression; she knew it would be a forced congratulatory acceptance of her win.

"Aye, Pip has a new fella working with her. Some bloke called Andrew."

"Yes, we met him. He seems nice."

"Aye, I mean, he's a bit square. Wouldn't want to go for a pint with the bloke, if you know what I mean, but at least he doesn't take offence to every comment."

"Give him time, Jim," Ben said. "I'm sure you'll find a way to upset him."

"Aye," he said quietly. "Anyway, Andrew pointed out some grazing on one side of the wound."

"Grazing?"

"The way he described it made sense," Cruz cut in. "If you belt someone with something heavy and sharp—"

"Like a spade," Gillespie added.

"Right, then the spade's blade will strike the skin a little way before the actual full force of the blow damages the skull. He suggested a sweeping motion." Cruz acted out the description of events, precisely where it would have taken place. "In a downward motion like this."

"I get it," Ben said. "Makes sense with the blood spatter, too."

"He also pointed out a few anomalies in the blade."

"A few what?" Nillson said.

"Anomalies," Cruz said. "Something out of the ordinary."

"I know what an anomaly is," she said. "I meant, specifically."

"Oh, right," he said.

"Dents," Gillespie said, taking over from Cruz. "The blade wasn't perfectly flat. It had a couple of little dents in it, like whoever used it hit some...I don't know, rocks or something, I suppose."

"Right," Freya said. "So, presumably, if we find the spade, then we can tie it to the murder, even if it's been cleaned."

"We can also eliminate other such tools from the investigation," Gillespie said.

"Okay," Freya said. "Okay, this is good. But I get the impression you're saving the worst until last."

"Aye, well," he began. "Time of death."

Freya steeled herself. What he said next would dictate who they went after, in addition to Godolphin and Bowen.

"She's given a window of nine p.m. Saturday night and two a.m. Sunday morning."

"You're kidding?"

"Nope," he said.

"That's almost identical to John Tyler's."

"Sure is," he replied.

"So, we still don't know who died first?" she said. "Bloody brilliant."

"Hold on," Ben said. "This works in our favour."

"Oh, really? I was hoping we could at least finish this with some kind of direction. Now, we still have two theories, none of which have progressed anywhere, and we still have no motive. It's been what, three days, and we're still getting nowhere."

"If it helps, we also paid a visit to the Halls."

"Who?" Freya said, allowing her irritation to come through.

"The Halls," he said. "The couple that took John Tyler in."

"Oh, I see. That's where you were hiding, was it?"

"Apparently, the wife took the news quite badly, so we only spoke to the fella."

"Go on. What did he have to say?"

"Well, I asked when they saw John Tyler last, and according to Mr Hall, he hadn't been to see them for years."

"Okay, so?"

"Well, doesn't it strike you as odd, boss?" he said. "Why would a man who, from the age of twelve, was taken in, given a home, and loved by this couple choose not to visit them."

That softness showed in Gillespie's eyes once more, and Freya altered her approach with him.

"I suppose, when you put it like that."

"Hadn't seen them for years, apparently."

Freya watched him speak, and that pang of guilt she often felt post-grilling him raised its ugly head.

"I assume you can empathise?" she asked, injecting a cushion into her tone.

"Aye," he said, shaking his head. "But I can't understand it, boss. Honestly, if I'd had a nice couple like that take me in and give me a good home, I'd...well, I'd go and see them, I know that much."

"Did he give a reason for not going to see them?"

"Nothing believable," Gillespie replied. "He said the wife was upset that he didn't bother to see them. She felt like he'd used them and as a result they'd had a row."

"And what did she have to say about it?"

"She was having a wee lay down," he replied.

"Right, I'm going to need to trust your judgement on this, Gillespie. You obviously have something in mind."

"Ah, I don't know. I just don't trust him. He's cagey."

"He's just lost his son," Nillson said.

"Aye. Aye, I know."

"He's right," Cruz said, to Freya's surprise. "I doubted it too. But there was definitely something off with him."

Freya nodded along, absorbing the information, and trying to find the line between feeling and a thread of fact to work with.

"Presumably, you asked where he was at the weekend?"

"Where do you think he was?" Gillespie asked.

"At home with his wife?" Freya suggested. "Who you were unable to speak to in order to verify it?"

"Got it in one," Gillespie replied.

"Are you looking to make a move on him?"

"With what?" he said. "I can't just knock on his door and tell him I've got a feeling about him and that he needs to come with me to the station."

"No, sadly not," Freya replied. "Alright, well, how do you want to progress?"

He shrugged, and she was instantly reminded of Benjamin Godolphin.

"Talk to him, I suppose, but how do we do that?"

"How did you leave it?"

"He doesn't know that we're suspicious if that's what you're asking."

"Do you think you can get in and talk to his wife?"

"With a little creativity, aye," he said, to which Freya nodded.

"Wait for the formal ID," she said. "Once we know it's him, then pick your moment to deliver the news. I'll let your imagination come up with a plan."

"Aye," he said, a little cheered by the support.

"But, Gillespie," she started. "Tread with caution. Don't break the rules."

"Me?" he scoffed. "Ah, we've got it, boss."

She turned her attention to the rest of the team.

"Chapman, are you still with us?"

"I am," she said, her light voice coming loud and clear over the phone.

"Okay, can you do some more digging? We're not short of people without alibis, but what we don't have is a motive. Let's look deeper into Tyler and Dean. Let's build up a picture of their last days. We know some of what they were up to, but not all. I believe the answer we're looking for is in one of those blanks."

"Will do," Chapman replied.

"Which, I suppose, leaves it for us to give you our news," Freya said. "We now have confirmation that the call was made by Benjamin Godolphin."

"The lad?" Gillespie asked, to which Freya nodded.

"We know the three boys all came over to the farm on Sunday. They spent the day in the fields and in the woods behind the farm. According to them, they spotted Bowen on his tractor, and knowing that he had a habit of throwing people off his land and that all of their parents forbade them to go to the farm—"

"All of them?" Nillson said.

"All of them," Freya said. "It seems our friend, Bowen, has a somewhat tarnished reputation."

"Because?"

"Because of a historical event," she announced. "Most likely the investigation into him back in the nineties, which I'm sure they would be loath to describe to their children."

"Right, that's why they weren't allowed over here, then?" Cruz said. "What did they do when they saw him? He didn't say anything to us about them, did he?"

"They ran," Ben chimed in. "Hid in here until his tractor went past—"

"Which is when they found the body. They didn't hang about. They ran up the lane, where they agreed not to say anything in case their parents found out where they were. Benjamin Godolphin turned right and headed back to Tattershall, leaving Henry Hyde and Liam Jackson to turn left. As we know, Liam's house is a couple of hundred yards away, and Hyde's house is in the estate on the other side of the river." She watched them all take the information in. Nillson stared at Freya with barely any reaction at all, Cruz had his head cocked to one side, presumably imagining the boys as she narrated their movements. Gillespie, however, clearly had questions. "Go on," she told him.

"Ah, sorry, boss. I just want to understand if they touched him or not?"

"No," she said. "They hid here beneath the window, then when the tractor passed, they legged it. Does that answer your question?"

"One more," he said, raising an index finger. "Did any of them recognise him?"

Freya found herself in a state of surprise that he had asked the question that Ben had raised when she hadn't even thought to ask it.

"As it happens, yes," she said. "Henry Hyde."

"Not Godolphin?"

"Not Godolphin," she said. "And not Liam Jackson."

"What's the connection?"

"He said he recognised him. He was a friend of his mother's, who last visited the Hyde house a few weeks back. In answer to your question, we don't know what the connection is," she said, once more checking her watch. "But it's something Ben and I will be working on for the remainder of the day."

CHAPTER FORTY-THREE

THE HOUSE on Church Street was brick-faced and modest, and had it not been for the river that cut through the village, it would have been but a stone's throw from Liam Jackson's house. There was no frontage to the house. Access was gained via a side entranceway, down which it wasn't hard to picture days gone by when coal men would have hauled sacks of black gold into a garden bunker.

It was usual for Freya to wait for Ben to knock while she prepared her warrant card, but such was her hurry to speak to the occupant that she tapped twice on the window set into the door and then stood back before Ben had even caught up with her.

The door was snatched open in less than three seconds as if somebody had just been passing the door when she had made their presence known.

The woman before them stared down in a fluster. Her lank hair, loosely curled, lay flat against her head. Her make-up appeared to have been done by a child or a teenager, and the smell of her perfume was enough to make the weeds that grew through the cracks in the little footpath wilt.

"Yes?" she said, eyeing them both curiously.

"Mrs Hyde?" Freya said.

"Yes, can I help?"

Freya opened her warrant card and held it up for her to see.

"I'm Detective Chief Inspector Freya Bloom. I wondered if we might have a word."

"Police?" she said, clearly confused. "Sorry, I...I thought you were selling something or other."

"Afraid not," Freya told her cheerfully.

"Is it, Henry? Is he okay? He's not done owt, has he?" It was Freya's turn to look confused, which was far better than an outright lie. "My boy. Henry. Is he okay?"

"I'm sure he's fine," Freya said. "Wherever he is." She gestured inside. "May we?"

"It's a bit of a mess, I'm afraid."

"We're not here to judge," Freya said, beckoning Ben inside before her. The house was what her father would have called a two up, two down, and the hallway would have been cramped even before the pile of shoes had been discarded on the floor and the mass of coats had been hung from the wall.

Hyde closed the door behind them, then ushered them into a small living room, which, back in the day when the house had been built, would have been ample but proved restricting with modern living standards. There was room for a two-seater sofa and an armchair but little else. The TV had been hung over the fireplace, and nearly every free space of was filled with toys or some other clutter. The carpet was predominantly red in tone, comprising a floral pattern with shades of oranges and yellows, all of which had faded over time, and, in patches, had earned another colour to the palette: a brown gravy stain, a deep red wine stain, and various other areas stained with little more than everyday grime.

"I'm guessing this 'int about me speeding, is it?" Mrs Hyde said, a nervous addition to both fill the void and fish for clues as to their reason for being there. She smiled weakly at Freya's look.

"Got caught up the road. One of them bloody vans on the side of the road. Didn't see it, did I? Should have known better, really. He's always there. You come round the bend a few miles over, and he's got you. Must make a fortune, those vans. I'll bet they're on commission, too—"

"Mrs Hyde, we're not with the traffic police," Freya said, cutting her off. "We're actually hoping you could help us with our investigation."

"Investigation?"

"I'm afraid it's rather serious," Freya continued, which seemed to hit home with the house owner, who beckoned for them to sit. "We recently discovered a man's body. Not far from here, in fact."

"Oh," she replied, which was perhaps the most feminine of her reactions so far. "How sad."

"It is rather," Freya said. "The thing is, Mrs Hyde, it took us a few days to identify him, and as a result, for us to build a picture of who he was, we've been led to believe that he was acquainted to you, somehow."

"To me?" she said. Then her eyes narrowed as the grips of deep thought took hold. "Is this about the farm? Brinkleview? I saw the commotion, and—"

"Tommy Dean," Freya said, displaying every card in her hand in the hopes of knocking the woman off her game. And she had. Her reveal was a widening of her eyes, albeit brief, and a slight intake of air, both of which were hurriedly concealed by two plump hands and an apparent bewilderment.

"What makes you think—"

"I'm afraid I can't go into too much detail," Freya said. "But our sources are reliable, and perhaps I should mention at this point that, due to the circumstances in which Mr Dean died, this is being treated as a murder investigation."

"He was murdered? But surely, you don't think that I—"

"I think you can help us, Mrs Hyde," Freya said. "That is all. I can assure you, if we believed anything more than that, then it would be very unlikely that we would be sitting here in this... charming room." Freya repositioned herself, seeking a little more comfort whilst avoiding too much contact with the grubby sofa. "Now then, perhaps we can start with how you knew Mr Dean?"

Mrs Hyde dropped her hands from her face, turned her head, and was, in Freya's opinion, about to begin a work of fiction.

"I'm sorry—"

"He was here a few weeks ago. Is that right?" Freya said, providing enough detail to let the woman know that their visit was more than a hunch. "Why was that? Were you close?"

Mrs Hyde stared at her, perhaps contemplating an extension of the lie but seeing sense in the end, as most of them do.

She nodded.

"Alright," she said. "Yeah, I knew him, and if it makes a difference, I'm...I'm quite saddened by the news. He was a good bloke, Tommy. Is his wife—"

"She's grieving, as you can imagine," Freya said, to which Hyde offered a glimpse of a smile that hid behind the sadness as the sun might peek from between the clouds on a wintery day. "How did you know him, Mrs Hyde?"

"How?" she said, shrugging. "Known him since we were dots. We went to the same schools, the same playgroups. It's hard not to know people round here. Well, it was back then, anyway. Not so much, now."

"So, you knew him from school?"

"I did, yeah," she said. "We sort of kept in touch, you know? Nothing like that. Just mates, I suppose, everyone else has moved away. Well, most of them. I stayed. He stayed."

"Who are these others you speak of, Mrs Hyde," Freya asked. "You make it sound like a large group of friends."

She laughed a little.

"Not really. I was never really in a group of friends. I had a few, I suppose, but never many. But I did get on with people, I'll say that. I suppose I was always one of those faces nobody noticed. I was never really the butt of anybody's jokes, but I was never in the limelight either. I suppose I was a nobody. Still am, but it doesn't seem to have hurt. I've a home, a family, which is more than some."

"As did Tommy," Freya said. "I'm keen to understand who his friends were. We've been speaking to a Geoff Godolphin—"

"Geoff?" she scoffed. "He spoke to you, did he?"

"You sound surprised."

"I am," she said.

Freya waited for her to add some detail to the reaction, but in the end, she had to fish for it.

"And why are you surprised? He's actually been quite helpful."

"Oh, I'm sure he has been helpful," Hyde said. "But if I were you, I'd take everything he says with a pinch of salt."

"I'll bear that in mind," Freya said. "It sounds like you know him well."

"Oh, I wouldn't say I know him well. Not anymore, anyway. His boy knocks about with my Henry, so he calls from time to time. You know, pickups and drop-offs and all that. He waves from the door sometimes, but we don't really talk. Not like Tommy and me spoke, anyway."

"Would you say that he and Tommy were well acquainted?" Ben asked, the new voice seeming to take her by surprise.

"Oh, I wouldn't know," she said. "Tommy never spoke of him, and look, Tommy used to pop round every now and then, but he never really spoke about anyone else."

"So why did he pop round?" Freya asked, and again she shrugged.

"I don't know. I think it was more out of duty than anything else. Tommy was alright. He had a strong sense of loyalty. He struggled a bit. You know? With the lockdowns and all that. You know he changed his job, right?"

"We do," Freya replied. "Quite the shift."

"Yeah, well. He was doing all right. I reckon he could have run that place. The accountants, I mean. I reckon he would have gone far, but we don't really know what people are thinking, do we? But I tell you this much. When he changed his job, he was a different bloke. He was like a kid again. Excited, you know? Hopeful. They probably had a drop in income, but I don't think he cared. I hadn't seen him like that since before his dad. You know?"

"No," Freya said. "What about his dad?"

She looked perplexed, checking each of their faces for a sign they were pulling her leg.

"You don't know?" she said, "about him going missing?"

"No," Freya said. "When was this? During the lockdowns? Do you think it was partly why he changed vocation?"

"No, no," she said. "It was years ago. Part of the reason why him and Geoff stopped speaking, I think."

"Oh, they had a fall out, did they?"

"Yeah, I mean, it was years ago, but.... You don't know about any of this?"

"Like I said, Mrs Hyde, we're trying to build a picture," Freya told her. "When was it that his father went missing?"

"Oh God, now you're asking. It was when we were kids. Course, nobody really spoke about it. Upped and left by all accounts."

"Mrs Hyde, you said it was part of the reason why he stopped talking to Geoff Godolphin," Freya said. "What was the rest of the reason?"

"Oh, right," she said. "Well, him and Geoff used to be close. Them and John. They were like a threesome."

"John Tyler?"

"That's right," she said. "He was a local kid. Lost his family in—"

"A fire, yes, we heard about that," Freya said, keen for her to finish the story.

"I see," she said. "Well, Tommy's dad buggered off about the same time as the fire. Course, nobody really cared. Everyone was just sorry for poor old John. I think it got to him, you know? I think deep down, it really got to him that his dad had left, and all people spoke about was John's family. Tommy told me about it once. They were all friends right up until they turned eighteen. John was about to go off to the RAF, Tommy had got into university, and they were all together for one last time." She laughed to herself. "They even gave each other tattoos.—"

"Why was that? You're referring to the crosses, I presume?"

"Yeah, that's them. Tommy told me once it was supposed to mark a change in their lives. Like a symbol, you know? To mark John's family and Tommy's dad. So that wherever they ended up in the world, they would always look in the mirror and know they had mates. Bloody stupid, if you ask me, but they were drunk. And then, according to Tommy, John kept going on about how hard his life had been in care, and when Tommy tried to talk about his dad leaving, they both laughed and said he'd probably run off with a younger woman. So, Tommy walked out. Never spoke to them again." She clicked her fingers. "Eighteen years of friendship, gone, just like that."

"Do you think he was jealous of the attention John Tyler's family received?"

"I don't know if jealous is the right word," she said. "I mean, it was devastating. They all burned to death, and John had to see it. I mean, he saw them being dragged out, right?"

"Quite the tragedy," Freya said.

"It was," she said quietly and thoughtfully. "They say it comes in threes, though, don't they."

"What does? What comes in threes?"

"Bad news. Tommy's dad, the fire," she said. "And then there's the girl. What was her name?"

"The girl?" Freya said.

"Yeah, she went missing. Rocked the whole village, I tell you. Everyone was out looking for her. My mum wouldn't let me out of her sight for a year. Petrified, she was."

"That was the previous year, wasn't it?"

"It was, yes, but it was still talked about. You know, with the villagers and that."

"And what about John Tyler?" Freya asked. "Do you see him at all?"

"John?" she said. "No. No, he changed after that. I suppose you would, wouldn't you? When you lose your entire family and then... anyway."

"And then, what?" Freya said, and Mrs Hyde silenced.

"Oh, don't mind me. I'm blabbing."

"Not at all," Freya said. "Please. Blab away."

"Well, Geoff and Tommy were all he had. I mean, he had his foster parents by then, but as far as his roots go, Geoff and Tommy were all he had."

"And because of the argument, he lost them?" Ben asked.

"Yeah, that's right. It's sad, isn't it?" she said. "Tommy never stopped looking for his dad, you know? He did those DNA things; he scoured the Internet for him."

"He didn't believe his dad had run away?"

"Didn't want to believe it, more like," she replied. "But I'll give him this; he never gave up on him. Not once."

CHAPTER FORTY-FOUR

"Is this alright?" Cruz asked. They were parked more than one hundred yards from the Hall's house and had been for some time. "I mean, couldn't he come back to us at a later date and say we tricked him? Like entrapment or something."

"It's not entrapment, Gabby," Gillespie said, bored of listening to Cruz whine. "And there's nothing wrong with what we're doing."

"Well, then, why can't we just knock?"

"Because, Gabby," he started, just as the front end of a sleek Jaguar nosed from the Hall's driveway. "Hold on. Here we go."

Gillespie slid down in his seat and beckoned for Cruz to do the same, although the young DC probably didn't need to; he could barely see over the bonnet, anyway. The Jaguar eased from the driveway and idled to the end of the road. A few seconds later, it was out of sight.

"Right, let's do this," Gillespie said, shoving himself upright. He started the old Volvo and crept forward, coming to a squealing stop in the shadow of the Hall's tall trees. "Just remember, she's frail. Leave the talking to me, alright?"

They hurried up the driveway, Cruz having to take three steps for every one of Gillespie's. The doorbell seemed obnoxiously loud, and Gillespie found himself urging the old woman on. He rang the bell again just as the door opened, and a familiar face stared out at them.

"Ah," Gillespie said, a little taken back. "It's a pleasure to see you again, erm..."

"Group Captain Shaw," the woman said, then shook her head as if to confirm that titles and rank meant nothing outside of the base boundaries. "It's Felicity when I'm not in uniform. Felicity Shaw. I assume you're here to see Mr Hall. If so, you're out of—"

"Did I hear my name?" a voice said, light in tone but far from frail. Mrs Hall edged into view. She dressed older than her years, and apart from the bags beneath her eyes, she seemed as strong and determined as before. "Oh, it's you again, Detective..."

"Gillespie, ma'am," he said. "Sergeant Gillespie, and this is DC Cruz."

"Of course," she said. "I suppose you've heard Mrs Shaw's news."

"News?"

"About..." she cleared her throat. "About John."

"Oh...aye, I have, and I'd like to offer my sincere condolences. I can't imagine what you're going through, and well, if there's anything we can do, please, you've got my details. Just call."

"Thank you," she replied. "I would like to see him if that's at all possible. I don't know that it is."

"I'm sure it can be arranged, Mrs Hall."

"Thank you. Perhaps you could arrange it with my husband."

She smiled sweetly as if expecting him to turn and leave.

"Speaking of your husband. I don't suppose I could have a wee word, could I?"

"Well, I'm afraid my husband's just popped out—"

"Ah, that's a shame," Gillespie replied, nudging Cruz with his elbow. "Eh, Gabby."

"It is," Cruz said reactively.

"But if it's not too much bother, maybe you could help us." He looked to the RAF Officer by her side. "I mean, if I'm not interrupting anything, that is."

"I was just leaving anyway," Shaw said, but the elder of the two ladies grabbed onto her arm.

"Could you stay dear?" Mrs Hall asked. "I'd feel more comfortable, and well, you knew John, didn't you?"

"Of course," Shaw said, checking her watch and offering a pleasant, albeit reluctant smile. "I'd be happy to."

They were seated in the same lounge as before, and Gillespie and Cruz occupied the same seats. Mrs Hall took her place beside the telephone while Felicity Shaw perched on the edge of Mr Hall's seat.

"Now then," Mrs Hall said by way of spurring them on. "What can we do to help? I feel a bit redundant if I'm honest. Helpless, if you know what I mean?"

"That's understandable," Gillespie replied. "We felt that, given John's condition, that it was best if we asked Mrs Shaw here to attend the hospital. It can be quite upsetting."

"She also said there was some kind of foul play," Mrs Hall said, shaking her head. "Who would do that to him? Who would do that to my John?"

"Aye, well. That's what we're hoping to find out," Gillespie said. "We're making progress, but these things take time. We have to be sure of the information we're given, which, as I'm sure you can imagine, is significant."

"I see," Mrs Hall said. She spoke as they were discussing the weather as if she had put up some kind of mental wall behind which her emotions were wrapped in cotton wool. "How long do these things usually take?"

"I'm afraid that varies," he said. "It all depends on the complexities of the investigation, but I assure you, we have a team dedicated to John's death. We're working hard, Mrs Hall and

I can assure you, nobody wants to draw this out any longer than we have to."

"I see," she said.

"You said before that you took John in when he was twelve. That's right, isn't it?"

She nodded.

"He was thirteen or fourteen when we adopted him. It seems everything takes time these days."

"Out of interest, do you happen to remember any of his friends, Mrs Hall? Specifically, a Tommy Dean and Geoff Godolphin? Do you know those names?"

"Godolphin?" she said, almost allowing a smile to break through. "I haven't heard that name for years."

"So, you do know him, then?"

"Know him, no. *But I knew* him. Him and little Tommy. They were all good friends once."

"But not anymore?"

"Not as far as I know," she said. "But then..."

Gillespie waited for her to say more, but she seemed to lose herself in thought.

"But then, what, Mrs Hall? I'm sorry; I realise this is a difficult time, but..."

"But then we didn't see him," she said. "Not often anyway, and certainly not often enough to know who he spent his time with."

"Oh, I think your husband mentioned something like that," Gillespie said, seeing a way in. "Why is that, do you think?"

"Why's what, my dear?"

"Why didn't you see him? I mean, like I told you before, I was raised in care, and I tell you that, if I'd have landed in the loving home of a couple like you and your husband, Mrs Hall, I'd have sainted you." She laughed and dismissed the notion. "I'm serious," he told her. "Did something happen for him to stop coming around?"

Her face stiffened in a scorn, and for the first time, Gillespie saw something in her other than the charming, mature lady he felt sorry for.

"What are you implying?" she asked, to which Gillespie shrugged and held his hands up defensively.

"I'm not saying anything. I just find it odd that a man like John, who's been through what he has, should shun a loving family. I'm just trying to understand him, that's all."

"Well," she said. "He joined the RAF, you know?"

"Aye, I know—"

"And if you must know, I was incredibly proud of him."

"I'm sure you were—"

"Why don't we have some tea?" Shaw said.

"I don't need tea," Mrs Hall said. "But you help yourself, dear."

"Mrs Hall, the last thing I want to do is make this difficult for you," Gillespie said, noting that Shaw had dropped the idea of tea. "I'm just trying to build a picture of John. Who was he friends with? Where did he spend his free time?"

"Oh, I can answer those," Shaw added. "Until he retired, John spent much of his time in the gym. He had a few friends. He was well-liked, and as far as I know, nobody had a bad word to say about him. People like him do well in the forces. He was very... driven."

"By what?" Gillespie asked but gained no response. "I suppose there are some things we'll never know, eh?" Mrs Hall turned her head and blinked away her tears, forcing Gillespie to press on. "I'm sorry to ask Mrs Hall, but we need to clarify your whereabouts last weekend. It's merely procedure."

"My whereabouts?"

"Aye. Your's and your husband's. He said you were both at home all weekend. I just need you to confirm that."

"We were," she said. "I hope you're not—"

"It's just procedure," Shaw cut in reassuringly. "It's quite common. It means they can move the investigation on, that's all."

"I see," she said. "Well...well, yes. I was here. I had a turn, you see?"

"A turn?"

"A dizzy spell. I get them from time to time, and I'm often laid up. My husband tends to me."

"Oh, I'm sorry to hear it. You're better now, I hope?"

"When you get to my age, you take each day as it comes," she said stiffly.

"That's a good attitude," he told her. "So, he was with you, was he? Your husband? All weekend?"

She hesitated for a moment, then nodded.

"Yes, he was."

"He didn't pop out for a bit?"

"No. Not that I recall."

"And to recap, you can think of no reason why John stopped coming to see you?" Gillespie asked. "I know this is all a bit fresh, but your husband mentioned an argument or some sort of falling out between you and John, I mean."

"An argument?"

"Aye, he said you and he had clashed heads over John not coming round very often, and since then..."

"How dare you?"

"I'm sorry, I'm just saying what your husband told me, Mrs Hall—"

"I supported John through his entire career," she said with more than a little indignity. "He was busy. He was forging a future for himself, and he did well." She looked to Shaw, who nodded enthusiastically. "I might have been hurt, but if he was alive, I can assure you, he would be as welcome here now as he was when he was twelve years old."

"I see," Gillespie said, then braced for the toughest question he had to ask. "In that case, Mrs Hall, can you think of any reason why your husband would have told us otherwise?" She looked away, finding solace in various inanimate objects on the bureau:

the telephone, an old photo, and a brass dog. "Mrs Hall?" Gillespie said again, keeping his voice low and soft. "If there's something you want to say, now's the time to say it."

She stared at him, seeing the metal inside her, a steely strength that only develops with age.

"I've nothing more to say," she said. "Now, if you'll excuse me, I think I'll have a little lie-down."

"Of course," Gillespie replied. "Thank you so much for your time, Mrs Hall. We'll see ourselves out."

He gestured for Cruz to follow, leaving Shaw to help the elder lady. They had barely descended the steps to the house when the front door opened.

"Sergeant?" Shaw said, pulling on a light jacket.

"Mrs Shaw?"

"I wondered if I might have a word," she said as she pulled the front door closed behind her. "I don't know if it'll help, but it's about John."

CHAPTER FORTY-FIVE

"DETECTIVE SERGEANT JIM GILLESPIE enters the room," Gillespie announced as he and Cruz burst through the incident room doors just as Freya was about to start a briefing.

"Well, perhaps Detective Gillespie can take a seat and conduct himself more appropriately in future?" Freya told him, which did little to deflate whatever bubble it was he had floated in on. She amended the timeline to reflect the findings they had already discussed. Adding Tommy Dean's name beneath John Tyler's to indicate they died at approximately the same time and adding a mark at 5 p.m. on Sunday to indicate when the boys discovered Tommy Dean's body.

Had she been asked which of her team had something else to add, she could have pointed them out in a heartbeat. Gillespie's winning expression and slouch suggested he and Cruz had learned something; but how useful it would be was yet to be known.

Gold sat upright, pen in hand and her notebook opened to a specific page of notes. Had she merely been ready to attend the briefing, she would have turned to a clean page. As it was, the double page of notes, suggested she would be referring to them while delivering her news.

Nillson, however, was less than attentive. She looked glum in both expression and body language, indicating that her time spent leading the search had been less than fruitful.

Chapman was the anomaly. Rarely was she anything other than ready to listen and take notes, and rarely did she ever fail to come up with some fact or data that would steer the ship one way or another.

Ben watched from his seat near the back of the room. He was casual in his posture, with one leg crossed over the other and his fingers linked across his stomach as if he were waiting for a play to begin.

"Sometime between nine p.m. on Saturday night and the early hours of Sunday morning, both John Tyler and Tommy Dean were murdered. One murder was clearly designed to inflict pain, and his body was left for us to find, while the other was far less planned, and his killer made quite a vigorous attempt to conceal the body. It's for this reason that I believe we are dealing with two murderers, and in light of the fact that this is not Hollywood and murders are not a daily occurrence in rural Lincolnshire, I would suggest that Tommy Dean was responsible for John Tyler's death, and as a result, Tommy Dean was murdered. His death was far more reactive, and his body was hurriedly buried." She paced back and forth. Verbalising the facts and theories were of little benefit to the team, but it helped her to build a picture behind that which could be conjured from staring at a whiteboard. "The three boys discovered Tommy Dean's body at around 5 p.m.," she said, tapping the time she had written on the board. "Which means that at some point between 5 p.m. and eleven p.m. when we arrived, the murderer, or an accomplice, returned to the scene to bury him."

"Frank Bowen was seen near the scene," Ben added. "The boys said they saw him in his tractor."

"Very good but bear with me. We'll get to MMOs in a moment," Freya said, clinging to her train of thought. "If that theory is correct, then somebody cared enough about John Tyler to avenge his death or lash out."

"Which crosses a line through Julie Dean," Gold said.

"If what she said about not knowing him is true, then yes, it does," Freya said. "But not only would they have had to care about John Tyler enough to enter into some kind of fit of rage and beat Tommy Dean to death, but given the close proximities of the two deaths, they would have had to either witness the murder or stumble on it and know, for whatever reason, that Tommy was behind it."

"Then they'd have to know where to find him," Gillespie said. "It's far more likely that somebody caught him in the act."

"My thoughts exactly," Freya agreed. "And given the trail of blood from the outside of the old farmhouse to the inside, then I don't think it's much of a jump to suggest that they acted right there at the scene."

"It would have been pitch dark," Ben said. "What if they were looking for John, happened upon the scene, then clobbered Dean?"

"And how would they happen upon the scene?" Freya asked. "You said it yourself; it's the one spot on the farm that can't be seen from the main road."

"Well, I don't know. But it makes sense they used the darkness to their advantage. Maybe they were too late to save Tyler? So, they clobbered Dean and dragged him off?"

"In what?" Freya said. "They certainly couldn't carry him that far."

The furrows in Ben's brow smoothed as a knowing smile formed.

"He used Dean's truck," he said, and Freya clapped once and pointed at him.

"He used Dean's truck," she repeated, adding a childish truck outline to the whiteboard between the murders and the 5 p.m. mark and then denoted the direction of travel with two equally childish arrows. She turned back to the team. "Where's the truck?"

"No hits on ANPR, ma'am," Chapman said. "We've got all units on the lookout for it, but nothing yet."

"Remind them," she said. "It's been a few days now."

"Will do," Chapman replied, making a note of the task.

Freya turned back to the board.

"Frank Bowen and Geoff Godolphin," Freya said, striking a line through Julie Dean's name. It was a temporary measure. Had they proven that Tommy Dean's wife could not have been involved, then she would have removed the name altogether. "Which of these men could have arrived at the scene, finding Tommy Dean in the process of murdering John Tyler?"

"Either of them," Gold said.

"Okay, which of them could have been upset enough to go after Dean?"

"Godolphin, maybe?" Nillson said. "I can't see any reason for Bowen to do anything about it. There's not even a link, is there?"

"He knew Tyler's father," Ben said. "It's a farm cottage on his property. Maybe he feels some kind of obligation to keep an eye on him."

"There's obligation, and then there's *obligation*," Freya said, which he seemed to accept. She looked about the room. "So, Godolphin? Is that where we focus our efforts?"

"Hold on," Ben said. "We're talking about this theory like it's gospel. We don't know that Dean killed Tyler. It's just a best guess."

"So, what do you suggest we do?" Freya asked, to which he had no reply. "That's what I thought. We *must* press on. We must pursue a course of action if we are to get any further. Even if it's wrong. In fact, I wouldn't be surprised if most of what we have—"

"Which is almost nothing," Ben added.

"Is entirely wrong," Freya continued, raising her voice to quash his remark. "A theory can be adapted, remoulded, or reimagined."

She pressed the cap onto the marker. "We can't reimagine nothing, Ben." She tapped the board with the marker. "This is our best chance."

"Actually, I have something to add," Gillespie said. "We managed to have a word with the wife."

"Tyler's adopted mother?"

"Aye," he said, his voice low like a distant rumble of thunder.

"Okay," she said, perching on her desk.

"See, when we spoke to him, he said that John and the mother had had a falling out over him not visiting often enough. He said she felt like he'd used them; ungrateful, you know?"

"I can imagine," she said, but he was shaking his head.

"She found the whole idea that her and John Tyler had fallen out abhorrent."

"I see," Freya said. "So, you think the husband lied."

"Aye, and not just about that," he continued, finally getting his moment in the limelight. "See, I think he and John had a falling out."

"Okay, do you have anything to support that, or is it gut?"

"A bit of both," he replied. "See, I still can't get my head around the fact that a wee lad loses his entire family yet shuns the people that gave him a loving home."

"Gillespie, I do hope you're going to get to the point sometime this afternoon. I'd like to get away before any of you claim overtime."

"Aye, boss. It's just...it's a big jump. I don't want to make any claims. Not yet, anyway."

"So..."

"The wife says she has these funny turns. A tight chest or something. Has to go and have a wee lay down."

"Should we send a card?" Freya asked.

"And he said something," Gillespie said, clearly trying to pull the fragments together in his mind. "Cruz made a comment about his garden. He said how nice it was, and the fella, Mr Hall, he said his doctor had recommended gardening."

"Right..." Freya said, coaxing him on.

"And Gabby said something about gardening being good for the soul and the mind or some claptrap. Anyway, the point is that Mr Hall is on blood pressure tablets."

He let that statement hang there until somebody grabbed it.

"You think he's been giving his wife his blood pressure tablets?" Chapman said, and all eyes turned on her, expecting an answer. She spoke as if it was common knowledge. "Blood pressure tablets lower your blood pressure. It goes without saying."

"But if you don't have high blood pressure and you take the tablets..." Gillespie added, leaving the ending for somebody to pick up.

"Then you end up with low blood pressure," Freya finished for him. "There was a case like that before. Quite a famous one. The man drugged his wife to make her feel like she was ill, which gave him the opportunity to do what he wanted to do. Are you suggesting that he...? What are you suggesting?"

"I don't know," he said. "I just...there's something about him. If he hadn't lied to us about the whole falling out thing, then I wouldn't have thought twice, but..."

"Is his wife his alibi?" Freya asked.

"Aye, boss. They both said they were home all weekend."

"And presumably, she had one of these turns?"

"Aye, boss," he replied. "She's been having them for years. She takes herself off to bed and is normally better in a day or so."

Freya nodded, and Ben shifted in his seat to pay close attention.

"Is it out of the question to suggest that he could be making his wife feel ill to buy him a little freedom?" he asked.

"That's what I'm thinking," Gillespie said. "I think..." he cleared his throat. "I think there could be a very good reason that

John Tyler left the Hall house aged eighteen and almost never went back to visit."

CHAPTER FORTY-SIX

FREYA STARED AT GILLESPIE. He was handsome in a rogue-ish way. There was no doubt his hair was too long for regulation, and seldom was his shirt tucked in completely. He shaved less than she would have preferred, but the overall shabby look only added to the charm that she just couldn't put her finger on. But he had a heart. Nobody could doubt that.

"Can you add some meat to the bone?" she asked.

"I'll do my best, boss," he replied, uncharacteristically quiet and thoughtful.

"Can you do it in a way so as not to kick a hornet's nest?"

"Aye, boss," he said.

"Because if he gets wind of what you're doing, the repercussions could be serious. I'm not sure there'll be any coming back from it; put it that way."

"I get it," he said.

"Good. What do you need?"

He rocked his head from side to side while he thought.

"The usual, medical, bank, and phone records," he said, and Freya turned to Chapman, eyebrows raised.

"We'll need disclosure forms," she said.

"I can arrange those," Freya said, returning her attention to Gillespie. "What do you hope to do?"

"Well, if we can prove he's been on blood pressure tablets for a significant amount of time, then that'll add weight to our claim that he's been inducing his wife's sickness."

"It won't prove it," Freya said.

"No, but it'll put us on a good footing," he replied. "Then, if his phone records come through, we could place him at or near the crime scene, slash scenes plural."

"How far is his house from the farm?" Ben asked.

"Not far. Five minutes by car."

"I'd be surprised if they do. The crime scene is probably covered by the same masts as his house."

"They could triangulate," Cruz suggested, and Freya nodded supportively.

"It's worth a shot," she said. "And the bank records? What do you need those for?"

"I just want the full picture, boss," he said. "I really think he's up to something. Hiding something. I don't know."

"It's okay, I get it," she told him. "What about Tyler's home? Have you been there yet?"

"He didn't have one, ma'am," Chapman chimed in.

"He what?"

"He didn't have a home," she repeated. "Not on any records, anyway. He was in forces accommodation until he retired a few months back, and since then, he's had no fixed abode."

"Actually, I was coming to that," Gillespie said. "See, when we were leaving the Hall's house, Group Captain Shaw stopped us."

"What was she doing there?"

"I don't know. Offering support?"

"Okay," Freya said.

"She said that during his exit interview, she asked John where he'd go. Apparently, he told her that he was buying his dad's old house."

"The cottage? The one that burned down?"

"That's what she said," he replied. "Said something about him rebuilding it. Reconnecting or something. In her words, boss, he was a lost soul."

"But he could have gone back to his adopted parents' house while all that went through, surely?"

Gillespie shook his head.

"He was adamant he wasn't going back there. She couldn't say so in front of the old lady, but apparently, there was no way on earth he was going back there."

"What about his mail?" Freya asked.

"I suppose there's a pile on the floor of his RAF house," he said. "Which I assume he's had to give up."

"So, where was he living?" Freya asked.

"How about in a tent?" Ben said, and he gave her that look that suggested his idea was so far-fetched that it could almost be true.

"Of course," she muttered. "But why? Why would he choose to live in a tent in his retirement? I see why he might want to rebuild his family home, but for God's sake, rent somewhere until it's done."

"He was broken," Gillespie said, taking the room by surprise. The brash tones he was known for gave way to a gentle narration of the picture Gillespie had formed of John Tyler. "He lost everyone he knew in a fire when he was twelve years old, boss. He watched the firemen drag his mammy and pappy out, along with his two kid sisters. He gets taken to a home where, if I'm right, he's...taken advantage of. So, what would you do?"

"Get away the first moment I could," Freya said.

"Aye, you would. The moment he turned eighteen, he was out of there. He got his head down, kept himself to himself. Aye, he had a few friends, but nobody special. Not like his old buddies, Geoff Godolphin and Tommy Dean, but he'd fallen out with them or lost touch or something."

"They fell out," Freya told him, then gestured for him to continue.

"In the RAF, he took up boxing, no doubt to give him a means to vent his anger and frustration. He did well. The base champ, according to Shaw. He forges a fine career. He's not a highflyer; he didn't win medals for valour, but he did alright." Gillespie stopped, and the image he conveyed raised a bitter grimace on his lips. "And then, after so many years of service, he was forced to retire. It's a young man's game, boss, the RAF, and he wasn't officer material."

"So, he finds himself out on civvy street," Freya suggested.

"Aye, and had you been through all that, and if you felt you couldn't go back to your adopted home, where would you go?"

"The house," Nillson said.

"Aye," he replied, a string of saliva connecting his jaws. "He went home, boss." He straightened and cleared his throat. "My problem is understanding how Mr Hall knew he was there."

"The phone records?"

Gillespie nodded.

"He wouldn't have called the old man," he said. "He might have called the wife, though."

"Do we have his number?"

"Group Captain Shaw supplied the number. Now we've a positive ID, we just need the disclosure form."

"Right," Freya said. "What about the wife? Mrs Hall? Does she have a phone?"

"No, she's not really a mobile type of woman, if you know what I mean."

"Damn," Freya said.

"But she does sit next to the house phone," Cruz said. "My mum does the same. I only call her on the house phone."

"And if he hadn't been in touch for some time," Ben started, "maybe he didn't even know their mobile numbers. Maybe all he had was the house phone."

"If he had a problem with the dad, all he would have had to do was call, and if the man of the house answered, he'd hang up," Gold said. "But if *she* answered, then he could have spoken to her. He could have told her he'd left the RAF or that he was leaving. He could have told her he'd be at the house or nearby or something. She would have asked. Any mother would have. It's not unbelievable to think that she could have mentioned it to her husband, especially if she was unaware of...well, if she didn't know he'd taken advantage of him."

"Gillespie?" Freya said. "Do you think she was hiding anything?"

"See, that's where it gets interesting," he said. "Just before we left, I gave her the opportunity to tell us if there was any reason her husband might have lied about the falling out."

"And what did she say?"

He shook his head.

"She just said that he must have got his wires crossed."

"Did you believe her?"

"No, boss," he said. "No, I did not."

She listened, applied some thought, and then responded.

"Chapman, you'll get those disclosure forms before I leave for the day," she said. "Gillespie, Cruz, good work. Stay on the trail for me."

"Aye, boss," Gillespie replied, but his expression suggested he was waiting for something else.

"What?" she asked.

"Well, I erm..."

"Gillespie?"

"It's just..." he started. "It's just a gut feeling. I don't want to waste resources—"

"I think it's a path we need to investigate," she told him. "And the pair of you are best placed to do so." It was as much of a compliment as she was prepared to offer, and she let him decipher it the best he could. "Gold, if you sat any straighter, you'll do yourself an injury," Freya continued, and she beckoned for her to provide whatever news she had.

"Oh, yeah. Erm, yeah. About the Dean house," she grimaced a little. "I don't think we're going to get away with a full search. She's really upset, ma'am."

"Understandably," Freya said. "But her husband, dead or otherwise, is a potential suspect in a murder investigation."

"I know, but I think if we press too hard, we risk losing her. She's on our side right now," Gold explained, and Freya was about to remind her that she's a police officer, not a social worker when Gold continued. "But I did manage to have a look about."

"Sorry?"

"I had a quick look while she was napping," Gold said. "She was exhausted after the—"

"What did you find?" Freya pushed.

"That's just it," she said. "Nothing. I checked the garage, the shed, and even the car. I couldn't find any rope. I couldn't find anything that suggests Tommy went after John Tyler."

"He would have taken it though, wouldn't he?" Ben said. "Was there a spade or a shovel in the shed?"

"There was, yes," Gold said. "All the tools were hanging up on nails."

"I don't suppose one of them was covered in blood, was it?" Nillson asked, her dry sense of humour shining through.

Gold picked up her phone and scrolled through the screens.

"Here, I took some pictures."

She reached across and handed it to Ben, who zoomed in on the image.

"There's a spade," he said. "But no shovel."

"So?" Freya said. "Aren't they the same?"

"Jackie, what's the garden like?" Ben asked.

"Eh? I don't know. It's a garden."

"Is it tidy or messy? Does it look like they enjoy gardening?"

"It's nicer than mine," she said. "It's neat, I suppose. There was fresh compost on the beds, and the grass was cut. I mean, if you're asking if it looked like Monty Don had been round there—"

"They would have a shovel," Ben said, smiling at her to apologise for cutting her off. He handed her the phone back. "There's a space where the shovel should go, and if they moved compost to put on the beds, then they'd have a shovel. A spade is for digging."

"And a shovel?"

"Well, you could dig with it if you had to, but it's mostly for moving soil," he said. "The shovel was his."

"And presumably, it's in the back of Tommy Dean's truck?" Nillson said, once more sprinkling joy onto the conversation.

"Alright, alright," Freya said. "Well, it might not be a huge leap forward, but it does support the theory. Right, tomorrow. Gillespie, Cruz, you're on Hall. Gold, stay with Julie Dean for me. Chapman, I'll draft those disclosure forms for you before I leave. We also need access to Tommy Dean's phone."

"Already done, ma'am," Chapman replied. "I'm just waiting for it to come through."

"Good. I'll request Godolphin's, too. Think you can manage that many?"

"Should be alright," she said.

"Thank you. This should give us a broader picture of who was where."

"Boss?" Cruz said, raising his hand.

"Yes, Cruz?"

"If having the phone, bank, and medical histories of the Halls, Godolphin, and Tommy Dean is going to help us that much, then why couldn't we have just done that a few days ago?"

It was a good question, and the answer was simple.

"Because Cruz," she started, "we live in a world where the rights of everyday people trump the pursuit of justice. This isn't Nazi Germany. This is Britain, and for us to gain access to an individual's bank records, medical history, and phone records, we need to provide a good reason. We need to be in a position to demonstrate the potential for them to be involved in a crime, and we need to demonstrate how the disclosure forms will drive our investigation forward. If we didn't need to provide good reason, then any officer in the force could simply investigate any member of the public, and we can all think of certain officers who might...abuse that privilege, can't we?"

"Jewson?"

"This is a game of jumping through hoops and cutting red tape, Cruz." She tapped the board again and raised her voice. "We're closing in. It might seem like we're going round in circles, but we are making progress. Think of it as a spiral more than a circle. The turns are getting tighter."

"Very poetic," Ben said.

"We have three names. Now, it's a process of elimination. While Gillespie and Cruz work on Hall and Gold finds out what she can from Julie Dean, the rest of us will look into Godolphin. I suggest you all get a good night's rest."

"And if all that fails?" Ben asked, stopping her in her tracks.

"If all that fails, Ben," she said. "Then we get to cross two more names off our list." She grinned and tapped the board again. "And that leaves only one."

The team bid their goodnights, and one by one, they left, leaving just Ben watching Freya create the requests for disclosure. It was one of those tasks that could have been summarised in a single sentence, yet somebody in a crummy little office somewhere, with nothing better to do, had decided to create a long-winded form. It was one of those hoops she had spoken of.

"You still think Bowen's involved, don't you?" Ben said, then waited for a response.

The only sound was the chorus of hums created by the idle printer and the overhead lights, so Freya spoke quietly.

"I do," she said. "Somehow, at least."

He said nothing for a minute or two, but she felt his eyes on her as she worked.

"What is it, Ben?"

"Nothing," he said. "Except, I was wondering."

"Go on."

"Well, how about we just call it a holiday?"

"Sorry?"

"The honeymoon. Why don't we just call it a holiday? Forget what I said about being right or wrong. The double or nothing. You win."

"Oh?" she replied, making a show of not giving him one hundred per cent of her attention. "That was easy."

"Yeah," he said. "Instead, I've had a new idea."

She inhaled, stopped typing, and looked at him, making it clear the pause in work was temporary.

"What?"

"The name," he said. "If you're right about Bowen being involved, you get to keep Bloom. But if you're wrong..."

CHAPTER FORTY-SEVEN

THE IDEA that Freya should ditch the family name and become a Savage was a long shot, and Ben knew it. Freya conveyed that sentiment with every muscle in her face but had the resolve to refrain from voicing her objections immediately. Instead, she licked her lips whilst considering her argument. He supposed he should have taken some kind of solace from the fact that she hadn't simply shot the idea down like a grouse on her father's acreage in shooting season and was at least searching for a gentler means to let him down.

She opened her mouth to speak, but before she could, the incident room doors squealed open, and that gentle hum of the printer and the lights became little more than the stroke of a cello against the percussive stomps of footfall and the melee of melody that was the team's chatter.

"Is it morning already?" Freya asked, making a rare joke to hide the fact that they had walked in on a sensitive chat. "I feel like you've only just left."

"We've had a change of heart, boss," Gillespie said as they each took their seats at their respective desks.

"Oh?"

"See, the way I see it, or the way we see it, I should say," he started, adopting the role of spokesman for the team. "We've got two days to get this one over the line before you two tie the knot and go off on your honeymoon."

"It's a holiday," Ben corrected him.

"Well, whatever it is," Gillespie continued. "If we don't push on, you two will miss your big day, and we can't have that, eh?"

"You mean, if Ben and I *do* go away, then it will be up to you to finish the investigation without us?"

"Aye, well. I mean, there's that, of course."

"He means it," Nillson said in a rare show of solidarity for Gillespie. "You were right. We're getting close on this one, and, well, to be honest, the whole Ben Savage and Freya Bloom saga has gone on for so long, it would be a shame to let an investigation get in the way."

"That's right," Gold said. "So, we're staying late."

"By my reckoning, if we can get those disclosure forms in now, I might be able to get my contacts at the phone companies to do me a favour," Chapman said. "The banks might be tricky, but the NHS offices are open until six."

Freya looked at them all in turn, then to Ben, who, in lieu of an argument to offer, held his hands up in defeat.

"I'll need to budget for the overtime," she said, which they all knew was a feeble argument, as there always seemed to be funds for unplanned overtime when push came to shove.

"I don't know about you lot," Gillespie said to them all. "But I'll not be claiming this one."

"Yeah, me neither," Nillson added, which then spurred a common agreement that rallied from desk to desk, leaving Freya with little option but to accept their offer. She nodded slowly and thoughtfully.

"In case you haven't noticed, ma'am," Gold said. "We want the pair of you to get married, and the only way we can make sure that happens is to make sure this investigation gets over the line."

"I'm not fussed about the wedding," Gillespie said, grinning. "I'm looking forward to the free bar."

"Personally, I want to hear your speech, Jim," Nillson said. "I can't wait to see you fall flat on your face."

"Okay, okay," Freya said calming them down. "Alright, if you mean it, then let's do it. But you will claim for overtime. I won't be accused of poor management. Chapman, I've sent you the disclosure forms. As for the rest of you, let's expand on our theory." She turned on her heels and strode back to the whiteboard, where she was about to begin what Ben assumed was going to be a monologue outlining her broader thoughts, when she hesitated, took one look at Ben, read into his questioning raised eyebrow, and then addressed a far more important matter. "Thank you," she said. "All of you. Thank you. It means a lot, and it's good to know that Ben and I have your support. It's lovely."

It was a moment Ben wished he could have captured on video. To see Freya at her most vulnerable, accepting thanks and speaking from her heart.

"Ah, what else were we going to do?" Gillespie said, his brash tone muddying the sentiment. "Like you said, we'd only be lumbered with it ourselves, eh?"

The comment was Gillespie's own way of dealing with sentiment, and Freya saw through it.

"Motives," she said, all sentiment put to one side. "If we stick to our theory, then we can assume that one of these men killed Tommy Dean for what he did to John Tyler. However, what we haven't discussed in any depth is why Tommy Dean felt the need to murder John Tyler." She paced a few steps, coming close enough to Ben to leave him with a waft of her fragrance as she turned and paced back. "Now, we know that the murder was planned. I've been over it and over it, and there's no way John Tyler's death was anything but premeditated, planned, and executed with almost infallible accuracy."

"Almost?" Ben said.

"Yes," she replied. "Almost."

"He left no evidence apart from the length of rope he used to pull him up off the ground. There's nothing. Nillson had the search team on their hands and knees, and they found absolutely nothing. I would have said he executed it to perfection."

"You're forgetting," she said with a smile. "He was caught." She tapped the three names on the board. "One of these men discovered him, presumably after Tyler had been set on fire; otherwise, I would imagine, he would have cut him down." She peered at them all once more. "So come on, why would Tommy Dean murder John Tyler in such an horrific way? Ideas. Anything. It doesn't matter how ridiculous they sound; we need ideas."

"An affair?" Cruz said. "It's always a bloody affair, and it's always a dog walker who finds the body."

"Unless we can prove a link between John Tyler and Julie Dean, I'd say this one is the anomaly, Cruz, but we'll certainly be checking when Tyler's phone records come through. Anybody else?"

Ben watched with fascination as Freya led the discussion, spurring them on and encouraging outrageous ideas. There was, of course, a very good motive that she had yet to share, but it seemed she was intent on letting one of the team stumble upon it. She was such a paradox, he thought. For the most part, she was self-centred and borderline narcissistic, but every so often, she demonstrated these little titbits that showed her in a different light.

"Maybe they'd had a row?" Nillson suggested. "I mean, we don't need to rewrite human nature, do we?"

"Okay," Freya said, showing more interest in the idea than she had in Cruz's. "Why would they argue?"

"Well, as far as we know, they hadn't spoken for years. Why was it they stopped speaking?"

"Aye, Mrs Hall said something similar," Gillespie said. "Said they were a proper threesome as kids."

"So, is this perhaps a childhood quarrel magnified by adulthood?" Freya asked.

"Just put them out of their misery, Freya," Ben said, and all eyes turned on him. He spoke to the team but held Freya firmly in his gaze. "Mrs Hyde had quite a lot to say about the threesome, and it all stems from Tommy Dean's father absconding."

"Absconding?" Cruz said, pulling his face into a confused grimace.

"Buggering off," Gillespie said.

"I know what absconding means, Jim. I was wondering why we haven't heard about this before now."

"It hasn't been relevant," Freya said, and she pushed herself off where she was perched and reached over to Chapman's desk, where she snatched up the scrapbook they had found inside what they now assumed to be John Tyler's tent. She opened it and flicked to the page with the newspaper cuttings. Instead of fingering the article on the Tyler family tragedy, she tapped one of the secondary articles with a fingernail. "Tommy Dean's father. George Dean. It's been staring us in the face all this time, and only now has it become somewhat pertinent."

"I don't get it," Nillson said. "How are they connected?"

"They're not," Freya said. "At least, not in this paper, which was printed two days after the fire, but according to Jennifer Hyde, Geoff Godolphin and John Tyler suggested that Tommy's dad ran off with a younger woman, to which Tommy took offence."

"So, twenty-odd years later, he kills him? Unlikely," Nillson said.

"There was also talk of George Dean being responsible for the fire," Chapman said, which was news even to Ben and Freya. The diligent researcher was focused on her screen. "I'm looking at crimes reported in the area at or around the time of the fire," she continued. "George Dean was reported missing, and his name also pops up in the investigation for the house fire as a possible suspect."

"But?" Freya said.

"But the fire was proven to be caused by the stove, and from that point on, it was treated as nothing more than a terrible accident."

The room fell into a silence, during which Ben gauged the team's expressions. Chapman was busy hoovering up more detail, Gillespie was probably imagining John Tyler seeing his family being carried from the blaze, Nillson was tapping her lip with the nib of her pen, deep in thought, and Cruz was scratching an itch inside his ear with his pinkie finger.

"As far as we know," Ben said, deciding to add his own pieces to the jigsaw, "Tyler, Dean, and Godolphin last saw each other when they were eighteen. Tyler had just been accepted into the RAF, Dean was heading to Uni, and from what Jennifer told us, they decided to mark the occasion with a few drinks, a needle, and some ink."

"The tattoos?" Nillson said, to which Ben nodded.

"Something was said while they were doing it, to which Dean took offence. He got up and left and never spoke to them again."

"Or at least until Tyler retired from the RAF," Freya added, turning to Chapman. "I need you to make that call. I think we might have just hit on something."

CHAPTER FORTY-EIGHT

"THE LAST ONE should be arriving in your inbox now, Denise," the voice said over the phone, and they heard him strike a button on his keyboard. The entire team watched on, and usually, Freya would have ushered them onto other tasks, but the information that was, at that moment, riding the light train through miles and miles of fibre cabling would dictate everybody's next move.

"Got it," Chapman said. "You're a star. Looks like I owe you... again."

"Well, you could always say yes to that drink," the voice said, and immediately, Chapman blushed.

"She'd be delighted to..." Freya said, waiting for his name.

"Erm, sorry. I didn't realise I was on loudspeaker."

"This is the police force," she said. "Secrets are difficult to keep. I'll see to it that Denise has ample time to meet, don't worry."

"Right," he said, sounding a little blindsided. "Okay, so, erm. See you then."

Chapman composed herself with a heavy, embarrassed sigh.

"Yes, thank you, Jason. I'll erm...I'll be in touch."

The line clicked, and she hit the button to end the call before busying herself with what he had sent.

"Get in, Denise," Gillespie said. "Keeping him at arm's length, eh?"

"That's enough," Freya said before the banter got out of hand. "I'm sure Chapman is quite capable of managing her own love life."

"I'll check John Tyler's phone records first," Chapman said, still red-faced but pressing on in the hopes of the conversation returning to the investigation.

"No, forward them to Gold," Freya said. "I need you to get onto the Hall's landline. Which company is it with? BT?"

"It is, ma'am, yes," Chapman replied.

"Do you have anyone there?"

"I do," she said, then called across the room. "Gold, it's heading to you now."

"Another wee fancy man? I bet you've got one in every service provider in the region, Chapman, you sly old—" Gillespie started, then silenced at Freya's warning glare.

"Right, get onto it," Freya told Chapman. Then she turned her attention to Gold, who was clicking away on her laptop.

"Yep, got it," she said, then made a show of taking in the data.

"We're looking for calls made to or from Tommy Dean and the Halls' landline," Freya said, stepping across the room where she dropped to a crouch at Gold's side.

"Well, he didn't use his phone much," Gold said. "Blimey, there's barely anything here."

"Who would he call?" Ben said. "He retired a matter of months ago, and by all accounts, he wasn't on speaking terms with his only known friends and had fallen out with his adoptive parents."

"Here we go," Gold said. "Call to a landline last..." She checked her calendar to put a day to the date, "Thursday."

"Can we check that landline?" Freya said. "Do we have the Hall's home number?"

"Aye, I've got it," Gillespie said. He opened his file as he walked, then leaned over the desk on the other side of Gold. "Aye, that's it. Ends in two-nine-two. That's their number."

"Right," Freya said as she strode over to the whiteboard. She added a cross at the far left of the timeline and denoted it with 'Tyler calls the Hall landline'. She stepped back, and while Gold searched for anything else of interest, she sought to extract every worthwhile meaning from the new information. "How long was the call?"

"Two and a half minutes," Gold replied. "Give or take."

"And when was the last time he called that number?"

"Hold on," Gold said.

While she checked, Freya found Ben in a state of deep thought, which she interrupted gladly.

"What can you say in two and a half minutes?"

"Me?"

"What does one say to their mother? Adoptive or otherwise?"

"No more calls to that number in the past three months," Gold cut in.

"Thank you, Gold," Freya said, still fixated on Ben. "So, you haven't spoken to your mother for more than six months. What do you say?"

"Personally, I'd be horrified she even answered the phone," he replied. "She's been dead for years."

"Tyler, Ben," Freya said. "What would he have said?"

"I don't know. Maybe he told her he'd retired? I mean, if he hasn't spoken to her for six months or more, who knows? Maybe he just told her he'd retired and he wanted to meet?"

"Maybe," Freya said. "And what would she have done with that information?"

He shrugged.

"Told her husband the good news?" he replied. "If Gillespie is right, then she had no idea what happened between her husband and Tyler. Why wouldn't she have told him?"

"Right," Freya said. "Do we have the husband's phone records? What's his name, anyway?"

"Terence," Gillespie said. "Terence Hall."

"Right, do we have his phone records?"

"We do," Gold said. "I'll pull them up."

"Landline records are being emailed to me now," Chapman called out by way of an update. "I'll forward them to Gold as soon as they're in."

"Good. Can you get back onto your man on the mobile network for me? I want to see where the husband was during the time of death window. See if he can pinpoint a location, will you?"

"I'll try," Chapman replied, leaving Freya to ponder the board.

"Actually, have him get them all. Tyler, Dean, Godolphin and Terence Hall."

"That's a big ask, ma'am," she said. "It's getting late."

"Tell him you'll buy the drinks as a thank you," Freya said with a smile, which raised another blush. "See if we can pinpoint each of their locations. Are they all on the same network?"

"I think so. There's only one network with decent coverage around here," she replied. "Leave it with me." She looked across at Gold. "Landline details are on their way to you now."

"Righto," Gold said.

It was nothing short of exhilarating to see the team coming together. Even Cruz and Nillson, who were outside of the direct conversation, were beavering away.

"Nothing on Terence Hall's mobile statement," Gold said. "Looks like he gets calls from his home landline fairly frequently, plus there's some random oh-eight-hundred numbers. Want me to check them out?"

"No, they'll be sales calls," Freya replied. "So, John Tyler didn't call him directly, which supports our theory."

Ben nodded away, biting down on his lower lip.

"Jackie, have a look to see if he had any calls at the weekend," Ben said. "Specifically, Saturday night."

Gold did as requested, and Freya, seeing where Ben was going, waited in hope.

"Just one," Gold said, a little confused. "From his house."

"Time?"

"Nine forty-five," she said, then added, "p.m."

"Nine forty-five p.m.," Freya repeated, and Ben, who was never one to gloat, was lost in thought. "So, he wasn't home when he said he was."

"Ah, I knew it," Gillespie, who never missed an opportunity to gloat, spat. "Lying toe rag—"

"Here we go," Chapman said, waving a hand above her. She braved the loudspeaker again and averted her eyes. "You're on loudspeaker, Jason," she announced to prevent any further embarrassment. "Can you tell them what you just told me?"

"Erm, yep," he said, still retaining the flavour of a blush in his tone. "The number you need, belonging to a Terence Hall, made contact with three masts on Saturday evening."

"Where are they?" Freya asked, impatient to put an end to the saga.

"For the most part, the phone seems to have been..." His voice trailed off as presumably he was referring to a map. Freya clicked her fingers to get Ben's attention and mouthed the word map at him. He stood and strode over to the rear wall where the map was pinned. "Fen Road," Jason announced. "I can't give you an exact location; it's a fifty-metre splodge on the screen."

"That's his house," Cruz said, checking with Gillespie, who nodded his agreement, and Freya's heart sank.

And then Jason spoke again.

"Then, the signals change," he said.

"Sorry?"

"Sorry, the strength of the hello signals to each of the masts changes later on. Looks like he was on the move."

"Really?"

"Yeah," Jason said, speaking slowly as if he was translating the data in real-time. "He stays within the masts, so he doesn't go far, but from what I can see, he spends some time at..." Again, he was converting the data from whatever software he was using to a map. "Labour in Vain Drove?" he said. "Does that mean anything to you lot?"

"That's where the old farmhouse is," Cruz announced, speaking before he thought.

"Yes, it does mean something," Freya called out, catching Gillespie's eye and giving him the nod to plan his next course of action. "It means everything to us. What about the other numbers?"

"I'm just working through them," he said, sounding a little perplexed. "It's hard to say for sure. Triangulation isn't an exact science, but if you ask me, all of them are in the same area."

"All of them?"

"Yeah," he replied, and Freya checked the expressions of her team. Gillespie waved his phone to indicate he had an incoming call and stepped out of the room.

"What time are we talking about?" she asked, to which Jason expelled a breath of air through pursed lips.

"Most of the night," he said. "I'll send Denise a summary, but it looks like they were moving about a bit. Like I said, it's hard to be sure, but they're not always together. They're in the middle of a field; then they're on the lane. It's tricky because the phones send a signal to the masts every sixty seconds, so I can't pinpoint them exactly. If I'm honest, I'm not sure what went on out there."

"You don't want to know," Freya assured him. "Thank you, Jason. You've been a great help," she said, then waited for Chapman to end the call.

"Terence Hall, John Tyler, Geoff Godolphin, and Tommy Dean all in the same area, at the same time," Cruz said, voicing his thoughts aloud.

"And only two of them walk away," she said, catching Ben's eye, who displayed a rare winning grin, presumably in reference to the updated wager he had proposed.

"Boss?" Gillespie said as he burst back into the room with little consideration as to whether or not he was interrupting anything important. His face was an unhealthy shade of white, and his eyes a fiery red. "Just had Group Captain Shaw on the blower."

"And?" Freya said.

"She didn't say anything earlier, as she felt it was a betrayal to Tyler, but..." He slowed, then stalled, and not for the first time during the investigation, his voice cracked. "She read between the lines and worked out that I suspected Terence Hall of taking advantage of Tyler."

"And?" she replied quietly, to which he simply nodded, and his top lip curled in distaste.

"She didn't agree in so many words, but she did say Tyler had regular sessions with the base therapist. That's all she could say on the matter."

"Which, of course, will be confidential," Freya said, and again he nodded. "I suppose that leaves me with two questions."

"Boss?" he said, and she resumed her position, perched on the edge of her desk.

"How many uniformed officers do you need," she started, "and when do you want to bring him in?"

CHAPTER FORTY-NINE

"AND THEN THERE WERE FOUR," Nillson said, as the incident room doors closed behind Gold, Gillespie, and Cruz, and their voices faded to nothing.

Ben eased back in his chair. To some, Gillespie and Cruz heading off to bring Terence Hall in and Gold heading to Julie Dean's house might have suggested the beginning of the end. But there were far too many hurdles to overcome, and most of those were not yet in sight. By the way Freya was keeping her anxiety in check, she was thinking along the same lines.

"Let's put Terence Hall to one side for the moment," Freya said. "We've spent three days with almost nothing to go on, and the same names keep cropping up. Finally, we can place people at the scene of the crime, which means that, finally, we can bring them in. However, if we're going to keep them in, then we'll need more than a fat, triangulated dot on a map offering little more than circumstance."

"You want some meat on the bone, then?" Ben suggested.

"In short, yes," she said. "Specifically, Geoffrey Godolphin's bone."

"I'd be careful how you word that—"

"And I'd remind you that I cannot bear vulgarity, Ben," she said. "Chapman, do we have anything from your man regarding the times Godolphin was at the crime scene?"

"He's sent through a summary, ma'am," she replied. "For indicative purposes only, though, I'm afraid. It looks like he is in Tattershall until about nine-thirty p.m.—"

"His house is in Tattershall," Ben added.

"Right. If I'm reading the data correctly, then Tattershall is on different mobile data masts. He doesn't move onto the Billinghay masts until nine-forty-two."

Ben caught Freya's attention.

"Didn't the lad say he saw his dad leave the house?" he asked.

"That was Sunday night when he made the call," Nillson added.

"And the night before. I'm sure that's what he told us," Freya said. "And now we know where he went. Benjamin Godolphin made the call at nine-fifty, which ties in with his story." She looked to Chapman and Nillson. "He waited for his dad to go out, then walked up the road so we couldn't trace the call to his house. He said he'd seen it on the TV and didn't want us knocking on his dad's door."

"Well, he had the right idea," Nillson replied.

"Chapman, when did Godolphin leave the crime scene?"

"That's just it," she replied. "It's hard to be sure. It looks like he went to the old house first, then if I'm right, he goes to the first crime scene."

"The site of the hanging?"

"Yes," she said. "Then he goes back...." She shook her head. "Sorry, ma'am. It's just difficult to follow. The sixty-second delay is giving me trouble. He's jumping about all over the place."

"Okay, when does he get back home?" Ben asked. "Let's have a window of opportunity."

"Ten-oh-six," she said. "And he doesn't leave the house again."

"His phone doesn't, but he might have," Nillson said.

"Let's hold that thought, Anna," Freya said. "We have enough possibilities to deal with for now. Should we hit a stumbling block, then we can pursue the fact that he may have left the house again without his phone." She turned back to the board and clicked the lid from the marker. "Godolphin was at the scene for what, twenty minutes? From nine-forty to around ten p.m.?" She noted the information onto the timeline. "And Hall? We might as well do the same for him."

"He's on the scene at eleven minutes past nine," Chapman started, "and like Jason said, he moves about a fair bit, eventually leaving at eleven-o-four."

Freya made a note of the timings on the timeline.

"Right," she said, gazing for some clarity. "So, if we're correct about a historic argument being the reason that Dean murdered Tyler, then is it plausible that Dean had arranged for Tyler to be there?"

Ben, along with Nillson and Freya, looked across at Chapman, who took the hint.

"There's no record of a call to Tyler's number," she said.

"Alright," she said, nodding. "Is there a record of a call from Dean to Godolphin?"

"No," she replied. "Dean did make calls, but none of them are to Tyler or Godolphin."

"Who are they to?"

"One of them is his wife's," she replied, then looked up, defeated. "I'll need to look into the others."

"Bowen?" she said, and again Chapman shook her head.

"Nice try," Ben said under his breath, which Freya clearly heard but chose to ignore.

"Alright, see who else he called and get a message to Gold, will you? Have her ask Julie Dean what her husband said on the call. It would have been nice to know about that sooner."

"Will do," Chapman replied.

"Right, while we wait—"

"Ma'am, sorry," Chapman said, a rare look of confusion spreading over her delicate features. "It's just..."

"Take your time, Chapman," Freya said to avoid her getting flustered.

"Well, it's just that...if I'm reading this data right, then Tommy Dean arrived at the old house at five p.m.," she said. "Then he left and drove round for a bit and returned at six-thirty. He was there long enough for the phone to talk to the masts three times, so three minutes, and then it looks like he went back to the main road and headed to the first crime scene. His phone talks to the masts every minute for..." they watched her counting the lines on the document she had been given by Jason. "Nearly three hundred minutes," she said eventually. "Two-hundred and eighty-something."

"What's that? Four, nearly five hours? "Ben said.

"And then?" Freya asked.

Chapman took a deep breath and pushed herself away from the lines of numbers.

"Back to the house, ma'am," she said. "He's there for nearly ten minutes, then the signal stops."

"Dead phone?" Nillson suggested.

"Turned off, more like," Ben said.

"I agree," Freya said, picking up on the thread, and Ben watched her struggle with the facts because these were facts. The entire investigation to date had been based on theories, and to her credit, she had led them through the darkness adeptly. But now there were facts, and facts couldn't be manipulated. They were set in stone. "So, Dean was back and forth to the house, then at around six-thirty p.m., he leaves the old house and goes to the site of the hanging."

"And if John Tyler was living there in a tent..." Ben said, leaving that little thread for her to grip onto.

"Then it's plausible that Dean went to the house to get Tyler, and from there, either reluctantly or not, he took Tyler to the first crime scene."

"Why?" Nillson asked. "If he was going to hang him and burn him, then why not do it in the house?"

"History?" Ben suggested. "Maybe it was too poignant?"

"I think if the whole murder was based on a historical event, Ben, then poignancy is the whole point," Freya replied. "Dean was bitter about Tyler's comments about his father and the fire."

"Tyler and Godolphin," Ben said, which seemed to stall whatever she was about to say.

"You don't think..." she started, then shook her head.

"What is it?"

"Nothing," she replied. "I almost had it." She stared through him for a moment, her eyes flicking from side to side. "You don't think Godolphin was supposed to die, as well, do you? I mean... sorry, I don't quite know what I mean. But there's something there. There's a link. The fire. Tyler was burned, just like his family."

"To be honest, Freya, I'm still struggling with the fact that Tyler and Godolphin could have said anything bad enough to warrant death, let alone being bloody burned and hanged."

"Yes," she said, distracted by what Ben could only assume was a whirlwind of ideas and theories. "Yes, I hate to admit it, but I agree."

"It's pain he was after," he said. "Dean wanted Tyler to die slowly and painfully."

"Then he got his wish," Nillson added.

"But why?" Freya said. "It's not enough."

Ben acknowledged the comment but said nothing more. His attention remained firmly fixed on Freya.

"Godolphin was there. We know that."

"You want to bring him in?"

"I think we should," he replied. "If only to ask why he was there."

"I've got two numbers," Chapman said. "Neither of which means anything to me, and both are unregistered Pay-as-You-Go phones."

"Go on," Freya said.

"Well, Dean called the first one at six-forty-five p.m., which must have been just as he arrived at the first crime scene. The call lasted less than a minute. But the second call, to the second number, lasted for two minutes."

"What time was that?"

"Oh Jesus," Chapman said as she flicked and scrolled her mouse.

"What?" Ben asked.

"The second number," she said. "Hold on. Give me a minute, will you?"

Freya turned back to Ben, eyebrows raised.

"Where were we?"

"Godolphin."

"The timeline doesn't work," she said, looking back at the board. "Godolphin was there from nine-forty until just gone ten p.m."

"But he *was* there," Ben told her, and he flicked his eyes up at the horizontal line and the surrounding scrawls. "If you want to cross names off, then let's bring him in."

"Here we go," Chapman said. "Sorry, I just wanted to check."

"What is it, Chapman?" Freya asked.

"The number. The second number. I knew I'd seen it before," she said. "It was the one used to report the body in the house. It's Benjamin Godolphin's phone."

CHAPTER FIFTY

ON SUCH A QUIET STREET, the task ahead was akin, in Gillespie's mind, to being on stage or in a circus. Curtains flicked, and he was sure that tongues would be wagging. The flashing blues on the liveried Astras would have seen to that. Ten years ago, such things mattered very little, but in the age of video phones, everything he did in the next ten minutes would be captured in perpetuity.

Terence Hall was waiting for them, no doubt alerted by the lights, much as his neighbours had been.

"Terence Hall," Gillespie said, loud and clear, and he strode across the driveway. "I'm arresting you on suspicion of murder—"

"You're doing no such thing—"

"You do not have to say anything, but it may harm your defence if you do not mention, when questioned, something which you later rely on in court. Anything you do say may be given in evidence. Do you understand?"

"Not really."

"Do you want me to repeat it?"

Gillespie came to a stop at the foot of the steps, beaming up at Hall, who peered down with a face like he'd swallowed a lemon.

He shook his head, defeated at the sight of the various uniformed officers who waited on the sidelines should he make a run for it.

"No," he said. "No, but…"

"But what, Mr Hall?"

He glanced back into his house, then back at Gillespie.

"Can we do this…respectfully?"

"You're being arrested on suspicion of murder, Mr Hall. You'll be afforded every privilege you're entitled to," Gillespie told him and then leaned forward and spoke quietly. "And trust me. It's not much."

"I mean…my wife."

"Ah, the delightful Mrs Hall," Gillespie replied. "I'll ask somebody to sit with her if it makes you feel better. Unless you want her to come to the station with us?"

"No," he said. "No, she's… she's in bed. It's best not to disturb her."

"Ah, having one of her spells, is she?"

"She is, as it happens," Hall said, slightly perplexed at how Gillespie could have known.

Gillespie glanced back at the uniformed officers, then pointed at one male and one female in turn.

"You two," he said. "Inside, please."

"Excuse me," Hall said. "You can't go in there."

"Actually, we can," Gillespie replied.

"Where's your warrant?" he asked, to which Gillespie grinned.

"We don't need one," he said.

"You cannot search my house without a warrant. Even I know that—"

"Oh, you're right," Gillespie told him. "Well, nearly. You see, usually we do need a warrant to enter a house, except for a couple of…" he wound his hand around a few times, feigning to think of the right word. "Unique circumstances."

"Excuse me?"

"Well, if, say, we knew you were in the house refusing to come out, we wouldn't need a warrant to come in and get you."

"I came out. I was standing on the bloody doorstep."

"And if we believe that somebody is in danger," Gillespie added.

"Danger?"

"Aye, danger," he said again, then glanced across at the officers. "Bedroom. Call the medic if you need to."

"No," Hall said. "No, you can't disturb her. She's unwell."

"Listen," Gillespie told him. "You can argue all you like. They're going in." He manoeuvred himself so that he stood in front of Hall, blocking his view of the house. "And if they find a wee glass of water beside her bed, and if perchance there's a little trace of something what shouldn't ought to be inside that glass..."

Hall closed his eyes to block out Gillespie's purposeful, improper use of the English language.

"Anything you want to say to me?" Gillespie asked, to which Hall opened his eyes and sneered at him.

"I have a hundred things I'd like to say to you, but I have a feeling that none of them will do me any favours."

"Aye, you may be right. Do you have a solicitor you can call? We can provide one if necessary."

"Considering the fact that I'm not guilty of anything, I shan't be needing one."

"I'll get a duty solicitor," Gillespie said, and he nodded for Cruz to do the honours, and as the little DC pulled Hall's arms behind his back to cuff him, one of the officers returned to the front door with a glass in her gloved hand.

"Sarge!" she called out, holding the glass up.

"That needs to go to the lab," Gillespie told her. "Is she breathing?"

"She's out of it," she replied and nodded once. "But yes, she's breathing."

"There's no need for any of this—" Hall started.

"Aye, well. Better safe than sorry, eh?" Gillespie beckoned two officers over to remove Hall, then gave Cruz another nod. "Best get the medic here, Gabby. Best get the medic."

"This is wrong," Hall shouted as the officers led him away. "You're wrong on this, and I'll prove it, and then I'll bring a world of pain down on you, Sergeant Gillespie. You are so wrong about this."

"I hope I am," Gillespie called back. "I doubt I am, but I hope I am. For your wife's sake."

His phone began to rumble in his pocket, and the screen was alight with Chapman's desk phone number.

"Aye, Denise. We're on our way back."

"Hi Jim, DCI Bloom asked me to give you a quick heads up. She and Ben have gone to get Godolphin."

"Gonna be a busy night, eh?"

"We've developed a timeline. Your man, Hall, arrived on the scene at around ten past nine on Saturday night. He was there until around eleven o'clock. The next timestamp is eleven-oh-four when it looked like he was at home."

"Two hours?" Gillespie replied. "That's a long time to be running around in a dark field."

He paced as he walked and rounded the corner of the house, where the garden opened up. He had to admit, it was well done but must have involved a great deal of faff to maintain.

"Are you bringing him in?" she asked.

"Aye, and he's well chuffed at the invite."

"Have you spoken about a brief?" she asked. "Will he need a duty solicitor?"

"He says he won't need one."

"I'll arrange a duty, then," she said. "What about Godolphin? Do you think he'll have his own? Does he seem like the type?"

Gillespie moved across the lawn toward the far corner of the property, where a wooden shed had been erected.

"Doubt it," he replied, growing ever more distracted by the shed. He tugged on the padlock, and it turned in his hands.

"Alright," Chapman said. "I'll make some arrangements. No point in us hanging about waiting for them to arrive, is it? I mean, I don't mind working late, but I can't stand waiting for people. Especially bloody solicitors."

Gillespie checked behind him to make sure nobody was looking, then opened the door a few inches to peer inside.

"Jim, you there?"

"Aye, sorry," he said as he pulled the door open wider, and his eyes fell on the one thing he had been looking for.

"So, you'll be back soon, will you?" Chapman asked. "In case DCI Bloom asks."

"Aye," he said again, then gave her his full attention. "Although, I might need to take a wee detour."

CHAPTER FIFTY-ONE

SERGEANT PRIEST HANDLED the custody suite melee like the seasoned pro he was. There were no hurried questions or processes to expedite the suspects through the space. He took his time, dotting the Is and crossing the Ts with infallible detail.

"Go on," he called to an officer, nodding at Hall. "Cell two."

"I was hoping to take him straight through," Freya said, checking her watch and glaring at Ben. "Where the hell is Gillespie?"

"Need an answer, guv," Priest said apologetically. "Cell or interview room?"

"You could always drop me off at home," Hall said, which Priest politely ignored as the door to the car park opened, and Gillespie came to a sudden halt at the sight of the full custody suite.

"Full house, Michael?" he called out above the heads of the uniformed officers who had brought Hall in.

"It's even fuller now," Freya replied, and Gillespie startled at the sound of her voice.

"Boss?"

"I want him interviewed now. Are you ready?"

"Aye, boss," he grumbled as if he'd been longing for the oppor‑tunity. "With pleasure."

The uniformed officers led Hall through to the interview rooms with Gillespie and Cruz in tow.

"I would have thought you would have been here to check him in," she said quietly so that Hall didn't hear.

"Aye, sorry 'bout that, boss,' he said. "Had to make a wee detour."

"Who's next?" Priest called as Gillespie and Cruz nodded assuredly, then headed into the corridor towards the interview rooms.

"Geoffrey Godolphin," Ben said, nudging Godolphin forward. "Arrested on suspicion of conspiracy to murder."

"Geoffrey Godolphin," Priest repeated as he typed one‑fingered into the computer. He then continued to run through the standard questions, date of birth, address, if he was aware why he'd been arrested, aware of his rights, and if there were any health concerns, leaving Freya and Ben to develop a hushed plan.

"I don't think we need one," Ben said. "I think we just let him tell his side of the story and then correct him if he deviates from what we know as facts."

"We already know he lies," Freya said.

"Then let him lie," Ben replied, and he closed in to ensure Godolphin didn't hear a single word. "All I want is to know what he was doing over near the crime scenes, how he found out about them, and why the bloody hell he used his kid's phone."

"All yours," Priest announced. "Room one?"

"Thank you," Freya replied. "It's clean, I assume?"

"You could eat your dinner off the floor, guv," he replied.

"The way things are going, it might come to that," she said. "When the brief gets here, send them in, will you? We're on a bit of a tight schedule on this one."

"Leave it with me," Priest replied, the bass of his voice accen‑tuating his Yorkshire accent.

A uniformed officer led Godolphin into the corridor and then ushered him into the interview room, but before Ben followed him in, Freya tugged on his sleeve, and they conspired in the corridor like two naughty teenagers.

"Is Gillespie alright in there?" she asked.

"Of course he is. He knows what he's doing."

"I know, but...you don't think we should have, I don't know, swapped."

"What? Freya, for God's sake, he's a Detective Sergeant. I'm not sure what it was like when you passed through that particular rank, but he worked hard to get where he is—"

"I'm not doubting his competence, Ben," she said. "I'm doubting his..." she sighed and hissed quietly at him. "I'm doubting if he can hold it together. Emotionally, I mean."

"Jim?" Ben said. "He'll be fine."

"I just think it's a bit close to home, you know? You didn't see him the other day at the old house. The man was on the edge, Ben."

"Oh, he'll be alright," Ben said. "And yeah, I know it's a bit close to home for him, but he can't pick and choose. If his past gets in the way of his work, then he's in the wrong job. He's managed fine up until now."

She moved away and edged closer to Gillespie's interview room.

"He's fine," Ben hissed, just as the doors at the far end of the corridor opened and in walked somebody who, even before she had introduced herself, could only have been a solicitor.

"I'm Kelly McCarthy. I'm from Johnson and Cleverly. I'm looking for DCI Bloom. Here to represent Geoffrey Godolphin," she said, her voice deeper than Ben's. She wore a visitor's lanyard around her neck and neither smiled nor sneered at them. To her, the entire process was business. It was a transaction. She would listen to Godolphin's story, and if there was any chance of culpability, she would advise him to offer a no-comment response, leaving them no better off than they had been but with a ticking custody clock to work against.

"Then, you've found her," Freya told her, then stepped out of her way, presenting the open interview room door. "Mr Godolphin is waiting inside." She checked her watch. "I'll give you a few minutes, then we'll come in."

"Thank you," McCarthy said, then made a point of closing the door behind her.

She looked back at Ben, whose face mirrored her thoughts precisely.

"Where do you think he went?" Freya asked.

"Jim?" he said, shaking his head. "No idea."

"Do you think he popped home? Maybe he stopped for a quick drink. A wee dram, as it were, to calm his nerves."

"No," Ben said. "He's a bit of a wildcard, but he's not an idiot."

"No?" Freya said. "I'll take your word for that."

"Godolphin," he said. "What do we have?"

"He lied during his initial chat with us," she said. "He said he didn't know Tommy Dean when clearly, he does. Plus, we've placed him at the crime scene, and we've got a call from Dean to his boy's phone a matter of hours before Tyler died."

"So, why isn't the boy here? Why haven't we got Benjamin Godolphin in that interview room?"

"Because he didn't make the call," Freya said, to which Ben looked utterly bemused.

"How do we know that?"

"We don't," she said. "But I'm sure we're about to find out."

"Freya?"

"Have you ever interviewed a minor?" she asked.

"Of course, I have—"

"Right, so where are the appropriate adults? Where is the evidence that he was involved?"

She smiled at his frustration and gave the door three gentle knocks before pushing in.

"Thank you for coming," she announced to Godolphin and McCarthy, holding the door for Ben. She let him settle in and begin the recording, giving her files a quick checkover during the delay. He hit record, and they waited for the lengthy buzzer that sounded before she announced the date and time. Once she had introduced herself and Ben, she gave McCarthy and Godolphin an opportunity to follow suit. "Geoffrey Godolphin, do you understand why you are here?"

"Not really," he replied.

"Okay, well, for the benefit of the recording and for the purposes of transparency, my colleague will remind you of your rights." She looked to Ben, who then cleared his throat.

"Geoffrey Godolphin, you have been arrested on suspicion of conspiracy to murder. You do not have to say anything, but it may harm your defence if you fail to mention, when questioned, anything you later rely on in court. Anything you do say may be used against you. Do you understand?"

He looked across to McCarthy, who gave a brief, single nod.

"Yeah," he said.

"Thank you," Freya said, taking the reins. "Right then, I'll start with what is perhaps the most puzzling question." She peered over her folder at him for sincerity. "It should be easy after that."

He raised an eyebrow and held a neutral expression.

"I'm all ears," he said.

"A few days ago, you were invited here for an informal chat with two of our colleagues. A DC Cruz and DS Gillespie."

"Yes," he said.

"You remember that, do you?"

"It was a few days ago."

"Good, well. Let's see how well you remember the discussion you had," she said, referring to Gillespie's notes. "Actually, it should be easy to recall, seeing as it was the last thing you said before you walked out of that door. Do you remember?"

"Not specifically," he replied.

"I'll remind you," she said, setting the tone. "DS Gillespie asked you if you knew of a man named Tommy Dean. Does that ring any bells?" Godolphin stared at her, his mouth ajar and his fat tongue licking at his teeth.

"No comment," he said.

"Oh, come on. We can do better than that, can't we?" Freya said. "It was, as you said, only a matter of days ago. It was the last thing you said during the interview. Surely you can recall such a significant detail?"

"No comment," he said again.

"That's a pity," she said, eventually. "I was rather hoping you'd be a little more forthcoming, but we are where we are." She moved on to the next item on her list. "Perhaps then, you can explain where you were between the hours of nine forty p.m. and ten p.m. on Saturday night?"

"I've already told you," he said. "I was at home. I've got a boy. Can't leave him on his own, can I?"

"Oh, that's right," Freya said. "Benjamin."

"S'right."

She smiled, showing her disappointment.

"Do you want to know what Benjamin was doing on Saturday night?"

"Eh?"

"Your son, Mr Godolphin, watched you leave the house on Saturday night. He told us so."

"He did what? You've spoken to my boy—?"

"It was all above board. We spoke to a few pupils at the school with the headteacher present, so there's nothing to worry about."

"You can't do that—"

"Oh, I think we can," she said. "You see, your son's mobile telephone was involved in our investigation—"

"It's what?"

"He called the emergency services the next day," she said. "A few hours after he and his friends discovered a man's body."

He sat dumbstruck while he processed the news.

"Body?"

"And do you know what I find interesting? We found that same phone number on Tommy Dean's call history. Why would he have called your son?"

"No comment."

"Perhaps they knew each other?"

"No comment."

"Although, if I'm right, you weren't on speaking terms so it doesn't make sense."

"No comment."

"It wasn't a question, but thank you for making your position so clear," Freya told him. "So, perhaps now you can understand why we're so keen to talk to you. You say that you're not acquainted with Tommy Dean, yet your son's phone was used to make the initial emergency services call, and then we found it on Dean's recently dialled numbers. Something doesn't stack up here."

"No comment," he said, and Freya closed the file before her.

"You're involved, Geoffrey. You know you're involved, I know you're involved, and even Miss McCarthy knows you're involved, and she's only known you for ten minutes."

"It's *Mrs* McCarthy," McCarthy corrected her with an obvious glance down at Freya's bare third finger. Freya offered a rather disingenuous smirk by way of acknowledgement.

"Perhaps we can move on," Freya said. "You see, while we were looking into you and a number of other persons of interest, we made a rather startling discovery. You were there, Geoffrey."

"Where?"

"At the crime scene," she said. "Brinkleview Farm."

"It's a big farm."

"And you should know. You trampled over much of it on

Saturday night between the hours of nine-forty and ten pm,"
Freya said. "Why was that? I mean, you had a small boy at home
in bed, so clearly, you couldn't have left him on his own. Yet, you
were in a field, in the dark. Had you lost something, perhaps?"

"No comment."

Freya softened her tone and relaxed her shoulders, hoping to
appear less confrontational.

"You've met DS Gillespie, haven't you?"

Godolphin debated on whether or not he should give a no
comment response but elected to play along with Freya's news
approach.

"You know I have."

"Then perhaps it might be worth speaking to him. I'm sure
he'd be happy to talk to you."

"About what?"

"About what it's like to grow up in a care home. I don't think
he'd mind me telling you, but his upbringing was...less than
perfect, shall we say? It had quite a profound effect on him."

Godolphin shook his head.

"I'm not following."

"Your boy," Freya said. "I need you to think about your boy,
Benjamin. That's what will happen to him while you're inside. You
may even have to fight for custody when you're eventually
released. I mean, it's not unheard of."

"Sorry?"

"I think perhaps we should stick to fact rather than fiction,"
McCarthy said. "And if we could not speculate on potential
outcomes regarding minors, I think it would be in all of our
interests."

Freya recollected her thoughts, then went for the jugular.

"Mr Godolphin, you should know that I have spoken to the
Crown Prosecution Service. They've given the green light for me
to charge you with conspiracy to murder."

"Based on what evidence, please?" McCarthy asked.

"Your client, *Mrs* McCarthy, was at the scene of the crimes. He is proven to have lied to us during the investigation, and a phone belonging to his son was one of the last numbers dialled by a man who we believe murdered John Tyler and then subsequently died himself. Is that enough for you? Because it's enough for the CPS."

"I'll be contesting the relevance of the phone records," McCarthy added.

"You're welcome to," Freya told her, then turned her attention to Godolphin. "You will be held on remand until the date of your trial—"

"What? You can't do that."

"Oh, I can," she said, and she leaned forward to look him in the eye. "Two men have died, Mr Godolphin. You knew them both; you were in the area when they both died, and your responses so far have been less than helpful." She let that statement hang there for a few moments while he digested it. "Tommy Dean called your son's phone on Saturday night. Dean was in the northernmost field on Brinkleview Farm. Your son was at home." She waited while the true meaning of what she had said registered. "I think it's time you told us what really happened out there, Mr Godolphin."

CHAPTER FIFTY-TWO

"I DON'T NEED LEGAL REPRESENTATION," Hall said while Cruz was arranging the recording. "I told you at the house. I've done nothing wrong."

Gillespie waited patiently. The brief made a show of pausing, his notebook half open on his lap as if waiting for somebody to tell him if he had wasted his time or not.

"Can I be honest with you, Mr Hall?" Gillespie said. "This is a murder investigation. It's serious stuff. Now, whether or not you feel you want legal representation, it's in your best interest. If this goes to court, which it's highly likely to, then you're going to need all the help you can get."

"I won't be going to court," he replied.

"Well, that's to be seen—"

"I won't be going to court," he said again, and he glanced ruefully at the brief. "Thank you for your time. I can only apologise."

The brief closed his notebook, pocketed his pen, and before he stood, offered Hall one more chance.

"I mean it," Hall said. "I'm sorry to have wasted your time."

Cruz's finger was poised over the record button, and Gillespie held his hand up for him to hold fire while the brief rushed from the room with his leather satchel in one hand and his jacket slung over the other. The door slammed behind him, and Gillespie gave Cruz the nod, then waited for the buzzer to finish before announcing the time and date and those present.

"Now then, Terence. You have been arrested on suspicion of murder. You do not have to say anything, but it may harm your defence if you fail to mention, when questioned, something you later rely on in court. Anything you do say may be given in evidence. Do you understand, Mr Hall?"

"The statement, or how it pertains to me?"

"I'll take that as a yes," Gillespie said. "Now then, for the benefit of the recording, the murders in question are those of one John Tyler and one Thomas Dean, both of whom died sometime between nine p.m. on Saturday night and the early hours of Sunday morning." Hall closed his eyes as if steeling himself for what was to come, and Gillespie opened his folder. But instead of going straight in for the kill, he sat back in his seat. "I'm at a loss, Terence. Honestly, I just don't know where to begin."

"Well, why don't you let me go, and perhaps we can discuss this in a more civilised manner in..." He glanced around the room. "In a more appropriate setting."

"Oh, I think this is fairly appropriate," Gillespie told him, then placed his hand on the topmost sheet of paper in his folder. "Shall I tell you what bothers me most?"

Hall adopted a professional posture. He crossed his legs and linked his fingers around his knee as if the two of them had sat down for tea and cake.

"Okay," he said.

"Your attitude," Gillespie said, to which Hall gave a laugh and shook his head sadly. "The lad you adopted, John Tyler, is dead, Mr Hall," Gillespie said, which wiped the smile from his face. "I don't get it. You give a twelve-year-old lad who lost his entire family a home. There's honour there. The world needs more people to do that kind of thing. Yet, the moment he turns eighteen, and is no longer under your care, he joins the RAF and doesn't come back. Why?"

"He had his own life," Hall said. "What can I say? What did you expect me to do, force him to come round?"

"He shouldn't have needed forcing. He should have *wanted* to come and see you. *I* would have. If somebody had picked me up and dusted me down, I'd have wanted to see them. It's not even like he was posted on the other side of the world. He spent most of his career two miles away in RAF Coningsby, yet in nearly three decades, he doesn't come to see you once?"

"He did come," Hall said. "You're blowing it out of proportion—"

"Weekly?"

"No, just every now and again. Like I said, he was busy," Hall replied. "And when he did come round, I'm afraid to say that my wife didn't exactly make it an enjoyable experience."

"Ah, yes. The guilt trips."

"It's not her fault," Hall said. "She was so happy when John came to us. It was everything she ever wanted. So, when he stopped coming, she became..." He looked down at his lap and then up at Gillespie, for the first time displaying humility. "She became quite resentful."

"Is that right?" Gillespie said, allowing him to spin the yarn a little more.

"The truth is," Hall continued, "that ever since we lost James, all she's ever wanted is to have somebody to call her own, you know? I blame myself, really. I should have seen something like this coming. I knew he'd leave one day, and well, let's face it, it's not like we're in a position to have any more of our own, is it?"

"I'm sorry, can we just go back a wee bit?" Gillespie said. "James?"

"Yes," he said. "Yes, James was our son."

"You had a son?"

Hall inhaled long and hard.

"He died. He was a few weeks old. Eighteen days, to be precise."

"I'm sorry," Gillespie said, setting all traces of his sour opinion to one side for a moment. "I didn't realise—"

"It's okay. I've had decades to learn how to deal with it," he replied. "My wife, however, she still feels it. It's the maternal thing. You understand that, right?"

"I do," Gillespie said.

"I suppose you'll want to know how."

"No," Gillespie said. "No, I have no intention of delving into something so personal. Unless, of course, I feel the need."

"Well, there is a need," Hall said. "That's why we're here, isn't it? To understand each other?"

"In a fashion," Gillespie replied, but Hall wasn't listening. He was remembering.

"He was a normal, healthy child. He wasn't heavy; he wasn't thin. He was...he was perfect. It's me who wasn't quite perfect. You see, after a week or so of him being at home, I made the decision to go back to work. I mean, I could barely do anything anyway. My wife wanted to breastfeed. She wouldn't let me even try a bottle. She wanted that connection, and I suppose, like so many other fathers out there, I let her. I mean, it's better for the baby, isn't it? Anyway, I did what I could. I fetched and carried. I woke up in the night and helped where I could. But mostly, she did it all. She controlled every aspect of our little baby's life. So, in the end, I went back to work. Somewhere, I could be useful. Somewhere, I didn't feel like I was in the way." It was far more than Gillespie had intended on learning, but Hall was talking, and given the subject, he understood why the brief had been dismissed so readily. "My wife probably didn't even notice me gone, truth be told," Hall continued and then stiffened. "Until she needed me. Until she truly needed me, that is." His gaze rose slowly and landed on Gillespie. "James had a seizure. It was out of the blue. Something that nobody could have foreseen."

"My God, I'm sorry—"

"She called me. She was in a panic. So, she called me, and I called an ambulance, but in the end, it was all too late. She doesn't drive, you see? Never has done." His nostrils flattened as he inhaled and prepared to finish. "And I wasn't there." The tone in those final four words carried decades of grief and blame, and after a few moments, Hall was able to continue. "After a year or so had passed, we felt ready to try again. Not to *replace* James, but..." his voice trailed off, perhaps remembering those moments, those tepid conversations of hope that were flavoured with bitter resentment. "I don't know. Anyway, we couldn't. They say that, don't they? The harder you try, the harder it becomes. I'm sorry, is that too much detail?"

"No," Gillespie said. "No, not at all. I'm just sorry you had to go through it."

Hall nodded his appreciation.

"John came along following two years of failure. It seemed right. We went through all the tests with social services, we put ourselves on the list, and then bam, there he was. A young boy on our doorstep looking for a home. Looking for somebody to love him and dote on him." He looked up and stared firmly into Gillespie's eyes. "And dote on him, she did. She poured everything into that boy. Smothered him. Suffocated him. I warned her. I said that one day he'd grow old and fly the nest, but she just kept on and on at him. She was into every detail of his life. He wanted a motorbike, but she told him they were too dangerous. He would go out with friends, and she would follow him or call around to friends' houses to check up on him. And then he did grow older, and the RAF offered him a place. They offered him a life of his own. They offered him a chance to breathe, I suppose, and what would you do if you'd been suffocated for that long? Would you choose fresh air, or would you hold your breath and endure it for longer?"

"You're saying she was a little overbearing?"

"A little?" he scoffed. "The lad couldn't make a cup of tea when he signed up. He'd never had to. Couldn't boil an egg. Christ, I even had to help him get driving lessons behind her back. She was terrified something would happen to him. I told her. I said she needed to ease up on him. Let him live life. Let him make mistakes, but she used to just get so...so bloody tense. She'd do herself a mischief."

Mr Hall, I think I see what you're saying here," Gillespie said. "But it's wildly different from the picture you've painted to date."

"Picture?"

"What you've told me," Gillespie said. "You and your good wife. Something doesn't add up. I've been to see you twice at your home, and all this is only coming up now when you've been arrested. You'll have to humour me here, Mr Hall, but in my experience, that usually suggests that somebody is hiding something."

"Well, perhaps I was," he said quietly. "Perhaps...I don't know. I was trying to protect her."

Gillespie watched him closely but picked up on no visible signs of deceit.

"Mr Hall, I'm going to lay my cards on the table," he said. "I'm going to tell you everything I have on you, and I'll be honest, if I don't receive a straight answer, then I'm afraid...well, you can use your imagination."

"Everything you have on me?" Hall said. "You've nothing on me. You can't have because I've done nothing. The only thing I'm guilty of is protecting my wife." He leaned forward in his seat and resumed that confrontational scowl he had worn outside his house. "And if that's a crime, then so be it."

"John's dead, Mr Hall. Do you understand that?"

"Of course, I bloody well understand it," Hall spat. "I loved the man. He was..." his tone softened. "He was our boy."

"Do you know where he died?" Gillespie asked.

"In the fields," Hall replied. "You haven't said as much, but there's been enough activity over the past week for us to put two and two together."

"Aye, in the fields," Gillespie continued. "In the fields where you were on the night that he died." Hall's head cocked to one side. His eyes narrowed, and his tongue wet his lips, then shot back into his mouth. "We checked with your mobile phone provider. They gave us access to your account."

"They can't do that. Not without good reason."

"And we had good reason," Cruz said, to which Gillespie held up his hand to stop him from butting in any further.

"What?" Hall said. "What is it? What's this reason you have for invading my privacy?"

"Mr Hall, what were you doing there?" Gillespie asked. "From where I'm sitting, I've got a man who has admitted to lying to us—"

"I didn't lie."

"You withheld information," Gillespie said. "It's as good as. You clearly had some friction with John, and now we discover you were in the area when he died. You're hiding something. What is it? Why were you there?"

Hall shook his head in disbelief.

"You think I could have killed John? I loved that boy," he said. "That man. I loved him like...like James. Do you want to know why I was there? Because he asked me to come."

"What?"

"He asked me," Hall said. "He called me, and he asked me to come."

"There's no record of John Tyler ever calling your mobile phone number, Mr Hall."

"He didn't call my mobile. He used the landline. I doubt he even knew my mobile phone number."

"Your house phone?"

"Yes," Hall said, exasperated. "He called me, and he asked me to bring him something. A scrapbook. It was something we did with him when he first came to us, so that his family were always there. Pictures, you know? Newspaper cuttings." The anger in his voice abated. "We added to it over the years. Every now and then, we'd receive a photo in the post. His way of staying in touch, I suppose. So, we'd add it in there. Him with his RAF friends. His squadron. We were proud. Proud parents, if you can believe that."

"And he called the landline? Did he not speak to your wife?"

"He wouldn't speak to her. I suppose he knew if he spoke to her, he'd get an earful for not coming to see us. He used to call the house every so often, and if she answered, then he would hang up."

"But you said he hadn't called."

"Of course I did. I couldn't bloody well let her find out, could I? She'd be heartbroken."

"And tell me, Mr Hall," Gillespie said. "What was said when he called?"

"Not a lot," he replied. "I happened to be near the phone when it rang. As soon as he recognised my voice, he told me what he wanted and then told me where he'd be. My wife came in before I could really speak to him, so I pretended the caller had just hung up."

"Which I suppose she bought, considering John had done the same thing to her."

"Precisely," he grumbled.

"And so, you took him the scrapbook?"

"I did," he said, nodding. "And before you ask, no, I didn't see him. I looked for him everywhere. I could hear people out in the fields, and I even traipsed through the bloody mud to find him. In the end, I left it there. In his tent."

"How did you know it was his tent?"

"How? Because he told me where to find him." He closed his eyes and composed himself. "Had I known what was happening, I wouldn't have left. But I have to live with that, Sergeant Gillespie. I have to live with the fact that I wasn't there to save him." He stabbed his finger into the desk and gritted his teeth as he delivered the final line. "For the second time in my life, I wasn't there when my child needed me the most."

The air in the room was thick, and Gillespie was awestruck at Hall's composure. It was as if the cloud of shame that had lingered over Hall had passed and now hovered over Gillespie.

"Mr Hall, did John say why he wanted it?" he asked. "The scrapbook, I mean. Did he have time to say why he needed it?"

Hall shook his head dismissively.

"Not really," he replied. "He just said he'd learned something recently and wanted to remember them."

"But he didn't tell you what he'd learned?"

"There wasn't time," he said. "He said a friend of his was going to help him rebuild the house."

"The house?" Gillespie said. "The farmhouse?"

"Yes. I think John fully intended to live there. He always said he'd buy it if he could—"

"Which friend, Mr Hall? Who was helping him?"

"The other lad," Hall said. "Tommy Dean."

CHAPTER FIFTY-THREE

"I DON'T KNOW," Godolphin said, his frustration rising with every syllable he spat. "Alright? I don't know why I went. I don't know why I didn't bloody well just ignore him."

"Who, Geoff?" Ben asked. "Who should you have ignored?"

"Tommy," he said. "Who else?" He looked away, clearly disappointed with himself. "He came to the house."

"When?"

"I don't know. Last week sometime," he said. "Hadn't seen him for years, but I recognised him immediately."

"What did he want?"

Godolphin's head snapped back as he glared as if Ben should have known better than to interrupt him.

"He wanted help," he said. "I don't know what he was planning. I don't know what he did, and if he died, well...well, that's a shame, and truly, I'm sad about it. But do I know anything?" He shook his head. "No. No, I don't. All I know is that he was as bitter when he came to my house as he was when he stormed out all those years ago."

"When you were doing the tattoos?" Ben asked.

"Yeah, when we were doing these." He turned his head and

pulled his collar down. "The man was born bitter. I closed the door on him, you know? But he kept on knocking. Knocked so loud the bloody neighbours came out. Then he started shouting."

"Shouting what?"

"That I was a coward. That this was his chance and that if I was any kind of a friend, I'd help them."

"Them?"

Godolphin hung his head and sighed.

"Him and John."

"I'm sorry. I thought you said that they'd fallen out."

"They did. We all did. Haven't seen either of them for years. John joined up, and Tommy lived a life of resentment, I suppose."

"So, you hadn't even thought about them?"

"I thought about them every day," Godolphin said and presented his neck again. "How could I not? But I hadn't seen them or spoken to them. Happens, don't it? You grow apart. An argument, no matter how small or irrelevant, seems to fester. Makes it worse. Anyways, he comes around, knocks on the doors and shouts and whatnot, and so I have to let him in, if anything, to keep the neighbours from calling you lot."

"You seem to care about your neighbours' opinions," Freya said.

"Yeah, well. If we all cared about our neighbours' opinions, the world would be a better place, wouldn't it?"

"What did he have to say for himself?" Ben asked, before Freya managed to get his back up and cause him to reassess his decision to give them something other than no comment.

"He said he'd been doing some digging. He reckons he found out something about his dad."

"His father, who you had previously suggested, had run away with a younger woman?"

"Yeah, well. That might not have been my best moment," he said.

"We all have them," Ben told him, hoping to offer some

encouragement. "So, am I right in saying that Tommy walked out all those years ago because of what you said?"

"Partly," he admitted. "I suppose it was a build-up, really. If it was a fight for sympathy, then John won. Not that there *was* a fight for sympathy, but you know? The bloke lost his entire family. Tommy's dad left. What was I supposed to do, ignore John, who was devastated, and put my arm around Tommy?"

"Well, when you put it like that?"

"There's no other way to put it," Godolphin said. "We all knew what Tommy's dad was like. He was always hanging off the latest barmaid. The chances are that he had met a younger woman and had buggered off."

"But Tommy thought otherwise, did he?"

"He did," Godolphin said, and he glanced across at his brief, who was as enthralled as Ben was. "You writing this down, are you?"

Clearly, McCarthy wasn't used to such interactions, and her mouth opened like a drawbridge, but she retained enough professionalism to refrain from responding directly.

"And so, what was it that Tommy wanted when he came to visit?" Ben asked.

"He wanted help," Godolphin replied flatly. "He said he'd finally worked it out and that he needed help to get him?"

"Get who?"

There was a knock on the door, and it was immediately opened by Gillespie, who leaned in and offered his apologies.

"Quick word, boss?"

"Now?"

"Aye, now," Gillespie said.

She looked disapprovingly at Ben, and had it been an ordinary investigation, she would most likely have let him continue without her. But seeing as Godolphin was just getting into the meat of his story, she gestured for him to pause the interview.

"How about we take a break?" Ben suggested to Godolphin

and McCarthy, who was still reeling from her telling him off. "Interview paused at nine-seventeen p.m." Freya stood, and Ben followed suit, taking their folders with them. At the door, Ben stopped and looked back at Godolphin. "I'd take this opportunity to get your story straight if I were you."

"It's straight enough," Godolphin replied.

Ben closed the door behind them and was met by Freya, Gillespie, and Cruz in the corridor.

"This had better be good, Gillespie," Freya said.

"It is," he replied. "Look, I've just had Hall spill his guts, and I, erm, ...well, I was wrong, boss. I was wrong about him, and..." He looked at Cruz, who offered a sympathetic smile. "I let my emotions steer me. I shouldn't have done that."

"What do you mean you were wrong?"

"His story," he replied. "It stacks up. It wasn't him who John Tyler was avoiding. It was his wife. She was overbearing, and John couldn't hack it."

"I'm sorry, Gillespie, but you've just dragged me out of an important interview to tell me this? If you have a conscience enough to warrant an apology, that's one thing, but this is a testament to obstruction. And anyway, who's to say he isn't lying? We have him at the crime scene."

"Yeah, we have him in the area, but even Chapman said they couldn't be sure who was exactly where due to the triangulation limitations, boss. He's telling the truth."

"Based on what? Your gut? I trusted your gut once, Gillespie—"

"And this," he said, and he held up his phone to display a message. The sender was Katy, and her name had been marked with a red heart on either side. But the message was clear.

Garden tools clear. Water clear. Sorry xxx.

"What does that mean?"

"It's why I was late checking him in, boss," Gillespie said. "I found a shovel and a spade at his house, and one of the uniformed lot found a glass of water next to his wife's bed. She was out of it, apparently."

"So, you took them to the lab."

"Aye, I did," he said. "I thought that if I can prove it, it might just get this investigation over the line, you know?"

"But what?"

"But all it's done is prove he's telling the truth," he said.

"And what about him dosing his wife?"

He shrugged.

"I suppose she's genuinely ill?" he said.

"And the abuse?"

He shook his head.

"Please tell me you haven't accused him of anything?"

"No," he said. "No, that's the joker up my sleeve."

"Well, keep it there," she said. "In fact, rip it up." She paced back and forth. "What else did he have to say?"

"Aye, well. That's where it gets interesting. See, Tyler called him on his landline. He refused to speak to the wife but eventually got through to him and asked him to bring him something to the house. He reckoned John had always wanted to buy the house and restore it. His mate was going to help him."

"The scrapbook?" Freya said, to which even Cruz's head snapped to attention.

"How the bloody hell did you know that?" Gillespie asked.

Freya looked at them all as if they had gone mad.

"There was nothing else there apart from an old sleeping bag and a stove, and I doubt he'd call up a man he hadn't spoken to in years to bring him camping equipment," she said. "Who was the friend?"

"Ah, Tommy Dean."

"Tommy Dean?"

"Aye, and that's not all," he said. "He reckons John had recently learned something about his family. That's why he wanted the scrapbook."

"Who owns the house now?" Freya asked, and she turned to Ben.

"Bowen, I suppose. It's on his land."

"Actually, from what Hall was saying, the sale might have gone through already."

"Then why hasn't anybody mentioned it?" Freya asked. "We've spoken to Bowen enough times now."

Freya's eyes grew wide and bright, and she brushed through them to reopen the interview room door.

"Mr Godolphin, you said something about Tommy Dean asking you to get him. Who was he on about?"

"If we're reestablishing the interview, I'd prefer if we could record every detail," McCarthy said.

"Oh, shut up, you stuck-up cow," Freya told her and turned her attention back on Godolphin. "You'll be helping us. Who did Tommy want help getting?"

Godolphin shook his head and looked suddenly fearful at seeing Freya's wrath being unleashed on his brief.

"I don't know."

"Okay," she said, entering the room fully so that Ben and the others could follow. "I don't want to put words into your mouth, but can you think of anybody in that area that might have something to do with Tommy's dad's disappearance?"

"You don't have to say anything," McCarthy said quietly to him, unable to look Freya in the eye. "You should really stay silent until they start the record—"

"Bowen," Godolphin said, speaking over her. "Frank Bowen."

"And what makes you say that?"

"Because he's a dodgy swine, and we all know what happened to that poor girl, don't we? Alice Neal."

"Alice Neal? Do you think her disappearance is connected to Tommy, somehow?"

"Not Tommy, no, but Bowen and Tommy's dad, maybe. I don't

know the ins and outs. Tommy was flustered. Kind of excited, you know?"

"He called your son's phone, Geoff," Ben said.

"He called my son's phone because that's the number I gave him."

"If you felt that way about him, why give him a number?"

"Because he wouldn't leave me alone," Godolphin replied. "Honestly, he just kept on and on at me."

"So, you gave him your son's number?"

"It's just a Pay-As-You-Go number. I figured if Tommy called it and Benjamin answered, then he'd figure he'd got the wrong number, and if he didn't, I'd get my lad a new phone. A new SIM card."

Freya glanced back at Ben with a look that said something along the lines of, 'how the hell were we supposed to have worked that out?'

"So, he called your boy's phone. Who answered?"

"I did," he said. "I was expecting him to call sooner rather than later, and I always make sure Benjamin leaves his phone downstairs at bedtime." He sighed heavily. "He told me to meet him in the North field. He said he'd need all three of us."

"To do what, Geoff?" Ben asked. "What did he have planned?"

"I don't know, exactly," he replied. "He just said *he,* whoever *he* is, wouldn't go down without a fight, and if our friendship had meant anything to me at any point in my life, then I'd meet him there." Godolphin stared at them all as if to say, '*you work it out*'. "According to Tommy, he'd never get another chance. He begged me."

"Another chance for what?" Ben asked to which Godolphin stared blankly at him.

"At proving his old man hadn't simply run away with a younger woman. That something happened to him."

A door slammed somewhere in the corridor, followed by the slap-slap of flat shoes on the hard corridor floor. By the time Ben had leaned out of the interview room, Chapman was running towards him with a folder in her hand.

"Chapman?" he said, which then prompted Freya to join them.

"I've got something," she said, waving the folder. She stopped before them, opened the file and flicked through several pages until she found what she was looking for. Her fingernails were trim and clean but unpainted. A far cry from the manicured weapons on the ends of Freya's fingers. She pointed at a line of text. "These are the PAYE records from Brinkleview Farm. They were processed by Plant and Yale Accountants."

"So?" Freya said.

"Plant and Yale?" she said, "It's the same accountants Tommy Dean used to work for before the lockdown."

CHAPTER FIFTY-FOUR

BEN DROVE, and he drove hard. The gap between Freya's Range Rover and the convoy behind them grew wider by the second. Somewhere among the trailing units were Gillespie's old Volvo and Nillson's little hatchback. But they were just distant headlights in the rearview mirror by the time they had torn through Timberland and Walcott, a few minutes out from Billinghay.

"Right," Freya said, always a precursor to her getting her facts in order. "Alice Neal goes missing. Bowen is investigated but found not guilty. A year or so later, the Tyler family's house goes up in flames, and at about the same time, Dean's father is reported missing, presumed run off with another woman."

"I'm listening," Ben said, dying to engage but focused on the task at hand.

"What if Dean's father knew something about Alice Neal?" Freya continued. "What if he approached Bowen about it? No, no, how would he know? And why would he wait an entire year to speak up?"

"What if Dean's dad was responsible for Alice Neal's disappearance?" Ben suggested.

"What, and Bowen..." she paused. Something about the possibility had caught her attention. "Bowen killed him. Why would he do that?"

"For what he'd been put through?" Ben said, slowing to make the turn into the farm entrance. He checked his mirror. The convoy was nowhere in sight but would only be a minute or two behind. He eased the brakes on and brought the car to a stop. "Bowen lost everything when he was accused. His wife, his kid. I'm surprised he didn't lose his farm. How would you feel if you lost your family for no reason, and then you find out who was actually responsible?"

"I'd be upset. But would I be upset enough to murder somebody? Or would I go to the police?"

"We're not talking about you, Freya. We're talking about Frank Bowen."

"Okay, so how did Bowen find out who actually did it?" she asked.

"I don't know," he said. "That's something that will have to come out in the wash, I suppose. But fast forward a few years, and Tommy Dean and his mates all fall out because of it. Fast forward a couple of decades, and Tommy, through his job at the accountants, works something out. What does he work out? What would his position give him access to?"

"Everything," Freya said. "PAYE, corporation tax, profit, and loss. He'd see everything that Bowen bought."

"And if he had an idea that Bowen was involved, he would have access to historical data, too. He'd be able to go back and see exactly what Bowen bought the year his dad went missing, who was working for him, and how much tax he paid. He'd see the lot, right?"

"Right," Freya agreed. "So, the theory so far is that Bowen knew, or at least thought, that Tommy Dean's father had something to do with Alice Neal's disappearance, but we don't know how he knew."

"Right," Ben said.

"And years later, Tommy Dean was in a position to find out something about Bowen, but we don't know what."

"Right," Ben said again. "But we do know that it was important enough for him to give up his job at the accountants and pursue a course of revenge, under the ruse of lockdown and stress, or whatever it was."

"Okay," Freya said. "It's vague, but it's a start."

"We also know that Bowen was in the field by the old house on the day the boys found Tommy Dean's body. They saw his tractor."

"There's a lot missing here," she said.

"We've worked with less," Ben replied, and in the rearview mirror, he saw the line of flashing blues along the main road. "Ready?"

"We need something on him," she said. "We need something to make him talk; otherwise, we'll nick him, and he'll no comment his way through the custody window. We need something that will convince him to open up."

"We've got a warrant for his arrest, Freya. We've got three boys who all saw him at the crime scene. We've got Godolphin's statement saying that Tommy was onto him and had clearly planned some kind of revenge, and we've got the phone data to prove that both Tommy and John Tyler were here on the farm when they died. He's experienced firsthand what it's like to be arrested for murder. He's going to know what's coming, and if he's got any sense, he'll talk. I doubt a jury would be so lenient a second time around."

"I wouldn't bet on it," Freya replied as Ben eyed the convoy coming to a stop behind him. He put the car into drive and set off slowly. The four barns were a good five hundred metres away, and the farmhouse, which they had yet to visit, was another two hundred metres along the track. Freya flicked through every file in her folder. Chapman had photocopied the entire contents of Brinkleview Farm employee records folder, plus every page of the scrapbook. She flicked on the overhead light, licked her thumb, and lifted page after page. "Are we doing the right thing?"

"What? It's a bit late now, Freya."

"I know," she said. "We've got one chance at this, and quite frankly, this is laughable. We've got almost nothing we can make stick."

"Right, but we've got enough to convince a judge to sign a warrant at ten o'clock at night. He or she obviously felt we have enough to go on."

"What if we're wrong?"

"Well, then it won't be the first time, and I doubt it would be the last," he told her. "What are our options? You said all along it was Bowen. All roads lead to Bowen. What do we do? We can't leave a bloke we suspect of killing three people over the course of a couple of decades to roam free, Freya. That would be tantamount to negligence."

"I know, but—"

"Look, worst-case scenario, we nick him, we put a disclosure form into the accountancy firm for the records, and in the morning, we get the entire team to go through the company accounts, starting with the years Alice Neal and Dean's father went missing. In the meantime, Nillson will lead the search of the property. She's good. If there's anything here, she'll find it. The local units are all looking out for Tommy Dean's pickup. Everything's in motion, Freya. We've got to trust the theory, right? That's what you always tell me. We've got to work the theory, and if it's proven to be wrong, then we regroup and go again."

"I know, but..." her words trailed off as Ben drew up to the farmhouse. It was a decent-sized building, built for function rather than form, as were many farmhouses, and it sat in a prominent position with a good view over to the barns. In the rearview mirror, several of the liveried units peeled off to begin the search of the barns, followed closely by Nillson's hatchback. One of the police Astras ambled along the track to support the arrest, followed closely by Gillespie's old Volvo, with one headlight brighter than the other.

"Freya, we need to do this," he said. "What are you thinking?"

The front door of the house opened, and dressed in an old wax jacket, heavy boots, and a beanie hat, Frank Bowen stepped into view.

"It's wrong," she said.

"Freya, for God's sake."

"I know, it's just...all roads lead to Bowen. I get it. I agree, and yes, throughout this entire investigation, I've said he was part of this. But if what Godolphin said was right, then our original theory is wrong, Ben. We said that either Tommy Dean killed John Tyler or vice versa, but if he's telling the truth, which I think he is...oh, I don't know. Why would one man kill another so violently and leave them on display, then do what he did to Tommy Dean? This isn't right, Ben. Something is off. It's wildly off."

Fifty feet away, Bowen leaned against the doorframe, the crevices in his face exacerbated by the hallway light behind him. Beside them, Gillespie's car came to a stop, and two faces peered up at the Range Rover. Ben gestured for them to wait, and in turn, they signalled the uniformed officers in the Astra.

Cruz lowered the passenger window, and Gillespie leaned across, so Ben lowered his window.

"Everything alright?" Gillespie asked.

"We're just piecing it together," Ben replied quietly so that Bowen didn't overhear.

"Well, if you can, you're a better copper than me. We've been trying to do that the entire journey. Can't make sense of it."

The Astra's flashing blues washed over the old house and Bowen, adding an ethereal contrast to the old farmer's granite-like skin.

Freya squeezed her eyes shut as if to block out the noise and focus. Then, finally, she slapped the folder closed, unclipped her seat belt and reached for the door handle.

"Sod it," she said. "Change of plan."

"Go, go, go," Ben said to Gillespie, kicking off an explosion of activity.

Gillespie and Cruz led the uniformed officers to the house, presenting the printed warrant sheet as they walked.

Bowen made no effort to move. He watched them walk by, his eyes firmly fixed on Ben and Freya.

"It'll all work out, Freya," Ben muttered when they convened at the front of the car. "Just pray that you're wrong."

"That's precisely what's troubling me," she said as they started towards Bowen. "I'm never wrong."

CHAPTER FIFTY-FIVE

BOWEN WAS a statue right up until Freya was just five feet from him when he finally shoved himself off the doorframe and held his hands out ready to be cuffed.

"Took ya time," he said.

But instead of slapping a pair of cuffs onto him, she gripped his arm and yanked him into the house, dragging him deeper and deeper, following her nose until they reached the kitchen.

"Sit," she said.

The kitchen was as she had expected it to be and not too dissimilar to Ben's father's farmhouse. It had been designed to accommodate a large family and, like the exterior, was a product of function over form.

"Aren't we going to the station?" Bowen asked. "I packed and everything."

Freya snatched a chair out from beneath the table and dropped into it.

"You and I are going to go through every little detail, Frank. I've got a team of officers searching your barns and more upstairs searching the house, and while they do that, you are going to relive every bloody moment if we have to."

"Don't I get a lawyer?" he asked, almost amused at Freya's outburst.

"Yes, you get a lawyer when I nick you. For the time being, you're afforded liberty. I suggest you make the most of it."

"It's a little unorthodox."

"I'm a little unorthodox," she told him. "And you should be thankful. Every officer in my team believes you were involved. If it was up to them, you'd be face down in the back of a van on your way to the nick right now, and that fresh air out there..." She pointed out of the window to accentuate the point she was making. "That would be the last time you breathed it. You've got one chance, Frank. One chance. Do I make myself clear?"

He looked across at Ben, grinning from ear to ear, and then back at her.

"Crystal," he said eventually. His smile faded, his voice gained depth, and the glint of humour in his eye dulled to reveal new depths of bitter hatred.

"Alice Neal," she said. "Go."

"Eh?"

"Talk to me about Alice Neal."

"I've nothing to say about the lass," he said. "Nothing I haven't told you lot already, anyway. Is this going to take long? I could make us a brew."

"You're going to sit right there, Frank, and you're going to stop pretending this is a game. You got away with it once. Not again. Not on my watch."

It was as if the message that he was there for the long haul had finally hit home, and he settled into the old carver seat and crossed his legs.

"I've got nothing to say about her," he said, "except that I didn't touch her, and I didn't kill her."

"But you know who did."

"What?"

"You know who did, don't you?"

He looked up at Ben, slightly bemused.

"Is she always like this?"

"Answer me, damn it," Freya snapped, and she slammed the palm of her hand down on the old pine table. "You say you had nothing to do with her, but you know who did, don't you? I'm trying to help you, Frank. I'm trying to save your skin, but for the life of me, I'm running out of reasons why."

"I don't want your help, lady," he said, leaning forward in his chair. "I don't need your help, and I don't want your help."

"People have died," she yelled. "At least two, maybe more. They're dead, Frank. Dead. They're not coming back. How long do you think you can go on like this? How long do you think you can lie your way out of what's coming your way? You say you didn't touch Alice Neal, and I accept that. Honestly, I really do. But I think you know who did. I think you know, and either you're scared or..."

"Or what?"

She stared into his eyes, and watched as his pupils grew in size, then shrank to tiny dots in the bright kitchen light.

"Or you did something. You found out somehow, and you took matters into your own hands. If you admit to knowing who did it, then you open up a whole new raft of enquiries. And frankly, I don't think you'd survive a second investigation." She sat forward to meet him eye to eye and held a hand up to put Ben at ease. "Talk to me about George Dean."

"What?" Bowen said convincingly confused.

"George Dean. Tommy Dean's father." She opened her folder, found the photocopied sheet of paper she had in mind, and slid it before him. "Do you know what this is?"

"Newspaper," he said. "Next question."

"Read it."

"I've read it," he replied without giving it a second glance.

"Well, read it again, Frank."

"It's about the fire," he said. "Christ, don't you think I've been over that a hundred times?"

"Not the fire, Frank," she told him, and she tapped the second article on the sheet. "This one."

Reluctantly, he glanced down at the sheet, and his eyes roved from left to right.

"Aloud," she said, and as a sulking schoolboy might, he sighed but did as requested.

"Police call off the search for a missing man," he said.

"That's the headline." She waited for him to get the message, and he continued.

"After two days of searching surrounding farmland and a sweep of the River Witham, police have called off the search for a man reported missing by his loving wife. Local man, George Dean, was reported missing on Tuesday night, and despite attempts, police have had no luck in finding him. His wife was informed yesterday that they believe he has absconded and that the investigation will now be closed. Dean, aged forty-three, is Caucasian, six-foot-one, with a medium build. He is not deemed to be a vulnerable person, and police do not suspect foul play. His wife and son live in hope that he will return."

"How does that sound?"

"That he was as mad and unreliable as his boy is," Bowen replied.

Freya delved into her folder again, producing the sheet of paper that Chapman had alerted them to.

"And this?"

He glanced over, craning his neck.

"My accounts," he said.

"This in particular," she said, again stabbing the sheet of paper with her nail.

"Plant and Yale? Yeah, so?"

"Have they looked after your accounts long, Frank?"

"Long enough," he said. "As long as I can remember, anyway."

"I suppose after years of dealing with them, you must know the accountants quite well."

"Not really," he said. "I speak to Joan, but she has various teams who do the work. What? What's this got to do with anything—"

"Do you know who used to work for Plant and Yale?"

He flopped back in his seat.

"I don't know," he said. "Father Christmas?"

"Thomas Dean," she said. "Tommy. An old employee of yours. In fact, he gave up a lucrative career with the firm to come and work for you."

"Like I said, he's as unreliable as his dad."

Freya laughed the comment off. She glanced up at Ben briefly but bit her lip to refrain from reacting.

"Frank, what if I told you that I have two witness statements suggesting that Tommy had discovered some piece of news regarding his father and, last Saturday night, had planned his revenge?"

"What?"

"I believe that Tommy Dean worked it out," she said. "I believe that during his time at Plant and Yale, he worked out that you were responsible for his father's disappearance."

"Rubbish—"

"Did you meet them, Frank?"

"Who?"

"Tommy and John Tyler. Did you meet them on Sunday night? In the north field. Did they jump you? Is that it?"

"You have lost the plot, lady—"

"We know that Tommy Dean made a series of calls before he died. We know who most of them were to, but there's one number, Frank. One number that we cannot account for."

"Check my statement," he said shrewdly. "Although I'm sure you've already done that. In fact, I'm pretty sure that if you had found a call from Tommy to me, then you'd have mentioned it already. What are you doing? Scratching for something. Is that it? Trying to find something to put on me?"

"And if we find that phone in your home?" Freya said. She bit down on her lip in thought and studied those tiny, subconscious twitches of facial muscles, the dilation of his pupils, the flaring of his nostrils, but found no North Star to guide her to the truth. But the game was in motion. She had, despite her lack of conviction, played the part of the lead detective. She had applied pressure and, as a result, had shown her cards. There was no turning back now. "My team are upstairs as we speak. If you've hidden that phone, then we'll find it. And what then, Frank? Can we agree that this little charade will be over? Will you put a stop to this nonsense? I don't know about you, but I gain nothing from this. Just as I would have gained nothing from dragging you down to the station, it's gone on for far too long. People are dead. Others are grieving. If it's not you, then for God's sake, just say so. If you know the truth about Alice Neal, and you, for one reason or another, took matters into your own hands, then for God's sake, let's put an end to it because unless you do, in ten or twenty years' time, or however long you live, people won't remember you for the kind old man who brought a little girl's family justice. They'll remember you for the callous and cruel monster you really are. And all this," she said, waving her arm around. "This farm? Gone. Houses, most likely. They'll throw a party and have a bonfire when the demolition team come in and tear these walls down. There'll be effigies of you tossed into the flames. And your name? The name you somehow salvaged from the original investigation. That will be gone, too. People won't even mention it. You'll be referred to as that monster, and they'll say 'good riddance' when they see the hundreds of houses rise from the earth. And if that doesn't bother you, Frank, if that doesn't cut through to your heart, if you have one, then picture this. It's mid-morning on A-wing. The hard cases are in their cells after the morning shift so that those who are vulnerable, the sex offenders, the child killers, and rapists, of whom you will be marked as one, I can assure you, can walk through to the shop or to get your lunch. But the word is out, Frank. The other prisoners know who you are. They know about Alice Neal and in prison, there's plenty of time for imaginations to fester. All it takes is for one prison officer to leave one door unlocked. Or maybe a few? A few well-known lifers who have very little to lose." She left that there for him to mull over and then leaned forward again, lowering her voice. "It might not happen on day one. It might not happen on day two. But one day, one day, Frank, it'll happen. One day, a hand will reach for you from an open cell and drag you inside. The question is, which day will it be? That's what you need to consider. That's what will be going through your mind every single day, like clockwork. Because prison is routine. It's monotonous. The same thing day after day. The same wake-up call, the same four walls, the same fear, Frank."

Her words did cut into his heart. Of that, she was sure. His grainy features dulled and paled, his gullet rose and fell like the piston of some ancient Victorian machinery, and his fists clenched and unfurled.

But his words belied what she saw.

"I don't know if I should cry or clap," he said.

"Neither," she told him, ready for such a response. "You just need to remember what I said. I just pray that you do the right thing before such a time comes when I'm proven right."

A noise at the kitchen door caught her attention, and she found Gillespie there, clearly aware that he had interrupted something.

"What is it?" she asked, her eyes never leaving Bowen's.

"It's clean, boss," he said. Three words that had the potential to dilute every syllable she had voiced. "There's nothing here."

The smug grin that formed on Bowen's face was like the earth's crust giving way to the depths of hell.

"So, I should clap, then," he said, with reference to his previous sardonic comment.

"Keep looking," she said, retaining control. "Frank, the opportunity for you to do the right thing is slipping through your fingers, and if you think that if we leave here empty-handed you'll somehow be spared, you should think again. Because we won't stop. I won't stop. Men have died, and every shred of evidence, every single witness, suspect, and even those who have died, all link back to you and this farm. Now, Frank. Now is your chance to tell me. If you're covering for somebody, then now is your chance. If Tommy Dean and John Tyler sought revenge and you got the better of them, then say so. You could plead self-defence or try, at least." She opened the file again and collected the farm's employee records. Where possible, Chapman had printed the various forms of ID to accompany each entry. Some were driving licences, and some, typically for the European farm labourers, were passports. "So come on. Let's go through this," she said, with a firm eye on any reactions. "Who do we have here? Kevin Barker. Left your employment in 2011." She placed the record on the far side of the table. "Justin Ellis," she said. "Left your employment in 1999." She slid the file beside Barker's and began to speed up the process. "Arben Hoxha. Albanian national. Dritan Berisha, Edmond Dervishi, and Petrit Shala, all Albanian, all left your employment in 2020. James Lewis, Matthew Moore, Daniel Scott, Frederick Green, Harry Green, brothers maybe?"

Bowen nodded, and she slid them all into place so that every one of the individuals who had ever worked at the farm was staring up at him. She slapped the next file down without calling the name. "Look at him, Frank. Is this who you're covering for? Or him, she said, slapping the next one down and the next until a single file remained. "Well," she said. "We know it wasn't him, don't we?" She pushed Thomas Dean's file into the last slot. Nearly the entire surface of the table had been covered by dozens of files, and yet still Bowen refused to look at them, as if in fear of betraying a confidence but to his own detriment. "Who is it, Frank? Which one of these men are you covering for?"

Outwardly, Bowen was calm as ice, but the heat of the moment was melting his steely resolve. The hard glares were gone, the deep furrows on his brow had softened, and tiny red arteries were visible in the whites of his eyes.

"None of them," he said, his voice thick with saliva. "And that's the God's honest truth."

"Not him," she said, jabbing a finger at Daniel Scott. "Or him?" She moved to Arben Hoxha. "Or the brothers? Maybe it was them?"

"I'm not covering for any of them," he said, and there was something in the way he articulated that phrase that caught Freya's attention.

The uniformed officers under Gillespie's control had moved into the room, and bottle by bottle, can by can, they began emptying cupboards. The fridge was pulled out of its recess, and even frozen food bags and boxes were being cut open.

Freya stared at the field before them and then back to Bowen, and somehow, in some yet unfathomable manner, they communicated. He offered very little, but she sought, nonetheless. Invisible tentacles that burrowed, not into his mind, but into his expression, into his eyes, and even into the words he had just spoken.

"He's not here, is he?" she said, and there it was. The reaction she had sought from him, and those tentacles of hers gripped and wrestled and writhed with their quarry, moulding and squeezing, and crushing, and tearing to expose the truth, and eventually, holding the shadow up to the light where she could see it, could breathe it, and could feel it, as intangible as it was, and she could say it out loud with nothing short of revelation. "It's the old man."

CHAPTER FIFTY-SIX

IT WAS QUICKER to run than to drive the short distance to the barns. Ben led, followed closely by Freya, and behind them, under Freya's command, Gillespie and Cruz dragged a resolute Bowen. The courtyard formed by the four buildings was awash with blue lights, and from every corner, voices could be heard. The huge doors to each barn had been opened, and torchlights glanced over every surface. Lockers had been emptied, the contents of storage cupboards had been strewn across the concrete floors, and at the centre of it all, Nillson stood as if directing the end of the world.

At her feet, a pile of shovels, spades and various other tools had been piled.

"Frobisher, get that container opened," she yelled. "If you need a gas kit, then get it. MacMillan, how are we doing over there? I can't hear much activity." She clapped her hands twice. "Come on, people. There's something here. There must be."

"Anna," Ben called as he tore between two of the barns and into the open space.

She turned on her heels and stepped aside to present the pile of tools.

"Not much so far."

"It's not here," he said.

"What?"

"It's not here," he told her again. "Get two men and come with us."

"Frobisher," she yelled again. "Leave that. You and Greaves, with me."

They ran to the edge of the courtyard and cut between the south and west barns into a patch of long grass where a makeshift path had been trodden by heavy boots.

It was as if they had stepped into another time, or another world altogether. Even the air felt different: stale and humid, stained with decades of decaying farm machinery, oil, and grease.

Ahead of them, the old caravan they had seen was little more than a shadow whose sharp corners cut into the night sky.

"Jesus, Ben," Nillson said. "What's this place?"

"It's a graveyard," he replied quietly, then turned to her.

"It's where they keep those things that have served their purpose," Freya added as she, too, rounded the corner. A series of heavy boots came in her wake, followed eventually by a series of scuffles as Bowen was pulled into view. Freya jabbed a finger at him and spoke directly to Gillespie. "He doesn't leave your sight."

"Aye, boss," Gillespie replied, increasing the pressure on his quarry's arm.

She nodded for Ben to lead, and aided by torches and mobile phones, they sought a path through the treacherous long grass, where the blades of old ploughs and cultivators threatened to gouge furrows in shins, and the spikes of old drills waited for the soft skin of a wayward foot.

They stopped ten feet short of the door, and despite their efforts, there was no way on earth anybody inside could have missed their arrival.

"George Dean," Ben called out. "This is Detective Inspector Ben Savage. Lincolnshire Police. If you're in there then make yourself known." Nobody said a word, and when Ben glanced back at Bowen, he found only amusement. Freya nodded again. "Last chance, George. We're coming in."

He took a step forward but felt Freya's grip on his arm, and she eyed him silently, conveying enough in that fleeting glance for Ben to comprehend her concerns.

"Over to you," he said to the uniformed officers, feeling more than a little uneasy at the delegation.

Frobisher and Greaves stepped up to the door. Frobisher took hold of the door handle while Greaves stood ready with a heavy torch in his hand. He signed that he was ready, and Frobisher tore open the door. Ben closed his eyes to the chaos. There was little to see. Against the gloomy night sky, the ancient caravan was a forbidding mass, but inside, the darkness was absolute.

The sound that erupted from within was volatile. Crashes of doors and aggressive shouting designed to disarm any attempts against the officers. But the space inside was small, and the melee was brief so that less than thirty seconds later, the officers appeared at the doorway and offered only a shake of their heads.

Bowen, even with Cruz and Gillespie holding an arm each, was enjoying every moment.

"You, stay there," Freya snarled at him, and as the two uniformed officers stepped down from the caravan, she took one of the torches and strode inside. Ben followed and breathed the damp air inside. The warm light from his phone washed over the scene like the receding tide, revealing a decaying wreck. The bed had been slept in. The old blanket that Dean had used had been tossed to one side, and Ben imagined the old man they had seen in the tractor on that very first visit to Brinkleview setting his gnarled feet down on the threadbare and stained carpet before pulling on a pair of old jeans and a grubby checkered shirt. The curtains hung from a plastic rod by a handful of hooks, and only one had been opened. He pictured Dean pulling one back to check the weather. It was the first thing Ben's father did in the morning and the last thing he did at night.

The caravan offered scant storage for clothing, and that cupboard that had been used as a wardrobe was open. Nothing hung from the rail inside, but on the floor of the cupboard, a few items of clothing had been piled. There were more hanging around the space, perhaps drying after a quick rinse in the stained sink.

"Here," Freya said, shining the torch on a ledge set above the seating area. He joined her, and among the few possessions on display was a handful of old Kevin Banner paperbacks, a broken watch, and a mobile phone.

Instinctively, Ben pulled a fresh latex glove from his pocket and tugged it on. The phone wasn't a modern smartphone, and there was no security PIN to deny him access. He held it out of the door for Nillson.

"There's one for you," he said, then resumed his search of the bed end of the caravan. With his gloved hand, he lifted the blanket and then the mattress, finding nothing beneath or hidden among either of them. But it was as he leaned across the bed to run a hand behind the mattress that something caught his eye. Something lighter in tone than its grim surroundings.

"Freya," he said calmly.

Stuck with Sellotape to the built-in cabinet beside the bed was a photograph. It was colour, but the shades and tones screamed the eighties or nineties, a sentiment the clothing each of the five subjects wore mirrored entirely.

"Christ," she said when she came to stand beside him. "Is that—?"

"The house," he finished for her. "It's the old farmhouse." Her perfume cut through the dank air, and in the gloom, the scars across one side of her face were porcelain. But it was her mind he sought to reach. "Why would George Dean have a picture of...?"

He didn't finish the sentence. It was one of those that required no voicing and to which the answer lay in the heart of every hurdle they had stumbled across, every detail they had disagreed on, and every theory they had disproved.

"Because that's not George Dean's family," she said, and that shining porcelain cracked into a smile. She pulled the photo from where it had been stuck and held it under her torchlight. Her thumb grazed the images of two little girls no older than seven or eight years old. She turned the photo, and Ben felt her gasp more than he heard it. On the rear of the dog-eared photograph, written in childlike lettering, were two words.

I'm sorry.

"Bloody hell," she hissed, and she bound over to the doorway, holding the photo up for those outside to see, but spoke only to one man. "Is this who I think it is?"

Ben came to stand behind her in time to see Bowen thrust his head back and issue a cackle before his eyes, bright in the gloom, settled on her, and the amusement, evident in those deep crevices, gave way to hatred.

"You got it wrong, love," he said. "You're too late."

CHAPTER FIFTY-SEVEN

THE CALL to Chapman's phone sang through the car speakers, the radio in Ben's pocket crackled and spewed garbled messages in frantic bursts, and the crops in Bowen's field collided against the front of Freya's Ranger Rover like rainfall on a tin roof.

Ben drove. He had insisted. He had run the two hundred yards to fetch the car and had drawn up in the adjacent field. All that had happened. She had seen it and lived it, but she hadn't been there. Not entirely. Those words had been sharp, and perhaps because of what Ben and she had planned to do in just three days' time, or perhaps because of what Granger had said, or perhaps because deep down, she felt the drain of age on her ability to think straight, her defences had weakened.

You were wrong.

Those three words had found her soft underbelly, and as a man might twist his blade beneath the ribs, Bowen's smug cackle had driven them home, so they were buried to the hilt.

And now Ben drove, following the lines of the crops with each wheel set into a furrow and a determination like no other on his face.

She said nothing. It all seemed dreamlike. Rows of crops

passed by in a flash and the entire world seemed bathed in the flashing blue lights from the police Astras that flanked them on the farm track.

The quiet, mild-mannered Ben that she loved had taken a back seat, and as if buoyed by the desire to be the first on the scene, he pushed the big SUV harder.

Where the old caravan had cut its form into the night sky, the house in the distance was masked by the surrounding trees and capped by that which sprouted from inside as if feeding on the lives that had been lost there.

He broke suddenly, aimed for the house, then reached one hand across to hold Freya in place and braced as they left the field and burst onto flat ground. The car came to a skidding halt, and the cacophony of sound died.

She could picture the scene now. She could picture the family and the old farmhouse as it was back then. As the photograph in her hand depicted. There were windows and doors in the empty spaces, there was a roof where now a tree grew, and where now there was only decay, there was life. Bright life. Children played, and she imagined a pot of something hot and filling on the stove. The man, the father and husband, Leslie Tyler, would come home and wash his hands after a day in the fields, and his children would fill those auditory voids with laughter and play. It was a simple life in a modern world. They had cut a simple existence on the fringes of modern life. In the photograph, a pair of bikes lay on the ground in the distance, no different to any house she might have seen on any street in Britain. The rear quarter of an old Ford Escort showed behind the house as if peeking around the corner. They were no different to any other family in terms of possessions or modern life, save for one thing.

The careless smiles on their faces beamed with freedom, innocence, and the joy of life.

Save for one.

"Freya," Ben said, his voice seeming to suck the image from her mind. "Freya?"

She roused herself.

"Yes?" She replied, feigning focus, and he nodded to the spot where, in the photograph, the Ford Escort had been parked.

"That's a pickup truck."

"Dean's?" he said. "It matches the description."

It was as if she had been dropped into the here and now and had to take a few moments to reestablish her senses. She glanced behind her. The convoy was close. Two hundred yards. So, she eased her car door open and stepped down, a little unsteady on her feet.

The empty windows and the front door revealed nothing of what lay inside. There was no movement, no sound, and no sign of life.

She made her way over to the pickup, giving the house a wide berth. Behind her, somewhere, Ben's door closed, and she heard his footsteps and the approaching cars. He could deal with them. There was something in the way that truck peeked from behind the house that led her on, drawing her forward into a time not so long ago when the driver had parked in the same spot, dropped the tailgate, and then dragged Tommy Dean into the house. She ran a hand across the cold metal and wondered how conscious Dean had been. There would have been tools. A shovel or a spade. But the killer would have had to return for them unless...

It was an old rerun. One she had seen before but so long ago the ending was obscured by the fog of time.

The passenger window was down, and she felt her pockets for her phone to light the interior. The driver's seat was torn and grubby from years of use, and a layer of grime lay across the instruments, like the dusty window of an old shed.

And then she saw it, protruding from beneath the passenger seat as if somebody had tucked it there for safekeeping. A lace.

Not the thin type you might find on a pair of Oxfords or brogues, but thick, like you might find on a pair of boots.

Carefully, she opened the door and bent inside to peer beneath the seat.

"One left boot," she whispered to herself, and a single laugh was forced from her throat.

There was no doubt in her mind that the boot had belonged to John Tyler and that he had been wearing it when this very truck had been used to hoist him into the air. He would have kicked and writhed. He would have been fighting for his life.

And there was no doubt in her mind that the truck had belonged to Tommy Dean, and there was even less doubt that his last journey had been on the back of the truck. His last moments of life could have been spent staring up at the stars, dazed and confused.

But the smell inside the cab she inhaled once the picture in her mind was complete cast a new light over the scene. Hues of oranges, reds and yellows, angry and relentless. It was a light that changed lives, changed people, and destroyed memories.

She straightened and checked around her, shining the light beneath the truck and the nearby bushes. She ran to the corner of the house and burst from the shadows where Gillespie, Cruz, and Nillson were regrouping with the uniformed officers.

"You alright, boss?" Gillespie called as Freya shone the light onto the ground at her feet and all around.

And then she saw them. Bright green in the torchlight, two jerry cans that had been discarded through the empty window space.

"Ben?" she said, realising he was nowhere to be seen. She turned to Gillespie, her heart belting a frantic rhythm inside her chest. "Where's—"

She was cut short by a distinct metallic clink to her right, and in the corner of her eye, in the darkness through the empty window, the flash of a spark lit the old man's tormented face.

There was no blast to deafen her, and there was no heat. Not at first. Just an angry rush of hissing air being sucked through those blank voids where windows and doors had once been, followed by the rumbling growl of hot and cold air converging in a fury way over their heads, reaching from the open rooftop into the night sky.

She knew it was Gillespie who hit her without even looking. Some part of her subconscious was aware of her surroundings far more than her conscious mind was. His huge bulk knocked her to the ground, covering her with his jacket, but she tore her face free to see newborn flames licking at their new world, tasting their surroundings. Others joined him, Cruz and Nillson, she thought, pulling her to safety. But she fought back, her boots scraping against the loose soil and her hands grappling for freedom. She tried to call out, but no words came. There were no words. There was nothing. She was senseless, and now there would be nothing. Just a perpetual emptiness marked by the tips of raging flames that danced in wild celebration in the dark sky above, and at its root, somewhere in the centre of that old farmhouse, that centre of death, was the entrance to hell.

CHAPTER FIFTY-EIGHT

GILLESPIE HELD HER. He had the clarity of mind to turn her away so that she stared wide-eyed into the fields. So bright were the flames that the crops were swathed in orange as if the sun was beating down on a hot summer's day.

Men yelled, though their words were muted tenor melodies that danced throughout the drum-like beating of Freya's thumping heart. She blinked away the tears, but like soldiers braving the whistle and going over the top, more stepped in behind to replace them.

She tried to turn, but Gillespie's grip was stronger, and somehow, despite all those times she had belittled him, berated him, and singled him out, he held her fast. And it wasn't that she wanted him to let go. His touch was the comfort she needed. She just needed to see. She needed to be sure.

"Don't," he said.

"Where is he?" she asked quietly. "Gillespie, I need to—"

"Just...just stay here a moment. They're dealing with it. There's nothing we can do. There's nothing anyone can do."

She listened to what he said. She let him guide her, and let her head rest on his shoulder.

"What do we do, Jim? What am I going to do?"

"You're going to stay calm, boss," he replied. "You're going to take deep breaths, and we're going to get through it." He applied a little more pressure to his hold on her as if to add weight to his words.

"Alright," she said after a while. "Alright, let me go."

"Boss, I don't think—"

"Let me go," she said again. "It's okay. I'm fine. I'll be fine."

He held her out before him, gripping her shoulders and staring into her eyes to be sure.

"I need to," she said, and he relented, easing his grip with every nod of his head but still holding onto her so that when she turned to see the blaze, he was there.

A gasp escaped her lips, and it was her who held onto him.

"I didn't see him. I wasn't with him, I mean. I—"

"Easy now," he said, pulling her into his side.

"I saw the truck," she told him. "He wasn't with me. I didn't even speak to him. I just went off—"

"Boss—"

"No, I mean, if I'd just told him to come with me. If I'd just been less bloody—"

"Hey," he said, as a father might call out a child's poor behaviour. He shook her and gripped her arms. "It's nobody's fault. You have to understand that, Freya. You have to understand it now. It's happened, alright? It's happened, and you need to be strong."

"But, if—" she'd barely started to reply when he shook her again.

"I said, you need to be strong, boss. Alright? You need to keep it together. You can worry about the what-ifs later, but right now, you need to hold it together."

There were a hundred of what-ifs that she could think of. More, in fact. A hundred or more variations of what had happened. A hundred or more beginnings, middles, and endings.

And every one of them began with one man.

She turned from the blaze and looked over to where the police Astras were parked beside Freya's car. Her doors were open, and Nillson was leaning against the bonnet, one hand holding her phone to her ear, the other gripping her hair. Her eyes caught Freya's, and the desperate expression she wore faded to sorrow.

Cruz was with a few uniformed officers, rallying around to shut the scene down and make space for the fire engines she could hear in the distance.

But of all the faces, one remained still.

Bowen looked on from the back seat of an Astra. The glow warmed his creased complexion, accentuating his simpering grimace.

"You," Freya hissed under her breath, and she tore herself free of Gillespie's grip.

"Boss, no," he said, but she shrugged him off and half-marched, half-ran towards the Astra. "Leave him. He's not worth it."

"You," she screamed as she neared the car, and his eyes followed her, beaming up at him from inside the car. She tore the door open, reached in, and grabbed onto his shirt collar. Gillespie's strong arm wrapped around her and began tugging her away, but she held fast. "Out," she screamed. "Get out of the car."

"Boss, no," Gillespie said, then calmly sought assistance. "A little help here, please."

It was as if the drama had only served to add to Bowen's amusement. With his hands cuffed behind his back, he allowed himself to be pulled from the car. Her grip on his shirt failed, and he fell at her feet. She landed three blows to his smarmy grin before Gillespie finally hauled her off him, and one kick as he lifted her away. "Boss!" Gillespie called out. She had her back to him, and her legs kicked wildly in the air.

"Let me go, Gillespie," she yelled. "Let go of me."

"Boss, you don't want to do that," he said, somehow maintaining a calm composure.

"You want to keep that bitch on a leash," Bowen yelled from the ground. "You're done, lady. Do you hear me? You're finished—"

His threats were cut off as Nillson and one of the uniformed officers dragged him away out of sight behind the car.

Gillespie set her down but held onto her until she calmed.

"You alright?" he asked, and she shrugged his hands from her.

"I'm fine," she said, averting her eyes, but wherever she turned her head, he moved into that space until she finally gave in and looked him in the eye. "I'm fine."

"If it helps, he deserved it," Gillespie said.

"He deserves a lot more than what I gave him," she replied. "If there was any justice in the bloody world—"

He held up a hand to silence her, and his eyes narrowed. He turned his head to the blaze and leaned in.

"What is it?" she asked, and irritated, he motioned for her to be quiet.

"Can you hear that?"

"Hear what?" The only noise she chould hear were the crackle of flames, her thumping heart, and the rush of blood in her ears.

He moved away from her, taking slow steps towards the burning building. But then he stopped, and with a shake of his head, he dismissed the idea.

"What is it?"

"Nothing," he said. "I thought I heard something, that's all."

"What, Jim? What did you hear?"

He opened his mouth as if he were about to say something but thought better of it, and the first of two fire engines rumbled into view, sparking another wave of action as doors opened and more bodies pounced on the scene, calling and yelling.

"Stay here," Gillespie said, holding a finger up as if commanding a labrador to sit and stay. "You stay."

She nodded and watched him walk between the fire engines. It was the first moment she'd had to stop and think, to let her mind wander and to really take it all in. It was one of those moments she had witnessed countless times before as a spectator. The victims of crimes and devastation stood in a state of shock. How many times had she wondered if they'd relive that moment, either in their dreams or while awake, staring out of a window? How many times would she relive the moment she was experiencing right now? How would what she did next affect that memory? Why did it have to be a fire? Was there some kind of force against her, using searing flames to grind her down, to break her, until she finally broke? Is this how life would be from now? Would the threat of fire live forever in her heart, for as long as she breathed air?

Would it get her in the end? Is that how it would end?

It was as if her demise was painted in vivid strokes of orange and red oils against the vague hues of dreamy blue watercolours.

"Boss?"

Gillespie's voice sang out from somewhere far off, pulling her from that lonely, dreamlike state.

"Boss?"

She found him standing between the two fire engines, and there was something about the way he was standing. Something in his posture that made it all too real, somehow. He beckoned her, holding an arm outstretched, his hand waiting for hers. She took his hand, although she couldn't recall walking over to him. Her hand felt small in his. It was as if she was a little girl once again, and an officer was leading her from devastation to safety. She went with him, following as he led her between fire officers to the truck. The solid brick walls that had stood for more than a hundred years and had endured two significant fires gave protection from the rage inside the house, and she felt the cool air on her scar. Beyond the truck, two police officers were grappling with the overgrown trees and thick brambles that had claimed the south side of the house. Torch lights bounced and waved, and as they neared, Gillespie stopped her. He turned to her, his eyes ablaze, shining in the gloom like glass marbles.

"You ready for this?" he asked, his expression solemn but hard as if he were her strength so that she didn't need to be strong. So that she could react and so she could break.

She nodded once, and gently, he tugged her on. But her feet were fixed to the ground like great weights had pinned her there. He turned back to her, still clinging to her hand.

"It's okay," he said and squeezed. He spoke to the officers, though his words were unclear in the haze of her mind. But they backed off to give them space, and he pulled her forward, beyond that dark corner of the building to a space where she doubted any man had been able to stand for decades and from where, with the aid of the officers' torches, she could peer into the thick brush.

And she saw him.

He was lying on the ground with Leslie Tyler, a tangle of limbs and brambles beneath the house's rear window. He wasn't, as her imagination had conjured, singed and burned, blackened and ruined. He was perfect.

She gasped, and Gillespie caught her as her knees gave way, holding her upright.

"Ben?" she said, and for the first time, her voice carried her emotion. "Ben?" She looked up at Gillespie. "Is he—"

"He's fine," Gillespie told her, his own voice cracking with relief.

He must have heard them over the sound of the fire and the hoses and the melee because his eyes opened, and although clearly pained, he grinned that boyish grin she loved so dearly.

"Alright, love?" he said, doing his best to sound jovial despite the thorns and the discomfort. "A little help here, please?"

CHAPTER FIFTY-NINE

"You bloody idiot," she said the moment the last of the brambles had been cut, and two large hands pulled him free. "You bloody, bloody, bloody idiot." She beat his chest with every syllable of every bloody she spat; he gripped her upper arms and held her fast. "I thought..." her anger gave way to emotions, and she piled into him, wrapping her arms around his neck.

"What?" he said, almost laughing. "You thought what?" Over her shoulder, Gillespie's eyes flashed a warning, and he shook his head.

"Just..." she started, her voice high in pitch, and she held him tighter. "You're a bloody idiot, Ben Savage."

She pulled herself off him and held him before smoothing his hair from his brow. He winced as her hand brushed over a graze.

"You going to tell us what happened, Ben?" Gillespie asked. "Doing a little gardening, were you?"

"I was inside," he said as the officer ushered them out of the way to get to Tyler. "But I saw him with the lighter, and...well, there was no way I was getting out. He'd doused the entire place. Remember all those pallets? He'd stacked them up against the walls. It was like a bloody funeral pyre."

"So, what happened?" Gillespie asked. "What did you do?"

Freya gave him some space but clung to his hands, staring up at him as if he was some kind of miracle.

"What do you think I did? I jumped him. Dragged him through the window. I've been stuck in the bloody brambles for ages. Didn't you hear me calling?"

Gillespie smirked at him, then bit his lip in case Freya saw him.

"No, mate. We thought you were gone, too."

"What? You're not serious? Really?"

"I was thinking I'd have to give your best man's speech at your funeral. I mean, it's much the same thing, anyway, eh?"

"*That's* not funny," Freya said, glaring at him.

"What do you want to do with this one?" one of the officers asked.

Leslie Tyler was in a far worse state than Ben. He was conscious but had clearly broken the brunt of Ben's fall. Two officers dragged him from the thicket on buckled knees.

"Over there, mate," Ben said, pointing to a spot away from the drama. He turned to Freya. "Do you want to read him his rights, or should I?"

Freya watched as they laid Tyler down in the long grass. There was little chance of the old man running. He lay staring up at a smoke-filled sky, where distant stars continued to shine, where the crescent moon bore witness to his actions with indifference, and where his dreams of sweet death faded.

"Not yet," she said, stepping over to him. Gillespie edged closer as if, somehow, he was keenly aware of Freya's fragility. He gave Ben a warning look but said nothing. "Get up," Freya said to which Tyler simply sighed and stared vacantly at her. "I said, stand up." She turned to Gillespie. "Help him, would you?" she said. "I want him to listen to what I have to say."

"Boss, he's—"

"Help him stand," she said, then her voice softened as if she regretted her tone. "Please, Gillespie."

He looked to Ben, who shrugged, and then together, they hauled him to his feet. The old man winced at the pain but remained upright, and Freya closed the gap between them. All it would have taken is for the old man to reach out, and he would have her in his grip. But there was no fight left in him. It was as much as he could do to stand there and brace for what she had to say.

"I'm going to tell you what I think happened," she started, her voice low and calm but confident and sure. "And then you're going to tell me if I'm right, Leslie. It's over for you. All of this." She waved a hand behind her. "It's over. It's time."

He said nothing but instead looked to Ben for some kind of explanation. Ben stared back offering nothing, which was far more than he deserved.

"I'll be honest," she continued. "I think you're a coward. In fact, I know you're a coward." He turned his head away, and she sought his gaze. "Did you hear me? Have you any idea what your boy, John, went through?"

Tyler closed his eyes at the mention of the name, and Freya, ever patient, waited for them to reopen. From her pocket, she withdrew the photo Ben had found in the caravan.

"Look at this," she said. "Look at this happy family. Happy son, happy girls, and even a happy you, Leslie." She tapped the face of the last person in the photograph. "But not a happy wife. Why is that? Why is it that, even though everyone else seems to be enjoying themselves, she is looking up at you like that?" She turned the photo to look at it again. "What is that? It's not fear. It's certainly not love, is it?" She held it up for him to see. "What is that? Hatred, do you think?"

"She rarely smiled," he told her, his voice grainy with age and nicotine.

"Not with you, anyway," Freya continued, and his expanding

chest belied his composure. "I'll bet she smiled with George Dean, though."

"You bitch—"

"You found them, Leslie. Didn't you? We've heard he was a promiscuous man. What did you do, come home early from work, and find them in the kitchen? Is that what happened? Did you lash out? What is that, some kind of instinct, do you think? Some kind of natural reaction? Talk to me, Leslie. I want to understand. I want to understand what drives a man to do what you did."

"You could never understand," he snapped, and if he were going to add to the comment, he thought better of it.

"No, you're right," she said. "I mean, I think all of us can understand how angry you must have been, but I can't condone you beating George Dean so hard that his skull fractured, and I can't condone you setting fire to the house to cover your actions. And your girls...?" She shook her head in disgust. "How could you?"

"I didn't know," he said, and he stared at her, his eyes burning with rage and grief. "They weren't supposed to be there. They were supposed to be at school. I didn't know."

"And your wife?" Freya said. "The man that, until now, the world thought was you was found with a fractured skull. They presumed you had fallen while escaping the blaze and hit your head, but your wife? She was so close to the door, Leslie."

He hung his head and closed his eyes, perhaps reliving a memory that had plagued him all these years.

"She tried to stop me," he said at last. "She saw what I had done to George, and she tried to stop me. I didn't mean to. I just..." his voice rose to an almost childlike pitch. "I just put my hands up to stop her, and I...I don't know. I only meant to stop her."

"You strangled her?"

"Not on purpose," he argued, then nodded slowly.

"And you burned the house down when you came to your

senses? When you realised you would never see the light of day again."

"I don't know. I just ran. I hid in the barns. I don't know how long for, but he found me."

"Who?"

"Frank," he said. "He found me in there. Said he thought I was dead. Told me the whole world thought I was dead."

"And so, you let them think that? You let your only living child think you were dead. You let him be carted off to live with foster parents while you hid yourself away like a coward."

"I didn't know what else to do!"

"Be a man," she suggested. "Face up to what you have done."

"But I didn't mean to—"

"You killed your own children, Leslie!" she snapped. "You killed them. And your wife. And George Dean. You killed him. His son has been searching for him ever since. Did you know that? Everyone said that he'd run off with another woman. You destroyed lives, Leslie," she said softly. "You destroyed the lives of countless people."

"Do you think I don't know that?" He barked at her. "Do you think I don't think about that every single day? What do you think I was doing in there? I was ending it all. I was paying my pittance. I was—"

"Running away," Freya said flatly. "That's what you were doing." She leaned forward, so close that Ben feared he might lash out. "Because that's what you've always done, you coward."

CHAPTER SIXTY

"BUT WHY NOW?" Freya asked, applying a little more pressure. "Why wait until now?" He looked away again, a scowl forming on his miserable face. "How long do you think you could have carried it on for? What, another five years? How long until somebody else worked it out? Because Tommy Dean did, didn't he? Tommy Dean worked it out. The little boy you left fatherless. Or should I say one of the little boys you left fatherless? We've been through the farm's files, Leslie. Here's what I think happened. I think that when you killed George Dean and your family and ran away like a coward, Bowen kept you on. What are you? Old mates? Old buddies? You know Tommy worked at the accountants, don't you?" she said. "I think he saw a pattern. His father was missing. His salary should have stopped. But for some reason, there was money unaccounted for. The same kind of money his father would have earned. It's the only way I can see he could have done it, and believe me, I'll be having my team go through every line on the farm's statements. I think he paid you cash. Gave you the old caravan to live in. Hidden away back there, out of sight, amongst the old crap that nobody needs. He must be a good mate."

"You know nothing," he growled.

"I know he came to work here. That must have been a shock, eh? To see a new boy on the farm when all the Europeans had gone back home during lockdown. How did you feel when he was introduced, Leslie? How did you feel when you learned his name?"

"Sorry," he said. "How do you think I felt?"

"Imagine what Tommy must have thought. Imagine it. He spent his entire life believing that his dad was still around somewhere. Then, finally, he gets a breakthrough. There's every possibility that his dad is alive and working on the farm, not two miles from his house. He tries to find him but to no avail. So, he joins the farm. That's how desperate he was, Leslie. That's how desperate Tommy was to find his dad. But he never did. All he finds is you. A washed-up old coward. Did he speak to you? Did he ask you about that day? The day the house burned down. Did he question you about it, Leslie?"

"He was a coward," Tyler said. "A no-good coward. You call me a coward, yeah? Well, he got me. He had me cornered not six months back. I offered myself to him. Here I am, I said. Come and get me. You want to see me hurting, come and get me." Tyler shook his head. "He hadn't the balls. Weak, he was. Disappeared, didn't he? Didn't see hide nor hair of him after that. But I know what he was doing. I know his type. He waited. He knew I weren't going nowhere, so he waited for me to think I was safe. Until I had my guard down. Then he called me, didn't he? Ain't nobody else but men on this farm got my number. I knew it was him. Told me to meet him in the North field. Said he wanted to put an end to it all and that if I didn't, he'd call the police."

"So, you agreed to meet him?"

"Course I did. What choice did I have? Then he jumped me. Bloody coward. Him and his mate. I knew something was up. Saw some bloke in the field on the way over here, another over here near the house. Nobody comes here, see? Old Frank doesn't like people on his land. Locals all know it, don't they? So, I knew what was going to happen." He tapped his temple as if he was some kind of genius. "I met him. He was on his own. Like some kind of cowboy movie, it was. He was over there, 'bout twenty feet away, calling out that he needed to hear me say it. Needed me to tell him what happened to his old man. I'm not silly. I weren't falling for it. I know what they can do these days with them phones and whatnot. So, I told him to go jump, didn't I? In not so many words, course. Anyways, that's when his mate got me. Started dragging me towards this old tree while Tommy got in his truck. Nearly had me, too. Strong bastard, he was. Anyways, I don't know what happened, exactly. He tried to get a rope around me so Tommy could haul me up. That was when I saw it. There was a noose in the tree. He'd already tied it. Bastards were going to hang me, weren't they?"

"What did you do?" Ben asked, enthralled by the account.

"What do you think I did?" he said. "I bloody gave it to him, didn't I? Fought back. Had the rope around him. See how he bleedin' liked it. He didn't, did he?"

"And where was Tommy when you did this?"

"Tommy? He was just bloody standing there, scared stiff, he was. Then he ran."

"He ran?"

"Yeah. Told you, didn't I? He was a coward. I knew he was out there in the fields watching. So, I figured I'd teach him a lesson. Show him what a real man does," he said, and his expression was tinged with shame. "I strung him up. His mate. I strung him up and torched the bastard. That's what they were going to do to me, so I did it to him. There. You've heard it. Straight from the horse's mouth, as it were."

He eyed them all, waiting for one of them to say something.

"What happened after, Leslie?" Freya asked, her voice quiet, forcing the old man to listen.

"Dunno. Thought Tommy would come for me, but he never. Saw him scarpering up the track, didn't I?"

"Was...was his friend still alive at this point?" Ben asked.

"Suppose so," Tyler replied. "He was kicking about something chronic. Had to pick one of his boots up. You know, in case you lot found it."

"Naturally," Freya muttered. "You had to cover your tracks, didn't you?"

"Then I went after him, didn't I?" He continued. "Went after Tommy." His eyes glazed, and the grin that formed was grotesque. "I chucked the rope in the dyke, got in the truck, and went after him. He was like a rabbit in the headlights. Bloody petrified, he was."

"You mowed him down?" Freya said.

"Yeah. Yeah, I did. Not full-on. I clipped him. Dazed him. Knocked him down so he couldn't get away."

"And then...?"

"I taught him a lesson," Tyler replied. "If he wanted his old man that badly, I'd take him to him. I'd make sure they never parted again. Know what I mean? Brought him here on the back of the truck. Parked it right there."

"Then you dragged him inside and beat him to death?" Freya suggested.

"Oh no," he replied, with a shake of his head. "He dragged himself in here. Trying to get away, weren't he? You should've heard him when he knew where he was, when he recognised the old place. Oh, did he sing. Bleedin' screaming, he was. Begging me not to do it. Kept crawling into that tent. Kept trying to get away, so I clobbered him."

"With?" Gillespie asked.

"The shovel," he said almost immediately. "It was on the back of the truck. Twice, I hit him. That's all it took."

"And you buried him immediately?"

"Buried him? No," he said. "No, not right away. There were people about, weren't there? The ones I'd heard in the fields. Told you. I'm not silly." He tapped his temple again.

"So, you ran?" Freya said. "Again."

"Yeah, I did, as it happens. I took the truck. Hid it on the farm. Somewhere no one won't go for a bit."

"And you returned later to bury him?"

"I did, yeah," he said. "There were some boys messing about. Had to see them off, if you know what I mean."

"Did you talk to them?"

"Course I bleedin' didn't. I was in the tractor, weren't I? Had a look about for them, but they must have scarpered—"

"Because everybody knows that Frank Bowen doesn't like people on his land?" Freya asked.

"S'right," he said. "Anyways, when I couldn't find 'em, I set to work. Buried him as close to his old man as I could," he grinned again. "And they say romance is dead."

"And the shovel?" Gillespie asked. "Where's that?"

"Under the caravan," he said. "Meant to get rid of it, but you lot kept coming back. Kept bleedin' pestering us, didn't you?"

"And the net was closing in?" Freya said.

"Something like that, yeah," he grumbled.

"And you just couldn't bear the thought of facing up to what you had done?" she said. "You are a coward, Leslie, and believe me, I've met some cowards in my time."

"I'm sure you have," he told her, eyeing Ben and Gillespie. "Anyways. I told you what you wanted to hear. Are we going to do this, or what?"

Freya took a step back and looked up in deep thought.

"I am," she told him. "But not yet. I want to take you somewhere first."

"What?"

"I want to take you somewhere," she said again, then glanced at Gillespie. "Can you fetch some support and one of those Astras?"

"What do you mean? What is this? I told you what you wanted to know."

"I want to give you a memory to take away with you. You

know?" she said. "Something to think about while you spend the rest of your life behind bars." She held his gaze and called out over her shoulder. "Gillespie?"

"Aye, boss?" he called back.

"Fetch Bowen, too, will you?" she said. "I think he needs to see this."

CHAPTER SIXTY-ONE

To Ben's surprise, Freya drove. He spent the journey picking thorns from his arms and hands.

"Are you okay?" she asked.

"I'm fine," he told her. "Apart from being half plant, now, I'm alright."

"I honestly thought you'd—"

"Well, I didn't," he said. "I scraped my shin, banged my head, and I've got more pricks in me than—"

"Ben!"

"A pin cushion," he continued. "Other than that. I'm alright. Tyler came off worse than me. He broke my fall."

"Yes, well. You should have bloody well left him in there."

"Oh right, yeah, and I suppose I'd sleep soundly for the rest of my life, wouldn't I? Knowing that I'd left a man to burn alive."

"No comment," she replied.

"What are you up to anyway?" he asked, glancing in the mirror. Another convoy followed them, comprising two police Astras, Gillespie's Volvo and Nillson bringing up the rear. "What are we doing?"

"It's...it's an idea," she said as she brought the car to a stop.

Before them, three little white vans were parked, each marked with the familiar police livery and Forensic Investigation in large red lettering. Beyond those, the old tree with its overhanging limb was stark against the night sky. He turned to look at her, and when she peered back, she wasn't the confident woman she was, in just a few days, about to marry. She was a little girl, filled with hope. "I'm not sure if I can ever remember a time when I've been so wrong."

"Freya, we all get it wrong—"

"No," she said. "No, not like this. Not as big as this. Yes, we let our theories veer off sometimes. That's all part of the process. But this?" She shook her head. "This was colossal. Every aspect of my theory was way off target."

"You said Bowen had something to do with it," he told her. "He was covering for Tyler all this time. He was bloody hiding him."

"Ah," she replied with a nervous laugh. "Yes, that's what brings us here."

She left that little cryptic nugget hanging there and climbed from the car.

"Freya?" he pressed, joining her as she marched over to the Astras.

"Everything alright, boss?" Gillespie called out from where he, Cruz, and Nillson were waiting by their cars. Ben raised a hand, asking them to hold off for a moment.

Two faces peered from the rear seats of both Astras. She pulled open the door to the first.

"Out," she commanded before striding over to the next. "You, too. Out." Tyler and Bowen were aided by the uniformed officers but kept well apart. "Walk with me."

She led the entourage, treading the old farm track with conviction. As they passed the forensics vans, she banged twice on the sides.

"Let's go," she called out, instigating a flurry of activity.

Southwell emerged from the foremost van and looked quizzically at Ben, who shrugged, and then to Gillespie, who broke from his trio to join his girlfriend, most likely sharing a moment of utter confusion.

"Right," Freya said, putting an end to the rumble of bemused hums. She stopped, turned with the tree behind her and watched as Tyler and Bowen were led into a position before her. "I imagine you're wondering why we're here. I expect you had envisaged a nice, warm interview room, a cup of lukewarm tea, and a hard seat. Don't worry. All that will come in good time," she continued. "I'm offering you both a chance. Not a chance for freedom; I'm afraid I don't have that power, but a chance at demonstrating to me, my team, the CPS, the judges, and ultimately, your peers that somewhere inside each of you, there is a heart. A conscience. A soul. This is your one chance. If you choose to let this chance slip through your fingers, all bets are off. Any attempts to appeal to my good nature will fall short. Any hope that I might employ empathy or pity even will be unfounded. Essentially, you will prove yourselves to be exactly what we think you are. Both of you. A callous, selfish pair of cruel individuals who will do anything to save your own skins."

"Christ, don't she go on?" Tyler started.

"Yes," she admitted. "Yes, I do go on. In fact, regarding the pair of you, I could go on for hours, days, even. Why? Because you baffle me. Because I cannot, for the life of me, begin to comprehend the sequence of events that took place on this farm a few days ago, and long before that." She turned away, slid her hands into her jacket pockets, and began to pace. "You see, when we piece this together, we begin to form a narrative, and I'll be the first to admit that what took place was way beyond my imagination. I was wrong. I know I was wrong, and I have to come to terms with that. I thought...no, I was sure that Tommy was responsible for the murder that took place here. Had I not been so bloody-minded, then perhaps we could have wrapped this up sooner. But here we are. I know now that you, Leslie Tyler, were responsible, and I know why. The entire story is laid out before me like a grotesque patchwork quilt." She stopped pacing and stared at them. "Except for two elements, and it's these two elements that bring us here, and if you can help me with them, then I'll do what I can to ease the process, and you can be sure that the jury will be made aware of your cooperation. I'll even make them aware myself. How does that sound?"

"You're all heart," Tyler said sardonically, to which she smiled.

"First of all, what I cannot comprehend is why you, Frank, hid this man for more than two decades. Why you lied to the police. Why you went out of your way to help a man who had just killed his entire family? It doesn't make sense."

"I'm an old mate," Tyler said.

"I'm not talking to you, Leslie. When I'm talking to you, you'll know because I'll look at you." She stared at Bowen. "Well?"

Bowen raised his gaze from the ground. There was defiance in his eyes, but it was shadowed by something far greater in power. Shame? Guilt? Ben couldn't be sure. It was like sipping one of Freya's fancy wines and trying to pinpoint an underlying flavour that she promised was there.

"Like he said. We're mates. It's what mates do, isn't it?"

"No," Freya said. "No, I don't believe that I would ask any of my friends to go to such lengths for me. I wouldn't want to think of myself as a coward." She waited, but Bowen offered nothing more. "Okay," she said. "For the record, the opportunity is slipping through your fingers with every second that passes." She waited again, and each of the men refused to meet her eye to eye. "That brings me onto the second part of my conundrum," she continued, and she held her hands up as if presenting her surroundings. "This place. This field. This tree. Why here? Why did Tommy Dean bring you here, Leslie?"

All heads turned to the old Londoner, who slowly raised his head and stared hard at Freya.

"It's dark," he said, and although constrained by the uniformed officers on either side of him, he looked about him. "Secluded. No one to see what he was doing."

"Wrong," she said. "That wasn't why Tommy brought you here, was it? There's something about this place in particular. Something secret. Something dark. What could that be? What could have happened here that...I don't know, but that stirred Tommy Dean enough to choose this place as the site for your death. As a site to hang you and burn you alive." She moved closer to them, stopping at a point from where she could address them both with equal distaste. "It was on this spot that Tommy Dean spoke to you, Frank, wasn't it? When he first asked if you had any work for him. He watched you from the footpath there, the one that leads into Tattershall where he lived, and he walked onto your land to ask for a start."

"I suppose so," Bowen said. "I can't remember if I'm honest."

"It was," she said. "But he wasn't the first person to walk up that path, was he?"

"It's a public footpath," he replied. "Hundreds of people have used it—"

"I'm talking about one person in particular," Freya said. "Alice Neal." She spoke the name clearly to avoid any misinterpretation, and she studied each of them for a reaction. "She's here, isn't she?"

Bowen said nothing.

"Where, Frank?" she said. "Where is she?"

"I've told you what I told them all those years ago. I had nothing—"

"I don't believe you," she snapped. "I don't believe you; nobody here believes you, and I'll wager that nobody within a square mile believes you. Do you know what I do believe, Frank? Do you know what I think happened? I think Alice Neal, a young girl out on her own, walked up that footpath all those years ago, and you, knowing how secluded and private this spot is, couldn't help yourself." He looked away but found only disgust on every face around him. "I don't know, nor do I want to know what you did to her, Frank. But I do believe she's here somewhere. I think you buried her here, and you," she said, turning on Tyler. "I think you saw it."

"You what?"

"I think you saw what he did, and you didn't say a bloody thing. I think that a year later, when you murdered your family, and Frank found you hiding in that barn, you used it against him. You're not friends. You're both vile human beings who use others to save their own skins. You'll have guessed by now why I've asked an entire team of forensic investigators to attend." She nodded slowly, allowing a grin to form on her face to match those that each of the men had lost. "I'll have every inch of this field dug up if I have to. I won't stop until I've found her." That grin faded to pity. "We've come to the end of the line, boys. This is it. Your final chance to buy yourself some semblance of leniency. A chance to show that you have a heart. That you are human." She waited, and when Ben thought she would instruct the officers to remove them, she waited some more until she could be sure. "Well," she said. "That is a shame." She turned to Southwell. "Katy, could you ask your team to begin, please? We're going to put this entire area under radar. Start with the area beneath the tree."

"Will do," Southwell replied, and with a few nods to her team, they set to work.

"Take him away," Freya said to the officer holding Bowen's arm, and then she approached Leslie Tyler. "Why do you keep quiet, Leslie?"

"Don't know what you're talking about," he replied.

"You're facing charges for the murders of six people. Six people. Six human beings who aren't here because of you," she said, and she stepped close enough to lean in and whisper into his ear. "And three of them are your own flesh and blood."

She eyed him curiously and took a few steps towards Ben while those words permeated.

"Wait," he said, and she winked at Ben before turning on her heels to face him. He stared at her, confused. "Three?"

"That's right," she told him. "Your two daughters, which you already know about, of course. But there is one more." She glanced up at the tree, now lit from underneath by Southwell's bright LED lights. "The man you hung and burned."

"What? What about him? He was just one of Tommy's..." His confused expression slipped away, and even in the dim light, his face paled. "No."

"His name was John Tyler," Freya said coolly. "You burned your own son alive, Leslie."

He fell to his knees, his arms held up by the officers on either side of him, and as his head fell back so that he stared up at the tree, he let out a wail like a wounded animal caught in a trap.

"You had your chance to be human, Leslie, and you blew it," Freya told him, then turned to the officers who hauled him to his feet. "Take him away."

CHAPTER SIXTY-TWO

THE REAR LIGHTS of the two police Astras had long since disappeared, taking the two men back to the station. Freya stood with Ben and the team by the cars, but where they usually might have shared a moment of celebration, the scene before them somehow put paid to any uplift they might have felt. They waited, each of them lost in their own sombre thoughts. But it was Nillson who broke the silence, holding a message up on her phone.

"They've got the shovel," she said, which Freya acknowledged with a curt nod of thanks.

"Does anyone mind if we just go over all this?" Cruz said. "So, Bowen attacked Alice Neal and buried her here?"

"That's the theory," Nillson said.

"Right, and we think Tyler saw it, or at least knew about it?"

"Why else would Bowen cover for him all these years?" Gillespie said.

"Right," Cruz replied, his face a picture of both disgust and bemusement in equal measure. "So then, Tyler caught his wife and George Dean in his kitchen and killed them both."

"In his defence," Freya cut in, "I don't think he intended to murder either of them. I think he hit Dean harder than he meant to, and well, I think at that point, something inside had taken over. A fight for survival, maybe?"

"Right, but then he torched the house to cover his tracks. He made it look like they'd died in a house fire, not realising his two daughters were upstairs?"

"How do you live with yourself?" Nillson asked.

"You don't," Gillespie said. "You exist. You get through each day, hoping that one day, either it'll become a distant memory or that you join them."

"But how did Tommy Dean know that Leslie Tyler had killed his dad?"

"He didn't," Ben said. "From the farm's records, he worked out that Bowen was still paying somebody cash and had been since the day his dad had apparently left. At that point, everyone thought that Leslie Tyler was dead, so who else could it have been?"

"And he went to work at the farm to find out?"

"Must have been a nasty surprise," Gillespie added.

"Right, and if Tyler was alive, then who did they drag out of the farmhouse?" Ben said. "It had to have been his dad. I suppose, from that point on, it was a matter of planning. How could he get his own back?"

"I think he enlisted John Tyler," Freya said. "I think that when Tommy Dean set Leslie Tyler up, it was designed to enact revenge for his dad, but also to somehow reunite him with his old friend. Somehow, it would have shown John Tyler who his father really was."

"Tyler said that Dean's mate came out of nowhere. That was John Tyler. Do you think he knew it was his dad?"

"Aye," Gillespie said. "I do. Can you imagine it? You spend your entire life thinking your family had died in a tragic fire, only to find out that not only is your dad alive, but he never even got in touch somehow, and not only that, that he bloody killed them. Can you imagine that?"

"Alright," Cruz said, playing devil's advocate. "All that makes sense. But how did Tommy Dean know that this was the spot where Bowen killed Alice Neal? I get that Leslie Tyler could have seen it. He could have been working in the next field. But what about Tommy Dean? How did he know?"

Freya looked at each of them in turn, enjoying each of their perplexed expressions, although there was something about Ben's face that suggested he had an inclination.

"Do you want a stab at it?" she asked him, and he puffed his cheeks.

"It's a wild stab."

"It's been a wild investigation," she said, to which he agreed.

"Alright," he started. "I think that, first of all, Tommy Dean was smart. Very smart. I think that when he found out about Tyler killing his dad, he must have realised that Bowen was covering for him."

"Good so far," she said.

"And I think that he, like us, formed some kind of theory. Except that, unlike us, his theory was right. He was right because he knew things that we didn't."

"Such as?"

"Such as what Bowen was doing when he approached him to ask for work," Ben said. "You wouldn't run alongside a working tractor to get the driver's attention. The tractor must have stopped."

"Okay," she said, encouraging him to go further.

"The driver wasn't even in the tractor. By which I mean Bowen. He was out of the tractor. He was..." he turned to Nillson. "What did you find? When this place was searched, what did you find?"

"Rope," she said. "Over there in the dyke,"

"No, there was more. There were a few other bits."

"Coke cans, an old sock, some wire—"

"No," he stopped her. "There were flowers."

"Oh, right, yeah. Just a few old roses that somebody had pulled up."

"Roses?" he said. "There aren't any roses here. The only roses I've seen on this farm are—"

"At the house," Nillson finished. "He was laying flowers?"

"Bloody hell, he picked flowers from his own front garden and dropped them on her grave."

"Just like he does every year," Freya told them. "The newspaper cutting in the scrapbook. There was an article to one side on the anniversary of Alice Neal's disappearance."

"The dates work," Ben said.

"Why?" Cruz said. "He bloody killed her. He...I don't know what he did with her, but he bloody well buried her."

"Guilt," Freya said. "Guilt, shame...I don't know. I don't know what drives these people, and we likely never will. Other than Tyler, Bowen was the only one who knew what he'd done. I suppose he felt she deserved something. Some...I don't know, recognition? A thought, maybe?"

"It's bloody sick," Gillespie said.

"One more thing," Cruz said, to Freya's surprise. He pointed at the forensics team working one hundred metres away beneath the tree. "What if we're wrong? What if she's not there?"

"What if I'm wrong, you mean?" Freya said. "It wouldn't be the first time during this investigation, and if it turns out that way, we still have Tyler on multiple counts of murder, and we reduce Bowen's charges to conspiracy to murder, perverting the course of justice, and aiding and abetting. Either way, they're both going down."

"Sounds good to me," Nillson said.

"Aye," Gillespie grumbled.

"On another note," Freya continued. "While I have most of you here, there's something I'd like to say."

"Freya—?" Ben said, but she stopped him with a single raised hand.

"You may have noticed I've been somewhat short-tempered this week," she said. "A little quick to react, maybe?"

She peered around at each of their blank expressions.

"No more than normal, boss," Gillespie replied on their behalf.

"If it helps, I have," Ben said. "Presumably, now's the time you tell us why."

"Thank you, Ben," she said, then addressed the team. "Well, you all know what we're doing in a couple of days' time. You'll all be there, I hope," she said. "What I'd like to tell you is that you have nothing to worry about, but it's very likely that this is the last time Ben and I will be working side by side, as we have been."

"Eh?" Cruz said.

"Boss?" Gillespie asked.

"Last Monday, Detective Superintendent Granger pulled me into his office. He made it quite clear that the powers that be will not permit a married couple to work in the field together."

"The Assistant Chief Constable, you mean?" Nillson said.

"Ben and I shouldn't even be on the same team, by rights, but he's done what he can. When Ben and I return from our holiday—"

"Honeymoon, you mean?"

"No, it's a holiday," Ben said. "Trust me, it's a holiday."

"When we get back, Ben and Sergeant Nillson will pair up, and I'll be office-based. I'll still be leading the investigations, only from my desk."

"What about me?" Cruz asked. "What do I do?"

"You'll be fetching coffee and walking the streets, Gabby," Gillespie joked.

"You'll continue as you are," Freya said, overriding Gillespie's comment. "Anna? Are you happy with that?"

"Beats working on my own, boss," she replied.

"Good," Freya said. "Let's not make a big deal of it. We need it to work. If it doesn't, then I'll be forced to seek alternative configurations."

"Hold on," Ben said, stepping into the centre of them all. "You're going to work in the office? Full time?"

"It's either that or one of us transfers," she said. "Granger did what he could, but it seems the ACC has had a change of heart."

"You'll go mad," he said.

"Madder," Gillespie added under his breath.

"What choice do I have?" she said quietly. "That's why I wanted to get this one right. It's why I *had* to get this one right."

"Because it's your last one?" he said.

"Over here," a voice called, and Freya looked across at the tree, where three individuals in white forensic suits were peering down into a freshly dug hole.

"Well, then, let's not do it—," Ben started as Freya began walking towards the tree. She stopped and felt every eye in the team on her when she turned. "Let's forget the whole thing."

"I have had an incredible career," she told them all, but focusing on Ben. "Granted, I was held hostage once, and more recently, I was burned quite badly, but aside from those incidents, it's been good," she said. "I want to go out with a bang. I want my last job in the field to make a real difference." She glanced over her shoulder briefly. "I think the timing is nothing short of perfect."

CHAPTER SIXTY-THREE

It wasn't the first time that Ben had felt that small. Nor was it the first time that every eye in the room had been fixed on him. He stood with his back to the congregation, his eyes planted on the arched window in front of him, waiting for it all to begin.

St Peters Church, Dunston, boasted character with every sweep of his eye. From the tall, arched windows and mouldings to the old wooden pews that looked as if they had been in place for centuries. It was, he thought, the perfect setting.

He checked his watch. There were three minutes to go.

"Alright, Ben," a voice said, far smaller than the one he had been expecting. He turned to find Cruz standing beside him, wearing a smart, three-piece suit.

"Gabby? You okay? I think you're sitting on Freya's side to make the numbers up."

"Actually, no. I'm here, mate," he said.

"Eh?"

"I'm going to be right here, next to you."

Ben peered down at him, studying his expression for some kind of telltale sign that he was pulling his leg.

"I don't get it. Where's Jim?"

Cruz pulled a face.

"He sends his apologies."

"He what?" Ben said as the organ began to play. He looked back at the church behind him and at the small congregation, which comprised a handful of Ben's family, the remainder of the team, Pippa Bell and Andrew Fox, who looked weirdly like a couple, and a few close officers from the station, including Detective Superintendent Granger and his wife. "You have got to be kidding me."

"Sorry, mate," Cruz said, and he tapped this pocket. "I've written a blinding speech, though. You wait."

A hand tugged on Ben's left arm, and in a flash of imagination, Ben saw the joke. He turned, expecting to find Gillespie standing there, beaming at the little prank.

But it wasn't Gillespie; it was somebody far more senior.

"Just thought I'd wish you luck before it all kicks off," the Assistant Chief Constable said. Like Granger, he was dressed in full dress uniform, his insignia shining and his cap tucked neatly beneath his arm. He offered his hand for Ben to shake, and then, with a sweep of his arm, he introduced his wife, who Ben graciously smiled at and nodded his thanks. "My daughter-in-law is around here somewhere, too," the ACC said, looking behind him. "I do hope you don't mind. She wanted to wish you well. She's a big fan of yours."

"Sorry, who?" Ben asked, hoping not to appear rude but still reeling from the bad news that Cruz had just delivered.

"My daughter-in-law," the ACC replied. "Ah, there she is. Third row from the back. Sitting with Detective Superintendent Granger."

He leaned back a little for Ben to see, and he pointed, and in the third row from the back, beside Granger, PC Jewson smiled back at him knowingly. She even had the gall to offer a little wave.

"Your daughter-in-law?" Ben said.

"Yes, she's a year or so in and doing well by all accounts. We try to keep the connection under wraps, as you can imagine. We don't want people to think she has an unfair advantage, do we?" the ACC replied. "Anyway, we'll catch up at the bar afterwards."

He gave Ben a friendly shoulder squeeze, then ushered his wife to their seats, leaving Ben staring across the church at Jewson who was in the throes of conversation with Granger.

The rear doors opened, and light spilled across the stone floor, and slowly, the congregation rose to their feet.

"For God's..." he stopped himself from cursing, but every substitute he thought of seemed somewhat inappropriate. "He better have a good bloody reason," Ben hissed, earning himself a curious glare from the vicar, who peered at him from behind her neat fringe.

"He said something about the speech," Cruz said. "Said he was worried he'd let you down and that perhaps it was better if he didn't bother."

"I don't care about the bloody...I don't care about the speech," Ben told him. "He said he'd be here."

Cruz shrugged, perhaps a little disappointed that he hadn't been welcomed into the role.

The vicar gave a little cough, and the organist entered into the first few notes of the bridal chorus.

Ben let his head fall back as Cruz settled in beside him, and a few female members in the gathering let out a collective gasp. Presumably, Freya had entered. He checked his watch. Eleven-oh-one. At least she had turned up. He waited a few moments, time enough for her to be somewhere along the central aisle, and then slowly, he turned.

And then a gasp of his own found its way out, somehow competing with the organ.

There was no blue dress, light or dark. She wore what Ben could only describe to himself as the most beautiful wedding gown he had ever seen. It hung from her arms as if held in place by little more than the girlish grin she wore and seemed to wrap around her and meet in a petite bow to one side. Her hair had been pulled back, contrary to nearly every one of her planned styles, and that shiny patch of skin on her cheek shone brightly in the light that streamed through the tall windows.

But as if her change of heart regarding the dress and her hair wasn't enough, the man by her side beamed proudly at him as they approached.

"Sorry, pal," Gillespie whispered as he placed her hand in his. "Had a better offer."

He was speechless, not just by how she looked, but at seeing him beside her. And behind them, wearing the darker blue of the two dresses Freya had been contemplating, was Katy Southwell, holding a bouquet in her folded hands.

"Are we ready?" the vicar asked, and with a wink that only he could give, Gillespie gave Freya a peck on the cheek, then backed away. "Good morning," the vicar continued, addressing the congregation and reminding Ben of Freya standing at the white-board in the incident room. "We are gathered here today to witness the joining of two people in the sight of God..."

Her voice trailed away, and Ben stared up at the ceiling some forty feet above them.

"Is everything okay?" Freya whispered, to which he had no answer and therefore gave no answer. "It's too late to back out now."

He saw her, and he heard her, and he heard the vicar saying something about vows. He looked across at Gillespie, who must have read something in his expression as he frowned back at Ben quizzically.

"Now comes the time where I invite you all to participate," the vicar said, rousing Ben from his thoughts, "but secretly hope that you do not." She smiled to herself, and a few laughs rumbled around the eaves. "Should anyone present know of any reason that this couple should not be joined in holy matrimony, speak now or forever hold your peace." She waited and eyed Freya and

Ben before adding her own witty comment. "This is always the tense part," she said, raising another few polite laughs.

Ben peered behind him at the collection of faces. His father and his two brothers, an aunt he hadn't seen since his mother was alive, and her husband who rarely uttered a word, the team with Gold biting nervously down on her lower lip, and those people he'd seen in the station since forever and day.

And then Jewson, who had, by all accounts, played her hand so well that she almost rivalled Freya's cunning and tenacious desire to win.

"Well," the vicar said. "Thank goodness for that. Even after nearly twenty years, it's always a relief—"

"Me," Ben said, and the room fell silent.

"Excuse me?" the vicar said.

"Ben?" Freya stared up at him, not with anger in her eyes but curiosity.

"I do," he said. "Not, I do. But I do. I know of a reason."

"Ben, it's really quite late—"

"I can't do it," he said, and a hushed murmur ran riot from stone pillar to stone pillar.

"Are you saying that you no longer wish to go on with the ceremony?" The vicar asked.

"Yes," he said. "No. I don't know."

"Ben, this is embarrassing—"

"I can't do it," he said, looking down at Freya. "I'm sorry, but I can't marry you. I can't be the reason you have to give it all up."

"We've been through this—"

"No. No, you've been through it. I haven't."

"I think perhaps we should take a little break—" the vicar started, gaining control of the room, much as Freya often did.

"No," Ben said. "No, we go on."

"Ben, make your mind up," Freya hissed.

"We go on," he said. "We do it. We do the ceremony. We do

the rings, and we kiss, and we walk out of here arm in arm. We'll go to the pub, we'll have a party, and that'll be that."

"Ben, make your mind up—"

"I'm not signing," he said. "The wedding certificate. I'm not signing it." He turned to the vicar. "We can do that, can't we?"

"Well. I suppose—"

"We've paid for the church and the organ and the pub and everything else. Nothing changes except the certificate."

"Technically, you won't be legally married."

He pondered that statement for a moment, then nodded.

"I know."

"Ben, what's the point?" Freya asked.

"Ah, Ben," Gillespie started. "Do you want to take a wee walk, maybe?"

"No," he said. "No, it's never been clearer. You get to keep your name. We get to have a wedding with all our friends and family. Everyone that means anything to us," he said, and he looked to the back of the room. "And others. We'll have our wedding, and we'll go on as we were."

"Unmarried?"

"Unmarried," he said, staring down at Freya. "If the choice I have to make is between calling you my legal wife but not working alongside you every single day, or not signing on the dotted line, but getting to be with you every day, then there is no choice. I'm not signing."

"Christ, Ben," Freya said, which earned her one of the vicar's frowns.

"That's alright, isn't it?" Ben said, turning to Granger at the back of the room. "If we're not legally married, then can we go on as we were?"

Granger fingered his collar, and all eyes turned on him.

"Well..." he began, then leaned forward to refer to the ACC, who shrugged.

"Technically, yes," the ACC said. "There's no reason for anything to change."

"Then, that's what I want," Ben said. "I want a wedding. I want the rings, and I want a party. A bloody big party. Excuse my French, vicar. And I want to go on as we were." He peered down at Freya again. "I want to work with Freya Bloom," he said, then realised his potential mistake. "If...if that's what you want." He waited a moment, but the suspense was murder. "Is it? Is that what you want?"

There was little in her expression that belied any of her thoughts. But slowly, ever so slowly, that smile he had come to adore revealed itself in all its glory.

"I do," she said, and she dabbed at her eye with a handkerchief before beaming up at him with every single one of her emotions etched into every single muscle in her face. Happiness burst from inside, and she held her hands up to her face, then let them fall to her sides so that she stood there as a little girl, staring up at him hopelessly in love. "I do."

The End.

Click here to download Waiting For Death, book 17 in the Wild Fens Murder Mysteries.

WAITING FOR DEATH - PROLOGUE

THERE WAS something about lying in the mud, in the pouring rain, with a gun pressed into his shoulder that reminded Zack Cummings of old war films. How they romanticised death, calling on that inane drive that thrives in every schoolboy, but usually fades when common sense develops, along with empathy, a respect for life, and the opposite sex.

None of that mattered now, though. Now, all that mattered was winning. All that mattered was showing Melissa's dad he wasn't a pushover and was able to defend himself and his family if push came to shove, and any minute now that chance would present itself.

He'd watched one of his oldest friends, Joseph, move from tree to tree, staying low, staying quiet. Of all of them, Joseph had always been into war films and games more than anyone, and Zack supposed he thought he had an advantage. But as the redhead stepped from behind a tree, he walked firmly into Zack's crosshairs.

He could take him anytime he wanted. There was a power there, a power not to be wantonly exhausted, but to be savoured, cherished, and drawn out.

Somewhere behind him, shots rang out, too far away to be any threat to Zack, but enough for Joseph to drop to the ground.

Slowly, Zack lowered his weapon until those two fine lines in his scope met over Joseph's head.

Head shot or body?

A body shot would hurt more.

A slight adjustment until his plump backside was the focus, and Zack grinned to himself. He'd have to be quick though. A shot in the backside would send Joseph writhing in pain, so he'd have to follow up with a kill shot. To be sure. That's what did, didn't they? In the films. They always made sure. Never take a kill for granted.

There were shouts from behind him now, and a few shots were fired off. He hoped his dad was okay. He hoped it wasn't too much for him. Even if it was too much for his knees, there was no way the old man would sit back and let his boy defend the Cummings' name.

But now was not the time to worry about his dad. He had to get rid of Joseph before the others came, before the melee behind him grew closer. Before they came to look for him.

He lowered his head to the sight again, but Joseph wasn't there and for a terrible moment he imagined the tables turning, and that Joseph would be standing over him, laughing and grinning before he let a few rounds off. He wouldn't take any chances, that's for sure. He wouldn't fire just once. He'd make sure.

But the shot didn't come and nobody was standing over him, and from behind a tree not fifteen metres away, Joseph's backside came into view.

Zack wouldn't make the same mistake again. He tracked his every move as his old friend dragged himself along on his elbows.

"Wrong way, Jo," he whispered to himself as his finger curled around the trigger and the crosshairs settled on that sweet spot between the legs where no man wants to be hit, kicked, punched, or even flicked.

He controlled his breathing, remembering what his dad taught him. Breath in, breath out, fire.

"Jesus bloody Christ," Joseph yelled, his voice reminiscent of his Northern Irish heritage. He rolled away from his gun onto his knees, squeezing his eyes closed and turning his face to the sky. "Hit. I'm hit."

Twice more Zack fired, each one finding its target. One in his back and one in the back of his head.

They would come for him now Joseph had given his position away, so he rolled into the ditch, stayed low, and then scampered over the other side, checking his surroundings as he went.

"Joe?" Somebody called out, and Brendan ran into view, seeming oblivious to the danger. He stopped less than ten metres from where Zack was hiding. "You over here, mate?"

Zack's next shot caught him behind the knee and he went down like a sack of rotten spuds, screaming blue murder. The next shot made sure he wouldn't come for Zack.

"Is he here?" Another voice said. It was Dan, who appeared to have a bit more common sense than Brendan had. He saw Brendan on the ground and dropped, searching the trees for movement. Zack was still. He wasn't best positioned, but moving now would get him shot. He had the cover of a bush to his advantage. All he had to do was wait for Dan to move into a better position, to come closer. But Dan, apparently, was smart. He slid backwards into the next ditch, and then took the cover of a tree. Every so often, Zack would see his shoulder move, or the barrel of his gun.

"Smart bastard," Zack said, assessing his own predicament. If more came, they'd see him for sure, but if he moved, then Dan would pin him down.

There was only one thing for it. He'd have to go on the offensive. Instead of waiting for them to come to him, he'd have to go after them, starting with Dan. He checked his weapon and his surroundings, then shoved himself forward towards Dan's position, keenly aware that whatever was going off on the far side of the forest was growing closer with every passing minute.

Dan had his back to a tree looking left and right, probably waiting for Zack to show himself. So, Zack edged as close as he dared, until he could be sure his shot would find its target. There would be no second chances this time.

When he was ten metres from Dan's tree, he settled in and took aim, waiting for Dan to turn his head to the right and for those crosshairs to line up.

The barrel of his gun rose and fell with each breath, but he held his aim true.

And then it happened. Dan's patience failed him. He chanced a look to his right, revealing enough of his head for Zack to take a shot, and he was just about to squeeze the trigger when three whistle blasts echoed around the forest and the trees seemed to erupt with laughter, shouting, and good old-fashioned banter.

Zack released the trigger and lowered his head, sliding the visor from his head. The tension had been high, and he still had no idea if his team had won. It didn't matter though; Brendan and Joe would take a few well-earned bruises home.

Dan shoved himself to his feet and made his way to the assembly point, where the marshal was calling for them to regroup. Reluctantly, Zack rolled on his back to join them, and was stopped in his tracks by a knife held inches from his throat.

"What the—"

"Shhh," he said, and the face grinned. "I never thought I'd get the chance."

"What the bloody hell are you doing?" Zack said, loud enough that somebody might hear. He dragged himself away until a heavy boot on his stomach pinned him down, and his assailant leaned in, peering deep into his eyes as if searching for some kind of understanding.

"What am I doing?" he said, his voice deeper than Zack recalled, almost guttural. "What I've wanted to do for years."

And he lashed out with the blade.

Zack tried to call out, but no words came. Had that just actually happened? He reached up to his throat, but his hands became sticky, warm, and wet.

"Oh, God," he tried to say, but coughed up a lungful of blood, and as the energy inside him waned, along with the fight for life, he lay back, feeling the warm spread of blood surge across his chest with every beat of his heart.

And that face, that taunting face, slipped into the trees, into the world that darkened around him.

And then there was nothing but the black silhouettes of trees, the cold embrace of death, and the knowing what should have been, would never be.

Click here to download Waiting For Death, book 17 in the Wild Fens Murder Mysteries.

ALSO BY JACK CARTWRIGHT

The Deadly Wolds Murder Mysteries

When The Storm Dies

The Harder They Fall

Until Death Do Us Part

The Devil Inside Her

Secrets From The Grave

The Wild Fens Murder Mysteries

Secrets In Blood

One For Sorrow

In Cold Blood

Suffer In Silence

Dying To Tell

Never To Return

Lie Beside Me

Dance With Death

In Dead Water

One Deadly Night

Her Dying Mind

Into Death's Arms

No More Blood

Burden of Truth

Run From Evil

Deadly Little Secret

Waiting For Death

The DCI Cook Murder Mysteries

A Winter of Blood

A Secret to Die For

VIP READER CLUB

Your FREE ebook is waiting for you now.

Get your FREE copy of the prequel story to the Wild Fens Murder Mystery series, and learn how Freya came to give up everything she had to start a new life in Lincolnshire.

Visit www.jackcartwrightbooks.com to join the VIP Reader Club.

I'll see you there.

Jack Cartwright

A NOTE FROM THE AUTHOR

Locations are as important to the story as the characters are, sometimes even more so.

I have heard it said on many occasions that Lincolnshire is as much of a character in my work as Freya, Ben, and the team. That is mainly due to the fact that I visit the places used within my stories to see with my own eyes, breathe the air, and to listen to the sounds.

However, there are times when I am compelled to create a fictional place within a real environment.

For example, in the story you have just read, the towns and villages mentioned are all real places. However, most of the houses and buildings in the story are entirely fictitious, and any references to farms and businesses highlight little more than figments of my imagination.

The reason I create fictional places is so that I can be sure not to cast any real location, setting, business, street, or feature in a negative light. Nobody wants to see their beloved home described as a scene for a murder, or any business portrayed as anything but excellent.

If any names of bonafide locations and businesses appear in my books, I ensure they bask in a positive light, because I truly believe that Lincolnshire has so much to offer and that these locations should be celebrated with vehemence.

I hope you agree.

Jack Cartwright

AUTHOR

AFTERWORD

Because reviews are critical to an author's career, if you have enjoyed this novel, you could do me a huge favour by leaving a review on Amazon.

Reviews allow other readers to find my books. Your help in leaving one would make a big difference to this author.

Thank you for taking the time to read *Deadly Little Secret*.

Best wishes,

Jack Cartwright
AUTHOR

COPYRIGHT

9 781916 986657